ALICE CAMPBELL
JUGGERNAUT

ALICE Campbell (1887-1955) came originally from Atlanta, Georgia, where she was part of the socially prominent Ormond family. She moved to New York City at the age of nineteen and quickly became a socialist and women's suffragist. Later she moved to Paris, marrying the American-born artist and writer James Lawrence Campbell, with whom she had a son in 1914.

Just before World War One, the family left France for England, where the couple had two more children, a son and a daughter. Campbell wrote crime fiction until 1950, though many of her novels continued to have French settings. She published her first work (*Juggernaut*) in 1928. She wrote nineteen detective novels during her career.

MYSTERIES BY ALICE CAMPBELL

1. *Juggernaut* (1928)

2. *Water Weed* (1929)

3. *Spiderweb* (1930)

4. *The Click of the Gate* (1932)

5. *The Murder of Caroline Bundy* (1933)

6. *Desire to Kill* (1934)

7. *Keep Away from Water!* (1935)

8. *Death Framed in Silver* (1937)

9. *Flying Blind* (1938)

10. *A Door Closed Softly* (1939)

11. *They Hunted a Fox* (1940)

12. *No Murder of Mine* (1941)

13. *No Light Came On* (1942)

14. *Ringed with Fire* (1943)

15. *Travelling Butcher* (1944)

16. *The Cockroach Sings* (1946)

17. *Child's Play* (1947)

18. *The Bloodstained Toy* (1948)

19. *The Corpse Had Red Hair* (1950)

ALICE CAMPBELL

JUGGERNAUT

With an introduction
by Curtis Evans

DEAN STREET PRESS

ALICE IN MURDERLAND

CRIME WRITER ALICE CAMPBELL, THE OTHER "AC"

IN 1927 Alice Dorothy Ormond Campbell—a thirty-nine-year-old native of Atlanta, Georgia who for the last fifteen years had lived successively in New York, Paris and London, never once returning to the so-called Empire City of the South, published her first novel, an unstoppable crime thriller called *Juggernaut*, selling the serialization rights to the *Chicago Tribune* for $4000 ($60,000 today), a tremendous sum for a brand new author. On its publication in January 1928, both the book and its author caught the keen eye of Bessie S. Stafford, society page editor of the *Atlanta Constitution*. Back when Alice Ormond, as she was then known, lived in Atlanta, Miss Bessie breathlessly informed her readers, she had been "an ethereal blonde-like type of beauty, extremely popular, and always thought she was in love with somebody. She took high honors in school; and her gentleness of manner and breeding bespoke an aristocratic lineage. She grew to a charming womanhood—"

Let us stop Miss Bessie right there, because there is rather more to the story of Alice Campbell, the mystery genre's other "AC," who published nineteen crime novels between 1928 and 1950. Allow me to plunge boldly forward with the tale of Atlanta's great Golden Age crime writer, who as an American expatriate in England, went on to achieve fame and fortune as an atmospheric writer of murder and mystery and become one of the early members of the Detection Club.

Alice Campbell's lineage was distinguished. Alice was born in Atlanta on November 29, 1887, the youngest of the four surviving children of prominent Atlantans James Ormond IV and Florence Root. Both of Alice's grandfathers had been wealthy Atlanta merchants who settled in the city in the years before the American Civil War. Alice's uncles, John Wellborn Root and Walter Clark Root, were noted architects, while her brothers, Sidney James and Walter Emanuel Ormond, were respectively a drama critic and political writer for the *Atlanta Constitution* and an attorney and justice of the peace. Both brothers died untimely deaths before Alice had even turned thirty, as did her uncle John Wellborn Root and her father.

Alice precociously published her first piece of fiction, a fairy story, in the *Atlanta Constitution* in 1897, when she was nine years old. Four years later, the ambitious child was said to be in the final stage of completing a two-volume novel. In 1907, by which time she was nineteen, Alice relocated to New York City, chaperoned by Florence.

In New York Alice became friends with writers Inez Haynes Irwin, a prominent feminist, and Jacques Futrelle, the creator of "The Thinking Machine" detective who was soon to go down with the ship on RMS *Titanic,* and scored her first published short story in *Ladies Home Journal* in 1911. Simultaneously she threw herself pell-mell into the causes of women's suffrage and equal pay for equal work. The same year she herself became engaged, but this was soon broken off and in February 1913 Alice sailed to Paris with her mother to further her cultural education.

Three months later in Paris, on May 22, 1913, twenty-five-year-old Alice married James Lawrence Campbell, a twenty-four-year-old theatrical agent of good looks and good family from Virginia. Jamie, as he was known, had arrived in Paris a couple of years earlier, after a failed stint in New York City as an actor. In Paris he served, more successfully, as an agent for prominent New York play brokers Arch and Edgar Selwyn.

After the wedding Alice Ormond Campbell, as she now was known, remained in Paris with her husband Jamie until hostilities between France and Germany loomed the next year. At this point the couple prudently relocated to England, along with their newborn son, James Lawrence Campbell, Jr., a future artist and critic. After the war the Campbells, living in London, bought an attractive house in St. John's Wood, London, where they established a literary and theatrical salon. There Alice oversaw the raising of the couple's two sons, Lawrence and Robert, and their daughter, named Chita Florence Ormond ("Ormond" for short), while Jamie spent much of his time abroad, brokering play productions in Paris, New York and other cities.

Like Alice, Jamie harbored dreams of personal literary accomplishment; and in 1927 he published a novel entitled *Face Value*, which for a brief time became that much-prized thing by publishers, a putatively "scandalous" novel that gets Talked About. The story of a gentle orphan boy named Serge, the son an emigre Russian prostitute, who grows up in a Parisian "disorderly house," as reviews often blushingly put it, *Face Value* divided critics, but ended up on American bestseller lists. The success of his first novel led to the author being invited out to Hollywood to work as a scriptwriter, and his name appears on credits to a trio of films in 1927-28, including *French Dressing*, a "gay" divorce comedy set among sexually scatterbrained Americans in Paris. One wonders whether in Hollywood Jamie ever came across future crime writer Cornell Woolrich, who was scripting there too at the time.

Alice remained in England with the children, enjoying her own literary splash with her debut thriller *Juggernaut*, which concerned the murderous machinations of an inexorably ruthless French Riviera society doctor, opposed by a valiant young nurse. The novel racked up rave reviews and sales in the UK and US, in the latter country spurred on by its nationwide newspaper serialization, which promised readers

> . . . the open door to adventure! *Juggernaut* by Alice Campbell will sweep you out of the humdrum of everyday life into the gay, swift-moving Arabian-nights existence of the Riviera!

London's *Daily Mail* declared that the irresistible *Juggernaut* "should rank among the 'best sellers' of the year"; and, sure enough, *Juggernaut*'s English publisher, Hodder & Stoughton, boasted, several months after the novel's English publication in July 1928, that they already had run through six printings in an attempt to satisfy customer demand. In 1936 *Juggernaut* was adapted in England as a film vehicle for horror great Boris Karloff, making it the only Alice Campbell novel filmed to date. The film was remade in England under the title *The Temptress* in 1949.

Water Weed (1929) and *Spiderweb* (1930) (*Murder in Paris* in the US), the immediate successors, held up well to their predecessor's performance. Alice chose this moment to return for a fortnight to Atlanta, ostensibly to visit her sister, but doubtlessly in part to parade through her hometown as a conquering, albeit commercial, literary hero. And who was there to welcome Alice in the pages of the *Constitution* but Bessie S. Stafford, who pronounced Alice's hair still looked like spun gold while her eyes remarkably had turned an even deeper shade of blue. To Miss Bessie, Alice imparted enchanting tales of salon chats with such personages as George Bernard Shaw, Lady Asquith, H. G. Wells and (his lover) Rebecca West, the latter of whom a simpatico Alice met and conversed with frequently. Admitting that her political sympathies in England "inclined toward the conservatives," Alice yet urged "the absolute necessity of having two strong parties." English women, she had been pleased to see, evinced more informed interest in politics than their American sisters.

Alice, Miss Bessie declared, diligently devoted every afternoon to her writing, shutting her study door behind her "as a sign that she is not to be interrupted." This commitment to her craft enabled Alice to produce an additional sixteen crime novels between 1932 and 1950, beginning with *The Click of the Gate* and ending with *The Corpse Had Red Hair*.

Altogether nearly half of Alice's crime novels were standalones, in contravention of convention at this time, when series sleuths were so popular. In *The Click of the Gate* the author introduced one of her main recurring characters, intrepid Paris journalist Tommy Rostetter, who appears in three additional novels: *Desire to Kill* (1934), *Flying Blind* (1938) and *The Bloodstained Toy* (1948). In the two latter novels, Tommy appears with Alice's other major recurring character, dauntless Inspector Headcorn of Scotland Yard, who also pursues murderers and other malefactors in *Death Framed in Silver* (1937), *They Hunted a Fox* (1940), *No Murder of Mine* (1941) and *The Cockroach Sings* (1946) (*With Bated Breath* in the US).

Additional recurring characters in Alice's books are Geoffrey Macadam and Catherine West, who appear in *Spiderweb* and *No Light Came On* (1942), and Colin Ladbrooke, who appears in *Death Framed in Silver*, *A Door Closed Softly* (1939) and *They Hunted a Fox*. In the latter two books Colin with his romantic interest Alison Young and in the first and third book with Inspector Headcorn, who also appears, as mentioned, in *Flying Blind* and *The Bloodstained Toy* with Tommy Rosstetter, making Headcorn the connecting link in this universe of sleuths, although the inspector does not appear with Geoffrey Macadam and Catherine West. It is all a rather complicated state of criminal affairs; and this lack of a consistent and enduring central sleuth character in Alice's crime fiction may help explain why her work faded in the Fifties, after the author retired from writing.

Be that as it may, Alice Campbell is a figure of significance in the history of crime fiction. In a 1946 review of *The Cockroach Sings* in the London *Observer*, crime fiction critic Maurice Richardson asserted that "[s]he belongs to the atmospheric school, of which one of the outstanding exponents was the late Ethel Lina White," the author of *The Wheel Spins* (1936), famously filmed in 1938, under the title *The Lady Vanishes*, by director Alfred Hitchcock. This "atmospheric school," as Richardson termed it, had more students in the demonstrative United States than in the decorous United Kingdom, to be sure, the United States being the home of such hugely popular suspense writers as Mary Roberts Rinehart and Mignon Eberhart, to name but a couple of the most prominent examples.

Like the novels of the American Eber-Rinehart school and English authors Ethel Lina White and Marie Belloc Lowndes, the latter the author of the acknowledged landmark 1911 thriller *The Lodger*, Alice Campbell's books are not pure puzzle detective tales, but rather broader mysteries which put a premium on the storytelling imperatives of atmosphere and suspense. "She could not be unexciting if she tried," raved the *Times Literary Supplement* of Alice, stressing the author's remoteness from the so-called "Humdrum" school of detective fiction headed by British authors Freeman Wills Crofts, John Street and J. J. Connington. However, as Maurice Richardson, a great fan of Alice's crime writing, put it, "she generally binds her homework together with a reasonable plot," so the "Humdrum" fans out there need not be put off by what American detective novelist S. S. Van Dine, creator of Philo Vance, dogmatically dismissed as "literary dallying." In her novels Alice Campbell offered people bone-rattling good reads, which explains their popularity in the past and their revival today. Lines from a review of her 1941 crime novel *No Murder of Mine* by "H.V.A." in the *Hartford Courant* suggests the general nature of her work's appeal: "The excitement and mystery of this Class A shocker start on page 1 and continue right to the end of the book. You won't put it down, once you've begun it. And if you like romance mixed with your thrills, you'll find it here."

The protagonist of *No Murder of Mine* is Rowan Wilde, "an attractive young American girl studying in England." Frequently in her books Alice, like the great Anglo-American author Henry James, pits ingenuous but goodhearted Americans, male or female, up against dangerously sophisticated Europeans, drawing on autobiographical details from her and Jamie's own lives. Many of her crime novels, which often are lengthier than the norm for the period, recall, in terms of their length and content, the Victorian sensation novel, which seemingly had been in its dying throes when the author was a precocious child; yet, in their emphasis on morbid psychology and their sexual frankness, they also anticipate the modern crime novel. One can discern this tendency most dramatically, perhaps, in the engrossing *Water Weed*, concerning a sexual affair between a middle-aged Englishwoman and a young American man that has dreadful consequences, and *Desire to Kill*, about murder among a clique of decadent bohemians in Paris. In both of these mysteries the exploration of aberrant sexuality is striking. Indeed, in its depiction of sexual psychosis *Water Weed* bears rather more resemblance to, say, the crime novels of Patricia Highsmith than it does to the cozy mysteries of Patricia Wentworth. One might well term it Alice Campbell's *Deep Water*.

In this context it should be noted that in 1935 Alice Campbell authored a sexual problem play, *Two Share a Dwelling*, which the *New York*

Times described as a "grim, vivid, psychological treatment of dual personality." Although it ran for only twenty-two performances during October 8-26 at the West End's celebrated St. James' Theatre, the play had done well on its provincial tour and it received a standing ovation from the audience on opening night at the West End, primarily on account of the compelling performance of the half-Jewish German stage actress Grete Mosheim, who had fled Germany two years earlier and was making her English stage debut in the play's lead role of a schizophrenic, sexually compulsive woman. Mosheim was described as young and "blondely beautiful," bringing to mind the author herself.

Unfortunately priggish London critics were put off by the play's morbid sexual subject, which put Alice in an impossible position. One reviewer scathingly observed that "Miss Alice Campbell . . . has chosen to give her audience a study in pathology as a pleasant method of spending the evening. . . . one leaves the theatre rather wishing that playwrights would leave medical books on their shelves." Another sniffed that "it is to be hoped that the fashion of plumbing the depths of Freudian theory for dramatic fare will not spread. It is so much more easy to be interested in the doings of the sane." The play died a quick death in London and its author went back, for another fifteen years, to "plumbing the depths" in her crime fiction.

What impelled Alice Campbell, like her husband, to avidly explore human sexuality in her work? Doubtless their writing reflected the temper of modern times, but it also likely was driven by personal imperatives. The child of an unhappy marriage who at a young age had been deprived of a father figure, Alice appears to have wanted to use her crime fiction to explore the human devastation wrought by disordered lives. Sadly, evidence suggests that discord had entered the lives of Alice and Jamie by the 1930s, as they reached middle age and their children entered adulthood. In 1939, as the Second World War loomed, Alice was residing in rural southwestern England with her daughter Ormond at a cottage—the inspiration for her murder setting in *No Murder of Mine*, one guesses—near the bucolic town of Beaminster, Dorset, known for its medieval Anglican church and its charming reference in a poem by English dialect poet William Barnes:

> Sweet Be'mi'ster, that bist a-bound
> By green and woody hills all round,
> Wi'hedges, reachen up between
> A thousand vields o' zummer green.

Alice's elder son Lawrence was living, unemployed, in New York City at this time and he would enlist in the US Army when the country entered the war a couple of years later, serving as a master sergeant throughout the conflict. In December 1939, twenty-three-year-old Ormond, who seems to have herself preferred going by the name Chita, wed the prominent antiques dealer, interior decorator, home restorer and racehorse owner Ernest Thornton-Smith, who at the age of fifty-eight was fully thirty-five years older than she. Antiques would play a crucial role in Alice's 1944 wartime crime novel *Travelling Butcher*, which blogger Kate Jackson at *Cross Examining Crime* deemed "a thrilling read." The author's most comprehensive wartime novel, however, was the highly-praised *Ringed with Fire* (1943). Native Englishman S. Morgan-Powell, the dean of Canadian drama critics, in the *Montreal Star* pronounced *Ringed with Fire* one of the "best spy stories the war has produced," adding, in one of Alice's best notices:

> "Ringed with Fire" begins with mystery and exudes mystery from every chapter. Its clues are most ingeniously developed, and keep the reader guessing in all directions. For once there is a mystery which will, I think, mislead the most adroit and experienced of amateur sleuths. Some time ago there used to be a practice of sealing up the final section of mystery stores with the object of stirring up curiosity and developing the detective instinct among readers. If you sealed up the last forty-two pages of "Ringed with Fire" and then offered a prize of $250 to the person who guessed the mystery correctly, I think that money would be as safe as if you put it in victory bonds.

A few years later, on the back of the dust jacket to the American edition of Alice's *The Cockroach Sings* (1946), which Random House, her new American publisher, less queasily titled *With Bated Breath*, readers learned a little about what the author had been up to during the late war and its recent aftermath: "I got used to oil lamps. . . . and also to riding nine miles in a crowded bus once a week to do the shopping—if there was anything to buy. We thought it rather a lark then, but as a matter of fact we are still suffering from all sorts of shortages and restrictions." Jamie Campbell, on the other hand, spent his war years in Santa Barbara, California. It is unclear whether he and Alice ever lived together again.

Alice remained domiciled for the rest of her life in Dorset, although she returned to London in 1946, when she was inducted into the Detection Club. A number of her novels from this period, all of which were published in England by the Collins Crime Club, more resemble, in tone and form, classic detective fiction, such as *They Hunted a Fox* (1940). This event may have been a moment of triumph for the author, but it was also something of a last hurrah. After 1946 she published only three more crime novels, including the entertaining Tommy Rostetter-Inspector Headcorn mashup *The Bloodstained Toy*, before retiring in 1950. She lived out the remaining five years of her life quietly at her home in the coastal city of Bridport, Dorset, expiring "suddenly" on November 27, 1955, two days before her sixty-eighth birthday. Her brief death notice in the *Daily Telegraph* refers to her only as the "very dear mother of Lawrence, Chita and Robert."

Jamie Campbell had died in 1954 aged sixty-five. Earlier in the year his play *The Praying Mantis*, billed as a "naughty comedy by James Lawrence Campbell," scored hits at the Q Theatre in London and at the Dolphin Theatre in Brighton. (A very young Joan Collins played the eponymous man-eating leading role at the latter venue.) In spite of this, Jamie near the end of the year checked into a hotel in Cannes and fatally imbibed poison. The American consulate sent the report on Jamie's death to Chita in Maida Vale, London, and to Jamie's brother Colonel George Campbell in Washington, D. C., though not to Alice. This was far from the Riviera romance that the publishers of *Juggernaut* had long ago promised. Perhaps the "humdrum of everyday life" had been too much with him.

Alice Campbell own work fell into obscurity after her death, with not one of her novels being reprinted in English for more than seven decades. Happily the ongoing revival of vintage English and American mystery fiction from the twentieth century is rectifying such cases of criminal neglect. It may well be true that it "is impossible not to be thrilled by Edgar Wallace," as the great thriller writer's publishers pronounced, but let us not forget that, as Maurice Richardson put it: "We can always do with Mrs. Alice Campbell." Mystery fans will now have nineteen of them from which to choose—a veritable embarrassment of felonious riches, all from the hand of the other AC.

Curtis Evans

CHAPTER I

When Esther rang the bell of Numéro 86 Route de Grasse, she felt within her that pleasant sort of stage-fright—a mixture of dread and exhilaration—which one is apt to experience when venturing into the unknown. The thrill might be out of all proportion to the prosaic character of her mission—for what is there exciting in applying for a post as a doctor's assistant?—yet there was no gainsaying the fact that when this door confronting her opened, anything, everything, might happen. That is the way Youth regards things.

"Opportunity—a door open in front of one." So in earlier years her Latin teacher had dilated on the inner meaning of the word. Esther smiled reminiscently and congratulated herself that she was not going tamely back to her work in America, choosing instead, when she found a door open, to enter and explore on the other side.

Numéro 86 was a conventional and dignified villa, noncommittal in appearance, like a hundred others. Clean windows blinked in the sunshine, the doorstep was chalky white, the brass plate on the lintel glittered with the inscription, "Gregory Sartorius, M.D." Beside the gate a mimosa shook out its yellow plumage against the sky. Mimosa—in February! ... New York, reflected Esther, was in the clutch of a blizzard. She could picture it now, with its stark ice-ribbed streets, its towering buildings, a mausoleum of frozen stone and dirty snow. As for flowers— why, even a spray of that mimosa in a frosty florist's window would be absurdly expensive; one would pay ...

"Vous désirez, mademoiselle?"

She turned with a start to find the door open, framing the squat figure of a man-servant, a brigand in appearance, French of the Midi; black hair grew low on his forehead; his beetling brows met over sullen shiny eyes which scanned her with a hostile gaze. Diffidently she mustered her all-too-scanty French.

"Est-ce Monsieur le docteur est chez lui?" she ventured, hoping for the best.

To her relief the brigand broke into a friendly smile.

"Mademoiselle come about job?" he replied in English. "Yes, come this way, please."

He led the way through an entrance hall into a large salon of chill and gloomy aspect.

"Take a seat," he bade her, grinning cheerfully. "I go tell doctor."

The salon was plainly a reception-room for patients. Looking about, Esther wondered why physicians' reception-rooms were invariably so uninviting, so lacking in personality. This one was particularly drab and cold, though she could not say that it was shabby or in more than usual bad taste. It was furnished in nondescript French style, a mixture of periods, with heavy olive-green curtains at the windows shutting out most of the light, and pale cotton brocade on the modern Louis Seize chairs. A plaster bust of Voltaire on the mantel-piece was flanked by Louis Philippe candlesticks, the whole reflected in a gilt-framed mirror extending to the ceiling. Across the middle of the room stretched a reproduction Louis Quinze table with ormolu mounts, and on it were stacked regular piles of magazines, French and English. Everything was in meticulous order. The parquet shone with a glassy finish. From the corner a tall clock ticked loudly, deliberately. The house was very still.

Suddenly Esther felt uncomfortable, oppressed. Yet why? There was no reason to dread the coming interview. Indeed, she could think of no plausible explanation for the absurd panic which overtook her in a flash. Why, for a single instant she had half a mind to bolt out of the house before the doctor appeared. What utter nonsense! How ashamed she would have been! To steady herself she picked up the folded copy of the morning paper facing her and opening it re-read the advertisement that had brought her here. It was plain and to the point:

"Dr. Gregory Sartorius of 86, Route de Grasse, wishes to find a well-educated young Englishwoman, trained nurse preferred, to assist him in his work. Good references essential. Applicants may call between two and four."

It sounded just the thing. Suitable jobs were not plentiful in Cannes, her three-day search had been sufficient to convince her of that fact.

She hoped she would land this one; if not, it would probably mean New York again, and the blizzard. She hated to be beaten.

A shadow darkened the glass doors. She sprang to her feet, slightly disconcerted to feel that the doctor had been silently inspecting her from without, perhaps for several seconds. Again she was impatient with herself for the odd suggestion of alarm which came upon her. She was not usually nervous like this.

What an immense man he was! That was her first thought as he paused for an instant in the doorway, scrutinising her. Big and rather clumsily built, with awkward, slow movements. He had a student's stoop, and his skin was brownish and dull, his whole heavy person suggesting the sedentary worker. His low forehead, receding into a bald head, was oddly flattish in shape. It reminded Esther of something—she couldn't think what. He stood with his head slightly lowered and regarded her deliberately, appraisingly, before he uttered a word. She could hear his breathing.

"Good afternoon, Miss . . ."

He stopped inquiringly.

"My name is Rowe. I've come about the advertisement, doctor."

He approached slowly, showing a sort of lethargic reluctance towards effort which extended even to the muscles of his almost expressionless face. To some he might have appeared dull and stupid, but Esther knew this was not true. There was life in the flicker of his small eyes, deep-set, bilious in tinge, and as she looked into them she received the impression of a great inner concentration of energy.

"You are American, I see."

"Well, Canadian, as a matter of fact. I trained in New York."

"A nurse, then. Where did you train?"

"St. Luke's."

She thought this made a good impression.

He made a chary movement of his hand towards a chair and at the same time sank into a fragile fauteuil, which creaked with his weight. He sighed, obviously bored with the prospect of the interview.

"What are you doing in France?"

"I came here as companion to a patient of mine who hates travelling alone. We stopped a week in Paris; then I brought her here, where she met some friends with whom she went on to Algeria. It was arranged beforehand. I was only to come as far as Cannes. I've been here a week now, and I was going back to New York, only—"

"Well?"

Esther smiled with the complete frankness which was one of her greatest assets.

"Well, doctor, I've never been abroad before, and I may never come again. It seems so stupid, having come so far, not to stay more than two weeks. I love it here. Only in order to stay I must get some work; I can't afford to be idle."

He seemed to find this reasonable, though not interesting, glancing away from her in a bored fashion.

"I see. Now about this place. What I want is a nurse who will be in attendance here from nine in the morning till six in the afternoon; someone thoroughly responsible, who will make appointments, do a little secretarial work, answer the telephone, and, of course, assist when there are examinations. The usual thing."

"Yes, doctor, I understand."

"Can you typewrite?"

"A little. I'll improve with practice."

"Know French?"

"Not too well, but I mean to study."

"It's of no great consequence, most of my patients are English. How old are you?"

It was a medical, impersonal question. He might have been inquiring the age of her grandmother in Manitoba.

"I'm nearly twenty-six."

"You look younger, but no one can tell these days. Now as to references. What can you show me?"

"I have brought my certificate from the hospital, and I have my passport, of course—"

"Let me see them."

He examined both, not omitting to look at the libellous photograph on the passport.

"Still, these are not really sufficient, Miss—Miss Rowe. They tell me nothing of your reputation, your character."

"I'd thought of that," she replied quickly. "I've got a letter written by Miss Ferriss, the patient I came with. She's known me several years."

"Ah! And how am I to know you didn't write the letter yourself?"

She was on firm ground now.

"I thought of that, too. I got her to write it in the presence of the manager of the Carlton Hotel and deposit it with him. You can ask him to show it to you."

He raised his brows slightly, seeming to admit, though with a bad grace, that she might not be as much of a fool as he first thought her. She suspected that his opinion of women was low.

"I see. Of course it won't tell me what I chiefly want to know, but I'll look it up. What I must have," and he brought his hand down weightily on the table, "is accuracy. Accuracy and precision . . . you see, I shall want you sometimes to help me in the laboratory."

"I thought you were a scientist!"

He looked at her with a flicker of interest.

"Oh? Why did you think that?"

She felt confused.

"I'm not quite sure. Something about you suggests a scientist. I worked one summer with a Rockefeller Institute man who was doing research. Perhaps that's why."

"Who was he?"

"Dr. Blumenfeld. He was working on infantile paralysis."

He nodded. "Blumenfeld; yes, I know him. He's on the wrong tack."

Slowly he hoisted his big body up out of the chair, giving the impression that the interview was finished.

"What am I to understand, then, doctor? Do you think you will want me?"

He bent his cold and impersonal gaze on her and again she felt oppressed. Her eyes dwelt on his rather ugly, flattish forehead, which somehow fascinated her. He appeared to be thinking of something else and trying at the same time to bring his attention to bear on the problem of the moment.

"Ah yes. I'll probably let you know this evening, after I've seen that letter. What is your address?"

She gave him the name of her small hotel and he wrote it down. Then suddenly she recalled the question of salary, which had escaped his notice altogether.

"One thing more, doctor. You haven't told me what you pay."

He mentioned a sum in francs; she put it quickly into dollars. It was a much smaller amount than she made in America, but she thought she could live on it. After all, was it not worth a little managing to stay on in this beautiful sunny place?

"You'll get your lunches here—and your tea," the doctor informed her.

He moved towards the door, plainly anxious to be rid of her. It crossed her mind that seldom had she seen a medical man with a less genial personality. She found it an effort to answer naturally, suddenly wondering what it would be like to have her lunch in this house, and whether she had to have it with him.

"All right, doctor, I won't look further till I've heard from you."

At the front door she looked up at him and was about to hold out her hand, but one glimpse of his dour, preoccupied face made her change her mind. Still, it was so incurably her habit to be trusting and friendly that on the doorstep she turned to shed on him her candid smile—only to find the door already closed. The rebuff was like a cold shower; it made her catch her breath. Had she made a bad impression on the man? Did he consider her rather confiding simplicity unbusinesslike? She resolved hastily to cultivate a severer demeanour for European use.

"Never mind," she reflected philosophically. "I have a feeling I'll land the job, which is the main thing. And as for the doctor—however queer he is, he'll be safe in one respect—he'll never make love to me!"

This, in her eight years' experience on her own, she had learned to consider. Not that all doctors and male patients made love, but there were a sufficient number who did, in spite of what certain invidious colleagues might say about girls getting only what they asked for.

For a moment she looked up at the house, its red-brick front and painted door so blank and non-committal, so little revealing, then with a laugh at her recent discomfiture she drew her fur closer about her throat and set off briskly towards the centre of the town.

She had not taken a dozen steps when the loud bang of a door made her look suddenly behind. Yes, it was the doctor's door, the same that had been shut in her face a moment ago. A young man—English by the look of him—had issued hastily from the house and was now getting into a small, rather smart car that stood by the curb.

In another moment the car and its occupant glided past her, the young man sullenly intent on the road ahead. Esther had a close view of his face, clean-shaven, healthily bronzed, with a sort of neat and inconspicuous good looks, somehow marred by a shallow hardness in the eyes and fine lines that spoke of high-living. Not a person one would notice very especially, yet at sight of him the girl's thoughts were instantly diverted into a new channel. She frowned as she watched the disappearing car.

"Now where is it I have seen that man before?" she pondered.

She had certainly met no one in Cannes; she knew few if any Englishmen, yet the face, with its combined hint of cynicism and petulance, was undoubtedly familiar. It stirred some vibration in her memory, recent, and in an indefinable way unpleasant. Where had she seen him?

She gave it up.

CHAPTER II

An hour later Esther sat at a table in the magnificent Restaurant des Ambassadeurs, drinking her tea with enjoyment and revelling in the scene before her. She felt a little guilty at being here, for she was a conscientious young woman, averse to throwing money about when there was nothing coming in. Still, she had not indulged herself to any great extent since Miss Ferriss departed, having bent all her efforts towards finding work, and now that there was employment in prospect she thought she had earned the right to a little relaxation. Gaiety was all about her, the very air of this holiday place held the suggestion of it like a pervading perfume. Consequently, when she had roamed about for an hour and finally gravitated towards the Croisette, the temptation came upon her to satisfy her longing for tea in some place where she could look upon the care-free world that flocked here to play. Not that she belonged to that world, heaven knows!—though, travelling de luxe with patients, as she often did, she knew a good deal about it, and it was always fun to pretend for a brief time that she did not have to work for her living.

The huge room was filling rapidly; it was the hour of the *thé dansant*. An orchestra, rich with saxophones, played a waltz that everyone in France was singing. It was from the latest musical success now running in Paris, and it pleased Esther to think she had seen the piece itself, ten days ago: it made her feel herself *au courant* of things new and smart. Leaning back in her chair she listened to the insidious little tune that grew more captivating with each repetition, meanwhile letting her eyes wander happily over the circling figures of the dancers. Glamour over-spread the scene; she was in the mood to see only the gracious and gay. For the moment the obvious boredom of confirmed pleasure-seekers escaped her entirely; the efforts of spoiled youth and jaded old age to escape from themselves had no place in the pattern of the life she saw before her. No, on the contrary, as she gazed through half-closed eyes, she fancied she saw a multi-coloured bed of flowers—flowers in rhythmic motion, that was all. Delicious frocks, swirling, floating, delicate shades of rose, mauve, periwinkle-blue, accents of black, graceful bodies, slender legs and ankles . . . not all so slender, she amended presently, becoming more critical. There were lower extremities of the grand-piano type, and short, fat feet with a look of pincushions resolutely stuffed into shoes.

Her own slender, well-shod feet would do more than pass muster here, she reflected with satisfaction. Indeed, although she was more plainly dressed than most of the women present, she rejoiced to feel she did not suffer too much by comparison. Esther was never dowdy. She was not ashamed of her well-tailored coat and skirt, marron in colour—which went well with her eyes and hair—nor of her little new felt hat, purchased in Paris. Her small choker fur was of good stone-marten, even her gloves and the handkerchief peeping from her pocket had the correct touch. Trifles, perhaps, but trifles that mattered. She made "good money," and she had always found it paid to dress well and carefully. . . . Of course, she would not be able to buy clothes on her salary from Dr. Sartorius—but what did it matter, for six months or so? It was surely worth a sacrifice to remain in France. Besides, she had a little saved up.

The doctor . . . that rather odd, cold creature. The prospect of working for him did not fill her with enthusiasm. What exactly was it she felt about him? She strove to analyse her impression, and found herself thinking only of his small, dull eyes and queer, flat forehead. . . . He was an able man, no charlatan, of that she was sure, instinctively. Primarily, a student, no doubt. What was his practice like, if indeed he had any? Not a good manner for a doctor, too remote, too negative, too lacking in humanity.

"For a moment I felt positively creepy!" she told herself. "What was it he reminded me of? Something that fascinated and repelled . . . or am I merely imagining things?"

After all, what did it matter? She always got on well with people. . . .

"My Dinah's gone away to Carolina,
My Dinah's gone and broke my heart in two.
Lonesome and blue,
Nothin' to do,
I roams around a-feelin' like I had the 'flu . . ."

From the region of the saxophones a gorgeous baritone had soared forth. Glancing around she saw the glistening black face of a faultlessly attired American negro. The song, one of the mournful type now emanating from Broadway, was the last word in banality, but the honeyed voice, suave, insinuating, gave it the charm of a narcotic. Even the waiters stopped where they were and gazed as they listened, transfixed. Conversation died, the great room was stilled to drink in the notes. A storm of applause, the chorus was repeated once, twice. Then fell a moment's lull and ordinary sounds began again.

It was at this moment that, tea-pot in hand, Esther heard close at her elbow the choking sound of a woman's sob. It startled her so that she very nearly looked around, curious to see the person who was so moved by the sentimental tribute to the lost Dinah. Then she was glad she had not turned, for she caught these words, low, passionate, distinct:

"Arthur—if *you* go away from me, as you speak of doing, I think, quite quietly, I shall kill myself!"

Good heavens! The woman, whoever she was, said it as it she meant it. It was no joking voice, its owner was deeply moved. She was evidently French, though her English was nearly faultless, the accent a mere flavour. Esther recalled that a man and woman had taken the table on her right and a little behind her. She longed to look at them, but controlled her impulse, out of curiosity to hear more. There was a silence that seemed interminable. Then the woman spoke again, her voice vibrant, urgent:

"You heard me! Why don't you answer? Why? Ah! My God, it is like beating against a stone wall!"

At last a man's voice, low, cold and a little sulky.

"What do you want me to say, Thérèse? You know as well as I do I've got to live."

"Ah, but is that the reason—the only reason for your going?"

"Good God, what else would it be? You don't imagine I'd choose to bury myself in a rotten hole like that, do you?"

There was a long sigh, quavering with tears.

"I know how fearfully difficult it all is, only, Arthur, why must you decide at once? Why not wait a bit?"

"If I wait, I lose the job. That's why. I thought you understood. Besides, what is there to hang about here for?"

"Well . . . There's always a chance, isn't there?"

An exclamation of contempt followed by the scratch of a match, then again silence, fraught, so Esther felt, with tension. Who, what were these people? She must try to steal a glance at them. Cautiously she turned her head, then, finding both the occupants of the next table were looking the other way, she indulged in a good inspection.

The woman claimed her attention first. Young—a very young thirty-five, Esther decided—blonde with delicate transparency, and lovely; her natural beauty was accentuated by careful make-up and clothes so exquisite that they could be called "elegant" without a misuse of the word. It seemed evident that she was wealthy. Her gown of filmy black had the cachet of an exclusive house, the expensive simplicity that serves so well as a background for wonderful jewels. Against it gleamed a heavy strand of glistening pearls—"Real ones, too!" thought Esther—on one slender arm slid negligently half a dozen diamond bangles, on the hand which supported her chin an enormous square diamond blazed. Her skin, shadowed by her little close black hat, was dazzling, her eyes large, grey flecked with gold, and shaded by long dark lashes. Altogether there was about her the clear beauty of a star, which even the traces of emotion now discernible could not dim.

And her companion—what was he like? Esther glanced at him and gave a start. It was the young Englishman who had come out of the doctor's house, the man she had seen before somewhere—she still did not recall where. Studied at close range he revealed points of interest. He was dressed with that perfection crowned with negligence which the Englishman of the upper classes so admirably achieves. He was, in fact, unmistakably a gentleman, at least by birth, though his bored manner held a hint of insolence, a suggestion of the bounder. His hazel eyes, glancing about with irritable restlessness, were curiously devoid of any depths, his mouth showed a mixture of weakness and obstinacy, devil-may-care courage and lack of moral stamina. An after-the-war product, no doubt, nervy and jumpy, frayed by stimulants and late hours, and yet, with all this, attractive. Yes, curiously attractive, there was no denying it.

"Waiter—where's that blasted waiter gone?"

He turned in Esther's direction, and for an instant his eyes met hers and took her in, though with little show of interest. Seeing him full-face she suddenly recalled him. Of course! When she and Miss Ferriss had first arrived, they had seen him on two occasions lunching in the Carlton grill, in company with a swarthy over-dressed Spanish-looking woman and her daughter. She remembered now. Shrewd old Miss Ferriss had said about him:

"Esther, that young Englishman over there is very nice-looking, but I can tell you he's what we call at home a *cake-hound*. I can always spot them!"

Esther smiled at the recollection.

"Waiter—bring me a 'doctor'—will you? And hold on—what do you want, Thérèse?"

"*Rien—rien du tout. Non, tenez—du thé de Chine, simplement.*"

She took care of her looks, that was evident. The waiter gone, Esther saw the Frenchwoman lean across to her companion with an obvious effort of self-control.

"Arthur—tell me once more. What is it, this job you speak of?"

"What, the Argentine? I don't know. The Toda woman wants to take me out there as a sort of manager or something. She sails on the eighth; she expects me to go with her."

"T'ck! I knew it!"

The beautiful woman's voice rose shrilly with a strident note which was an odd revelation.

"So that is it! Manager—ha, ha, ha! But, of course, I might have known, it is quite plain, she wants you for herself—the old cow! *Naturellement!*"

"S'sh, Thérèse, for God's sake—"

"Well, isn't it true? What can you do on a ranch? Why does she want you if not for herself? Do you deny it?"

"What's the use of denying anything? You'll believe what you want to believe."

He sounded cold, indifferent. The woman made an impulsive gesture.

"Ah, *mon cher*, now I have hurt you! Naturally I know you cannot care for this creature, this mountain of fat, *cette espèce de vache espagnole*"—she uttered the epithet literally through her teeth—"but all the same I know that she wants you, and I also know that if you go so far away—thousands and thousands of miles—it will be the end. You know it too."

Out of the tail of her eye, Esther saw the young man merely shrug his shoulders. She grew more and more interested.

"Listen, Arthur. Can we not find you something here?"

"Good God, in Cannes?"

She answered the utter contempt of this with a burst of self-reproach. *"Mon Dieu, mon Dieu, c'est de ma faute, si j'avais su—"*

"Oh, cut it, old girl, what's the good of post-mortems?"

"But it was my fault! If only I hadn't let him think it was baccarat—if I'd thought of some other excuse! But I never knew, I never dreamed—and now, of course, I'm so utterly helpless, my hands are tied!"

She made a hysterical gesture which shivered the diamond bangles in a mass together.

"Oh, well—"

"Arthur, tell me! Is there no other way, absolutely no other? Must you go with this creature?"

A pause while the returning waiter set before them tea and a cocktail. Then the young man's voice, wearied and irritable.

"I tell you I've got to live. And I can't live on air."

Another long pause and Esther began to fear they would say no more. She had become so interested, too, it seemed a shame. After a wait of at least three minutes the woman spoke once more in an altered, quieter tone:

"I forgot to tell you something. Yesterday I went again to Fleurestine. You remember Fleurestine?"

"Oh, *that* woman!"

"Oh, I know you don't believe in her, but . . . well, anyhow, yesterday she went into a trance. She was quite, quite unconscious. She saw things. She saw Charles . . ."

"Oh, she did, did she?"

As if moved by a common impulse, both turned and took a brief survey of the neighbouring tables. On Esther they bent but a casual glance. She was apparently quite absorbed in the contents of her bag.

"She saw him in bed, ill, very ill. There was a nurse beside him."

"Oh, ill enough for a nurse . . . Well, did she see anything more?"

"No, that was all, except that she described the doctor."

"Not my friend Sartorius?"

"Yes, she described him perfectly."

Esther strained her ears to catch all they said. Dr. Sartorius—so these people were patients of his!

"What then?"

"Nothing. She woke up."

"She would!"

He gave an ironical laugh.

"Still, Arthur, one can't help thinking . . . after all, he's seventy-three. . . ."

"Yes, and he'll live to be ninety. You'll see."

"Ninety!"

"I'm not joking. It wouldn't surprise me if he outlived us both."

There was a gasp of horror from the Frenchwoman.

"Oh, Arthur, it's cruel of you! Besides, I tell you, it's impossible; it's—"

"Yes, I know, it's simply not done. But he'll do it, you'll see."

"I will not see. I refuse to believe it. He cannot, he—"

"Steady on, Thérèse!"

There was a note of warning in his voice the cause of which Esther perceived when a moment later the couple were joined by a plump Frenchwoman with hennaed hair and a burnt-orange make-up.

"*Comment ça va, Thérèse? Ah, Captain, on me dit que vous avez l'intention de nous quitter. C'est vrai?*"

What ensued was lost in a cackle of French interspersed with high-pitched laughter. The friend sat down for a few minutes, joked with the "Captain," drank the remainder of his cocktail, and patted him famil-iarly on the cheek. Esther stole a glance at the beautiful blonde woman and found her calm, gazing across the room with narrowed eyes and an expression of thought. At last she got out her mirror and made herself up, as delicately as a cat washes its face, little touches here and there.

"Going?"

"Yes, I shall see if the doctor will give me a *piqûre*. I am very tired."

"I thought you had them on Mondays and Thursdays."

"Yes, but sometimes I have an extra one. They pick me up."

"*Ah, les piqûres! Je suis, très bien, ça!*"

In two minutes all three had risen and disappeared into the crowd about the broad stairs that led into the room. Left behind, Esther felt a sense of flatness and anti-climax. She had begun to take such a keen interest in the blonde woman and her young Englishman, that the thought of not finding out more about them filled her with disappointment. Still, they were patients of the doctor she was perhaps going to work for; there was a chance that she might learn something more. She sat turning over in her mind all she had overheard. Though not particularly worldly wise, she was no fool, and while she was not quite clear about the situation of these two and their relations to each other, the various implications they had let fall were not entirely lost on her.

She had not seen the last of the Captain, as it happened. Five minutes later she caught sight of him sauntering about near the entrance with a vacant eye and a restless manner. Simultaneously there approached her corner a short, enormously fat, overdressed woman, barging aggressively ahead towards the vacant table, her huge bosom well in advance like the prow of a ship. As the swarthy face drew nearer she saw that it and the bosom belonged to the Spanish woman of the Carlton—no doubt the very one who was trying to entice the young man to the Argentine. Yes, and there was the daughter coming in her wake, a clumsily built girl in pink satin, her swart arms bare to the shoulder. The elder woman attacked the waiter almost bodily, and in hard, guttural French commanded him to move the table closer to the dancing floor—an operation causing considerable annoyance to the surrounding guests. For a moment the Spaniard pressed her hulk so close to Esther that the latter was nearly choked with the fumes of her chypre. Then suddenly there was a shriek of delight. The lady, as Esther expressed it to herself, had discovered her "boy friend."

"What will be the end of it?" wondered Esther as she paid her bill and rose to go. "Which of these two women is going to get her way?"

With amusement she watched the stolid daughter led away by a "professional" to dance the tango, leaving her mother in eager conversation with the Englishman, tapping his arm with her pudgy hand, her black eyes like burnt holes in the whiteness of her powdered face. Then she threaded her way out of the restaurant and through the main entrance of the Casino.

When she reached her hotel the sallow clerk called to her as she passed his desk.

"Oh, Mees, I have here a note for you. It has just arrived."

She tore open the envelope. It contained two lines in a small, slovenly hand, on thick, engraved paper.

"Dr. Sartorius will expect Nurse Rowe to-morrow, Wednesday, at nine in the morning."

So that was that!

CHAPTER III

ESTHER was not mistaken in her surmise that the doctor was by choice
at least more of a scientist than a physician. Patients he had to be sure,
a respectable number, composed mostly of English and American tourists, well-to-do people. Esther thought that if he had been more keenly
interested or a better business man he might have developed his practice
into a large and lucrative one. She recognised in him the sure instinct of
the natural diagnostician, she knew enough to realise that his methods
and knowledge were up to date. Even that manner of his, though a little
forbidding, had the merit of inspiring confidence. One felt he was a big
man and could afford to dispense with geniality. Yet it was perfectly
apparent that his practice never came first with him. Esther had not
been in the house with him half a week before she made that discovery.
Every free minute of the day found him engrossed in his experiments, to
the utter exclusion of all else, so intolerant of interruption that he more
than once kept patients waiting a quarter of an hour in the gloomy salon
while he finished some piece of work.

The laboratory, with which Esther quickly became familiar, was
at the top of the house, up two flights of stairs, a bare, L-shaped room
built originally for a studio. A sloping skylight admitted a strong north
light, which streamed down on the long table covered with all the paraphernalia of research. There were two glass cabinets containing bottles
of many descriptions, and a plain Normandy oak armoire, fitted with
shelves upon which were specimens and materials for work. A fibre mat
and a couple of kitchen chairs completed the furnishings of the main part,
but in a sort of alcove which formed the base of the L, and which was
curtained off by thick red hangings, was a camp bed with a table beside
it and a chest of drawers. Here, so she was told by Jacques the servant,
the doctor not infrequently slept when he had carried on his labours far
into the night. He would drop down on the hard bed at perhaps five in
the morning, just as he was, in his shirt and trousers, with only an old
army blanket over him, and there he would sleep like a dead man till
Jacques brought him his tea.

Esther learned a good deal from Jacques who, despite his desper-
ado exterior, proved to be friendly and communicative, glad no doubt of
someone to chat with since his master was so particularly reserved. His
master, Jacques confided about the third day, was not a man at all but
a machine. Work, work, work—day and night, no thought for comfort,

no distractions, no voices. *Voyons!* It was against nature when a man lived like that. And what did he get for it?

"*Écoutez, mademoiselle,*" the little man of the Midi said to her earnestly, laying his finger on her arm, "if the doctor worked only one half so hard—only one half, now I am telling you—he could be a rich man to-day, with a palace, three, four cars, a chauffeur, a *valet de chambre*. It is only because he spends his time up there in that room that he makes so little money."

Esther knew that he was right, although she understood better than he the unworldly aims of the man.

Jacques had more to tell her. Such was the doctor's complete stupidity, not to be comprehended by rational beings, that whenever he had a little money put aside he would shut up shop and take a holiday, so as to be able to devote all his days to research.

"Mademoiselle knows that is not a way to do," complained Jacques in an aggrieved voice. "People think he not practise any more, they find another doctor. Many, many times he lose patients that way. *Quelle bêtise, voyons!*"

"He must have been practising pretty steadily now for some time," remarked Esther, "to have as good a practice as he seems to have."

"Ah, yes, it is long now, for him, and I think he gets now what you English call fed-up. I believe he would like to throw it all up to-morrow, but he cannot. It is the season, there are many English here. Later, in the summer, perhaps, he take a rest."

These confidences took place chiefly at *déjeuner*, which Esther ate alone in the *salle à manger*, a room more cheerful than the salon, being on the sunny side of the house. The doctor, consecrating the lunch hour to work, had his meal brought to the laboratory on a tray. The food was excellent, in the best French bourgeois style, cooked and served by Jacques, who did all the work of the place with the help of a *femme de ménage* in the mornings. He was frankly delighted when Esther did justice to his dishes.

"Mademoiselle will have a little more of the *blanquette de veau*," he would say pleadingly. "It is very good, yes, the *champignons* I choose myself. The doctor up there will eat whatever I give him. If it is bread and cheese it make no difference, but I, I say to him, '*Il faut que cette demoiselle soit nourié!*'"

He was the one human element in the establishment, Jacques, and his familiarity was not offensive.

As for her employer, Esther decided that she could live at close quarters with him for a year and know him no better than she did now. At the end of a week she regarded him as an unknown quantity. A man of one idea, extraordinarily concentrated, methodical, abstracted, without friends, no outside interests whatever. That is all she could gather. Silent, yet hardly secretive, he merely gave her the impression that he had nothing he wished to impart. He was not curious about other people, why should they want to know about him? Not by any stretch of imagination could she connect him with a human emotion. He never asked her a question about herself or her antecedents, and only once did he volunteer any information in regard to himself, and then it seemed as though for a moment he was thinking aloud. He referred absent-mindedly to a time when he lived in Algeria, mentioning the fact that for almost two years he was able to experiment without interruption.

"I had a bit of money," he remarked, "a windfall . . ."

"I suppose someone died and left you a legacy," suggested Esther, washing test-tubes at the basin in the corner.

He appeared to have forgotten the subject, but presently he roused himself to reply:

"Eh? What was that?" he murmured vaguely, holding a tube up to the light. "There is a sediment here, certainly. . . . Yes, that was it. A legacy. I lived on it for two years, then I had to go back to the grind again."

Esther was curious to know more about the research which so completely absorbed him, but he was not eager to talk about it. Still, by watching him and prodding him occasionally with direct questions, she discovered what she wanted to know. Two of his serums were in general use; she had heard of them. Indeed, she knew enough to be impressed. This was a valuable man of science; why, he might yet be awarded the Nobel prize; his discoveries were quite important enough to merit it. Yet she suspected that the idea of fame had never entered his head, he worked for the love of it. He was engaged now in trying to find anti-toxins for certain deadly diseases, tetanus for one. When she thought of the extent to which his efforts might benefit humanity, she felt inclined to forget the man's repellent personality in the dignity of his accomplishments.

As for what she had to do, she found it neither very difficult nor very tiring—not half so hard as ordinary nursing. While the doctor was out on a round of visits, she put the laboratory to rights, arranging everything neatly and in perfect order, for that was of paramount importance to her employer; then she attended to the small amount of clerical work that fell to her task, answered the telephone, and made appointments.

In the afternoon there was a fairly steady stream of patients for consultations, and she was kept moderately busy, yet with frequent moments in which to sit down and read or "have a go" at her French grammar.

The evenings at her hotel threatened to be a little dull; she did not care to go alone to the Casino and, barring the cinema, there was not much in the way of distraction. Still, she was far from regretting her determination to stay in Cannes. She wrote long letters to her sisters in Canada, to Miss Ferriss in Bousaada, to a certain young doctor in New York, who for years had lavished on her an unrewarded devotion. She thought of him dimly as belonging to another life. Already she had slipped into new habits, fresh ways of thinking. She planned excursions for Saturday afternoons and Sundays, meaning to see as much of this country as possible while she had the chance.

"If only Jean were here, what fun we'd have!" she reflected regretfully.

Jean was her favourite sister, now a librarian in Montreal.

At the end of the week something happened. Late one afternoon a patient arrived who had no appointment. Jacques admitted her, went up to tell the doctor, who had thought consultations over for the day, then, returning, spoke to Esther in the *salle à manger*.

"It is Lady Clifford," he whispered. "It is the second time now she come like this. Always before, the doctor he go to her."

Esther knew the name, her book had told her that the doctor paid regular visits to a Lady Clifford. She turned up the visits for the next day. Yes, there it was, Thursday, Lady Clifford, 11.30.

She heard the doctor's heavy step on the stairs, so she hastily replaced the crisp white coif she had removed a moment ago and repaired to the salon. A slender woman was standing at the window looking out and tapping her foot with nervous impatience. She was smartly dressed in black, with a magnificent silver fox about her shoulders.

"Will you come this way, please," said Esther. "The doctor will see you."

The woman turned suddenly and Esther received a shock of surprise. It was the blonde woman of the *Restaurant des Ambassadeurs*. As she was French it had never occurred to Esther to connect her with the unknown Lady Clifford. For a moment she felt self-conscious, afraid lest the beautiful patient should recognise her. But no, there was no need for alarm, the Frenchwoman passed her with a brief, incurious glance. Probably on that former occasion she had never noticed Esther at all, or if she had, the nurse's uniform was sufficient to effect a complete alteration. Who was this exquisite creature, French, but with an English name? All Esther's curiosity returned in full force.

Dr. Sartorius stood, heavy and uncompromising, beside the flat mahogany desk. He scarcely took the step forward which courtesy demanded. Surely his manners were the least ingratiating Esther had ever known in a professional man!

"Forgive me, doctor, for coming like this," the patient began impulsively. "But to-morrow morning I find I cannot be at home, and I do hate to miss my *piqûre!*"

"Very well, you can have it now."

That was his grudging response to an appeal full of winning charm.

Women and their fascination had evidently no part in his life.

"Ah, that is good of you! It puts strength into me—and I have need of all my strength. I"—she paused to moisten her lips—"I wish also to have a word with you again about my husband."

"Oh?"

She had stripped off her gloves and was clasping and unclasping her hands.

"Yes, I—I don't feel quite so satisfied about him as I did. I want to ask you some questions."

While she was speaking, the doctor, having signed to Esther to remain, had opened a drawer and was taking out several small bottles which he examined one after the other.

"Miss Rowe," he said, "all these are empty. On the top shelf in the oak cupboard in the laboratory you will find a full one. Bring it to me, please."

He extended an empty bottle for her to see the label.

"Yes, doctor, I won't be a minute," Esther replied, and hastened out, closing the door behind her.

She ran up the two flights of stairs without stopping to take breath, and looked into the Normandy armoire, but neither on the top shelf nor any of the others could she find what she wanted. She went over the contents of the cupboard a second time to make sure, examining the labels of various drugs, chemicals, serums, cultures. What was this new bottle? Tetanus—horrible! She gave a slight shudder, realising that the stuff in that bottle was enough to give lockjaw to half the inhabitants in Cannes. No, the doctor was mistaken, the mixture she sought was not here.

Rather more slowly than she had come up, she retraced her steps to the bottom floor. At the last landing she stopped, listening acutely.

"Non, non, je ne peux pas, je ne peux pas le faire!"

It was the Frenchwoman's voice, high-pitched, emotional, the protest wrung from her as if in agony. What was she saying? A rapid stream of French followed—Esther could not catch a word of it—then at the end a phrase or two that was intelligible.

"Je vous jure, je mourrais—je mourrais. . . ."

The doctor's voice cut in upon her, dominating, brutal even, a tone that caused Esther to gasp and clutch the stair-rail.

"Stop that! Stop that nonsense! Are you an utter fool?"

It was like bidding a dog to lie down. Silence followed, then a stifled sob.

CHAPTER IV

Esther's first thought was, "Why does she stand being talked to like that? I wouldn't, not for a moment."

It was as if all his latent contempt for the opposite sex was concentrated into that one vitriolic burst. Well—! Some physicians, she knew, practised with hyper-emotional subjects the method of "treating them rough." This was probably Sartorius's idea. Certainly she was ready to believe that Lady Clifford was of the uncontrolled, hysterical type, who easily gave way to her feelings; perhaps the doctor had found this the best way of dealing with her. As she still paused, hesitating to enter the room, the doctor spoke again. "Sit down and try to behave like a reasonable woman. Remember all I have told you. Why should you upset yourself like this?"

There was no audible reply. Esther retreated upward a few steps, then descended with a brisk step and opened the door. She observed Lady Clifford sitting with a submissive mien on the edge of a stiff François Premier chair, biting her underlip and pulling a small lace-edged handkerchief between her fingers. The doctor, with an immovable face, was filling a hypodermic syringe from a small phial.

"I'm sorry, doctor—" Esther began, when he interrupted her.

"No, no, it's all right, nurse, I found I had some here after all. Now, if you will assist Lady Clifford with her dress—"

"I suppose you give it in the thigh?"

"In the thigh."

Lady Clifford had crossed to the hard couch by the window, and was now seated, leaning up against the cushions at the end, cautiously, so as not to disarrange her hat. Esther drew up the narrow skirt, exposing slender legs encased in gossamer stockings and six inches or so of a diaphanous under-garment, pink georgette, delicate as a cobweb and scented like the rest of its owner with an indefinable and slightly cloying perfume. On the white skin just below the hip there showed startlingly a blue-black bruise, the size of a franc piece—the visible mark of repeated injections. Esther sponged a fresh spot and the doctor shot in the long needle with a casual indifference. Simultaneously the woman on the couch closed her eyes and stretched out her limbs with a feline luxurious movement. Esther was tempted to believe she enjoyed the stabbing pain. There were people who took a sensual delight in suffering, or at least she had heard that there were. She watched curiously the sort of rapturous twist of the patient's body, the convulsive grip of her hands on the rim of the couch.

Hands? For the first time Esther noticed them. What was it about them that was different, that filled her with a mixture of fascination and repugnance? They were not large; they were soft, milky-white, marvellously manicured, each nail a plaque of carmine enamel. Yet there was something wrong, almost like a deformity. Of course! It was the shortness of the fingers, or rather, of the first joint, a general look of stumpiness, the nails trained to long points to hide the deficiency. The thumbs, in particular—how squat, how stunted! They appeared to have only two joints instead of three. Somehow they gave her a feeling akin to nausea. . . . She sponged the puncture with iodine, smoothed down the skirt, cleaned and replaced the needle in its case, and all the time she was thinking of those oddly repulsive hands. Repulsive to her, that is. She knew that not many people would have noticed them specially.

Lady Clifford had risen, a sort of nervous expectancy in her manner.

The doctor glanced at her, then turned to Esther.

"You may as well go home, if you like, Miss Rowe," he said. "I don't think I shall need you for anything more."

"Oh, thank you, doctor!"

It still wanted half an hour until the time she usually left off. For a moment it flashed upon her that there was, after all, a spark of kindliness concealed in that big, slow-moving machine, and the thought warmed and pleased her. She always wanted to like the people she worked for, it was so much jollier. But when she smiled her appreciation she met with no answering gleam whatever. He had already forgotten her as a person, was merely waiting for her to leave the room.

"There's no use," she sighed ruefully as she closed the door. "I might as well try to be fond of the Woolworth Building!"

"Oh, nurse," Lady Clifford called to her suddenly. "Perhaps you will be so good as to give a message to my chauffeur. Tell him he is not to wait, but to call instead for Sir Charles at his club."

"Yes, Lady Clifford."

She quickly got into her things and slipped out of the front door. The car waiting by the curb was a luxurious Rolls, the sandy-haired English chauffeur was smoking a cigarette and reading the *Sporting Times* by the aid of a tiny electric light. Inside the car on dark blue cushions a small Aberdeen terrier, the picture of patient good-behaviour, sat gazing resignedly out of the window. The rug heaped beside him showed a lining of sable pattes. Clearly Lady Clifford, whoever she might be, possessed an abundance of this world's goods. How doubly odd that she should allow her physician to order her about in so peremptory a fashion! Probably no one else dared to, she looked arrogant enough herself, for all her fairness and fragility.

The chauffeur stared at Esther attentively while she delivered the message, then with a stolid face, "Right-o, miss," he replied and, touching his cap, started the engine.

"How do you do, Miss Rowe? Is this the place where you are employed?"

Esther jumped, astonished at anyone's knowing her name. Then, seeing who it was who had come up behind her, she smiled in recognition.

"Oh! Miss Paull! I had no idea."

It happened that Miss Paull was the one person at her hotel with whom she had any extensive conversation. She was a tall and angular Englishwoman, clad always in voluminous black, a wide-brimmed, old-fashioned hat resting uneasily atop her mountain of snowy hair.

"Yes, that is the doctor's house," added Esther in reply to her acquaintance's question. "I'm just off for the day."

"Shall we walk along together then?" suggested the other, slightly modifying her tremendous strides. In spite of her elderly and quaint appearance—rather in the style of an ancient Du Maurier drawing—the lady was a tireless pedestrian, covering miles daily, armed with an umbrella, a water-colour box, and a folding camp-stool. Esther had more than once met her, racing along, not the least impeded by her paraphernalia, her black cloak and veil streaming behind her in the wind.

"Do you know this neighbourhood?" Esther was inquiring, when she noticed that her companion had stopped stock still and was regarding with frank curiosity the Rolls Royce, which had just succeeded in reversing its position.

"I seem to know that car," remarked Miss Paull. "I certainly know the chauffeur's face. Can it be—yes, now I know." She walked on again with a satisfied air. "That car belongs to a countryman of mine; he has a villa over there"—she waved a black-gloved hand—"in the part that they call La Californie."

"Really!"

Esther's tone was one of lively interest. Now she would hear something.

"He's a Mr. Clifford—or no, he is Sir Charles Clifford now, he was knighted for something or other during the war. He's a big mill owner in Lancashire—cotton, you know. Perhaps you've heard of the firm of Seabrook & Clifford?"

Esther had not.

"No, of course not. I forgot you don't know England. It's an important firm, though, several big factories. They make the Seacliff Fabrics. Sir Charles was our Conservative member for years. He has a place near my home, between Chester and Altringham. I've often seen him."

"There is a Lady Clifford with the doctor now. What is she—a daughter-in-law? She's quite young."

"Is she French?"

"Yes."

"Ha! That's his wife. His second wife, of course. He married again about six years ago, some Frenchwoman he met down in this part of the world. There was a great deal of excitement about it at the time, the whole neighbourhood was astonished. It must have been a shock to his family."

"Then he has a family?"

"Only a son, he lost another boy in the war. And then, of course, there is a sister, unmarried, about my own age. I've met her sometimes at charity bazaars and so on."

"Do you know Lady Clifford?"

"Heavens, no! Though I've seen her here in Cannes. I believe she was an actress."

There was no mistaking Miss Paull's sentiments in regard to the stage. Esther was secretly amused.

"They spend nearly all their time here now," continued the spinster, "though whether on account of Sir Charles's health or because his wife prefers it I can't say. I daresay it wasn't gay enough for her in Cheshire— not enough distractions. You know how it is with these young women who marry old men, they don't want to sit at home and do needlework."

She ended on an expressive note, as though implying more than her delicate maiden mind would permit her to say. Esther thought of the young Englishman in the restaurant at the Casino, and was silent.

Their walk led them through the older, more picturesque part of the town, a portion Esther loved, finding in its steep winding streets and irregular architecture the charm that was missing from the modern cities of her knowledge. Here, she thought, one could imagine anything happening—intrigues, romantic incident, crimes even, all the material that went to form tales of adventure. This was its habitat. From the newer, cleaner streets, the luxurious Promenade de la Croisette, the heterogeneous Route de Grasse, or that region of plutocrats, La Californie, one expected nothing of the kind.

"Fascinating, isn't it?" remarked her companion, echoing her thoughts.

"I am so fond of all this part. When the weather gets a little warmer I am going to bring my sketchbook out one day and get a few nice bits. That corner, for instance—delightful, don't you think?"

They dawdled a bit, through a littered street of open markets where they examined the contents of barrows—flowers, cheap lace, stockings, furs, trays of battered coins and bits of china, brass and copper vessels—now and then peering into a provocative alley-way, held by the spell of the exotic. Hatless women with smooth shining heads bustled past them, children in black pinafores played noisily in the gutters, *ouvriers* in dust-coloured corduroys bound about the waist with red sashes lurched along, often with a clatter of black varnished sabots. In a doorway one of these fellows, a swarthy brigand, was feeding a particularly ill-favoured mongrel, kneeling beside it and admonishing it to eat. *"Allez, vite, mange donc, Hélène!"* he was saying, and Esther found entertainment in the mangy cur's rejoicing in the name of Hélène.

It was dark now, lights flared in the windows. Leaving the market, they turned into a street of shops which Esther had several times explored, and paused before an antiquaire whose windows showed a display of old majolica, silver-gilt, and Limoges enamel against a Flemish tapestry.

"This is one of my favourite shops," said Miss Paull. "You know it, too? But of course I never buy anything, the things are too dear for my purse. Cannes is like Chester when it comes to antiques—too many tourists."

As she spoke a taxi rattled up the street at a characteristic break-neck speed, stopping abruptly at the shop next door, a dingy jeweller's. From the taxi stepped a woman, young, smartly dressed. She paid the fare, then stood looking somewhat uncertainly at the name on the shop door.

"C'est bien vingt-quatre, madame," said the driver, as if to help her.

"Oui—ça va bien," she replied, but still hesitating.

Esther had turned at sound of her voice just in time to see her gather her silver fox closer about her neck, clutch her red morocco *pochette* against her chest and enter the shop. The taxi, with a little "cling" of the meter, shot off down the hill. Esther touched her companion's arm.

"That was Lady Clifford who went into that shop," she said.

Miss Paull dropped her tortoiseshell lorgnon.

"Was it? I didn't notice, Where? What shop?"

"This one, just here."

"Really! That's an odd, dirty little place for her to go into!"

She raised her lorgnon again and examined the printing on the door. It was *"Abel Klement, achat de bijoux, anciens et modernes."* Then, not content with this superficial inspection, she went close to the door and, bending, gazed with frank curiosity into the interior. Lacking her indifference to appearances, Esther made a pretence of looking into the window.

"She's taking something in a small box out of her bag," announced the Englishwoman after a deliberate scrutiny. "Ah, of course, some bit of jewellery to be repaired. No, she's not opening the box, after all. She's following the man out through the door at the back of the shop. Now she's gone."

Satisfied that she could ascertain no more, Miss Paull turned away from the door.

"Doesn't look at all her sort of shop," she remarked thoughtfully as they pursued their way. "Such a dingy little second-rate place. And why do you suppose she came up in a taxi instead of her own car?"

She appeared to ponder this question so deeply that Esther was amused at what seemed to her a morbid desire to scent a mystery in an affair which, no doubt, had the most ordinary explanation.

"Now *I* should say," her companion added, confidentially, "that that fashionable lady is up to something she doesn't want known. That is *my* conviction—you can take it or leave it."

CHAPTER V

"I say, have you got any matches anywhere?"

Esther jumped at the sudden sound of a man's voice close to her ear, and looked up from the accounts she was writing. She had heard someone moving about in the salon, but she had thought it must be Jacques, who a few minutes before had been cleaning the brass on the front door.

The voice, which addressed her casually and without any preliminary greeting, stirred something in her memory. She rose from her desk by the window and shot the intruder a glance, at the same time reaching the matches from the sideboard.

"Here you are," she said, holding out the box.

The visitor, cigarette in mouth and hands in pockets, sauntered into the room and took it from her. He was young, English, immaculately dressed, except for a rather baggy Burberry, worn loosely over his tweed suit, and he carried a pair of very smart motoring gloves, which he cast upon the table. His manner was at once hard and immature, languid and curiously restless. A second glance assured Esther that her first suspicion was correct. Undoubtedly he was the young man she had seen on several occasions, notably with the Frenchwoman at the Restaurant des Ambassadeurs.

Puffing contemplatively, he let his eyes roam about the room.

"Doctor still out?" he inquired in a vacant tone.

"Yes, but he'll probably be home in a few minutes. It's nearly lunch-time."

She was going to ask if she could do anything for him, but she decided the question was superfluous. He had the air of a friend, not a patient, of an intimate dropping in for an informal call. It came to her that she must amend her opinion that Dr. Sartorius was quite without social ties. She was about to return to her work when the young man's roving eyes reached her in their tour and rested upon her face for several seconds, their vacant gaze giving way to speculative attention.

"You have a familiar look, you know," he remarked. "I seem to recall seeing you somewhere. Where was it?"

Esther met his scrutiny for a moment, then slowly shook her head.

"Odd. You've not been here before, have you? With Sartorius, I mean?"

"No, never."

He carefully flicked an ash upon the rug, then looked at her again.

"Yet I'm positive I've seen your face somewhere about Cannes." The problem appeared mildly to interest him. "Have you any idea where it could have been?"

She regarded him for some seconds, considering what to say.

"Yes," she replied deliberately. "I can tell you where it was. At least, I believe I know."

"Where?"

"In the grill-room of the Carlton. About a fortnight to three weeks ago, at lunch."

"Oh!"—he weighed the suggestion for a moment. "You may be right. I daresay."

Resolved not to mention that other encounter when he had been with Lady Clifford, Esther grew bolder.

"Weren't you there with two ladies, rather Spanish-looking, one much older than the other?"

He raised his brows and blew out a cloud of smoke.

"I shouldn't wonder," he assented, and seemed to dismiss the subject from his thoughts.

While Esther resumed her task he roamed aimlessly about, winding up again in the salon, where she heard him rustling a newspaper. Jacques, coming in to lay the table for *déjeuner*, glanced across the hall and whispered to Esther.

"That *capitaine* will stay for *déjeuner*. It is good I have a *ragoût* to-day, there will be *assez* for three. I need only to put another egg in the omelette."

He laid three places, then from the recess at the bottom of the sideboard he produced a cocktail shaker and a variety of bottles.

"That young man he stay here once for three weeks," remarked Jacques. "Always he mix the cocktails, many different kind. But to-day he will not like it that I have no ice."

A latch-key grated in the outer door, the doctor's heavy step resounded along the hall, pausing at the salon.

"Ah, Holliday," he said without surprise. "I saw your car outside."

"About the last you'll see of it, doctor," the visitor replied, joining him. "I'm going to sell it. Know anybody who wants a decent little car cheap?"

The two entered the *salle à manger* together. Esther saw the doctor give his friend a slow ruminative glance before inquiring:

"Why do you want to get rid of it?"

"Oh, I'm thinking of leaving this part of the world in a few weeks' time. No good carting a car as far as I'm going—too damned expensive."

"And where are you going?"

The doctor stood blinking down on the young man with his odd, sluggish little eyes. He appeared tired and not specially interested, yet there was a sort of negative friendliness in his attitude which Esther had not seen before.

"I may go out to the Argentine. There's a job offered me out there."

"South America!"

The sleepy gaze flickered over the whole slight, dapper person of the captain, betraying frank scorn.

"So that's it, is it?" He began feeling in his pocket for a cigarette, adding as an after-thought, "I suppose you've made up your mind about it?"

"Not entirely. But there's no point in sticking around here . . . as things are. There's precious little, I want to tell you, between me and starvation. Still, I'm taking a few weeks to think things over."

"Won't you lose the post if you let so much time go by?" inquired the doctor, with the heavy air of making conversation.

His friend's lip curled in easy contempt.

"Not *this* post," he answered laconically, and turned his attention to the sideboard. After a brief inspection of the array of bottles he called through the little passage that led to the kitchen:

"Jacques! Here then! Got any lemons?"

"Des citrons? Oui, monsieur, j'en ai."

"Squeeze a couple and bring me the juice."

"Entendu, monsieur."

With a thoughtful face Holliday measured equal parts of gin and Cointreau into the shaker. Esther found herself watching the operation with interest. Still busy, he remarked without turning:

"Old Clifford seems a bit seedy."

The doctor had sunk heavily into a chair at the top of a table with a sigh of relaxation. He replied:

"Yes, so his wife mentioned to me a few days ago, but I have not seen him."

"I have. Last night. I was there to dinner. The old boy was quite off his feed, and pushed off to bed about nine o'clock. I daresay you'll be hearing from him before long."

Sartorius yawned. "I daresay," he agreed, and broke off an end of the long stick of bread before him. It occurred to Esther that it was the first time she had seen him sit down properly at the table for a meal.

The lemon-juice arriving at this point, the expert added it to the contents of the shaker and agitated the whole violently.

"It's a long, long way to that Argentine ranch," he remarked pensively. "See here, doctor, you're a far-seeing man. On general principles, what would you advise?"

The doctor looked up from his contemplation of the mustard-pot, and it seemed to Esther that his dull eyes met and held the young man's shallow hazel ones for an appreciable space of time.

"Well," he said at length, "do you particularly want to go?"

"Like hell," was the brief reply.

"H'm! In that case I should certainly leave the decision till the last possible moment. There's always some slight chance of something's turning up."

"No! Do you think there is, though?" demanded Holliday eagerly, stopping with the shaker in his hands.

"On general principles."

The visitor's face brightened noticeably. Whistling a bar or two of "Gigolette" he poured out two glasses of a pale straw-coloured liquid, then with the shaker poised over a third glass looked inquiringly at Esther.

"What about you?" he invited.

Esther hesitated and succumbed to the temptation. After all, why not?

"As a resident of a dry country," she said, smiling, "I can't refuse."

He filled the glass and handed it to her just as Jacques entered, bearing the hot and savoury *omelette aux champignons*.

"Well!"—and Captain Holliday raised his glass and his left eyebrow simultaneously with easy nonchalance, "may we all get what we want!"

"Hear, hear," murmured the doctor mechanically, and drank his cocktail at a gulp.

Esther sipped hers, finding it a subtle and delicious concoction. Later she decided it was a potent one as well. Soon she observed that a hint of unwonted animation crept into the doctor's manner and indeed as the meal progressed he became almost gay, though how much of the change was due to the cocktail and how much to the company she could not tell. Moreover he ate steadily and voraciously. She thought she had never seen a man eat so much, it was like stoking an engine. Holliday, on the contrary, had little appetite for the excellent meal and seemed strung up with a kind of nervous excitement.

Afterwards this scene recurred to her more than once, showing to her imagination like a close-up on the screen. In the light of subsequent happenings it held for her a curious fascination. She could at any time shut her eyes and see the three of them, so ill-assorted, sitting around the table in that bourgeois dining-room, eating and conversing, herself one of the party by accident and virtually ignored by the other two, yet linked with them in a sort of casual camaraderie that was somehow established when she accepted the cocktail. Out of all that followed, no incident remained for her so sinister and at the same time so paradoxically trivial and absurd as this chance gathering at *déjeuner*.

CHAPTER VI

ONE bright afternoon about ten days after this the Rolls Royce of the Cliffords drew up at the doctor's door, and when the sandy-haired chauffeur had descended and rung the bell, there emerged from the car in somewhat ceremonial order Lady Clifford, her sister-in-law, and Sir Charles himself. To the casual eye it would appear that the first of these three could have no possible connection with the other two, any more than a bird of paradise would have with a pair of rooks.

"She has brought the old man with her this time," confided Jacques to Esther *en passant*, having admitted the trio to the salon. "He is a very bad colour, that man! I don't like his look."

Nor did Esther, when a moment later she opened the salon door and caught her first glimpse of Sir Charles, a gaunt, heavily built old man with sunken eyes, unnaturally bright, and a dry, yellowish skin tightly stretched across his prominent cheek bones. He sat leaning forward in his chair, wearing his heavy overcoat with the fur-lined collar drawn up about his thin neck and his big bony hands clasped so rigidly over the handle of his stick that the knuckles shone blanched and polished. He shivered slightly at the opening of the door.

"Here, Charlie, put on your cap," commanded his sister quickly. "This room is always creepy."

"Yes, do put it on," murmured Lady Clifford gently, taking a grey tweed cap from the table and trying to fit it on his head.

He brushed her aside with a petulant gesture.

"No, no, I don't want my hat on in the house. What do you take me for?"

The two women exchanged resigned glances, which patently said, "Well, if he won't, he won't." Miss Clifford sighed as if a little anxious, and the furrow between her brows deepened. She was strikingly like her brother, with the same heavy features, but she was a good ten years younger, and with her ruddy red-brown complexion and bright brown eyes under rather bushy brows had a look of alertness and vigour, as well as certain kindly simplicity which attracted Esther. She was dressed in good plain country clothes, and her felt hat fitted badly because of the thick coils of her hair, brown, streaked with grey.

"Will you come this way?" said Esther, holding open the consulting-room door.

The three filed past her, Sir Charles walking with a firm if inelastic tread. There was about him a look of obstinate, almost rude, determination; he had the air of coming here under protest. Miss Clifford looked at Esther with a certain interest.

"I have not seen you before. When did you come?"

"Only a few weeks ago."

"Ah, I see you're American. No, Canadian, is it? Well, it's pleasant having someone here who speaks English."

Dr. Sartorius had come forward with a more cordial manner than he usually displayed. He positively smiled as he took Miss Clifford's hand.

"Well, you're not looking very ill," he remarked in a tone almost jovial. "Don't try to tell me there's anything the matter with you. I'll refuse to believe it."

"Oh, heavens, no, I'm all right," laughed Miss Clifford agreeably. "It's this tiresome brother of mine who's been bothering us a bit. He's been feeling seedy for several days, haven't you, Charlie?"

Sir Charles shook his head, though whether in dissent or simply out of an ingrained desire to contradict was not apparent.

"Feeling seedy, has he? Well, and what seems to be the trouble?" inquired the doctor with that sort of purring patter which one can readily believe to be the first thing learned by a student of medicine. "Caught a slight chill, perhaps? The weather's been a bit tricky."

"Ah, I think it is that," put in the Frenchwoman eagerly. "That Wednesday at the polo, Charles, when it came on to rain. . . ."

"Not a bit of it," denied her husband positively. "If it comes to that, I had all these feelings before I ever thought of going to the polo."

"I begged him to let me send for you, doctor, but you know what he is like," interpolated Miss Clifford. "He hates to admit he is ill."

"What sort of feelings?" blandly inquired the doctor.

Sir Charles thrust out his lower lip. He had planted himself in an armchair, while his wife remained standing a little behind him, her face, it seemed to Esther, full of anxiety.

"Oh, headaches, backaches. The back's the worst. Goes on steadily. Had it for days."

"Sharp pain?"

"No, dull. Not like lumbago."

"He has no appetite," added his sister.

"Well, well, let's have a look at you."

The doctor drew a chair beside Sir Charles and reached for the gaunt brownish hand. At the same moment Lady Clifford made a little movement of solicitude, laying her gloved hand on the old man's shoulder.

"Are you quite comfortable there, *mon cher*?" she whispered. "You're not in a *courant d'air*?"

He let her hand rest, but shook his head impatiently.

"No, no, I'm all right. My God, doctor, what with these two women for ever fussing about my health and asking me how I feel a hundred times a day, the wonder is I manage to keep going at all."

He closed his eyes while the doctor counted his pulse. During the ensuing silence it struck Esther that both women were more worried than was necessary. The Frenchwoman in particular watched with an air of tense apprehension.

The doctor shut up his watch with a snap.

"Now the tongue," he said non-committally.

He examined the tongue, then the eyeballs, after which he held out his hand without looking round and took the thermometer Esther had ready for him. The silence continued while the old man sat sucking the little glass tube.

"Well," said the doctor at last, holding the instrument to the light, "he certainly has got a slight temperature."

Miss Clifford let her breath escape explosively.

"Thank Heaven for that!" she ejaculated in a tone of relief.

All eyes turned towards her in surprise.

"I suppose you're glad I'm ill, are you, Dido?" queried her brother dryly.

"Nonsense, don't be absurd! I'm only glad you'll have to admit you're ill and be put to bed properly where we can look after you. You should have been there days ago."

"Oh, very well, I'll go to bed. You'll never be happy till you've laid me by the heels, you and Thérèse both. What have I got, doctor? Touch of 'flu? They call a lot of things 'flu these days."

The doctor smiled and clapped him on the back reassuringly.

"Oh, perhaps. It's impossible to say yet. However, your sister's right; you mustn't be walking about with a temperature, however slight." He rose and the others followed suit. "Go home, get comfortably to bed, and I'll drop in early in the evening and have another look at you."

"Then you think it's nothing serious?" inquired Lady Clifford with a sudden appeal, her beautiful eyes glancing from her husband to the doctor.

"You know, doctor," broke in Miss Clifford eagerly, "I've sometimes wondered if there was anything wrong with the water. I . . ."

"Rubbish, Dido, I never drink the water."

There was a general laugh at this.

"I'm not sure that you don't," insisted the old lady defensively. "And I've always been told the water in France is only to be used externally."

"And precious little of it is used in that way," commented Sir Charles, moving towards the door, where he looked back with a curt, ironic gesture of leave-taking. "It's au revoir then, doctor, and not good-bye. Coming, Dido?"

His wife followed him to the outer door.

"In a minute I will join you, darling. Get into the car and put the rug well around you."

She bundled the fur collar closely about his throat and patted him affectionately on the shoulder. He was well over six feet, even though he stooped a little, so that she had to stand on tiptoe to reach him.

"There, I'm all right," the old man objected testily, but he was not displeased.

Perhaps, thought Esther, she was mistaken after all in regard to Lady Clifford's sentiments towards her husband. She could not, of course, be supposed to be wildly in love with him, but she undoubtedly did appear to be fond of him, even though her feeling might be that of a daughter for a father. At any rate, when it came to the point, she seemed genuinely concerned over the idea of his being ill. Most likely, in common with many very emotional women, she dramatised and exaggerated her slightest feeling, professing far more than she meant. This would easily explain that conversation at the tea-table. She might have meant all she said at the time, but she had probably forgotten it completely by now.

Waving aside all offers of assistance, Sir Charles made his way slowly to the car. His sister let him go ahead, then halting on the doorstep, took hold of Esther's arm confidentially. "One moment, nurse," she said in an undertone, "I'd like to ask you something. Tell me frankly, do you think the doctor saw anything alarming in my brother's symptoms?"

Her plain, pleasant face was puckered with anxiety, her eyes searched Esther's.

"Why, no, I honestly think he meant what he said, that it is too soon to tell anything definite."

"I wonder! Doctors are all alike, they never give anything away," and she frowned thoughtfully. "I daresay you think me foolish, but the fact is I am extremely apprehensive. You see, I'm afraid it may be typhoid."

"Typhoid!"

Esther could only repeat the word, unwilling to admit that the same suspicion had occurred to her.

"Yes, there's a great deal of it about the Riviera this season, as you may know."

"I've heard so."

"There have been several cases quite close to us, and one actually in the house, one of the maids. She went down with it four weeks ago, and has had a severe case. She's in a nursing home now. An attack of typhoid as violent as that would probably prove fatal to a man of my brother's age and in his state of health—for he hasn't been at all strong for several years. So you can understand how I—how we—feel about it."

With an impulse of sympathy Esther grasped the gloved hand on her arm and gave it a warm squeeze.

"You mustn't think such things," she admonished earnestly. "It may be nothing at all serious, over-fatigue, a slight cold. Besides, typhoid fever needn't be fatal, even at his age."

The elder woman's face lit up with a sudden, grateful smile.

"You're right. I shouldn't cross bridges—and I mustn't let him see I'm worried. Thank you, my dear!"

She took a step downward, then turned and smiled again at Esther with friendly curiosity.

"What is your name," she asked, "and how do you come to be here?"

Esther told her.

"Well," remarked Miss Clifford, "you're a very different sort from the young Frenchwoman the doctor had here before you came—all paint and powder, busy making herself up whenever she thought you weren't looking, always ready for a flirtation." She made a grimace. "Not that she got very far with the doctor, I may tell you," she added, then nodding good-bye, joined her brother in the car.

Esther went into the salon and straightened the disarranged pile of magazines. Then going to the window she peered through the net curtain at the two occupants of the Rolls Royce. The old man was leaning back with his eyes shut and his haggard face sunken into lines of weariness; his sister was adjusting the rug more comfortably about him, watching him with troubled eyes. What a good sort she was! Esther liked her downright honesty and warm-heartedness; she thought she had never met anyone of that age so utterly guileless. How did she get on with her temperamental sister-in-law? What did she think of her really?

She heard the door of the consulting-room open, the other one, leading to the hall.

"You *think*—but are you *sure*?"

It was Lady Clifford who put this question in a voice which, though low-pitched, had a note of sharp insistence.

"Sure! Can one be absolutely sure of anything?"

All the geniality was gone from the doctor's voice; he sounded cold, as though wearied by a tiresome topic.

"Yes, but you know what my nerves are like! Can't you say something more?"

A short silence. Then:

"You say he had his milk regularly—the pint and a half a day?"

"Yes, yes, of course—every day."

"Oh, then, I don't think I should worry."

The front door closed; a moment later the car drove away.

Puzzled and slightly curious, though not intensely so, Esther found herself wondering what meaning there was in the doctor's last words. Was the old man ill—or wasn't he?

As she continued putting the room to rights the doctor pushed open the glass doors and stood regarding her undecidedly. There was no clue to his thoughts, but then there seldom was.

"Fools, these people," he remarked at last. "The more money they have the bigger fools they are. Always insisting that you tell them more than you know yourself, never willing to wait for a disease to declare itself."

With a kind of contemptuous snort he lumbered back into the consulting-room and closed the door. Had he been offering an explanation in case she had overheard? Or merely expressing aloud a general opinion regarding patients, all of whom he evidently held in scorn? For the life of her she could not decide.

CHAPTER VII

SEVERAL days slipped by, during which she heard nothing further of the Cliffords. Nor indeed did she think about them very much, there being more vital matters to occupy her attention. Esther was but mortal. There was a particular chestnut-coloured crêpe-de-Chine jumper in a shop-window along the Croisette that drew her like a magnet—her colour, and what a background for her golden amber beads, brought her recently by a patient from Peking. Should she give way to the extravagance, or ought she to save her money? The problem was a weighty one. Besides this, there was a young Italian, merry and good-mannered, whom she had met at her hotel, and who was beseeching her to come out one evening and dance. What ought she to say to him? Her soul longed for gaiety—Italians were good dancers, as a rule. There was, moreover, a letter from New York from the devoted doctor who wanted to marry her, a long letter, fraught with complete understanding and fidelity which left her cold, but gave her something to think about. On the whole she had quite enough to occupy her idle thoughts.

Yet now and again she recalled the sudden liking she had felt for Miss Clifford, and at these moments she wondered what was happening to the old cotton manufacturer up there in La Californie. She knew the doctor called twice daily. She decided to question him.

"Doctor, what happened to Sir Charles Clifford?"

"Happened?"

The doctor frowned into a test-tube and waited for her to explain.

"I mean, if he is ill, what has he got?"

"Oh, typhoid fever," replied the doctor indifferently, intent on his experiment.

"So it was typhoid after all!" Esther exclaimed, conscious of a certain regret.

He lowered the tube and slowly levelled his small dull eyes upon her.

Without knowing in the least why, she felt uncomfortable.

"Why do you say 'after all'?"

"I merely meant that his sister told me she was afraid it might be that. One of their housemaids had it."

"Yes, that is so. There's enough of it about."

She wanted to inquire how the old man was, but she could not bring herself to continue the subject with a person who somehow made her feel that her questions were superfluous, if not actually impertinent. She watched him fit a slide into his huge microscope, entirely absorbed by the matter in hand. Patients as human beings meant nothing to him. Two days later the thing occurred which altered her whole mode of life.

She was aware that something had happened when she arrived as usual in the morning, for Jacques, who met her in the hall, had a somewhat mysterious and wholly ironical manner.

"Ah, mademoiselle, what have I told you? Did I not say it would be so?"

"Say what? What do you mean?"

"Did I not say he was what you call fed up?"

"Jacques, what are you talking about?"

He shrugged his shoulders and shook his head.

"Go in there; you will soon know. He is waiting to speak to you."

Considerably puzzled, she tapped on the consulting-room door and was bidden to come in. As she did so, the doctor looked up from what seemed an unusual confusion on his desk, and as his gaze encountered hers she thought that the dull heaviness of his demeanour was oddly lightened by a spark of something she could not define.

"Ah, Miss Rowe, you see me about to make a rather sudden change. The fact is I have been persuaded to put aside my practice for a short time—I can't say exactly how long it will be—and during the interval to act as private physician to Sir Charles Clifford."

Frankly taken by surprise, Esther could at first only exclaim, "No, really!" and wait for him to go on. Whatever had induced him to do this? She reflected that the Cliffords must have offered him a good deal of money.

"I have arranged with a colleague to take over my practice for the next few weeks," the doctor continued, busy sorting papers as he spoke. "Although naturally my patients can please themselves about going to him. He is a competent man. Needless to say Sir Charles will make it worth my while, and for the rest I badly need a holiday. The change will do me good."

So this was why he looked more cheerful. Even a machine needs a rest once in a while. Then Esther thought of that other work of his, the research of which he seemed never to tire.

"What about your experiments?" she ventured.

"I shall be able to snatch a couple of hours now and then," he replied. "But of course I must resign myself to giving up really serious work in the laboratory until the case is finished. It is regrettable, for, as you know, I am in the midst of that series of tests in regard to the anti-toxin for tetanus. Every week I lose increases the chance of some other fellow's finding it; there are a number of experimenters hot on the trail. However, it can't be helped." He sighed and added to himself, "You can't have it both ways."

It now occurred to Esther to inquire how this alteration of plans affected her.

"Then I suppose, doctor, you won't be wanting me for the next month or so?"

"I was coming to that. No, I shall not; and I don't know that it would be worth my while to pay you to stay on while I have nothing for you to do."

"Oh, no, naturally. I understand."

"If, however, you still wish to remain in Cannes, I have an offer to make you. There is an English nurse looking after Sir Charles, but he is going to require another. Perhaps you'd care to take on the job of day-nurse to him?"

It was a second surprise.

"Oh! Would they like me to come?"

"It was Miss Clifford's suggestion. I believe from what she said to me she took a liking to you when she saw you here the other day."

The detached tone in which he made this observation implied that such a thing as taking a liking to a person did certainly exist and therefore must be scientifically recognised, incredible as it might appear.

The image of the simple, friendly eyed, north-country woman flashed across Esther's mental vision, obscuring the less comprehensible figure of her sister-in-law. She thought for a moment.

"Why, yes, if you like, I'll be glad to come," she agreed.

The doctor raised a corrective hand. "It's if *you* like," he amended. "I can get another nurse from the British Nursing Home in an hour's time, it is all the same to me. If you come, however, they will pay you at the rate usual in your country—more than an English nurse gets, as you know."

"I wasn't thinking of the money," declared Esther hastily and with truth. "I was only wondering . . . but it doesn't matter. I'll come. When do you want me?"

"At once. How soon can you be ready?"

"Oh, I can be ready in an hour or so. I've only to pack my things and settle my hotel bill."

"Very well, try to get to the house before lunch. I will telephone to say you are coming. Here is the address."

He scrawled it on a slip of paper and handed it to her, instantly turning his whole attention to something else in the way he had when a matter was concluded. It was exactly like shutting a door in one's face, she thought with rueful amusement. In another minute she had left the house and was on her way back to her hotel.

In the little lobby she met Miss Paull, just drawing on a pair of black gloves preparatory to setting off on a ramble.

"And what are you doing here at this hour?" she greeted Esther cheerfully, curiously beaming in every line of her rather noble face.

Esther explained hurriedly.

"How extremely odd! The very people we were discussing the other day. And you say your doctor is giving up his entire practice to devote himself to Sir Charles? They *must* have money to burn. I wonder what you will think of them. I wonder if the son is there? Such a nice-looking boy he was. I used to see him often. And the beautiful French wife—you must tell me what she is like, to know, that is. Of course she *looks* like something on the films, doesn't she?"

Esther assented, anxious to get away.

"I should like to know what she was doing in that dirty little jeweller's shop, going into the back room and all," mused the spinster regretfully. "Well—good luck to you!"

Esther smiled to herself as she got into the tiny lift. Miss Paull extracted so much enjoyment out of life from inventing mysteries out of simple things. What a pity she could not be in her, Esther's, place! What capital she would have made out of her opportunities!

It was with a slight feeling of excitement that two hours later she toiled in a creaking taxi up to the steep streets of Cannes, her hat-box and neat dressing-bag reposing on the seat beside her, her small trunk in front. What luck, she reflected, to have brought her uniforms along! She had not really thought she would need them. A thin rain fell, but the sky showed signs of breaking, and the raindrops sparkled on the thick green foliage of the trees and added beauty to the feathery sprays of mimosa wherever it raised its yellow plumage. The town left behind, villa after villa came into view, many half-hidden in greenery. The drive seemed a longish one, but of course a good car would have done it in half the time. . . .

How strange to think that the very first woman who had in any way impressed her in Cannes should now be employing her to nurse her husband! It was a good thing Lady Clifford had never recognised her; no doubt if she had done so she would have thought twice about engaging her services.

Ah, here it was, the Villa Firenze—a spacious, even imposing mansion of pinkish brick, the front covered in wistaria. Acacias shut off the well-kept garden from the road and bordered the drive, a circular one, the approach terminating in wide, shallow stone steps, flanked by carved stone baskets of fruit. While she was paying the taxi, the door opened and a manservant, English, with sparse grey hair and a pleasant wooden face, came out and took her bag and hat-box.

"I daresay you'll be wanting to go straight to your room, miss?" he suggested.

"Yes, thank you."

She found herself in a large, irregular entrance hall with a sweep of stairs facing her. On the left was a high Gothic chimney-piece of grey stone, the fireplace banked with azaleas, flame-coloured and rose. There were a few tall Stuart chairs and a carved oak coffer. The long windows were curtained with old needlework. She followed the butler up the carpeted stairs and from a broad upper hall along a passage towards the back of the house, meeting no one on the way but a housemaid.

The room into which she was shown had the charm of harmonious simplicity. The plain furniture was painted black, outlined in mauve; the curtains and covers were of Toile de Jouy in one of those delightful reproductions of an eighteenth-century pattern, showing a dozen scenes of pastoral life, mauve on a white ground. The carpet was black, and on the mantelpiece was a black Wedgwood bowl filled with anemones, placed between crystal candlesticks.

"Your box will be up directly, miss," the butler said as he left her.

She went to the window and looked out over wet green lawns with hedges and oleanders. Rain dripped from the shrubs, but a shaft of watery sunlight had broken through the clouds. She breathed in the fragrance of the garden for several moments, then, her trunk arriving, set herself to work to unpack the belongings so recently stowed away. This done, she quickly changed into one of her pale buff uniforms with its accompanying snowy apron, stiff cuffs and coif—an uncompromising costume at the best of times, yet she had managed to have hers well-cut and of a becoming colour, which was the most that one could do.

As she was putting the final touches to her attire there was a tap on the door and the maid she had seen in the passage entered. She was a wholesome-looking Scotch girl with a strong Glasgow accent, and she smiled on Esther in a friendly way.

"If you please, nurse, Miss Clifford is wanting to see you when you've done dressing. She said there was no pertickler hurry."

"I'll come at once," said Esther promptly, and followed her out of the room, back to the central landing, and a few yards along another hallway to the right. Here, in an open doorway, Miss Clifford was standing. At once Esther noticed in her appearance a marked alteration; her strong colour had faded and she looked tired and distressed. However, she smiled in a welcoming fashion and extended her hand as to a friend.

"Ah, I am glad you could come, Miss Rowe," she exclaimed with an air of relief. "It was my first thought when Dr. Sartorius consented to come to us. I felt I should so like to have you look after my brother."

She drew Esther into her room, which was comfortable and bright in a solid, old-fashioned style.

"So you see," she said, closing the door and motioning Esther towards a large easy chair by the fireplace, "my fears were well-grounded after all. He has got typhoid—he had it then."

CHAPTER VIII

"I FELT it from the first," continued Miss Clifford. "You see, his symptoms were so exactly like Bannister's—that is the maid who is ill. There was only this difference, that my brother was a good deal longer developing his case. I don't know why, I'm sure, for he's so much older and not in robust health, either. You'd have thought he'd succumb more quickly than a young strong woman."

"You would think so," agreed Esther. "But of course there are different types of typhoid. I've even seen people who had all the symptoms fully developed, yet who never knew it and kept about the whole time."

"Really!" Miss Clifford looked frankly astonished.

"How is Sir Charles now?"

"Why, not so ill as one might have expected," replied his sister more cheerfully. "So far, we have much to be thankful for. The other nurse will tell you what she thinks, and of course you'll see the chart, but I believe I'm right in saying they consider it a mild case."

"I'm glad of that!"

"You'll see him after lunch. The other nurse is going off duty then until about eleven to-night. To-morrow will see you straightened out with regard to your hours. I thought we'd have you for the day, because"—she laughed—"without meaning to descend to barefaced flattery, you are rather nicer to look at!"

"I sha'n't know how much of a compliment that is till I see the other nurse," replied Esther, laughing too.

"You will think me very stupid," resumed the old lady after a slight pause, her face grown grave again, "but for weeks past, even before this happened, I've had such an odd sense of insecurity, a presentiment of trouble. I'm not given to feelings of that kind, which makes this one more noticeable. I can't explain it, but there it is—a kind of foreboding that I can't shake off."

"You shouldn't feel it now that your brother is going on so well."

"No, of course not, but I'm afraid I do."

"I expect you are tired and run down. That causes lots of premonitions."

"Yes, no doubt you're right. Was that the bell?" she asked, breaking off and listening alertly. "For two days I've been looking for a cable from my nephew. I sent him one nearly three days ago, but there has been no reply. That's one thing that's worrying me."

"Is that Sir Charles's son?"

"Yes. He has been in America on business since October. I sent the cable to Chicago, which was the last address we had, but he has probably moved about a good deal since then. I wish he were here!"

There was a knock and the butler entered with the blue form of a *dépêche* in his hand.

"Ah, here it is at last! This surely must be from Mr. Roger, Chalmers."

She took the telegram eagerly and tore it open, reading its contents with an expression of mingled joy and amazement.

"This is odd. It is sent from Cherbourg and says simply, 'Shall be with you Friday morning.' Friday! That's to-morrow. Why, he has arrived in France, and is catching the night train from Paris. That is a surprise, isn't it, Chalmers?"

"And miss, if you'll notice, it's addressed to Sir Charles, not to yourself."

"Is it? You are right, Chalmers. That looks as though he'd never got our cable, doesn't it? I suppose he couldn't if he was already on the water."

"Unless," suggested Esther, "they had sent it on by wireless to the boat."

"Of course, I didn't think of that. Anyhow, it doesn't matter now that he will be here so soon. He must have wanted to surprise us. We didn't expect him for another two months."

She turned briskly to the butler.

"Get the corner room ready, Chalmers. What a good thing we put the doctor at the back! And tell her ladyship we're expecting Mr. Roger—or no, I'll see to that myself."

"Very good, miss. It will be nice to see Mr. Roger, won't it, miss?" said the old man, preparing to go. "It will do Sir Charles a world of good."

"Yes, Chalmers, it's great good fortune. Find out the times the Paris trains get in, and order the car. I shall drive down to meet Mr. Roger."

"Yes, miss. I should hardly think he'd be on the Blue Train, as that's booked up so far in advance."

"Of course," mused Miss Clifford when the butler had departed, "if he hasn't had our news it will be a shock to him to find his father ill. I am very fond of my nephew, Miss Rowe," she added. "He is almost like my own son."

Her eyes brightened and her whole plain-featured face was irradiated with pleasure so that she seemed suddenly to have grown handsome. Then as Esther remarked this another change came over her, a sort of cloud descended, and her manner showed vague nervousness and hesitation.

"I suppose," she said, rising, "I'd better go and tell my sister-in-law."

She moved about undecidedly, and it occurred to Esther that the task she was contemplating was an uncongenial one, though why it should be so was not apparent. She turned suddenly to Esther.

"Come with me, Miss Rowe," she suggested, "I can show you your patient's quarters at the same time."

They quitted the room and turned back to the central hall. "This is my sister-in-law's bedroom," Miss Clifford informed her, laying her hand on the first door. "That third door leads to my brother's room, with his dressing-room and bath beyond. This middle one is a sort of boudoir or sitting-room—it is really Lady Clifford's, but I use it, too. . . . Are you there, Thérèse?" she called gently through the door.

"Yes, come in!"

A soft, cloying wave of perfume greeted them as they entered. It seemed a mixture of the scent Esther now definitely associated with Lady Clifford and some other of Oriental character. The room, filled with sunlight, was a perfect setting for its owner. Silver blue brocade filled the panels of the walls, grey carpet lay under foot, the furniture was walnut Louis Quinze, graceful in shape. The two long casement windows, opening upon a narrow balcony, were framed in heavy curtains of the same material as the wall covering. A thin trail of blue smoke hung in the air, and Esther discerned its source in a small incense-burner, a golden Buddha, resting cross-legged between trees of jade and amethyst on a table near the fireplace.

Lady Clifford was seated with her back towards the door at a writing-table placed between the windows. She did not immediately turn, but instead looked up, meeting the reflection of her visitors in a mirror on the wall. It was the first time Esther had seen her without a hat, and she found her not less lovely. Her golden-brown shining hair waved back from a side parting with that carefully contrived artlessness which is the crowning achievement of a coiffeur, and in colour it exactly matched her soft frock, which was of the sports variety with a finely pleated skirt. The skin of her throat was milky-white and of the fineness of a flower petal. Against it her pearls showed a faint rosy tinge. She was smoking a cigarette through a long holder.

"Thérèse, this is our other nurse, who has just come. You remember you saw her at the doctor's the other day?"

The Frenchwoman laid down her pen and turned towards Esther with a bright, perfunctory smile.

"Ah, yes, I remember."

Her grey eyes looked Esther over appraisingly from head to foot, then returned to the sheet of paper on the desk. Miss Clifford spoke again, with slight hesitation.

"What I really came to tell you, Thérèse, is that I have just had a telegram from Roger."

"From Roger?"

The younger woman stared blankly.

"A cable, you mean, not a telegram."

"No, a telegram, from Cherbourg. He says he will be here to-morrow."

With a bound Lady Clifford sprang to her feet.

"Roger here to-morrow?" she exclaimed almost sharply, her eyes fixed on her sister-in-law's face. "But it is impossible; you must be mistaken."

Her cigarette fell out of the holder to the floor, where it would have burned a hole in the carpet if Esther had not quietly picked it up.

"That's what he says."

"Let me see the telegram."

She snatched it rather brusquely from the other woman's hand and scanned it frowningly, her vivid red underlip caught between her teeth. Miss Clifford looked embarrassed. Esther moved unobtrusively across the room and examined the crystal lustres on the mantelpiece.

"Yes, but I do not understand. How is it he has come back so much sooner than he expected and without letting us know?"

"I can only suppose he has finished his work there and thought he would give us a surprise."

The younger woman gave back the telegram and turned with a slight shrug of her shoulders.

"I think he might have written us he was coming," she said with a sort of resentment. "Why do people want to take you by surprise?"

"At any rate," remarked Miss Clifford pleasantly, "it can't possibly make any difference. To me it seemed like an answer to prayer! It's just as though something had warned him his father was ill."

"How could anything possibly warn him of such a thing?" demanded the other with a touch of irritation. "A thing no one could have foreseen!"

"I don't know how, but I certainly felt a premonition of it, as I was telling the nurse a moment ago. If I had been away I am sure I should have come home at once, feeling as I did."

Lady Clifford carefully fitted another cigarette into her holder and lit it.

"I think the doctor is right, that we are all making far too much fuss over Charles's illness," she said abruptly. "After all, there has been nothing so far to cause us any alarm."

"Yes, you are quite right," agreed Miss Clifford simply. "And I am glad to hear you say so, my dear. You know you have really been more nervous than I have."

"Ah, that is the way I take things. I cannot help my nature!" sighed the Frenchwoman amicably enough. "I always fear the worst. I suppose now we had better ask the doctor if we can tell Charles about Roger's coming?"

"Is the doctor with him?"

"I will see."

She crossed to the door at the far side of the room and opening it spoke softly to someone inside. A second later the nurse stuck her head through the opening. She was a smiling, angular woman of forty, with fluffy, mouse-coloured hair, and a frosty tip to her nose.

"Do you wish to see the doctor, Lady Clifford?"

She spoke ingratiatingly, with a hiss of badly fitting false teeth.

"Yes, is he there?"

The nurse disappeared and was presently replaced by Dr. Sartorius, who came inside and closed the door behind him. Acknowledging Esther's presence by the merest flicker of the eye, he bent his head and listened attentively to what the Frenchwoman told him. As she spoke her eyes searched his face eagerly, but his heavy features remained impassive.

"Ah, it won't hurt him to hear good news," he replied indifferently. "Go in now, if you care to, he's wide awake."

To Esther's surprise, the Frenchwoman put out her hand to her sister-in-law with a gracious gesture.

"You tell him, Dido, dear," she said gently, "I know you would like to."

"Thank you, Thérèse."

With a grateful smile the old lady disappeared into the bedroom, followed by the doctor, and Esther was left alone with her employer. Lady Clifford did not glance in her direction, but put up her hand with a restless, irritable movement and swept the big wavy lock of hair off her forehead.

"*Qu'il fait chaud!*" she exclaimed, going to the nearest window and flinging it open with a jerk. "Stifling! There, that is better."

She stood for several seconds breathing in the fresh air, her body tense as if on steel wires, her head thrown back. Then, relaxing somewhat, she turned and spoke to Esther, as if suddenly recalling her presence.

"You come from New York, I hear," she said, with another keen glance; "do you like it, New York?"

Esther replied that she did, but Lady Clifford closed her eyes, not listening.

"Ah, New York, that is a place I have never visited. It must be marvellous. Some day I shall go there, some day when I am . . ."

She did not finish, for at that moment the butler came in to announce lunch. She had stretched out her arms with a sort of abandon, but now she let them fall abruptly, gave a sigh, and without looking in Esther's direction walked into her own bedroom on the right, perhaps to give a touch to her hair, or another brush of powder to her flawless nose.

The breeze, with wet freshness, cleansed the over-perfumed room, fluttering the papers on the writing-table. The top sheet sailed through the air and settled on the hearthrug. Mechanically Esther picked it up to replace it, the habit of order being strong upon her. Unavoidably she saw that it was covered with figures in angular French writing, money sums by the look of them, with frequent signs of the pound and the franc. She anchored the paper upon the blotter with a little carving of amethyst crystal, then, turning away, perceived Lady Clifford, motionless in the doorway, regarding her with eyes narrowed suspiciously.

"Your papers were blowing about," explained Esther. Inwardly she was asking herself: "What is the matter with me? I always seem to be imagining things with this woman!"

With one of her swift movements the beautiful Thérèse snatched up the rescued sheet and tore it to bits.

"It is of no consequence, this," she remarked indifferently, dropping the pieces into the waste-basket.

Again Esther noticed those stumpy, abbreviated fingers, so oddly at variance with the rest of their owner.

"*Bien,*" said Lady Clifford, flashing a charming smile upon her. "Let us have our *déjeuner.*"

She led the way downstairs.

CHAPTER IX

AT THE *gare* next morning, Miss Clifford, having selected a likely train, leaned forward in her brother's car and eagerly scanned each arrival as he issued from the exit. What if Roger did not arrive after all? These trains were so booked up at this season, he might not have been able to secure a *wagon-lit.* Still, he usually managed things. . . .

"Roger! Roger!" she shouted suddenly, so that at least half a dozen travellers turned in her direction.

The young Englishman in the Harris tweed coat wheeled at the sound of her voice, and reached the car in a dozen quick strides. He was nearing thirty, tall, but less tall than Sir Charles, with features similar but not so pronounced, and eyes intensely blue. He had his father's humorous mouth modified and softened, and to the old man's look of stubborn strength he added something which suggested more imagination and sensitiveness. He appeared in excellent condition, wiry and vigorous, his skin tanned from five days of sea and wind.

"Roger, darling!"

"Dido, my dear old girl!"

His bear-like embrace brought comfort to her heart. She held him off at last and gazed on him with deep affection.

"This is good of you, auntie, to come and meet me. I didn't expect it."

"As if I wouldn't!"

She kissed him again warmly, and the nature of this second embrace conveyed to him the knowledge that something was amiss.

"What's wrong, Dido? Anything happened?"

"It's your father, Roger—he's ill."

"Ill! Why didn't you cable?"

"I did, to your Chicago address, three days ago."

"It should have been Marconied to the boat. What's the matter with him?"

"Typhoid fever, my dear. We've been rather distressed."

His face grew serious.

"Good God, that's bad!"

"Don't be too alarmed, he seems to have a mild case, thank heaven, and naturally we are doing all that can be done for him. We've got two splendid nurses, and a doctor who is giving us his entire time."

"What doctor is it?"

The chauffeur, having strapped the luggage to the back of the car, was looking to them for instructions.

"What would you like to do, dear? Stop anywhere, or go straight home?"

"Oh, home. I want to see the old man."

In a twinkling they had left the *gare* and were heading for the heights.

"What luck to be here!" exclaimed the young man with a luxurious sigh. "I had hoped to get a fortnight later on, but as things have turned out I finished up much sooner than I thought I should. I found I could get a passage on the *Berengaria*, and I can tell you I didn't waste much time saying good-bye. Out where I've been, in the West, it's ten below zero, with the wind cutting like a knife. People can abuse the Riviera all they like, but after that sort of thing it seems like Heaven."

He glanced out at the town appreciatively, throwing back his coat.

Then he turned again to his aunt.

"I thought you always had Cromer when you wanted any doctoring?" he said.

"So we did, but he got so very fashionable we felt he didn't give us much attention. Too many kings and queens, you know! Then we heard of this other man through Captain Holliday. You remember Arthur Holliday?"

"Do I not?"

Her nephew made a slight grimace.

"Oh, I know you never cared for him, but this is quite apart from anything personal. You see, when Arthur was so terribly damaged from that last smash of his, he met this Dr. Sartorius out in Algeria. He was absolutely a wreck; none of the doctors who had seen him could do anything more for him. Well, this doctor took hold of him, experimented on him, and really made him over. I'm not exaggerating, the result was a miracle, everyone will tell you so. It was enough to give one enormous confidence in the man."

"Well, I'm glad you've got him."

"Yes, I'm thankful. He's unattractive to meet, indeed he is rather an odd, cold-blooded creature—a scientist mainly—but what does that matter if he is really so able?"

Roger nodded. Then, after a pause, he inquired casually, but in a faintly altered tone:

"And how is She?"

"Thérèse?" his aunt returned, understanding at once. "I was going to tell you. Do you know she has been so charming lately, that I am beginning quite to like her?"

"No!"

He raised incredulous eyebrows.

"It's true. Her whole disposition is improved. She is so changed that except for just a little petulance now and then, which I'm sure she doesn't mean, she's—she's—But you'll see for yourself."

"I can't believe it."

"I knew you wouldn't. But you'll see. She is nicer to Charles than she has ever been since just at the first."

"I am astonished! How long has she been so angelic?"

"Let me see—oh, about two months, I believe."

"Not very long, then."

"It began before Christmas. Before that we had a dreadful time. She and your father had a frightful quarrel. I wish I hadn't been there! She did most of the quarrelling, of course; he was merely firm, but for all that I have never seen him angrier. There were terrible scenes, so embarrassing. One hates so to have the servants get to know about these things, and really they couldn't help knowing."

"What was it all about? Do you know?"

"Oh, yes, I know. It was about the amount of money Thérèse had been spending. It seems your father suddenly for some reason took it into his head to go through her pass-book. Apparently he was horrified at the frequent large sums she was drawing to herself—oh, not for dressmakers or anything of that sort. Naturally he asked what she was doing with all that money, and eventually it came out she had been losing it at baccarat."

"Baccarat!"

"Well, you know your father has never much approved of gambling, beyond what he calls a mild flutter; so when he found she was throwing away several thousands a year—"

"As much as that?"

"I believe so. I never heard the exact amount, but it was staggering, that much I know. At any rate, he put a stop to it at once. He went carefully into all her legitimate expenses, and the result was he made her a fixed allowance—oh, a generous one—he has never been mean with her—only if she wants more, he must be told what it's for."

"Good boy!" murmured Roger with approval. "So of course she was in a devil of a rage?"

"Devil expresses it rather well, I'm afraid, Roger. I've only seen one other person so violent, and that was an Irish cook we had before you were born, who drank raw spirit out of the bottle. As for Thérèse, she stormed first, then she wept, and was pathetic, then she raged again. Altogether she must have tried everything, but you know what your father is like when he takes a stand. At last she shut herself up in her room and sent for the doctor. She declared she was ill, and threatened going into a nursing home. After a few days, however, she came to herself, very subdued, but much more pleasant and anxious to please. I can't help thinking she might have been better all along if Charles hadn't spoiled her so, if from the start he had taken a firmer hand."

Roger frowned a little dubiously.

"A woman, a spaniel and a walnut tree—" he murmured. "At any rate, I am very glad for the old man's sake, and yours, too!"

"Yes, as you know, I would never stay here if your father didn't insist on it, but now it is much more agreeable; there is scarcely any friction. She seems far less self-centred. Why, to give you one little instance; earlier in the winter your father was ordered to drink milk between meals. We had special milk in sealed bottles, and we kept it upstairs in a small refrigerator. I always opened the bottles myself and gave it to Charles at the right times—you know I have always attended to that sort of thing. But one day Thérèse came to me and asked if she might see to it herself. She said she felt she would like to do something for him. Of course I was delighted, so she has done it ever since. Still, it was unlike her, wasn't it?"

"Very," assented her nephew dryly, while his face grew a little more thoughtful. "Indeed, I feel almost inclined to question her motives. Don't you suppose this is just another attempt to get round him? *'Timeo Danaos,'* you know."

Miss Clifford shook her head.

"I never studied Greek," she said, "but I am sure you are unjust."

Roger gave a rapturous chuckle and squeezed her plump hand in his.

"Never mind. 'Kind hearts are more than coronets, and simple faith than Norman blood'—you know that quotation, don't you?"

"Certainly, though I scarcely see how it applies to Thérèse."

"It doesn't," retorted Roger, laughing anew. Then more seriously, "You spoke of Arthur Holliday. Is he still on the tapis?"

"Oh, we see a good deal of him, although I believe he's considering a position that's been offered him in the Argentine. He came recently to ask Charles's advice about accepting it."

"The Argentine! He must have pulled a wonderful bluff with some-one."

"Yes! I've never known him do anything serious. Yet he always appears to have money. He runs a car, dresses well and lives at a first-rate hotel."

"One of Life's little mysteries," commented the young man with a shake of the head. "I would like to know how these gentlemen of leisure manage. I always have to pay my hotel hills, or I would be put out, but not these fellows. Oh, no! There's some magic about them—no known means of support, yet they live like princes. There's one in Manchester now—he was up at Cambridge with me, I regret to say. The fact's cost me a good deal first and last. He comes regularly to borrow money and keeps a taxi ticking up outside for an hour while he's waiting to see me. Oh, he's to the manor born, just like Arthur Holliday. I take off my hat to them both."

Miss Clifford laughed tolerantly.

"What you say is quite true. In the ordinary way no one despises that type more heartily than your father, but he can't forget that Arthur was Malcolm's great friend, and for that reason he has a soft spot in his heart for him. Arthur comes and talks to him about the war and Malcolm's bravery, and you know what that means to Charles. And then of course he amuses Thérèse, who, after all, doesn't get much fun, poor girl."

Before they realised it the car was swerving into the drive of the Villa Firenze, whose door stood wide open, framing the butler's precise, black-clad figure. At sight of him Roger's eye lit up.

"Well, well, Chalmers my lad, how are you? You're looking fairly fit."

Chalmers's wooden face relaxed into so broad a smile as to reveal what was rarely seen, a missing tooth in the upper story. He greeted the young man with evident pleasure.

"And so are you looking fit yourself, Mr. Roger, in the very pink, if I may say so, sir. Had a good crossing, sir?"

"Rotten, thanks. I'm as covered with bruises as it I'd been having a round with Tunney. Same room, I suppose?"

"Same room, sir. I'll bring up your bags."

With an arm round the ample figure of his aunt, Roger mounted the stairs.

"I'll wash up a bit, and then do you think I'll be allowed to have a word with the old man?"

"I'm sure you will. He is eager to see you and to hear your news. I hope it is good."

"It is; it is absolutely one hundred per cent. good, as they would say on the other side. I—"

Here he broke off, for, on reaching the top of the staircase, he suddenly caught sight of a young and trim-looking girl of pleasing appearance, clad in a uniform of primrose-yellow, with white apron and cap. She issued from his father's bedroom with an enamelled basin in her hand, smiled at Miss Clifford for a brief instant, and rapidly vanished down the hall towards the back stairs. The glimpse was a short one, yet it was sufficient to disclose the facts of clear, very child-like hazel eyes, fresh dashes of colour in the cheeks, and an exceedingly shapely pair of ankles and legs. Roger remained spellbound on the top step for so long a space that his aunt turned back to discover the cause.

"That's your day-nurse, I take it?" he asked.

"Yes, such a nice girl, who has been working for the doctor. She only arrived here yesterday, but I am sure she is an excellent nurse."

"I'm sure she's an excellent dancer," remarked her nephew with the grave air of a connoisseur. "I wonder if she has any free time?"

The old lady looked slightly puzzled. There were so many times when she could not be quite sure whether Roger was in earnest or not.

"Come along," she chid him, pinching his ear gently, "I suppose, as usual, you are trying to pull my leg!"

CHAPTER X

A few minutes later Roger was shown into his father's room. His first sight of the old man, lying flat on his back, his emaciated arms limp on the smooth white coverlet, his face drawn and the colour of old parchment, gave him a distinct shock. It was but a momentary one, however. The room, filled with sunlight, was calm and cheerful, the fresh fragrance of violets scented the air, the whole atmosphere tended to allay his fears. The young nurse he had seen in the hall came forward as he entered, greeting him with a frank smile.

"The doctor says you may stay half an hour," she told him with friendly simplicity of manner. "Only you must promise not to talk very much, and not to excite him. You'll be careful, won't you?"

"You can trust me," he assured her.

Their glances met. He liked her naturalness, as transparent as the lucid brown-amber of her eyes. She seemed to him so straightforward, like an extremely nice child. He was sorry when she slipped quietly out and left him alone with the invalid.

"Well, father! This is very wrong of you."

The dull eyes brightened, one big bony hand stretched out to grasp the young man's firm one.

"Roger! I'm glad to see you. A welcome surprise! I never thought you'd be free for another couple of months. How did you manage it?"

"Oh, I succeeded sooner than I expected, that's all. I'm particularly pleased it happened, since you took it into your head to get laid up. Whatever do you mean by it?"

At his tone of cheerful banter his father's grim face relaxed into a smile.

"God knows. I seem to get everything that's going, and it isn't for want of taking care of myself, either. Never mind about me; draw up that chair and sit down."

Roger obeyed.

"Now let's hear all about America. You realise you have written me precious few details. I've no idea what you've been up to."

"I didn't want to say much until I had it all definitely fixed up. It was no good crowing too soon. I can set your mind at rest now, though, everything's O.K."

The old eyes riveted themselves on his face intently.

"You mean you've landed some good orders?"

"Some! A lot, all over the place. I tell you, we've done the trick at last; you can accept it for an absolute fact that our American market is established."

The gaunt face on the pillow glowed with triumph. Sir Charles would have hated to admit in words just how great was the satisfaction given him by this news, but his expression betrayed the truth. In his secret heart he had sometimes felt that the principal thing he lived for now was the firm establishment of a market in the United States for the output of Seabrook & Clifford. Until now the buyers across the Atlantic had shown little interest in their well-known materials, although salesman after salesman had been sent out, and money sunk in advertising to an extent that made him shudder to contemplate. Bitterly he had begun to fear that the wish of his heart would never be realised in his lifetime, yet now, behold! It had come about, and through the agency and judgment of his son. He felt a burning desire to know all details.

"What about those new patterns you took out with you?" he inquired, with an effort to appear casual.

Roger stared at him in astonishment, then laughed.

"Why, of course, it was the new patterns that did it! The old stuff was out of date, no one would look at it. Didn't I always say so? If there's any place in the world that wants modern ideas, it is America. And let me tell you something else: before you know where you are, the colonies are going to wake up and want them too!"

His father gulped. It may have been that he was swallowing his pride.

Still, he managed to nod, as if this were what he'd been expecting.

"Henry Seabrook will hate to admit he's been wrong all these years," was his game comment. "You recollect how he raved and carried on when you showed him those futurist designs?"

"Do I not? You'd have thought there was something positively immoral in them, evil enough to rot the very yarns!"

He refrained from alluding to the fact that his father had displayed an almost equal distaste and scepticism. Let old Seabrook shoulder the blame!

"As soon as you've pulled out of this, I'll go over the whole thing with you and show you the figures. For the moment, though, I don't want to tax your strength."

"I suppose you're right," admitted his father with a sigh. "I'm getting on pretty well, I believe, but the slightest effort does me up. This wretched fever leaves me as limp as a rag. Never mind—what you've told me is the best tonic I could hope for."

He closed his eyes with a look of contentment and lay quiet, the outline of his head sharp against the pillow. Roger leaned back in his chair, well pleased with his father's reception of his report, and realising more than ever before what his achievement meant to the old man. Up till now he had been chiefly concerned with his own satisfaction over a great personal triumph, the biggest thing he had accomplished in his entire career. To begin with, hampered as he had been by the two hard, conservative old men above him, Henry Seabrook and his father, this represented the only time he had been allowed to strike out a line for himself. Ever since he came down from the University and went to work to "learn the business," he had violently disagreed with certain details in the policy of the firm. Not that he was not proud of Seabrook & Clifford. No factories were run on better lines; there was nothing in their administration to hide up or apologise for, while "Seacliff Fabrics" were of an excellence recognised throughout England and the colonies. Only their designs were old-fashioned, the honoured firm had not moved with the times, as others and often less worthy competitors had done.

In Roger's opinion, the sign of this was their failure to capture the American market. He had tried hard to convince the old partners of this, but for several years his efforts had met with no success. In the end he had on his own initiative sought out young artists of a modern school of design in London and in Paris, wherever he could find them, and from them had obtained a whole collection of new drawings for printed cottons. Then, after a hard-fought campaign, he finally secured a grudging consent to put his idea to the test and, armed with his batch of Seacliff Fabrics brought up to date, he had set out four months ago for the United States—with the happy result just related.

Well! They would have to believe in him now, those two stubborn old men; they could no longer regard him as a hare-brained youngster full of mad theories. He wished suddenly that his mother could know of his good fortune. She, he was sure, would have had confidence in him from the start. He raised his eyes to the mantelpiece, where there was a photograph of her, taken in the dress of eighteen years back. The face was pleasing without being beautiful, the eyes seemed to look at him with humorous understanding, just as they had so often done in life. He had been a schoolboy when she died, yet even then he had realised her imagination and love of beauty, coupled with the ability for bringing out those same qualities in himself.

On the other end of the shelf was a large, shadowy photograph of his father's present wife, one of the sort known as a "camera study," the pose exquisite, hair and draperies fading into a dim background, the eyes wistful and dreamy. Without moving, he examined it appreciatively. There was no denying that Thérèse was a lovely woman.

Yet as he looked his face hardened, and he felt the blood slowly mount until his cheeks burned as though on fire. He was recalling an incident known to no one but himself, a thing which never failed to rouse in him sensations of shame and resentment. It belonged to the early days of his father's second marriage, and before relating it, it may be as well to explain how the cotton manufacturer came to meet the present Lady Clifford.

Some years back the old man had made the acquaintance of a Baron and Baroness de Rummel through the organisation of a musical festival in Manchester. The de Rummels collected about them at their London house a varied circle of smart, semi-artistic people. Sir Charles, first and last a simple business man, having only one point of contact with their world, enjoyed—perhaps a trifle guiltily—his excursions into so sophisticated a set, feeling, no doubt, that in some new way for him he was "seeing life." The men and women he met were ornamental and amusing, possessed expensive habits, spoke in thousands, and told you in the same breath that they hadn't a bean. Many might have been somewhat hazy as to antecedents, but all were well-provided with a certain stock-in-trade—personal charm. There were young men who composed music, others who designed everything from a lampshade to the *décors* of a ballet, young women who sang or danced, actresses who had not got on because managers would make love to them—or wouldn't, as the case might be. All types and many classes were represented, but a common object bound them together, namely, the hope that in the de Rummels' drawing-room they might chance upon a "backer," someone trusting enough to invest money in their enterprises.

In the winter of 1919, the particular star in this artistic zodiac was Thérèse Romain, dazzling chiefly on account of her ethereal beauty. She had a voice, which did not amount to much, and she had done a little acting on the stage and for the screen, but without conspicuous success. She had devoted years to war-work, and there were tears in her beautiful eyes when she spoke of her husband, killed in action. She refrained from mentioning the fact that when he fell he had been in the midst of divorce proceedings against her, nor was she explicit as to the nature of her war-work, though there were those, Roger among the number, who assumed that it must have paid pretty well. At any rate, the Baron took an interest in her referring to her as his ward—a sufficiently elastic term. Finding Sir Charles attracted, he took him aside and besought him to do something for Thérèse. Exactly what the Baron had in mind may have been shadowy; but what Sir Charles did was definite. He married her.

This action was as much a bombshell to the Baron as it was to the neighbours in Cheshire, perhaps even more than Thérèse herself had bargained for. It was a piece of amazing good fortune, but it entailed restrictions which soon grew tedious. Country life in the North Midlands proved a crushing bore. Tennis she cared little for once she had finished dressing for the part, and hunting she gave up after her third venture, when a fall strained a ligament in her back and laid her up for weeks. Altogether she loathed England and the English more every day. London she could have borne, but this life of the rural provinces spelled extinction, beginning with the climate and ending with the vicar for tea. At last she could not even be amused by the sensation she was causing, and, casting about for something to mitigate her boredom, she hit upon Roger as a possible distraction.

Roger, for his part, had seen trouble in the offing, though he was unprepared for it to take this form. He did not dislike the young woman, half French, half Belgian, with the qualities of both races, though secretly he thought his father a fool to have offered her marriage when something less permanent would have served the purpose. Still, for all his private convictions, he behaved to his stepmother with perfect courtesy, determined to make the best of things.

While Thérèse was recovering from her accident, Roger sat with her nearly every evening. His father went off to bed at ten o'clock, while Thérèse found herself with several hours on her hands. It was during this period that Roger became aware that his stepmother was using every means to make him fall in love with her. He tried to ignore the fact, he sought excuses to take him away, but this led to reproaches which made him still more uncomfortable. Beyond a certain point one cannot pretend denseness, and he was in an agony of dread lest his father would see what Thérèse was up to. She had begun kissing him good-night, and now more and more warmth crept into the embrace until he found himself trying to avoid it. He was no prig, and Thérèse was attractive, yet the distaste he felt for the situation neutralised her power to lure him. Moreover, she showed him a side which convinced him of what he had hitherto suspected—that Thérèse had all the instincts of a *cocotte*. Whether she actually was one or not was a matter of opportunity.

The climax came one night during an absence of his father in London. Thérèse deliberately came into his room when she knew he was in bed. It was a painful thing, and even after six years it embarrassed him to think of it. It was her bad taste that revolted him, the calm assumption that he was ready to enter light-heartedly into a liaison with his father's wife! He was filled with disgust. She had placed him in a position where whatever he did would be wrong; consequently he let his temper get the better of him and, taking her by the shoulders, put her out of the room. Naturally, she never forgave him.

Since that night he had seen little of her. He had moved into Manchester, on the excuse of being nearer the factory, while she, in turn, took to spending more and more time abroad. Three years ago his father had been persuaded to give up work and try the South of France for his health. That had made things easier.

"I'm afraid I shall have to turn you out now. We have to be strict."

He glanced up quickly, then jumped to his feet. The screen which guarded the door had kept him ignorant of the nurse's quiet entrance until she was beside him.

"Have I stayed too long?"

"Oh, no, and I'm glad to see he's resting quietly. You can come in again for a little while this afternoon, if he's going on well."

Roger took leave of the invalid, who opened his sunken eyes for a moment, then closed them again.

"Come outside a moment," he whispered to the nurse when he reached the door.

She followed him into the hall, looking up inquiringly.

"Do you consider he's very ill?" asked Roger.

She looked at him earnestly and shook her head.

"Why, no, Mr. Clifford, since you ask me, I can honestly say that it seems to both the night-nurse and me an unusually light case of typhoid—about the lightest I've ever nursed, I should say. It certainly *is* typhoid, yet he has never run as high a temperature as one expects."

"Considering his age, that's lucky, isn't it?"

"Yes, of course, oh, yes!"

He thought she seemed a little puzzled.

"Has the doctor's treatment of the case anything to do with it, do you think?"

She smiled and shook her head.

"No, there isn't much one can do in typhoid, it's mainly a question of what not to do. I only hesitated because we—the other nurse and I—both think it a little odd that Sir Charles, who's an old man, should have such a mild case, when the type that's going around is rather severe."

"Oh, I see. Well, I suppose there's no accounting for these things, is there?"

"No, and in any case we can't complain, can we?"

He liked her laugh and the frank way she looked at him. Her eyes were as clear as a sunny pool that mirrored brown leaves. He liked, too, the freshness of her skin, and her rather square white teeth, with a tiny space separating the middle two. They made her look so honest. It was a friendly, fearless face, yet there was sensitiveness about it, evident from the way the colour mounted into the cheeks at the closeness of his scrutiny.

"Where do you come from?" he asked suddenly.

"Manitoba," was the prompt reply, "the western part."

"Oh—the plains?"

"Yes, but I'm astonished at your knowing."

"Do I look so ignorant?"

"Everyone over here is ignorant about American geography. I never expect them to know anything. When I mentioned Manitoba to one man, he said at once, 'Oh, yes, Central America!'"

Roger laughed.

"I shouldn't like to be cross-examined myself, but I know a little about Canada. I think, too, that you have the look of the plains."

"What sort of look is that?"

He hesitated, and his eyes twinkled.

"An extremely nice look."

They both laughed at this.

"To be definite, it is a certain breadth across here"—he indicated the cheek-bones—"and then your eyes, the way they are set, and a sort of shining brightness about them. I should think you are very far-sighted. Are you?"

"Well, do you know, I am. I grew up in a country where one could see for miles and miles. When I first went into hospital training, my eyes began to trouble me. The doctors said it was only because I wasn't used to looking at objects at close range."

"You ought to be out of doors. Why, may I ask, did you take up nursing?"

She shrugged her shoulders and flashed a frank smile at him.

"I had to do something—there were such crowds of us at home. And I haven't any talents."

"It strikes me as remarkably plucky."

"Why?" she demanded promptly. "Thousands of girls are doing the same thing every day."

"I suppose they are, but that's quite another thing."

"I fail to see it," she retorted with an ironical sparkle in her eye.

"You wouldn't, of course, and I can't altogether explain. But perhaps when I've had time to think it over . . ."

Again they laughed. It was the sort of stupid little conversation to which enormous point is given solely by mutual attraction. However slight and evanescent that affinity may be, it yet hints at the possibility of other things, surrounding the most trivial remarks with a kind of roseate glow.

In this instance the glow lasted during what might have been an awkward interval, while the two stood looking at each other with nothing to say. Esther was the first to return to a matter-of-fact world.

"I mustn't stay here talking. I have things to do for my patient."

"I'm glad he's got you to look after him," said Roger impulsively. "It can't be so bad to be . . ."

But she did not wait to hear more. With a quizzical smile over her shoulder she vanished into the bedroom, leaving him to descend the stairs whistling, conscious of an agreeable warmth he did not seek to analyse.

Esther also felt oddly elated, but she did not neglect to enter very softly, in case her patient should be dozing. Her hand still on the door-knob, she peered cautiously around the edge of the screen.

Someone was in the room, she felt it instinctively even before she discovered who it was. A woman's figure was bending over the table at the other side of the room, her back turned, and something eager and tense in her attitude. It was Lady Clifford. But what was she doing?

Oh, of course! She was examining the chart.

CHAPTER XI

WHY should Lady Clifford show so much curiosity about a technical thing like a medical chart? She was told several times a day exactly how her husband was progressing. She seemed to Esther like an importunate child, probing to know the future, which no one could foresee.

As this thought crossed her mind, a quick movement on the part of the figure opposite caused her to halt on the brink of making her presence known. She saw Lady Clifford straighten up and come towards her with a cautious step to the foot of the bed. She saw her lean forward, without touching the foot-board, and gaze with frowning intentness at the ill man's face. His eyes were still closed, he had perhaps fallen asleep; but if he had suddenly chanced to look up Esther thought that his wife's expression would have given him rather a shock. For the moment her beauty was quite altered. With her lip caught between her teeth and her eyes narrowed with a sort of avid, calculating sharpness, she appeared a different person. It was curious how anxiety could change one's appearance.

Suddenly Esther woke up to the fact that Lady Clifford did not realise she was being watched. What an embarrassing thought! Esther had never willingly spied on anyone in her life. Yet spying was surely too harsh a name for it. Eager to atone for her involuntary fault, she removed her hand from the door-knob, meaning to enter boldly. It was too late. At this exact moment the eyes of the watcher by the bed lifted and met hers. Instantly a new expression flashed into them, for the moment they seemed more yellow than grey.

"I did not hear you come in," she murmured with that trace of accent which lent charm to her speech.

"I tried to be quiet because I thought he might be just dropping off."

"Yes, I think he is asleep. I slipped in to have a little look at him."

She glanced again at the motionless figure, then impulsively drew her arm through Esther's and led her towards the far side of the room.

"Tell me, nurse," she whispered with a little confidential appeal.

"Just how long does this illness last? Usually, I mean?"

"About six weeks, as a rule, Lady Clifford," Esther replied, puzzled, thinking surely the questioner must have found out all this.

The French woman gave a sigh which suggested nerves frayed to the breaking point.

"Six weeks! What an endless time to be in suspense!"

"But you won't be in suspense the whole of that time," Esther hastened to assure her. "If he passes a certain point safely, we needn't be anxious. Unless, of course, he should have a relapse."

"Ah, yes, yes, I remember! And when exactly does that point you speak of come?"

"Well, roughly, about three weeks from the start. By then his temperature ought to be down to normal."

Lady Clifford pondered this, her hand still on Esther's arm, the fingers drumming jerkily. Then she said suddenly:

"You will think me stupid to be so emotional. The doctor does; he has no sympathy with nerves! I know many wives would take all this quite calmly, but unfortunately for me, I am too sensitive, I feel things so terribly! I keep thinking, if anything should happen to my husband . . ."

"But I don't see why anything should happen, he's really getting on very nicely," returned Esther, more and more perplexed.

She was unprepared for the almost fierce way in which the other turned upon her, saying:

"You think that too, do you? He is, as you say, getting on nicely, quite safely?"

It was almost accusing.

"Why, yes. I'm sure there's no immediate cause for alarm."

The delicate brows knit into a frown, the hand on Esther's arm tightened its grip.

"Then *you* don't think that for a man of his age and in his state of health typhoid is—is a thing to—to be frightened about? *You* would not be frightened for him?"

Esther glanced apprehensively at the bed.

"If you don't mind, Lady Clifford, I think we'd better not talk in here. One can't always be certain if he's asleep."

As tactfully as she could she manoeuvred her companion towards the door. Lady Clifford went willingly enough, but on the threshold she paused and said, more distinctly than was necessary, it seemed:

"Yes, yes, you are quite right. But you see I have been afraid he had not the strength to resist any serious disease. You do understand my being so nervous, don't you?"

Esther closed the door with a feeling of annoyance. How silly of Lady Clifford, at the very moment when she had been cautioned! Had the old man heard? It was often difficult to tell about him, when he lay so quiet. She did not want him to be upset by thinking the family were apprehensive about him.

She went to the window and looked out. Her hand still smelled of Lady Clifford's distinctive perfume; she sniffed at it, trying to decide if she liked it or not. It was delicious, but heavy, clinging. What was it the night-nurse had said to her the evening before?

"Isn't Lady Clifford a dream?" the woman had confided gushingly. "Did you ever see anything so lovely? I do so adore her scent when she comes into the room. Yet for all she's such a picture, I never saw anything like her devotion to that old husband of hers—poor dear, she worries so she can't sleep—keeps coming in during the night in her lovely dressing-gown to ask me how he's going on, and if there's any change. He's a lucky old thing, if you want my opinion."

Yes, there was no doubt whatever, Lady Clifford's anxiety for her husband was genuine. She had worked herself into a state of tense nerves. Yet why? Was it possible she was as fond of the old man as the night-nurse believed? Esther could hardly credit that. To begin with there was that conversation at the tea-table, which made it impossible to think that the Frenchwoman loved her husband, at least enough to upset herself as she was doing now. What then could be the reason? Could it be—ah, now perhaps one was getting at it!—could it be that Sir Charles had made some will of which she did not approve? She might easily be anxious for him to recover, so that he might have a chance of altering it. Yes, that was distinctly possible.

And yet, after all, it did not quite fit in with all that her memory held in connection with that little scene at the Restaurant des Ambassadeurs. She made an effort to recall it in detail. Had not Lady Clifford said something about a visit to a fortune-teller of some sort? What was it? Of course! She said the woman went into a trance and described "Charles" lying ill in bed, with a doctor beside him and a nurse.

"Good gracious, it has come true! And I am the nurse!"

She almost exclaimed it out aloud, so great was her astonishment. The next moment she wondered how on earth she had failed to recall this astounding coincidence before. Most likely it was due to the fact that her first impression of Lady Clifford had been overlaid by subsequent ones. What was it she had thought as she listened to the subdued, eager voice? There was no question about it—she had been convinced at the time that the exquisite creature was passionately hoping for illness to come to her rescue and rid her of a tedious old husband.

Instantly the scales fell from Esther's eyes. Why of course! The woman was not anxious for fear Sir Charles might die, she was in a fever of dread lest he should recover! What a horrible thought! Could it really be true?

The habit of believing in people made her long to reject the explanation, yet she knew she could not. It accounted for everything, even the expression on the French woman's face a moment ago.

Guiltily Esther glanced at the motionless invalid. There he lay, with quiet breathing, ignorant of the fact that his own wife was wishing him out of the way, praying for death to claim him. Praying? What if the prayers of the wife had in some way *wished* an illness upon the unsuspecting old man? Of course that was purely grotesque, yet as the ghastly notion occurred to her, Esther felt a sudden longing to confide in someone—Miss Clifford, the son, even the doctor. . . .

Good heavens, what an idea! The mere thought of mentioning this sort of thing to Dr. Sartorius threw a dash of cold water over her heated fancy. She could picture the scornful indifference with which he would receive her communication, she could almost hear him say, "Well, what of it? How many wives do you suppose are daily wishing their husbands would die? Does it shorten anyone's life? We don't live in the Middle Ages!"

At thought of the man of science, rational and cynical, she felt her balance restored. She was even able to laugh at herself for getting so worked up. Granting her suspicion was true, Lady Clifford could not harm the old man by thinking, not even if she cherished an effigy stuck full of pins. Such things did not happen. . . .

"Nurse!"

She started violently. Without the least warning movement the ill man had roused to consciousness and was calling her feebly.

"Are you there, nurse?"

She went quickly to his side.

"Yes, certainly, Sir Charles. Did you want anything?"

"I suppose it must be nearly lunch-time?"

"In half an hour. Are you hungry?"

"Oh, I don't know. It depends. If I'm only to have that disgusting milk again, I don't mind waiting."

She smiled at his petulance.

"You mustn't have any solid food, you know," she told him gently. "You'll have to be on a liquid diet for some time."

"I know all about that," he replied with a fretful movement of the head. "It's the milk I detest. I was sick of it before ever I was taken ill. I've had so much of the damned stuff."

"Have you?"

"Oh, yes, gallons. The doctor prescribed it for me several months ago, to try to put some flesh on me."

"And did it do you good?"

"I gained a few pounds, certainly, but I got to hate the very sight of it."

He turned restlessly, seeking a more comfortable position, and a grim smile flickered over his sallow face.

"I did my utmost to dodge it, but it was no good. First it was my sister who kept forcing the stuff on me, then my wife took a hand. Between the two of them I hadn't a chance. Now, to cap the climax, I have nothing but milk. I don't know why I should be so punished."

She laughed gaily and with a deft hand put the covers right for him.

"Never mind, I'll fix it for you so you'll find it quite different. You'll see, it won't be bad."

Her words and the laugh were alike purely mechanical. Inside her brain she was listening to other words in the doctor's hall, ten days ago: *"I suppose he's had his milk regularly, a pint and a half a day? . . ."*

She had assumed that Sartorius had meant that the old man was fortified by the extra nourishment, but the conclusion she had come to in regard to Lady Clifford upset her former ideas. She heartily wished she had not thought of it, that she had never overheard the conversation between Lady Clifford and Holliday. . . .

"I'd far better attend to my own affairs," she told herself decidedly. "If I don't, I shall be in imminent danger of becoming known as Esther the Eavesdropper."

At this thought she laughed again, spontaneously, then was disconcerted to find a pair of sunken old eyes regarding her keenly.

"What's amusing you?" demanded her patient.

"This time I'm afraid I can't tell you," she confessed in confusion, annoyed to feel a tide of red sweep over her face.

"Well, you might think of it again when you want a little extra colour," commented the old man dryly, but with an approving glance.

As her eyes met his shyly, noting how the quizzical smile softened his rather grim features, she realised his resemblance to his son. Simultaneously Sir Charles became for her a human being. Up till now he had been merely a "case." Something about him roused her sympathy, a wave of pity swept over her, she felt that she would put her whole heart into the task of taking care of him and making him well. Odd! Was this the result of flattered vanity? Or was it because the old man happened to resemble a certain young one? There was no denying that the pleasant glow had persisted ever since that trivial conversation in the hall.

She was late for *déjeuner*, and on entering the dining-room found Lady Clifford just leaving, and Miss Clifford and her nephew lingering over their coffee.

"You've had a lot to do, haven't you, Miss Rowe?" Miss Clifford greeted her kindly. "It doesn't matter, everything has been kept hot."

As Esther sat down the old lady continued what she was saying to the young man:

"Yes, it is very nice of Thérèse," she remarked, "really most thoughtful."

"What is?" inquired Roger absently, his eyes on Esther.

"Why, to give the doctor a lift back to his house. It is quite out of her way, but she knows that he hates driving his own car."

"Oh!" he exclaimed briefly, as though the matter did not interest him. "I wonder if there's a car I can have this afternoon?"

"Certainly, the little Citroën; it's in good order."

"Good, I'll tell Thompson to get it out. I've got a few things to attend to. As a matter of fact I want to call in at the cable office and inquire about that message that never reached me."

"Do you think it is any use?"

"I don't know. I'm going to see what happened, anyhow. You're quite sure it was sent?"

"Of course! Thérèse saw to it herself. I recall it perfectly."

Roger dropped his cigarette end into his coffee cup and rose with a stretch of his long arms; then, with a smile that included Esther, he left the room.

On her way upstairs Esther met the doctor, hat in hand. He stopped her, laying a heavy finger on her arm, and spoke in a low voice.

"As far as possible," he said slowly, keeping his little lightish eyes upon her, "try to keep Lady Clifford out of the room. Make excuses. She is a highly emotional uncontrolled type, and she is likely to have a bad effect on the patient. Excitement," he added with careful emphasis, "is the thing we must do everything to guard against. To a man in his condition it might have disastrous results. You must see that he is not agitated in any way whatsoever."

"I understand," she replied quickly. "I'll do my very best. Perhaps it would be as well if you spoke to Lady Clifford yourself."

"I have done so, but I cannot promise that it will be sufficient," he answered. "She is a difficult woman to manage."

Looking after the ponderous figure as it creaked down the stairs, Esther wondered if by chance the doctor shared her suspicion as to Lady

Clifford's secret feelings. Did he fear that in some way her adverse desires might communicate themselves to the invalid with unfortunate effects? She half thought this was the case. In his cold-blooded way the doctor was conscientious. He was being highly paid to save the old man's life, and save him he meant to do, no matter whose wishes stood in the way.

Late that afternoon, while Miss Clifford was changing her dress for dinner, there was a knock at her door, and her nephew entered. With a look of moody thought on his face, he stood for some moments beside the dressing-table drumming with his fingers on the edge of the mirror in a way that betokened indecision.

"Is anything the matter?" his aunt asked when she had glanced at him the second time and still he had not spoken.

"Just this," he replied, frowning slightly. "Would you believe me if I told you that that cable you spoke of was never sent?"

CHAPTER XII

"Not sent!"

Miss Clifford laid down the comb she was using and turned upon her nephew a face of bewilderment.

"No, it wasn't sent."

"But that's impossible; it must have been."

"It wasn't. There's no record of it."

"Oh, there is some mistake. Why, Thérèse herself . . ."

Her voice trailed off; she stared before her in a puzzled fashion.

Then reluctantly her eyes met the young man's.

"Then you think," she said hesitatingly, "that she didn't send it after all?"

"There's no question about it; I know she didn't."

The old lady shook her head slowly, utterly perplexed.

"But why? I can't see the least sense in it."

Roger sank upon the Chesterfield sofa and pushed his hair back from his forehead.

"Why? Because she didn't want me to come, I suppose. Of course, you must realise that Thérèse isn't fond of me."

"But even so, it's so—so stupid! You were sure to hear about your father sooner or later."

"Yes. I should think she merely meant to postpone it a little. I have figured it out like this: she dislikes to have me here, so she omitted to send that cable in order to put off my knowing the old man was ill. Not hearing from me, in a few days you'd cable again. Then I should wire back to ask if there was any necessity of my coming over, she would show the message to Father, knowing perfectly well he would insist on my staying to finish up the business. She knows he would have to be in the last extremity before he'd be willing for me to quit in the middle of a big job. In the end the chances were I'd not have to come at all. Do you see?"

His aunt picked up the comb again and carefully smoothed her front hair.

"It sounds very complicated. Do you suppose she reasoned all that out and was prepared to take so much trouble to keep you away?"

"I do," he said simply, and lit a cigarette.

"It's hard to believe. And yet . . . Roger, why is it Thérèse dislikes you?"

He got up and strolled about aimlessly.

"Ask me another," he replied lightly, with a shrug of the shoulders.

"You've never quarrelled?"

"Oh, no, certainly not!"

He had no intention of revealing that hidden episode. After a moment, seeing the troubled look on his aunt's face, he put his arm around her ample waist.

"I'm sorry I mentioned the beastly matter, Dido, honestly I am! Don't attach too much importance to what I've said. We all have our little peculiarities, and I just happened to stumble on one of Thérèse's, that's all. She doesn't mean any harm. Stand up and let me look at you. Is that a new gown?"

It evidently was, as her frank pleasure showed. She added a long string of tortoiseshell beads which Roger had given her on his last visit, and surveyed the effect in the glass, thinking what a long time it was since anyone had admired her appearance.

"My dear," she said after a pause, "I think perhaps I ought to tell Thérèse about that cable, and give her the chance to explain."

"Don't," commanded her nephew quickly. "She can only say one of two things—either that she forgot it, or else she'll swear she sent it and blame the cable office. In either event we sha'n't believe her, and the result will create an unpleasant atmosphere. Better let it drop."

"I suppose you're right," sighed his aunt. "Only it makes me uncomfortable."

"It would make us much more uncomfortable to have Thérèse in one of her sulky moods, especially with strangers in the house. I don't care about the doctor chap, he doesn't appear very sensitive, but that little day-nurse, for instance . . ."

"She is nice, isn't she? Of course she is a lady. I realised that the moment I saw her. I recall now that she was in the room when I told Thérèse you were coming, and although she made no sign I'm sure she noticed how upset Thérèse was. I felt humiliated."

"Oh, so Thérèse was upset, was she?" mused Roger, pondering this confirmation of his theory. "I wonder what your little nurse thinks of her?"

"Oh, Thérèse is charming to both nurses. The night-nurse, who has been here from the beginning, would do anything for her. She is always saying how lovely she is."

"Oh well!"—he yawned and gave a lazy stretch—"that's all to the good. I'm glad. I have an impression that the little Canadian girl is a pretty good judge of character, for all she looks so young and innocent."

Quitting his aunt's room, he sauntered in the direction of his own. He was fairly satisfied with the explanation he had evolved regarding the cable. He alone knew the extent to which Thérèse hated having him under the same roof with her. Outwardly she was cordial enough, but he realised that he must be a thorn in the flesh to her, although he had never had reason to believe she would take so definite a step to keep him away from Cannes. How furious she must have been at the shipwreck of her little plan!

He laughed aloud, so absorbed in the mental picture of her chagrin, that he collided with a dapper young man in a dinner jacket at that moment about to enter Thérèse's sitting-room. Pulling up short, he looked to see who it was who made so free of the house, and, simultaneously, the visitor wheeled round with an expression of nonchalant arrogance.

"Holliday!"

"Ah, it's you, Clifford!"

The greeting, though not exactly unfriendly, lacked warmth on both sides.

"I heard over the telephone you were expected. How's the great New World?"

"Oh, flourishing. I suppose you're dining here?"

"Why, no. As a matter of fact, I thought of taking Thérèse out somewhere. She's a bit frayed out, poor girl; she thought it might help her to sleep if she got away for a couple of hours. Rotten shame about your father. Typhoid's no joke at his time of life."

"Still, he seems to be going on fairly well."

"So I hear. I've been having a chat with Sartorius. He's by way of being a pal of mine, you know."

"Yes, my aunt tells me he did great things for you."

"Great!"—with a short laugh—"I should think he did. You didn't see me at that time, did you? I was just about to 'pass in my checks,' as your Yankee friends would say. He's a wizard, that's what he is. Never will be a fashionable physician, not enough ambition. Well, cheerio. I shall be seeing you soon no doubt."

He disappeared into the boudoir and closed the door. Roger continued thoughtfully across the landing. Resentment stirred in him at the cool manner in which Arthur Holliday came upstairs unannounced and went into rooms without knocking. Not that he cared on his stepmother's account, but it seemed to him an indignity to his father, an old man, belonging to another and more formal generation. It was evidence of a vulgar streak in Thérèse that she should permit such familiarities, whatever her relations with Holliday might be. He was glad that his simple-minded aunt appeared to remain in the dark about an affair which was plainly apparent to him, had been so a year ago. Probably by now Thérèse had completely lost her head over the casual Arthur, who on his side would never lose his head over any woman.

"Odd, that boy's success with women," he reflected a moment later as he turned on his bath. "He makes no effort whatever, yet they all pursue him. Since he was a youngster he has always had some woman hanging around his neck, usually a rich one."

Here a sudden thought came to him.

"By George! I wonder if Thérèse has been taking care of him all this time? Funny not to think of it before. I suppose it never occurred to me such a thing could happen where the old man's money was concerned, and yet he is old, and—damn it all, that would account for her consuming rage when he put her on short commons. I'd give something to know if that baccarat story is true."

The speculation engrossed him until the bath was full; then, lying in the warm water, he ceased to concern himself with his stepmother's affairs and gave himself up to sheer exultation at the prospect of the month of idleness before him. Since October he had worked with every atom of brain energy he possessed; now he could revel in his holiday, knowing he had earned it. He thought of tennis, of motoring to Monte Carlo, of dining and dancing afterwards, provided he could find a girl he liked. Somehow, as this idea occurred to him, he had a mental "flash-back" of the little nurse, more particularly of her slender legs and ankles as she had hurried along the passage that morning. There was a girl, now, who looked as if she knew how to enjoy things. Why should not he ask her to come out with him one evening to sample a little of the night-life of Cannes? He felt that with her as a companion the usual round would have twice its savour.

Esther came out of Sir Charles's room just as Captain Holliday issued from the adjoining apartment, with the result that they met face to face in the hall. She was about to pass after a formal greeting, but he, bestowing on her a perfunctory salutation, suddenly came a step nearer and stared at her so pointedly that she stopped, thinking he must have something to say.

"So you've taken on this job, have you?" he remarked tentatively, his eyes boring into hers. "You know, I've never been satisfied with that story of yours about my seeing you—where was it you said?—at the Carlton."

"I said I saw you there. Perhaps it wasn't where you saw me," she replied simply.

"Anyhow, it's not the occasion I mean. I've seen you somewhere else, in different circumstances . . . not that it matters a damn, but . . ."

"But it makes conversation," she finished the sentence for him, laughing.

"If you hadn't that thing on your head, now," he suggested seriously, "I might be able to recall where it was."

With a quick gesture she whipped off her white coif. Her bronze hair ruffled up all over her head in a shining crop of short curls. She put up her hands to tidy the mass, enduring his exploring gaze with a twinkle in her eyes, perfectly sure the alteration in her appearance would not help him, since on that other occasion she had worn a hat. After a close scrutiny he slowly shook his head.

"I can't get it," he admitted reluctantly. "But I shall one day."

"Let me know when you do," she bade him with irony.

"I will."

Still he did not move, and his shallow eyes held her. Into them had crept what she knew to be admiration, though of a lazy and indifferent sort. Without knowing why, for the second time that day—or was it the third?—she felt the blood rise in a wave to her cheeks. How silly, this facile blushing! She was angry with herself. It was not as if she were really embarrassed or confused, it came simply from that kind of physical sensitiveness which causes the closing of leaves in those plants we call "touch-me-not."

At this precise instant Roger, ready for dinner, came out on to the landing. What he saw was the young nurse, her head uncovered and blushing as she had that morning blushed for him, her eyes upraised with a provocative sparkle in them, standing close to Holliday, who was staring at her with unnecessary intentness, a grudging smile just beginning to stir the corners of his mouth.

Involuntarily Roger halted, conscious of an acute displeasure at the sight before him, a feeling compounded of resentment towards Holliday, whom he regarded as a puppy, and a sort of hurt disappointment in the girl. Was she, too, one of the many women who fell victims to Arthur's charm? He had thought better of her.

Whatever the situation, his appearance put an end to it. He saw the nurse's slender, capable fingers replace the cap, watched her smooth the tendrils of her hair at the sides. She was demure once more, utterly seemly, and the sly glance she shot him conveyed the hint that she might, perhaps, admit him into the joke. He felt inclined to modify his judgment and give her the benefit of the doubt. "Probably," he heard her remark to Holliday, "you've got me confused with someone else. I've only been a very short time in Cannes."

A door opened: they all looked around to discover Lady Clifford, attired for the evening. The vision took Esther's breath. She was reminded of what the spinster from Chester had said about the fair Thérèse being "like something on the films." The Frenchwoman was wrapped in a chinchilla cloak, caught about her with a grace Esther felt she could never emulate, even granting the chinchilla cloak. There was a revelation of apple-green and silver beneath, of white skin, pearls, and the flash of an immense diamond brooch. Held high gleamed the impeccable golden head, one of those flawless marvels of our time. Thérèse looked radiant, younger than Esther had yet seen her. Her grey eyes, rayed round with black lashes, shone like stars. There was a sort of cold purity about her that dazzled.

"Ready?"

Holliday's voice sounded as nonchalant as ever. Glancing at him, Esther felt amazement that he could accept all this supreme feast of a woman's beauty without so much as the flicker of an eyelash. Roger, too, appeared unimpressed. What were the two men made of?

"Have I kept you long?"

Something slightly sharp in the tone caused Esther to turn back towards Lady Clifford. She was astonished to see that the grey eyes had narrowed a little and were searching her own face, even while the question was addressed to her escort.

"No, I've been having a chat with Miss Rowe," replied the young man negligently, and as he spoke, he turned to Esther and smiled, a sophisticated smile, holding the hint of conspiracy.

She wished he had not done that. It called up an expression on Lady Clifford's face which there was now no mistaking. Heavens! Could it be possible that this transcendently lovely creature was able to feel even the tiniest bit jealous of her? It was incredible—and yet her instinct assured her it was so. She felt all at once that she had a good deal to learn. Days later, looking back, she thought that Lady Clifford's manner towards her altered from this exact moment.

Roger, too, saw that glance, momentary though it was. It struck him that Arthur was very clever; he never let any woman be too sure of his affections. As this thought came to him, Thérèse turned in his direction with a little wistful, appealing manner that she sometimes had.

"Will you forgive me for running away on your first evening here?" she asked sweetly. "I think perhaps a little change of scene will quiet my nerves a bit. *Au revoir, mon cher—à demain.*"

She kissed the tips of her fingers to him and moved slowly down the stairs, followed by her indifferent swain. When the front door banged Roger spoke:

"Then you've met that fellow before?"

For the life of him he didn't know why he said "that fellow."

"He came to lunch at the doctor's one day," Esther informed him, then added with a reminiscent and faintly malicious smile: "He thinks he has seen me before, and it bothers him."

"Has he?" demanded Roger bluntly.

"Yes, but he can't recall where, and I'm not going to tell him. As a matter of fact, it was at the Restaurant des Ambassadeurs. I was sitting at the table next to him one afternoon."

"Oh, I see!"

Somehow this explanation was very agreeable to Roger's ruffled sensibilities.

"Coming down to dinner?" he inquired, feeling a glow of regret at having misjudged her.

"Yes, but I want to make a quick change first."

"I'll wait for you."

He didn't know why he said that either. It came out unbidden. Ridiculous, the interest he was taking in this girl, whom he had not set eyes on before this morning. Yet there it was, he felt a distinct desire for her company and a longing to know if he could again inspire that sudden blush. It still irked him to think she had been able to blush for Holliday; the little beast was not worth it.

Lighting a cigarette, he strolled to the window at the end of the hall near his own door and, parting the curtains, looked out. Through the black fretwork of the acacias showed the thin crescent of the new moon, clean and sharp as a knife-blade. He made a wry face. He had seen the new moon through both trees and glass!

"It's a good thing I'm not superstitious," he reflected; yet for all his avowal he was conscious of a sudden qualm, which irritated him.

A heavy, inelastic step creaked across the floor behind him. Turning, he found Dr. Sartorius beside him. The gravity of the large face, with its bald, slanting forehead and small lightish eyes, slightly alarmed him.

"Is anything wrong, doctor?" he asked quickly.

"No, no, nothing at all. I merely promised to tell you that your father would like you to attend to a small matter for him in the morning before you go out. I believe he wants you to open his safe and get out the copy of his will which is there."

"His will?" repeated Roger, slightly dismayed.

"There is no reason for alarm. He appears anxious to refresh his memory, that is all. It seems better to humour him. I fancy there is some point he would like to discuss with you."

"Very well, I'll come in the first thing after breakfast."

In spite of himself the thought took root that the old man believed he was going to die.

CHAPTER XIII

HAVING finished a late and lazy breakfast next morning, Roger ascended to his father's room. He found the old man lying tranquil if weak, his temperature fallen to normal with that curious abruptness characteristic of typhoid. The nurse, very fresh in a clean apron and cap, was putting the room to rights. She smiled at Roger, who was no longer a stranger, for the two had had a long talk over their coffee the evening before, and later, with Miss Clifford, had indulged in a little mild cutthroat bridge.

"The doctor said something to me last night about your wanting the safe opened," ventured Roger, after several minutes' conversation with the invalid, during which no mention was made of the matter in question.

The old man's face looked blank, he appeared struggling to recall. At last he nodded slowly.

"I believe I did speak of it, though it's not of great importance. It occurred to me I might as well glance through the will I drew up two years ago. I made a slight alteration in it this winter, which I want to speak to you about, but I'll look through it first. Something Sartorius said reminded me of it."

Roger felt relieved. There was no evidence of his father's expecting an immediate decease; he seemed calm and fairly cheerful.

"Right you are. I'll attend to it now, if you'll tell me the combination."

"Give me a piece of paper; I'll write it down."

Roger handed him an envelope and his fountain pen, and watched while the ill man laboriously traced the figures of a simple combination.

"You will find the will in the top left-hand pigeon-hole," Sir Charles instructed him, lying back once more and wearily closing his eyes.

In the dressing-room Roger discovered Esther, occupied in arranging flowers.

"Here's what you are looking for," she told him. "It's been moved to make room for my diet-kitchen."

She indicated a small safe almost hidden by a white-tiled refrigerator and an enamelled stand which bore a spirit-lamp and an array of shining saucepans.

Roger knelt on the floor and examined the knobs and dial. Then, raising his head, he sniffed the air, his nostrils detecting an elusive fragrance, exotic, vaguely familiar.

"There seems a good deal of scent about here," he remarked. "It isn't yours, is it?"

Somehow she didn't look as if she would use that particular perfume, or indeed any perfume, while in working clothes. She laughed and shook her head.

"Oh, no, it's not mine. It's Lady Clifford's. I could tell it anywhere now."

"I can't see where it comes from."

"I'll tell you. When I arrived I found one of her handkerchiefs on the floor behind the refrigerator. You wouldn't think an odour could be so lasting, would you?"

He busied himself with the combination.

"I suppose she had been in here seeing about the milk. My aunt says she used to look after that matter before my father was taken ill."

"Who, Lady Clifford? Did she?"

He did not look up, and so missed the brief, faintly puzzled expression that flitted over her face as she stopped in the doorway with a vase of tulips in her hands.

As it happened, she was wondering over this fresh instance of Lady Clifford's solicitude for her husband's welfare, and trying to make it fit in with the idea that had come to her on the previous day. More than ever the Frenchwoman appeared to her a mass of contradictions; try as she would she felt she could never fathom her. . . .

A moment later Roger brought a narrow folded document and handed it to his father.

"Is this it?"

"Yes, quite right. Lay it here on the bed beside me. I'll run over it presently. I suppose you'll be off somewhere now?"

"I thought of running down to the tennis-courts on the chance of getting a few sets. I'll not be back for lunch."

"Know anyone to play with?"

"Yes; I ran into Graham and Marjory Kent at the Casino yesterday. They said they'd bring a fourth."

"Well, make the most of your holiday. You've earned it."

It was high praise. In this one simple sentence the old fellow, hard, undemonstrative, more than a bit "Lancashire," expressed the utmost approval of which he was capable. Understanding what it meant, Roger glowed with appreciation, yet he contented himself with a bare "Thanks," because anything more would have caused his father acute embarrassment.

Esther, who had been in the room, now withdrew in quest of more flowers. When she was out of earshot the invalid spoke, with a slight movement of the head in her direction.

"Nice girl, that," he said laconically.

For an instant his son's eyes met his.

"I'm inclined to share your opinion," the younger man agreed with conviction. After a moment's hesitation he strode quickly across the room and re-entered the dressing-room.

"Miss Rowe!" he called.

She was in the bathroom beyond, washing her hands free of flower-stains. She looked up in some surprise to find the son of the house beside her.

"What time do you have free?" he demanded abruptly.

"Oh, an hour or so in the afternoon. I usually go out for a walk."

She shook her dripping fingers and reached for a towel. He noticed that her hands, though slender and long, were firm and capable as well—the sort of hands he admired in a woman.

"I see. Then supposing I came straight back from the courts after lunch, would you care to come for a drive with me? It wouldn't bore you?"

"Bore me! What do you think?"

There was no doubt as to her genuine delight. Her eyes shone, the flecks of red deepened in her cheeks.

"Right-o! That's understood, then."

He grasped her still damp hand and was gone, leaving her with a slight feeling of confusion the reverse of unpleasant. She continued drying her hands, slowly, painstakingly, her thoughts far away. She was realising a most important fact, namely, that never before with any man of her acquaintance had she experienced a similar elation, a like breathless flutter of the pulses. She had had more than one proposal of marriage; perhaps if she had ever felt like this . . .

Her cheeks were warm when she came back to her patient, and she was a little self-conscious when she saw the shrewd old eyes fix themselves upon her with a quizzical but not unkindly gleam.

"You're much better to-day, aren't you?" she remarked to cover her confusion. "I'm so glad—I'm feeling very pleased with you. Your temperature is coming down nicely; you must just keep it up and you'll be well before you know it."

It was true, she felt personal triumph and gratification in the progress he was making. It was as if she were definitely fighting for him against those malevolent wishes in which she had begun to believe, so that his continued improvement was "one up" for her side. Yet what an anomaly Lady Clifford presented! Why the elaborate pretence of caring for her husband, brought to the point of preparing his milk for him? It wasn't what one would have expected of her. Had she done it to throw dust in the eyes of his sister and himself, so that she could the more safely indulge her friendship with Captain Holliday? No doubt that was it. Unless, of course, she herself had made a mistake, was doing the young wife a gross injustice.

"Perhaps I'm too quick at jumping at conclusions," Esther reflected. "What have I got to go on except an expression on Lady Clifford's face when she didn't know I was watching her? In any case, she's doing her utmost for him; I've even heard her say if he got worse she was going to call a consultation. There's the proof, right there. Why should I worry?"

Whether from the firmness of her resolution or from the prospect of the drive in the afternoon, she did succeed in banishing the whole matter from her thoughts. She was happy at the anticipation of seeing something of the neighbouring countryside, happier still to think that Roger Clifford had cared to invite her to go with him. Her experience with men had taught her the great if simple truth that they did not ask one from a sense of duty.

She had just settled her patient for his afternoon nap when Roger returned, warm and sunburned.

"Get ready as soon as you can," he bade her. "Let's make the most of the sunshine. Put on a warm coat; the car's an open one."

In ten minutes' time she was seated beside him in the little Citroën, speeding along smooth roads out into the country. After the confinement of her work she felt gloriously exhilarated, leaning back with the sharp wind in her face, revelling in the view of the mountains, enthusiastic as a child.

"I suppose you've been to Nice and Monte Carlo?" he suggested.

"Me? Indeed I haven't; I've not been anywhere yet. I came here with a patient, and exactly a week later I started to work for Dr. Sartorius."

"Then you've everything before you. How I wish I could take you about sight-seeing a bit! If only these places were a trifle nearer! . . . Still, when my father is convalescent we must see what can be done."

"It would be heavenly! It's so stupid going alone, hardly any fun at all. . . . Of course, I don't know what the doctor would think if I began running about like that. He probably wouldn't approve."

"Do you like him?" asked her companion suddenly.

"Dr. Sartorius?" she replied, knitting her brows. "I hardly know. . . . I suppose the fact is I neither like nor dislike him. I admire him very much indeed; I think he's a frightfully clever physician and scientist."

"But as a man?"

"I don't believe he is a man, quite," she laughed. "At least, one can't exactly think of him as one."

"That's how he strikes me. Yet I suppose no one can be as phlegmatic as he seems; there must be a spark of enthusiasm in him somewhere."

"Oh, but there is! Don't you know? He absolutely lives for research; it's the one thing he takes an interest in. He practises medicine to make a living, but he devotes every spare minute to hunting for anti-toxins."

"Does he indeed? I know my aunt thinks very highly of him, but I'm glad you do, too. Your opinion is worth something."

The time passed with amazing quickness, as they discovered when they consulted their watches.

"Must you go back at once?" Roger asked as he tentatively reversed the car and slowly headed for home.

"I don't want to be late," she said with a sigh. "It's my first case here; I must be on my best behaviour! But—I've just thought of something. Would it be very far out of our way if we went to the doctor's villa in the Route de Grasse? I left my French lesson-books there, and I'd like to fetch them."

"We can do it easily; only show me the house."

Before long they came in sight of the villa, which looked as tidy, as smug and non-committal as it had done when she first approached it some weeks ago. Alighting quickly from the car, Esther rang the bell and waited, expecting momentarily to see the friendly Jacques answer the summons. There was, however, no response.

"Is anyone staying here?" asked Roger.

"Yes, the doctor's servant, but he may have gone out."

She rang again; from the distant kitchen they could hear the faint persistent peal.

"The place looks deserted for the moment, at any rate," Roger remarked, gazing up at the closed windows.

With a sudden wry smile, Esther fished in her bag and produced a latch-key.

"Isn't it stupid of me? I'd forgotten I still had it. I've meant daily to give it back to the doctor, but I never think of it at the right moment."

She fitted the key into the Yale lock, and in another moment the two were standing inside the dim and chilly hall, looking about them. A few circulars lay in a heap on the floor, there was a film of dust on the polished parquet. A man's overcoat and hat adorned the rack. From the salon a clock ticked loudly.

"Gloomy place, this," commented Roger, glancing into the cold and orderly salon. "Makes me think of funerals."

"Yes, that room is always like that, only used as a reception-room for patients."

She flung open the door of the *salle à manger* and entered, then stopped, looking about her.

"This looks as though Jacques had been entertaining his friends," she said, pointing to the collection of bottles on the sideboard and the syphon and whisky decanter on the table.

"By Jove, it does!"

Roger ran his eyes over the miniature bar.

"Martini vermouth, Noilly Prat, Gordon gin, Angostura, Bacardi rum, absinthe—pre-war, at that. If your Jacques mixes all these drinks—"

"I never saw Jacques take anything except a little *vin ordinaire*," Esther replied, shaking her head. "But there have certainly been two people here, whoever they were, for here are their two glasses."

As she spoke she picked up the tumblers from the table one after the other and examined them thoughtfully. One, she discovered, had had only soda-water in it, there was a little in the bottom now, with a cigarette-end floating about—a cigarette with a red tip, half uncurled from the wet. She frowned at it for a moment, then went to the book-shelves in search of her books, which she discovered among a pile of medical journals.

"Here they are. Shall we go?"

Roger was examining the tumbler she had recently set down.

"Jacques also seems to have a nice taste in cigarettes," he remarked. "Extravagant fellow altogether."

He indicated the floor, which was littered with stubs, mostly cork-tipped, though there was an occasional scarlet tip here and there.

"Jacques smokes only those cheap Marylands that come in a blue packet," Esther replied, laughing. "You see I'm acquainted with all his habits. No, I can't believe it is Jacques who's been here; it looks as though . . ."

She stopped and, bending down, picked up a tiny object from the rug.

"There was a woman, at any rate," she mused, with a considerable degree of curiosity in her voice, "for here is a hairpin."

It was a little bronze one of the "invisible" sort. Utterly unable to comprehend any woman's being in this house, she turned the hairpin over wonderingly. Then she noticed that her companion was staring up at the ceiling with a frown on his face.

"S'sh," he cautioned, laving a hand on her arm. "I thought I heard . . ."

"Who the hell is that down there? Answer, or I'll shoot!"

They jumped guiltily, astonished at the sudden angry voice that thundered upon them from the upper regions of the house.

"Goodness!" whispered Esther, gazing at Roger with round eyes. "Who do you suppose—"

"I say, whose bloody business is it to prowl about down there? Here, show yourselves, damn you!"

It was a man's voice, at once sleepy and peevish.

"Who on earth is it?"

"I'll soon see."

Roger pushed the door wide and strode into the hall, Esther closely following.

CHAPTER XIV

WITH one accord they peered up the dim well of the staircase. On the floor above, leaning over the rail, one hand clutching an army revolver, was a dishevelled young man, his hair tousled, his eyes swollen with sleep. He was clad in orange-striped silk pyjamas open at the neck, and even as he scowled darkly on the intruders below he stifled a capacious yawn. Although his face was in shadow there seemed something familiar about him. However, before anything had been said on either side, the belligerence faded from the young man's manner, his attitude altered, and he gave vent to a lazy chuckle, as with his free hand he fastened the top button of his sleeping attire and smoothed back his hair.

"Good God, I beg your pardon," he exclaimed. "I'd no idea; I thought it was burglars."

In a flash Esther saw that it was Captain Holliday. Roger also recognised him, and gave a nod, needlessly curt, Esther thought. After all, there was no good being indignant with the man for using profanity a moment ago when he could have had no knowledge that there was a woman present.

"We didn't dream anybody was here," Esther explained quickly. "We came to fetch something I left behind. I had a key, so we let ourselves in."

"Oh, I see! I woke up wondering who the hell was roaming about down there. I knew it couldn't be Jacques; he's off for a couple of days. I just roused up sufficiently to get my gun." He tossed the revolver lightly into the air and caught it again. "I'm hanging out here looking after things while Sartorius is away," he added, running his fingers over his unshaven chin.

"Well, we won't interrupt your siesta any longer," Roger returned, moving towards the front door and drawing Esther with him.

"Siesta! That's a good one. This is my first appearance to-day, old man. I say, if you hold on a minute, I'll shake you up a side-car. I feel inclined for one myself."

"No, thanks."

"No?" and the captain yawned again. "Then cheerio!"

The door slammed behind them, they descended the steps and got into the car without speaking. Esther could not see why her companion appeared to be so much annoyed. She stole a glance at him, and saw that his mouth had taken on a grim line that made him more than ever like his father, while his eyes were bleak and steely. An Englishman might have said that this was the Lancashire coming out in him.

"Think of anyone being able to sleep like that!" she ventured, laughing a little. "Why, it's nearly five o'clock. He must have been up all night."

She had not meant to say exactly that, on account of what was in her secret thoughts, but she was glad to see her friend's severe expression relax a little.

"Ah, that's the advantage of a care-free life," he remarked lightly.

"But doesn't he ever do anything?—any work, I mean?"

"Not that I know of, but I lost track of him after the war and only ran into him again about a year ago."

"He was in the air service, wasn't he?"

"Yes; he was at Marlborough with my brother, and the two of them went into the Flying Corps together as boys of eighteen. Malcolm was killed, and Arthur nearly so—he was in five or six bad smashes. He always had plenty of courage, a fine record for bravery. The old man has never forgotten that, nor the fact that he was Malcolm's friend."

"So that's how you came to know him?" mused Esther reflectively. "I'm glad to find out. He interests me rather."

"Does he, indeed!"

She was gazing thoughtfully at the road ahead, oblivious of the quick, faintly suspicious glance he bent upon her.

"Yes," she said slowly. "Merely, I suppose, because he is a new type for me. He's not in the least what I should ever have considered a lady's man, much too hard and indifferent, and yet I can see that he is extremely attractive."

"So you can see that, can you?"

"Oh, certainly! I can feel his charm myself, in a sort of way."

She failed to add that Holliday was not the style of man she particularly admired, partly because she was too busy thinking of Lady Clifford and the very evident fascination he possessed for her. She did not realise how long she sat absorbed in her speculations, and still less had she any idea that the man beside her was for the second time wondering if she, too, had fallen under the casual Arthur's spell, and reflecting regretfully that he could not well disillusion her without appearing caddish.

"It seems a bit of a come-down for him to be living in this comparative obscurity," he observed, half to himself. "I daresay he's comfortable enough, still, after the Ritzes and the Carltons . . ."

"I heard him tell the doctor a fortnight ago that he was absolutely stony, so I suppose that accounts for it. He was going to sell his car."

"Oh, I see!"

Indeed, Roger saw more than he would have cared to disclose. He felt nearly sure now of what he had at first only dimly suspected, namely, that Thérèse had been supplying Arthur with funds. He could comprehend now his stepmother's rage at being summarily cut down, as clearly as he understood the reasons back of Holliday's projected removal to the Argentine. The conclusions he was coming to appeared to him sordid and humiliating. He hoped his father had no suspicion of the truth.

They had reached the Villa Firenze; the car purred up the gravel drive under the curving branches of the acacias.

"I'm glad you asked me to come," Esther said sincerely as she alighted. "I feel like another person."

"So do I."

He looked at her gravely and for a longer space than the occasion demanded. Again there was the sense of pleasant confusion within her as she raced up the stairs to her room, a smile played about her lips, her pulse beat quickly. She had forgotten the matter that had been in her thoughts ever since she had entered the doctor's dining-room, but once she had closed her door it came back to her. That cigarette-tip with its scarlet edge uncurled—had her companion associated it with anyone in particular? She wondered. Opening her bag, she shook out the tiny hairpin she had picked up off the floor. So few hairpins were used at all these days of shingled heads . . . yet she had recently seen one identical with this. It was Lady Clifford who used it to anchor into position her big wavy lock of hair.

"She was there last night, I am sure of it," Esther said to herself as she threw off her hat and coat. "It was quite safe, Jacques was away. I'm the only person who knows, and that by the merest accident. . . . Well, it's just as well for her it isn't some malicious person. She's all right in my hands."

How odd it seemed to think that she, a stranger, should know more about Lady Clifford than her own family! Or perhaps it wasn't so strange after all. One's family was often the last to know things, its ignorance was proverbial. She felt a sudden wave of pity for the old man, lying ill and unsuspecting.

When she slipped back into Sir Charles's room, she found Miss Clifford in a chair by the window, knitting.

"He's just waked up," she said, rising and coming towards her. "You've had a good nap, haven't you, Charlie?"

"Oh, yes, once I managed to get to sleep. Thérèse would keep coming in and fidgeting around my pillow; she can't seem to let me alone."

"She does so want to be useful, poor child," the old lady made excuse gently. "You can't blame her if she doesn't know much about nursing. I finally insisted on her going and lying down. I thought she looked very tired, as though she hadn't slept well."

Esther felt annoyed, particularly after what the doctor had said about trying to keep Lady Clifford out of the room.

"I hope I haven't stayed out too long," she said with compunction, glancing at her watch.

"Not a bit of it. You must get fresh air. I hope you'll go often with my nephew; it is good for him too. I'll go and get my tea now. You'll be wanting yours, too, no doubt," and with a kindly pat on Esther's shoulder she quitted the room.

"Is my son coming in after tea, nurse?" inquired the old man feebly.

"Yes, in a few minutes."

"I have something I want to say to him. Will you leave us alone?"

"Of course," she promised, smiling.

Sir Charles closed his eyes, then spoke without opening them:

"Where's Lady Clifford?"

"I expects she's still lying down, Sir Charles, but I'm not sure. Would you like to see her?"

"No, no, not at all, not at all. I'd like to speak to my son alone; I don't want her to interrupt us."

"I'll see to it, Sir Charles; don't worry."

He appeared satisfied. When some minutes later Roger came in, Esther left him with his father, merely cautioning him against staying too long. Roger watched her till the door had closed behind her, then he drew a chair beside the bed. He saw that the old man was fumbling ineffectually in the effort to get at something under his pillow.

"Here, I'll do that for you," Roger said, coming to his aid. "What is it, anyhow?"

"Only that copy of my will. I want you to put it away again. No good leaving it about for people to pry into."

Roger smiled at the invalid's native cautiousness. He had to lift his head before he was able to extract the document, planted under the very centre of the pillow.

"Pretty safe there, eh?" Sir Charles commented with a gleam of humour. "Just as well, just as well. Take it now and lock it up, then come back. I've something to say to you."

When Roger returned, he had several minutes to wait before his father spoke again. The ill man seemed to be husbanding his resources as well as considering how best to begin. At last he moistened his dry lips and made an effort.

"You all of you assume I'm going to get well of this," he stated casually.

"Get well? Of course you are!"

"I'm not so sure. Not that it bothers me. I've had my day. Only, in case I do peg out, it seems fair to tell you beforehand about a slight alteration I have seen fit to make in my will."

"Yes, what is it?"

The old man drew a deep breath, then continued, pausing between sentences.

"It has nothing to do with the disposition of the property. That remains the same. Only, I have appointed you as executor and a sort of trustee of the whole estate."

"Me!"

Utterly unprepared for this information, his son regarded him in dismay.

"Why not?"

Roger could think of nothing to say. He was filled with chagrin, but afraid to voice his reasons for objecting.

"It struck me," went on Sir Charles in a laboured manner, "that as Thérèse is a young woman, the trustee ought to be a young man. An old one might not have so much understanding."

"Perhaps not, but why me? Wouldn't it be better to choose someone outside the family?"

"No, I don't think so. Who outside the family would take enough interest? Besides, frankly, I don't know any other young man whose judgment I'd trust as I would yours."

Great as was the compliment, it did not mitigate for Roger the onerous nature of the responsibility.

"Are you quite sure it's necessary?" he asked unhappily.

"Quite. I could not rest easy unless I had placed what I have to leave in the hands of a competent man of business. You know it as well as I do, Thérèse needs looking after."

Roger rose and walked to the window, where he stood for several seconds staring out, unable to bring himself to make a suitable comment.

There was but one thing he felt inclined to say, which was, "Oh, give her the usual amount for a widow, and let her go to hell!" which, of course, wouldn't do. Why had his father forced this irksome duty upon him? To be forcibly kept in contact with his stepmother, to be compelled to advise her, overlook her expenditures—it was intolerable. At all cost he felt he must get out of it—that is, at all cost save that of exciting and distressing his father. Ah, that was the difficulty! How could he refuse without giving the old man some hint of his feelings regarding Thérèse?

"Surely," he said at last, with great restraint, "such a trusteeship isn't necessary. Thérèse is not a child; she ought to be capable of managing her own affairs."

Sir Charles's face assumed an expression of obstinacy that Roger knew well.

"Where money is concerned, Thérèse is a fool. She has no judgment whatever, money drips through her fingers. I've no intention of allowing her to fritter away the property it has taken me a lifetime to get together. You will find I have tied it up pretty securely. She won't be able to throw it away, she won't be at liberty to do anything—I repeat, *anything*—without your full knowledge and consent."

He had spoken with such emphasis that he closed his eyes with an expression of great lassitude.

"I don't like it," protested Roger, helpless in the face of his father's iron determination; "it's too much responsibility."

"Not too much," retorted his father calmly.

"And besides, you know yourself that Thérèse won't like it, either. She—she may resent it very deeply."

There was a pause, then the heavy eyebrows went up with a slightly ironical movement.

"Don't trouble your head about Thérèse; leave her to me."

There was nothing to be done; any further objection might cause the old man serious annoyance. Roger's only hope lay in waiting till his father was well, when, perhaps, he might renew the argument. Accordingly he gave in with a good grace.

"Oh, very well, there's no more to be said about it. By the way, have you told Thérèse?"

"Not yet. I wanted to speak to you first. But I shall broach the subject to her . . . when I feel equal to it."

The dry humour in this last phrase caused Roger to wonder if, after all, his father was quite as blind as he thought him. Did he suspect the baccarat story? Was this a diabolical plan for getting even? There was no way of knowing; the old chap would keep his counsel till the last gasp. Yet, as Roger gazed on the mask-like face, he thought that his father's decision constituted a delicate and appropriate revenge for many a secret indignity.

He himself had no wish to score off Thérèse; his sole desire was to leave her strictly alone. It was true that the very perfume she used had become offensive to him—he fancied he could smell it now about the covers of the bed, which showed how she was getting on his nerves—but certainly he wished her no harm.

He was silent and thoughtful when a few minutes later he joined his aunt and Esther in the adjoining room. He had overcome his first avoidance of the boudoir, yet he still disliked the hint of incense that clung to its atmosphere. He drew a breath of slight distaste as he sank down on the pale blue chaise-longue and mechanically drew out his cigarette-case, only to find it empty.

"There are cigarettes on the table in that box, if you want to smoke," suggested his aunt.

He picked up the box, made of turquoise-blue shagreen, and opened it. There were three compartments within, holding three kinds of cigarettes. In the middle one was a single cigarette with a scarlet tip and a scarlet monogram—T. C. He lifted it between his thumb and finger and examined it with a slight frown.

"That's one of Thérèse's own special kind," observed his aunt placidly. "She has them made for her. They're scented with amber."

He let the little object fall and selected a plain cigarette. Then as he lit it, his eyes encountered for a fleeting instant the clear gaze of the nurse. Immediately she looked away and, rising, perhaps too hurriedly, left the room. However, that single glance had been sufficient to tell Roger what was in her thoughts.

His first impulse was one of regret. He felt a poignant humiliation to think that this young girl, a stranger in the house, should be aware of a thing of that kind concerning his father's wife. Yet, oddly enough, a second later, he realised that he no longer regarded Esther as a stranger. He felt as though he had known her for years; she had mysteriously become something quite personal. Strange, how the sharing of a secret knowledge can change a relationship.

When Esther opened the door into the bedroom, she was just in time to see Lady Clifford bending over the ill man, with one hand lifting up his head, while with the other she turned over the pillow beneath it.

CHAPTER XV

The Frenchwoman looked up with a slight start, then smiled.

"Ah, it's you, nurse!" she murmured. "You do not mind my being here, do you?"

Esther stood still for a second, trying not to betray that she was annoyed. Why couldn't the woman leave her poor husband alone? Recalling the doctor's injunction to her, she wondered how she could convey the needed hint to Lady Clifford without giving offence.

"Did you want anything, Sir Charles?" she inquired a little pointedly, coming forward and gently taking the pillow out of Lady Clifford's hand.

"No, nothing at all," the patient replied somewhat fretfully.

"I thought he seemed so—so terribly hot," explained the Frenchwoman with a note of apology. "I always think when one is ill . . ."

She left her sentence unfinished while her eyes took a quick survey of the smooth sheet. Words Sir Charles had spoken a little while ago in regard to his wife's "fidgeting about his pillow" recurred to Esther.

"Were you looking for something, Lady Clifford?" she asked, cheerfully bland.

The Frenchwoman shot her a glance, her beautiful eyes wide with surprised negation.

"*Mais non,*" she replied with a graceful shrug. "But why do you ask that?"

"I beg your pardon," murmured Esther, confused by the other's sweeping repudiation.

She settled the invalid on his pillow once more, noting the ghost of an ironical smile that flitted over his features. Between half-shut lids he watched the two women with an amused appreciation.

"I think, perhaps, it would be as well if you said good-night to him now, Lady Clifford," hinted Esther tactfully. "In a short time I am going to begin getting him ready for the night, and I like to have him absolutely quiet before-hand."

Hoping her suggestion would prove sufficient, she started removing flowers from the room. When she returned she saw Lady Clifford kiss the patient's cheek, then straighten up, wrap her négligé closer about her slender body, and move towards the door.

"*Bonsoir, mon cher,*" she called softly, kissing her finger-tips to him, "*dors bien!*"

So charming, so transparently appealing . . . yet she had been looking for something under the pillow, Esther was convinced of it. Sir Charles, she thought, realised it, too. But what was it she had been trying to discover? Suddenly she recalled the will that Roger had taken out of the safe that morning. Ah! Lady Clifford wanted to have a look at it; she was nervous for some reason. It was like old Sir Charles to keep his intentions closely guarded.

Several times that evening she noticed that Roger's gaze rested on her with interest. She was feminine enough to wonder if he thought she looked nice in the little wine-red frock she had put on. It was such a relief to get out of her stiff uniform that she always managed to change for dinner when there was sufficient time.

As a matter of fact, Roger was thinking as she sat there on a low stool, one foot curled under her, that she looked absurdly young, hardly more than a little girl. He believed she could be frivolous, too, gay without being silly, as he put it. So few girls could achieve that. . . .

"Do you like dancing?" he demanded abruptly.

"Do I not!"

"Then I'll tell you what we'll do. To-morrow evening we'll run down to the Casino for dinner and dance a bit. Would you care to?"

"It would be heavenly! But do I dare?"

She glanced at Miss Clifford.

"Why on earth not, my dear? When you're off duty, your time's your own. You needn't stay very late, if you're afraid of over-sleeping in the morning."

"Well, then, I will," Esther promised, her eyes shining with pleasure.

"Good girl! We'll have a regular beano. We both need it."

In the seclusion of her room that night Esther took out her best new evening gown, bought in Paris, and examined it with satisfaction. She had worn it only once; it had been a present from Miss Ferriss. Layers of filmy chiffon, peach-coloured, it presented a delectable picture as she spread it out on the bed. There was a shaggy diaphanous flower of silver gauze to wear on the shoulder, and the shoes that went with it were silver kid, well cut and severe.

"It is adorable," she sighed gloatingly, as she fingered the delicate mass. "What luck to have it here where there are so many smart dresses!"

She held it up in front of the mirror. Yes, this shade of pink suited her perfectly; it brought out the bronze tones in her hair and heightened the rose in her cheeks.

"I wonder if he likes me, too," she mused. "Or if I'm merely some-thing to dance with? Never mind, it doesn't matter. I do need a little gaiety. I hope the doctor won't object—but why should he? I'm not going to neglect my job. Still, he might; he's queer. That's the worst of having the doctor living in the house. Such a nuisance!"

She spent half an hour manicuring her nails and then, still feeling wide-awake, decided on a bath. The bathroom was between her room and the doctor's. On entering she found it, as usual, so stiflingly hot that she was obliged to throw open the casement window and let the cool, moist air steal into the room. For several minutes she leaned out, breathing in the night odours of the dark garden. With them came a heavier odour that was familiar, the acrid, pungent smell of the doctor's tobacco. By it she could tell that he, too, had his window open; he was sitting close to it, reading and smoking. She had no idea how he spent his evenings, but when she came to bed his light was always on. What an odd, self-contained, saturnine creature he was! There was something so ponderous, so logical, so crushing about him. Yes, that described him best, crushing. She always felt that he was ready to flatten her out. . . .

Somewhere near at hand a door opened and closed again. Before she could decide what door it was she heard the low rumble of the doctor's voice addressing someone.

"Well," she heard him say somewhat brusquely, "what is it now?"

It was the exasperated tone one might employ to a rather tiresome child. She found herself listening idly, wondering who it was who had come into his room. A second later, with a slight shock, she recognised the unmistakable tones of Lady Clifford. As on a former occasion, she was puzzled to know how it was the doctor spoke to her in so peremptory a fashion. She could not catch the words of the Frenchwoman, but the doctor's reply was clearly audible.

"That was wrong of you," he was saying. "I distinctly told you not to try. Besides, I am sure you exaggerate the importance of it."

Lady Clifford's next speech, uttered in a querulous tone, was distinguishable, from which Esther concluded she had come closer to the window.

"But I tell you I must know the truth! I cannot rest until I find out. Something warns me he has done something . . . damnable!"

"You will know soon enough."

"But, mon Dieu, when I know it will be too late!"

She seemed almost in tears. The doctor waited a little before replying, in accents of unmoved calm:

"Rubbish! How did this idea come to you?"

"I will tell you." The woman's voice was eager, importunate. "In January, when we were in Paris, he went to see Hamilton, his English solicitor. I thought nothing of it at the time, but a few days ago something he said made me think—made me afraid—I don't know what he may have done. He is capable of anything, everything! I tell you, I am terrified!"

Esther, by the bathroom window, nodded to herself with satisfaction at the confirmation of her theory. So it had been the will Lady Clifford was trying to see! Matters were clearing up. She heard Sartorius say sceptically:

"Don't be a fool! Go back to your room; this is neither the time nor the place for these conferences. I have told you that before."

There was a faint murmured protest, then again the doctor's voice, heavy and intolerant:

"Good God, woman, what possible difference can he make, or anyone else, for that matter? You appear to overlook the fact that all is being done for your husband that can be done. There is not the slightest cause for alarm."

Another murmur, longer than before, then in a slightly modified tone, though still dictatorial:

"I see no reason why you shouldn't sleep, but if you insist I will give you something. . . . Here, one powder, not more, or I'll not be answerable for the consequences. . . . And remember, don't come here again. If you want me, send your maid for me. Good-night."

There was the faint sound of the door dosing, then silence. Esther shut the window cautiously, so that her neighbour might not suspect he had been overheard.

Exactly why she minded his knowing was not clear to her. There had certainly been nothing wrong in the conversation. It was the doctor's manner towards his employer that was strange, that was all. She found herself puzzling about it after she was in bed. Her brain was very active; she could not compose herself to sleep, though when she tried to analyse her state of mind there seemed little to cause her vague discomfort. She knew that many women made confidants of their medical men; there was nothing surprising in Lady Clifford's unburdening herself to Sartorius on the subject of her husband's will. The overbearing familiarity with which the doctor treated her was harder to understand, yet even there it was difficult to say there was anything abnormal. It merely suggested that these two had known each other a long time, had not, indeed, the formal relation of physician and patient. Whatever the case, there was nothing one could definitely say was wrong, yet . . .

"I don't in the least know why," she said to herself as she lay in bed, "but I've got a feeling there is something queer going on in this house—something—something *underhand*. There! I've said it."

Yet, admitting this, what could be wrong? Not surely anything to do with Sir Charles's case, which was a straightforward affair? The patient was progressing well, with every reasonable hope of recovery. To the outward eye, at least, everything was smooth and normal. . . .

Why was it she suddenly recalled an incident of many years back, dating from her childhood in Manitoba? One of her sisters had played a trick on her. On going to bed one night, she had turned back the smooth, white counterpane of her bed to find, to her horror, a whole nest of young garden-snakes curled up together between the sheets. The exterior of the bed had given not the slightest inkling of the loathsome contents, so carefully had her sister tidied the clothes. Perverse that this particular incident should have come to her now out of the past!

Esther was not psychic, she was not even given to premonitions. Yet she knew that she was sensitive to the emotional states and conflicts of those about her. She had always been able, on entering a room full of people, to tell instinctively if anything was amiss, though whether her faculty was purely intuitional or merely the delicate functioning of a mental process she was unable to say, any more than a person suffering from "cat-fear" can tell how he detects the presence of the hidden cat, whether the warning comes out of the blue, or is the result of finely developed olfactory nerves.

In the present instance, having no tangible grounds for her conviction, she became exasperated and made repeated resolutions to put the entire thing out of mind. It was no use; she was wide awake, over-excited, the room felt hot, the cover got in her way. Why on earth were French sheets so many yards long? This one kept coming up about her neck and stifling her. Again and again she flung it back, until a final gesture of fury brought her hand in contact with a hard object, which fell with a clatter to the floor. It was her small alarm-clock. She picked it up and set it on the table beside her, where it ticked busily away.

How long it was before the welcome tide of drowsiness engulfed her she did not know. She hardly realised she had been asleep when gradually she became aware of something heavy lying across her body, pressing down upon her with an inert weight. The unpleasant consciousness grew, she wanted to rid herself of the incubus, but she felt curiously drugged, impotent. The weight increased; at the same time it seemed to have life of a certain sort, slow-moving and lethargic; it crept upward slowly, always pressing heavily upon her. She was cramped, her body ached, her breath came with difficulty, she turned and twisted, tried to free her arms, but they were pinioned close to her sides. What was the Thing thus crushing her? She strained to see, but the darkness was like black velvet; she could see nothing, only feel, breathlessly, chokingly. A horrible idea assailed her. Whatever it was, it was striving to suffocate her—yes, and it was going to succeed, unless she could muster the strength to cast it off.

Panic seized her. She struggled, possessed by a mad terror; she opened her mouth to scream, but no sound came, her voice was paralysed like the rest of her. Up and up crept the weight, it reached her throat, she felt it graze her chin. Its touch was cold and scaly; she shuddered at the contact. At the same dreadful moment she realised what the Thing was. Instantly her vision cleared as if an inky cloud had rolled away, and she stared with starting eyes into the small, cold eyes of a python!

The flat head was drawing slowly nearer, the mouth opened, she saw the darting tongue—the creature was going to bite. Then with a rush her voice came back; she screamed aloud . . .

CHAPTER XVI

SHE heard her own voice, muffled and unnatural. It seemed to work a sort of magic, for the python vanished, melted away like mist; she drew a great shuddering breath and found she was lying on her bed, unharmed, but with the sheet muffled about her throat and the thick eiderdown quilt resting in a roll across her. Her heart was still pounding, perspiration streamed from her while she laughed hysterically and repeated to herself:

"But pythons don't bite! Pythons don't bite!"

No, of course!—how absurd it was!—they crushed you to death. What an illogical creation of her sub-consciousness! It had been so vivid, the sensation so acute, the thing had had such solidity! Revelling in her sense of security, she lay quite still, listening to her breathing as it slowed down to normal. What had prompted the dream? Was it because she had been thinking of that snake episode of her childhood? Was it a python after all? Somehow there seemed more to it than that; the suspicion haunted her that the dream held some hidden significance.

A sharp tap came at the door.

"Who is it?" she cried, starting up and realising that it was morning.

The door opened a crack and the slightly prim accents of the night-nurse called through:

"It's after your usual time," she said. "I thought you would like to know."

Esther sprang out of bed.

"Oh, I'm dreadfully sorry! Something must have gone wrong with my clock."

It was true. Last night's accident had damaged the alarm. She raced through her dressing and hurried across the hall to her patient's room, devoutly hoping the doctor would not find out she had overslept. Luck was against her. For the first time since she had been on the case he was there before her, standing at the foot of the bed, looking down thoughtfully at the sleeping old man. It was not a heinous offence to be twenty minutes late on a single occasion, yet somehow the sight of the big, bulky figure, planted there as though lying in wait for her, made her suddenly uncomfortable.

"I'm afraid I've overslept a little," she murmured apologetically as she greeted him.

Instead of replying, he took his watch from his pocket and looked at it. Then, without moving his head, he turned his little greyish eyes upon her and regarded her fixedly. That was all, yet she felt completely crushed by his disapprobation. She started to make excuses, then felt that she could not. Her tongue clove to the roof of her mouth. She knew that any explanation would sound stupid and futile. Why was it the man affected her in this oppressive fashion? No other doctor had ever done so. Why was it that the mere physical presence of him, of his big, thick body and his little bald head with its small, glancing eyes, filled her at times with a sort of repulsion? From the first she had had the sensation vaguely, now it had become intensified a hundred-fold.

"I'm developing nerves!" she scolded herself severely as she went into the dressing-room to prepare her patient's morning milk. "Why should I be afraid of any man? . . . Yet it isn't that I'm exactly afraid. I can't explain it, quite."

She was glad when she returned to find him gone. She gratefully drank the tea which a maid brought her and began to take a more normal view of things. She recalled the fact that to-night she was going to dine and dance with Roger Clifford, and the thought cheered her immensely. By the time she had had her breakfast she was inwardly calm and ready to face the doctor when he came for his usual morning visit. Moreover, she was pleased about Sir Charles, who was making really steady progress. It astonished her that a man of his age and general health should be doing so well.

With this in her mind, she was unprepared for the sober, pessimistic expression of Dr. Sartorius's face when he had finished his examination. He withdrew a little distance from the bed, and beckoned her to follow him.

"We must do something," he said in a low tone, frowning at the carpet. "I do not like his extreme weakness. His pulse is bad, very bad. He needs boosting up."

"Why, doctor, I thought he was doing so well! I . . . that is, considering he's over seventy and all that, it seemed to me that . . ."

Her voice trailed off, blighted by the brief scorn with which he glanced at her before continuing steadily:

"We must put some strength into him—if we can. Iron and arsenic . . ."

"Oh, yes, doctor, certainly—injections."

"There are two things we have to fear now," he continued didactically, still in a whisper. "One is his general condition of weakness, the other is—excitement. He mustn't be upset in any way—or startled."

"No, of course not: I'll be very careful."

She wondered a little that he should a second time lay such stress on the matter of excitement. He seemed to have little confidence in her, but that, she suspected, might be owing to his low opinion of women in general.

"That is all. I'd better give him an injection now, I think."

"Yes, doctor."

She brought the usual accessories—a basin of water, cotton-wool, iodine—and placed them on the little table by the bed, feeling a sudden grave doubt about her patient. Had she been too optimistic? If she had, then so had the night-nurse, who only last evening had remarked to her how well the old man was going on. Yet she was impressed by the doctor's ability to discern things hidden from her eyes. Perhaps all along he had regarded it as a losing fight.

"Now then, nurse, help me to get Sir Charles over on his left side."

The invalid did not demur, merely made a grimace as the needle shot into his emaciated thigh. With the basin in one hand and a wad of cotton-wool in the other, Esther happened to glance at the doctor. He was stooping over, his thick body bent at the hips, his small eyes narrowed in cold absorption as he watched the mixture run through the needle into the flesh. Suddenly her eyes grew round, she stared fascinated. Something stirred in her memory, a suggestion that was horrible, frightening. What was it? Ah, now she knew: her nightmare—the python! He reminded her of a python.

"Good God! nurse, what are you about?"

The basin had fallen from her shaking hand to the floor. How stupid of her! She was on her knees in an instant, confused, apologetic, mopping up the puddle with a towel.

"I can't think how it happened," she stammered, feeling an utter fool, and conscious of the cold, amazed scrutiny directed at her from above. At the same time a voice inside her brain was repeating mechanically, "But pythons don't bite—pythons don't bite. . . . Of course, I was thinking of the hypodermic needle!" . . .

"Please try to be more careful. That sort of thing is inexcusable. Is there anything wrong with you this morning?"

"No, nothing, doctor. I can't tell you what made me drop it."

He still stared at her searchingly, his eyes probing her as if he had some suspicion regarding her sanity. A weak voice came from the bed.

"Anybody might drop a basin, doctor," murmured Sir Charles dryly. "You might yourself."

Esther laughed gratefully as she covered him up again, but she felt her laugh to be a trifle hysterical. She hated the doctor to think her an imbecile, yet for some reason her identification of the man with the creature of her dream now struck her as extremely funny. She wanted to laugh and laugh; it took all her resolution to restrain herself. . . . Of course, the whole thing was clear now. Psycho-analysis explained things so wonderfully. No doubt, now that she recognised the source of that vague shrinking she felt in regard to Sartorius she would experience it no longer. Odd, in more ways than one he did resemble a python. His heavy, slow movements, the feeling he gave one of having cold blood in his veins, his little, glancing eyes that so often seemed the only part of him alive. . . . Yes, and there was something else, though perhaps it was very fanciful of her to think of it in that way. Jacques had told her how whenever the doctor had sufficient money—a windfall, as he himself had called it—he would quit work, his practice, that is, and devote himself to research until the last penny was exhausted before bestirring himself again. Was not that the python's method, making a hearty meal of sheep, then lying by for a long period until he had absorbed it completely? What a curious idea—revolting, somehow . . .

At intervals all during the day she caught Sartorius looking at her in a meditative fashion, as though speculating about her mental condition. Each time she felt his gaze upon her she longed again to burst into laughter, her eyes danced, her mouth twitched. If only he had any idea!

When early that evening she set out for the Casino with her escort, Miss Clifford came out of the drawing-room to bid her good-night.

"Have a good time, my dear," she said in her friendly fashion. "It would be a pity to be in Cannes and not see something of its gay side. You look extremely nice," she added with a glance of approval.

Esther glowed with appreciation of the compliment, inwardly hoping Roger agreed with his aunt in her opinion of her. She felt his eye upon her as she stood there with her simple evening coat wrapped tightly about her, the grey of its fur collar soft against her throat, but he said nothing. A movement behind her made her turn towards the drawing-room door.

"Vous sortez?"

It was Lady Clifford who spoke. There was a brittle, intensely Gallic intonation about the query with its upward inflection, reminding one somehow of a postman's knock, a sort of rat-tat-tat.

Miss Clifford answered for them.

"Yes, Thérèse, Roger is taking Miss Rowe out to dinner. It is such an excellent idea for both of them to have a bit of fun."

"Ah!"

An indescribable glint came into the wide grey eyes, and there was a brief pause before Lady Clifford smiled and gave a little wave of the hand.

"Alors—amusez-vous bien!" she said, and turned away.

Could it be that she was displeased with her stepson for paying attention to a nurse in her employ? Esther was not quite sure, but she felt a moment's awkwardness. It vanished, however, when a moment later she climbed into the Citroën beside Roger.

"I hope you don't mind this plebeian way of getting about?" Roger said as he started the car. "I somehow feel I don't like to use the chauffeur and the Rolls in case my stepmother should want it."

"What do you think I'm used to, anyway?" demanded Esther with a light-hearted laugh.

He turned his head and surveyed her critically.

"I'm not sure what you're used to," he replied. "But as you sit there you look like a million dollars, as they say in your country."

She was satisfied he admired her. The evening was hers to enjoy.

The Restaurant des Ambassadeurs was rapidly filling when they entered and made their way to the table reserved for them. With keen interest Esther looked about her at the groups of sleek, well-dressed people, English, French, Russian, Italian. There was a large party of

Americans who had crossed on the same boat with Roger. Their voices rang out, their R's smacked of the Middle-West, Mommer and Popper seeing Europe, accompanied by a brace of coltish daughters, a reedy son with enormous spectacles, and the son's two college chums, who looked to be good at football. Farther along sat two Russians who never spoke, one an owlish young man with glassy eyes and damp hair raked smoothly back, his companion a woman much older than himself, with broad cheek-bones and a mouth that was a great blot of scarlet in the midst of her chalk-white face.

Esther spied the plump, hennaed woman whom she had seen speak to Lady Clifford that day weeks ago, sitting at a table with another French-woman equally plump and two men, fat and bald, both wearing a good deal of jewellery. The younger man, incredibly, had round his pudgy wrist a bangle set with turquoises! On the other side of this hilarious party was a large, sober-faced Englishman who looked like a stockbroker, Roger said, and with him a little humming-bird of a girl, starry-eyed, infantile—belonging to musical comedy, no doubt. What a medley!

"Look! Over there—"

Esther touched her companion's arm suddenly.

"Do you see? There's Captain Holliday—and with his fat Spanish friend. Isn't she dreadful?"

Following her eyes, Roger discovered across the room the redoubtable Arthur, nonchalantly ordering dinner for his *vis-à-vis*, a colossal, swarthy creature, dripping with pearls and glittering with diamonds like a chandelier.

"Spanish, did you say?"

"Yes, from the Argentine. I've seen them together before. It is she who has offered him the job." She almost added, "And it is she whom your stepmother is jealous of," but she pulled herself up in time.

"What a lot you seem to know about Holliday," remarked Roger half-quizzically, half-seriously, eyeing her over the menu.

She laughed cheerfully.

"I do. I told you he interested me—as a type. Caviare or grape-fruit? Oh, caviare. I feel like it, somehow."

"So do I. And after that what about some *sole spécialté de la maison*? How does that strike you? With a *pigeon en cocotte* to follow?"

"Marvellous! I'm glad I'm hungry. I missed tea on purpose."

"So did I miss tea, but for other reasons. I took a bank at baccarat—they've opened the room—and time ceased to be."

"Did you win?"

"No fear; I was down as usual. What about a simple Bronx to start with? And do you like a dry champagne?"

"Very dry, thanks!"

"It's a good thing; it saves me buying two kinds. Waiter!"

"I feel this is going to be really a spree," sighed Esther contentedly. "I have been abstemious for so long. You, too—I notice you confine yourself to Evian water."

"Oh, you've noticed that, have you? Yes, I take it for my complexion—like my stepmother."

"That's so, she does drink Evian, doesn't she? She scarcely touches wine. . . . How exquisite she is—don't you think? She is one of the loveliest women I have ever seen."

"I quite agree," he said slowly. "Thérèse will stand a good deal of looking at. Exquisite—that's the right word. There is only one thing about her that isn't exquisite."

"What is that?" she asked him curiously.

"Her hands."

She gave a quick understanding nod.

"I know—I've thought that, too. They don't seem to go with the rest of her, although she takes such perfect care of them."

"A psychologist chap once told me," he remarked after a thoughtful pause, "that hands like that—you mustn't misunderstand me, he was only speaking of the type—were the hands of the successful *cocotte*."

CHAPTER XVII

SHE was so silent he began to wonder if he had shocked her, though that didn't seem likely, she was such a sensible girl.

"Of course she can't help having that sort of hand," he hastened to add apologetically. "It's just a peculiarity."

Esther was repeating to herself that phrase, "the hands of the successful *cocotte*," which somehow seemed oddly illuminating. Lady Clifford's hands had a meaning for her now. The soft cushioned palms spelled love of luxury, the stumpy, curving fingers and talon-like nails indicated acquisitive greed. She could see them grasping, grasping . . .

"Ah, here are the cocktails."

She came to herself with a smile, and took the frosty glass which he held out to her.

"May we both get what we want!"

She touched her glass to his gaily and drank. Then with a flash of reminiscence she glanced across at Holliday, recalling the fact that a few weeks ago he had uttered exactly the same toast. What was it Holliday wanted? She had thought at the time it was something quite definite. . . .

The meal proceeded happily, they laughed and chatted with a sense of exhilaration derived only in part from the champagne. Although they told each other many things, as on a former occasion, it was not what they said that mattered. Each was intensely absorbed in the other's personality; what counted was mutual attraction, which invested every commonplace with vibrant inner meanings. They forgot the life about them; it was as though they were marooned upon a tiny island in the midst of uncharted seas.

"Do you feel like dancing?"

The coffee, sending up a fragrant steam, was too hot to drink; the saxophones sounded an insinuating invitation.

"Do let's—I'm dying to!"

As they mingled with the circling couples on the glassy floor, Roger gave her hand a faint pressure.

"I said you were," he told her.

"Said I was what?"

"A wonderful dancer. The first time I saw you."

"No—did you?" she replied delightedly and returned the pressure spontaneously. "I'm glad. I'd far rather you praised my dancing than my character."

"I don't know anything about your character," he disclaimed, laughing.

He was enjoying himself immensely. Of all the girls he knew, it struck him that not one would have fitted in so perfectly with his mood as did this little Canadian girl who worked hard for her living. Why was it? He had nothing to say against his own friends, jolly girls for the most part, excellent at games and only a little spoilt by having always had money—yet certainly they lacked the freshness which was so large a part of this particular girl's attraction for him. She was capable and intelligent, too, without sacrificing one whit of her femininity—he was a simple enough male to remark on this; for that matter, he reflected with pride, there was not a woman in the room who was smarter. She had a poise and grace of movement that were a delight to the eye, and she was *soignée* to the finger-tips. A thoroughbred, he summed her up, and felt pleased with his judgment.

When presently they were joined by his friends, Graham and Marjory Kent, he was not particularly elated.

"I hope you don't curse us for barging in like this," Miss Kent apologised, "but my brother is fed to the teeth with me and is going to try and cadge a dance or two off you, Miss Rowe, if you'll be good to him."

She was about twenty-six, tall and gypsy-like, her black hair in a bang and her thin brown arms jingling with bangles. Esther liked her, she was straightforward and jolly. The brother was younger and very shy, yet plainly one of those timid souls whose tenacity of purpose will carry them through agonies of embarrassment to a desired end. The end in this case was evidently Esther. His black eyes shone with frank admiration, even while he blushed a dusky red to the roots of his immaculate hair.

"May I have this dance?" he murmured almost at once.

She smiled and rose to join him. At the same moment she caught a certain glint in the eye of Roger which told her plainly how her value had risen by reason of competition. In so many ways was he a mere male—but she did not like him the less for that.

Roger, dancing with Marjory, whom he had known all his life, watched the slender figure in fluttering pink whenever it crossed his line of vision. The curly head had an upward tilt at times, for Graham was over six feet tall, and she had to look up to speak to him.

"You know, Roger, Graham's fearfully taken with that girl of yours," Marjory told him calmly. "He gave me no peace until I brought him over. Who is she? You don't mean it? A nurse! Well, who'd have thought anyone so useful could look like that? I call it genius."

"Nurses needn't be frights," he objected.

"But most of them are. . . . By the way, I saw Lady Clifford here last night, marvellous as usual. She was with a rather nice-looking Englishman I've seen about Cannes a good deal—no one I know."

"Yes, he is here this evening, or was. I saw him having dinner."

"So did I, with a comic-looking foreign woman, simply lousy with jewels. She's always about here. I used to wonder who in the world had money enough to buy those enormous diamonds and ropes of pearls you see in the shops in the Rue de la Paix. Now I know."

The dance went on and on; for the first time he noticed how frequently the orchestra responded to an encore.

"Do look at Graham," whispered his partner delightedly. "Isn't it amazing when you think how timid he is?"

The tall youth was not losing any time. In a brief interval Roger overheard him saying something very earnest to his partner on the subject of Saturday afternoon, evidently making a desperate bid for Esther's free hour. She in turn was shaking her head doubtfully, but, thought Roger, she did not look displeased. The idea came to Roger that young Kent, who was sole heir to one of the biggest mill-owners in Lancashire, would be counted a fine prize. . . . He looked at his watch.

"That little girl has to get up early," he murmured to Marjory. "I promised faithfully not to keep her out late. If this goes on much longer . . ."

It was a little after one o'clock when he tucked Esther into the Citroën. He drove slowly towards La Californie, reluctant to put an end to the evening, and intensely conscious of the girl beside him, wrapped in her velvet coat, warm and glowing in the darkness.

"I'm sure we ought to have left sooner," she said, a little conscience-stricken, "only it was so heavenly! I had the bad luck to oversleep this morning; it would be dreadful to repeat the offence."

"Why should you care?"

"How like a man! Don't you grasp the fact that my living depends on what doctors think of me?"

"In that case, you'll never be out of work."

She laughed.

"No, seriously, I was in the doctor's bad graces this morning. Not only was I late, but I dropped a basin of water on the floor. Wasn't it stupid? He looked at me as if he thought I was weak-minded."

"Pooh! I shouldn't let that worry me."

"I don't, only . . . do you know, that man has a curious effect on me, something sort of paralysing. . . . I can't explain it, quite."

"Does he? How do you mean?"

She told him, on an impulse, about her dream and her subsequent recognition of the python as a symbol of the doctor's personality.

"It sounds silly, but it was really quite horrible," she ended with a little laugh. "To feel I was in the creature's power, and that it didn't *care*, it had no feeling—I was simply something to be crushed, annihilated."

"He *is* a cold-blooded sort of person," said Roger thoughtfully. "Not that it matters much, if, as my aunt says, he is so good at his job. Only, of course, it is pretty apt to prevent his becoming exactly popular."

"That wouldn't worry him. He only wants to be able to live in order to carry on research."

When the car turned in at the drive Roger fancied he saw a thread of light from one of the drawing-room windows. The next instant it was gone, and he decided he had been mistaken; it must have been a trick of the moonlight. The house loomed dark before them. He garaged the car, and escorting Esther upstairs, parted from her at the end of the short passage leading to her room.

"Thanks for a gorgeous time," she whispered, careful not to make a noise.

He thought how lovely she was as she looked up at him, her lashes curving back from her lambent eyes, the soft curls of her hair ruffling back from her warm forehead.

"If you've really liked it," he said, detaining her hand a little longer than was necessary, "you'll come with me again?"

She smiled and was gone, the brief adieu leaving each of them to wonder how much more was meant than the polite commonplaces uttered.

Roger leaned out of his own window for ten minutes smoking, his mind full of a pleasant excitement. Disturbing, too, for with the unaccustomed feeling that perhaps at last he had found a girl he was willing to let himself fall in love with came a doubt, a cautious warning to hesitate, not to go too fast. She was delightful, he firmly believed her to be transparent and sincere, but men have been taken in only too easily when their senses have been stirred as his had been to-night. No, he must not rush things; he must wait a little and be sure, not so much of himself as of her; he must be convinced that she cared for him, that she was not merely dazzled by what he could give her one day. . . . That was the drawback of having money, if only in prospect. Already, for some years in fact, he had been pursued by mercenary maidens and their mothers. He had a rooted aversion to the whole breed, and a latent fear that one day he would be taken in after all. He knew himself to be impressionable and impulsive; still, behind these dangerous qualities lay a certain hard, deliberate common sense that had saved him in more than one perilous situation. Sternly he informed himself that he had known Esther Rowe about three days. In short, he must not be a fool.

Something, the champagne perhaps, had made him very thirsty. Finding his bottle of Evian water almost empty, he decided to explore the kitchen region below to secure another. He knew where the mineral waters were kept—in a small cupboard next to the wine-cellar. He sallied forth and descended the back stairs very quietly, in order not to disturb anyone. After poking about for a few moments he found what he wanted. There was nothing to open it with, however. Where was the thing kept? Ah, of course, in the sideboard, he remembered.

The swing-door into the dining-room made no noise; he discovered the little implement in the drawer with the table-knives and, wrenching off the metal cap from the bottle, turned to go back the way he had come. All at once he stopped stock-still and listened. Then he glanced towards the door that led into the drawing-room. Had he heard whispered voices?

For thirty seconds he remained rooted to the spot, his ears strained to catch a repetition of the fancied sound. It had been only a faint murmur; he might have been mistaken . . . yes, there it was again, a sort of choked, sibilant whisper coming from the adjoining room. Hardly had he made sure of it when there fell on his ears a small crash, sharp, as of some object dropped on the parquet. It was followed by a smothered exclamation in a man's voice, brief and profane.

With but one idea in his mind—burglars—he crossed to the drawing-room door and flung it wide. That he was unarmed did not enter his thoughts.

The drawing-room was in utter darkness. He reached for the nearby switch and flooded the room in a blaze of light.

CHAPTER XVIII

ABOUT an hour before this Arthur Holliday left the Restaurant des Ambassadeurs and, with a slight frown on his face, got into his car and drove rapidly to La Californie. When he reached the Villa Firenze all was in darkness. He left his car in a turning out of the main road, then quietly slipped into the garden and walked across the grass around to the paved terrace at the side of the salon. As he set foot on the flat stones the doors opened softly and Thérèse Clifford put out her hands and drew him inside.

"Ah, I thought you would never come!" she sighed a little fretfully, standing for a moment with her whole body against his.

His arms held her in a perfunctory embrace, while his eyes glanced restlessly about. The big room was lit by only a single lamp, which shed a pool of rose-coloured light over the satin-covered chaise-longue and a tiny table, upon which was a pile of illustrated journals.

"Damned silly getting me here like this," he remarked, turning and drawing the thick curtains carefully over the doors behind him. "I don't half like it."

"There is no risk, none whatever. Everyone is in bed except the night-nurse, and up in that room one can't hear anything."

"Still, if anyone did find me here, there'd be a devil of a mess. Roger'll be coming home, too; I saw him having dinner with that nurse girl."

She made a slight grimace.

"Oh, they will be hours yet. Listen! I sent you that message because I simply had to see you. You were dining with that creature to-night, and

I could not have closed my eyes till I had made sure you had done nothing stupid. Tell me, Arthur darling—what has she been saying to you?"

She clutched him tightly with both hands, probing into his shallow eyes as if to tear the truth from them.

"Oh, the usual thing; she's getting more and more fed up. She suspects now that I'm playing with her. She says she must make arrangements, send cables and so on, and she's got to have a straight answer—yes or no—at once."

"Yes, and then what?"

Her hold on his shoulders tightened avidly.

"She's booked sailings for herself and the girl for the 8th, and she wants to book one for me, too. Otherwise she says it's all off."

"Ah! What did you tell her?"

"I promised I'd go."

She drew in her breath sharply.

"You promised to go—on the 8th!"

"There was nothing else to do. I can't throw away an opportunity like that. I've told you so all along. Of course I could always change my mind at the last minute . . . if anything happened."

His wandering gaze came back to her, and for a long moment they looked at each other in silence. Then Thérèse bit her lip and turned away.

"What did Sartorius say when you talked to him yesterday?"

"Oh, nothing whatever. He won't express an opinion beyond the fact that the old boy's age and general condition are against him. There's not much in that. I wouldn't mind betting even money that he'll pull through this and go on for another ten or fifteen years."

She shook her head slowly, looking away from him.

"No . . . I do not think he will do that. Somehow I have a feeling . . . I am almost sure this time . . . he will not live."

"Why?" he demanded quickly.

"Fleurestine. You know what I told you."

"Rot! Besides, she only said he would be ill; she didn't pretend to see the outcome."

Again she shook her head.

"What I told you was not quite true. She told me he would not recover; she saw me dressed in black . . ."

"Good God! Why didn't you say so before?"

She gave him a shrewd glance.

"But, Arthur, you don't believe in these things."

"Well, I don't know. I don't say I disbelieve in them exactly. I— you might have said something before, you know," he explained in an injured tone.

"But, my dear, I couldn't! It seemed so—so cold-blooded, so calculating. I couldn't let you think of me as calculating, could I? You might not care for me so much."

He scarcely heard her. A change had come over him, he was apparently filled with a nervous elation, moving jerkily around the room, snapping his fingers, whistling softly under his breath, picking up small objects and examining them unseeingly, then setting them down again. Thérèse watched him narrowly, suspicion deepening in her eyes. At last she spoke.

"Arthur, come to me."

He approached her mechanically, engrossed in his own thoughts.

"No, closer. I want to look at you."

He met her gaze without interest, looking through her at some vision beyond.

"Arthur, all you are thinking about is the money. The thought of that makes you happy. Is not that so?"

He gave a forced laugh.

"Good God, what makes you think that? If you do think it."

"It's the way you look. You are not thinking of me one little bit. Arthur, if for one moment I thought you no longer cared for me . . ."

"What on earth are you taking about?" he retorted with a touch of irritation. "Why are you for ever harping on that theme? Naturally I care for you."

"Ah, but you torment me so! If I could only be sure, only for one little minute! How do I know it is me you want, and not what you will get with me?"

She spoke with a certain fierceness. He looked at her silently, then with a shrug of his shoulders turned away, moving towards the door.

"Where are you going?" she demanded quickly.

"What difference does it make to you where I go? Since that's the opinion you have of me, South America isn't a bad idea. The sooner the better."

"No, no, Arthur, come back; you don't understand . . ."

"Oh, I understand all right. You don't trust me; after a year and a half that's all you think of me. It doesn't matter, it's better not to see me again."

His hand was on the knob.

"Don't say such a stupid thing, Arthur! Come here."

"Why should I come? You don't want me really."

"Arthur, you know I want you—always."

Without replying, he opened the door and stepped outside. He was really going, his foot sounded on the flags. With a smothered cry she reached his side, clutched at him, half sobbing, drawing him back with all her strength. He resisted stonily.

"Don't make a scene, Thérèse, someone will hear you."

"Then come back. If you don't, I don't mind what happens, or who hears!"

Sulkily he took a step inside the door, then raised his head, listening. A car had come into the drive, was crunching around the gravel to the garage on the far side of the house.

"S'sh—it's Roger. Close the door quietly."

With a quick movement, Thérèse switched off the lamp.

"Damned silly, that," he whispered. "Why did you do that?"

"No, it is best. Wait—they will soon go upstairs."

They stood silent, listening. After a few moments they heard the front door close, then footsteps mounting the stairs, after which no sound whatever. Five minutes went by, while Thérèse pressed tightly against the unresponsive young man, clinging to his hand. At the end of that time he drew away from her.

"Now I'll slip out."

"No, not yet. I sha'n't let you!"

She sank down on the chaise-longue in the darkness, trying to draw him with her.

"I shall not stay, I promise you."

His voice was cold and indifferent. For all that she drew him to her, by main force, and pressed her mouth to his, her perfumed arms about his stubborn neck.

"If you do love me, Arthur, make me know that you do! Show me it is myself that you care for, show me, show me! You can if you want to."

After a brief struggle she felt his muscles relax.

"Ah . . . *Tu m'aimes encore! Tu m'aimes encore!*"

"Sh-sh—let me go, Thérèse . . ."

"No, no . . ."

A moment later, in the gloom, Thérèse's wide chiffon sleeve caught on something.

"Be careful—what is that?"

The little table toppled over with a crash. At almost the same instant, it seemed, the door to the dining-room was flung open and dazzling light poured down upon them from the central chandelier. In the doorway Roger stood regarding them.

It was one of those moments when there is simply nothing to say.

Explanations would only aggravate a situation already impossible.

Utterly confused, Holliday automatically straightened his tie, while Thérèse, seated, smoothed her tumbled hair and stared at the intruder with horror-stricken eyes. For several seconds no one spoke.

Roger, indeed, felt powerless to make any comment. After the first shock of discovery he was dumb from sheer fury. Indignant beyond words at what seemed to him a rank insult to his father, the emotion he felt struck to the very root of his being. For the moment he saw red. At last he addressed Holliday.

"Get out!" he commanded, and pointed to the door.

The young man had by now recovered a slight degree of his usual poise.

His eyebrows lifted with a touch of arrogance.

"Steady on. What right have you got to order me out of this house?"

"Never you mind what right I've got," Roger blazed at him, but keeping his voice low. "You get out, or I'll throw you out. You've heard me."

Holliday looked at Thérèse, who, pale and shaken, nodded slightly.

"Go," she murmured; "you can do no good by staying."

He made a faint show of standing his ground, then with a contemptuous shrug went out through the garden doors.

Roger took three strides after him and closed the doors, bolting them quietly. When he turned he saw a change in his stepmother. Her eyes regarded him with a Medusa-like stare; a spot of dull red smouldered in each cheek. Her lips seemed suddenly thin, were working slightly. He knew that her anger was even greater than his own, though she might express it in a different way.

"And now perhaps you will explain what you mean by coming into my salon and ordering my friends to leave my house?"

Her tone burnt like vitriol. All the suppressed hatred of six years had compressed itself into that single sentence. He paused, eyeing her curiously, and choosing his words with a certain care, trying not to let his anger run away with him.

"See here, Thérèse," he said at last, "I don't intend to discuss the matter of my right to do anything in this house. I am simply going to tell you something. It makes no difference to me what lovers you have, it is not my affair, so long as you conduct your liaisons with discretion. But while my father is ill and I am here to protect his interests, I shall make it my business to see that this sort of thing doesn't happen under his roof."

"Ah, indeed!" she exclaimed with a touch of bitter contempt.

"You know as well as I that anyone might have come in that door just now—my aunt, the nurse, one of the servants. You may not care yourself, but you've got to have respect for my father."

Her breath came hard, the spots of red throbbed like wounds, while all the time her eyes remained glued to his face with a stare of fascination. He thought she seemed torn between rage and a reluctant fear.

"Now listen to me: I shall not say it again. From now on Arthur Holliday is not to come inside this place until my father is well again. Is that quite clear?"

An odd mutinous gleam came into her eyes.

"Must I remind you that I am at liberty to do as I like in my own house?" she said monotonously.

"I don't think I have made myself clear, Thérèse. I am not arguing; I am telling you that Holliday must keep away."

He was anxious to go. The scene and her scent nauseated him.

"And suppose I do not choose to do as you say? What then?"

"I'm sorry you asked that, but of course I'll answer it. If I catch Holliday here again, I shall quite simply tell my father all that I know about you and him. You may be sure he will divorce you."

She made no sign beyond a little intake of her breath and a dilation of her nostrils.

"That is a threat, is it not?"

"Of course it's a threat. It is the only way one is able to deal with a woman like you," he retorted, too irate to soften his words.

"I see."

Her composure was greater than his. He had expected her to fly at him with abuse. Something in her manner egged him on to say more:

"You may pull the wool over my father's eyes, but you have never deceived me. You have been waiting for years for him to die, hoping every illness would finish him, so that you could spend his money. Well, he's not dead yet. Suppose, after all, you found he had altered his will? It's not too late for that; he could get a solicitor here in an hour, and he would do it, too, if he knew what had gone on here to-night. Oh, don't misunderstand me, I don't want him to know, for his own peace of mind. As long as you behave yourself decently inside his house you are safe from me. But this sort of thing has got to stop. That's all."

As he turned to go he glanced at her again. She was almost unrecognisable. Her eyes had narrowed to slits, her cheekbones showed an unexpected prominence under their patches of red. One hand fumbled and twisted the heavy pearls at her throat; he could hear her laboured breathing. How she was going to hate him now! The thought suddenly came to him that if there had been a revolver or a knife handy she would have tried to use it on him. Well, he had the upper hand of her; that was all that mattered. She could hate him as much as she chose. . . .

He left her standing there, staring after him fixedly. Once outside, he had to admit he had taken a pretty strong line. Of course, in a way it was not his business to issue ultimatums of this sort. Yet he would have done the same again. The thought that his aunt or Esther Rowe might easily have come upon the scene he had just interrupted filled him with rage. Of course, from now on it was going to be still more difficult to remain under the same roof with Thérèse; it would require a skin thicker than his to endure it. Still, it would not be for long.

When he reached his room he discovered with a reaction of amusement that he still held the bottle of Evian water upright in the crook of his arm. There it had been throughout the foregoing passage at arms. He laughed, and his anger began to recede. Still, he could not sleep, and it was three o'clock when he put out his light. As he did so he listened to a faint sound outside.

It was Thérèse, who, only after this long time, was coming upstairs to bed.

CHAPTER XIX

OF THE foregoing incident Esther remained in total ignorance. Accordingly, when next morning she heard Lady Clifford's maid, Aline, say that her mistress had had a bad night and was indisposed in consequence, it meant nothing special to her. She had come to regard the beautiful Frenchwoman as spoiled and self-indulgent, prone, like many others of her type, to exaggerate trifling ailments—though she concluded that the explanation of this tendency lay in the boredom of the woman's daily life. If she had been indulging in a round of gaiety she would have proved equal to enormous exertion, but there is a vast difference between dancing all night and lying awake in bed. Esther knew that fact well.

At about twelve o'clock the doctor sent Esther with a message to Lady Clifford. It seemed Sir Charles had been asking for her. The voice that called out *"Entrez!"* in reply to Esther's knock sounded sharp and strained.

Lady Clifford was sitting before her rather elaborate dressing-table, partly dressed, wrapped in a peignoir of heavy white crêpe. The face she turned upon Esther was pale and shadowed about the eyes, the lips tightly compressed. She really did look ill.

"As soon as you are dressed, Lady Clifford, would you mind going in to Sir Charles? He has been asking for you. I believe he must have something rather special to say to you."

"Ah?"

A quick look of both apprehension and suspicion sprang into the grey eyes. What was she afraid of, wondered Esther?

"The doctor thinks he's not up to much conversation, so perhaps you'll make it as brief as possible," added Esther tactfully.

"Yes, yes; I understand!" Lady Clifford replied, nodding impatiently.

"I will come at once."

She hastily dabbed some rouge on her cheeks, powdered her face and neck with her heavily scented powder, and followed Esther across the boudoir and into the other bedroom.

There Esther left her and, returning to the boudoir, sat down before the blazing log-fire with a magazine, less to read than to review with lazy enjoyment the whole of last night. She saw and felt it all again, the lights, the dresses, the music, the little table with its shaded lamp that shut the two of them into an enchanted circle, Roger's arm about her as they danced, the drive home in the dark. Why had it all been so thrilling? She had no doubt as to the answer, indeed her certainty on this point made her pull herself up sharply, resolving to restrain her errant fancy, not to allow herself to take too much for granted.

Suddenly across the fabric of her thoughts the old man's voice reached her in a faint, indistinguishable drone. She had not the slightest interest in what he wished to say to Lady Clifford, nor in the effect it would have upon the latter. All at once she heard the Frenchwoman shriek out with a piercing sharpness.

"No, no, it's impossible! You can't do it! You sha'n't!"

The words, half supplication, half angry protest, seemed wrung from their owner out of sheer anguish. A low monotone made reply, but it was interrupted by a fresh burst.

"But it is ridiculous, stupid! I am not a child, it's not in the least necessary. I don't have to be watched. *Ah! c'est insupportable!*"

Esther rose uncertainly, wondering if she ought to intervene. While she hesitated, a still wilder tirade decided her. She opened the door just in time to behold a startling spectacle. Lady Clifford was that instant seizing hold of her husband by his emaciated shoulders and shaking him furiously, crying in a strangled voice:

"*Pas lui, pas lui! Vieux monstre que tu es!*"

"Stop! Lady Clifford, what on earth are you doing?"

Wholly aghast, Esther forgot everything except that her patient was being bodily attacked—there was no other word for what was happening. Running forward, she grasped the wife forcibly by the arm and pulled her back from the bed, then, thoroughly frightened, bent over the old man, who had sunk back limp and panting. In her ear she heard the Frenchwoman's choked breathing, but she did not trouble to look at her.

"Are you all right, Sir Charles?" she asked as calmly as she could.

She was amazed to see a queer little flicker of humour in the sunken eyes.

"Oh, quite, quite," he gasped in a spent tone. "Don't trouble about me: but just get Lady Clifford away, will you?"

Turning, Esther beheld a look of baleful resentment in the black-fringed eyes. She remarked the stubby white hand with its carmine nails slowly rubbing a spot on the opposite arm, where she had grasped it a moment ago.

"You! You!" breathed the Frenchwoman in a suppressed voice. "What business have you to interfere in matters that do not concern you?"

"But I'm afraid this does concern me, Lady Clifford, very much indeed," replied Esther, as lightly as she could. "Do forgive me if I caught hold of you rather roughly. I am sure you didn't realise what you were doing. It—it was really dangerous for him, you know."

"Dangerous!" repeated the other with withering contempt. "For him! T'ck!—leave us, please. There is something I must say to him. I will not forget myself, I promise you!"

"No, Lady Clifford, really, not to-day. It wouldn't be wise. We must get him quiet."

Sir Charles interposed in a whisper:

"It's quite settled, my dear, I've nothing further to say. You will see that I am right."

She burst out hysterically, trying to get past Esther to the bed:

"No, no, you do not understand; you are doing a terrible thing! Charles darling, if you love me . . ."

She broke off abruptly, staring at the hall door.

Following her gaze, Esther saw that Roger had just entered and was looking gravely from one to the other of the three. It seemed likely that he had heard the disturbance and was come to investigate.

"There he is now!" cried Thérèse, pointing at her stepson. "Tell him you will make some other arrangement, that you have changed your mind; you will, you must!"

Esther noticed that Roger displayed no astonishment whatever, merely glancing expectantly at his father. The old man's lips twisted into a grim smile as he remarked dryly:

"You behave as if you were quite certain I was going to die, my dear."

A swift change came over her face. Pushing Esther aside, she threw herself on her knees beside the bed, grasping her husband's bony hand and pressing it against her cheek emotionally.

"Ah, why do you say such things. You are too cruel; you want to make me suffer!"

"There, there, don't make a song about it. Of course I don't want to make you suffer. Now go. I want to rest."

Still clinging to his hand, she began to weep, convulsively, without restraint. Esther, greatly embarrassed, made two attempts to lift her up, but she resisted. At last Roger bent over the huddled figure and touched her on the shoulder.

"See here, Thérèse," he whispered, so low that the rather deaf old man did not catch his words, "I don't like this arrangement any more than you do, but if we oppose him now it can only do harm. Leave him to me, and when he's well enough I'll tackle him again."

The weeping ceased, she stiffened to attention, her face still hidden. Then slowly she raised her head, her cheeks streaked with tears. Little rivulets of black coursed from her lashes. For several seconds her gaze swept his countenance, her expression strangely hostile, yet enigmatic. Watching her, Esther could not possibly guess what was going on behind that mask.

"Very well," Lady Clifford murmured at last in a detached voice, all passion gone. "You may be right."

She got up, smoothed her hair automatically, drew her peignoir close about her, and walked out of the room like a woman in a dream. Esther gazed after her, astonished but relieved. She had feared she would have to remove her by force. Now that the extraordinary episode was over she was quite unnerved, her heart beat fast, her hands trembled.

Roger eyed her sympathetically.

"Don't look so upset, Esther," he whispered reassuringly. "You must tell me presently what happened, though I have a pretty good idea."

They both glanced at the old man. His eyes were closed now, he was breathing more quietly.

"He seems all right," murmured Esther doubtfully. "I'm still a little frightened; it—it was terrifying."

He took her arm and drew her well out of earshot towards the window.

"Don't worry too much," he told her. "I shouldn't wonder if the poor old boy is more used to bursts of temperament than you are, you know!"

She smiled at him gratefully, feeling comforted. It was not till later that she realised he had a moment ago called her "Esther." It had seemed perfectly natural.

Soon after lunch she made an excuse to take her patient's temperature, for she was not yet sure he had suffered no bad effects. However, the thermometer registered no change. Sir Charles may have noticed the relief on her face, for he remarked hesitatingly, choosing his words:

"You mustn't take my wife's excitability too much to heart, nurse. It is true she goes up in the air sometimes, but she always comes down again. She's rather like a spoiled child, but that may be partly my fault."

"Of course—you mustn't think I don't understand," she assured him quickly, thinking what a generous explanation he had given for an unpardonable offence. The instance she had witnessed of Lady Clifford's "temperament" was unique in her experience, and she hoped it would remain so. Not readily would she forget those sharp accents of rage and—was it fear? She had thought at the time it was fear; she could not be certain.

It did not surprise her that Lady Clifford should fail to appear at *déjeuner*, but she was unprepared for the new development announced by Aline, the maid, who came into the dining-room at the close of the meal and somewhat portentously informed the doctor that her ladyship was *"très souffrante"* and wished to see him at once.

"*Souffrante*, Aline?" repeated Miss Clifford. "Is it a headache?"

Aline replied that it was both backache and headache. She was a steely-faced woman of middle age with gimlet eyes and dank black hair in a ragged fringe. As she spoke she eyed the company at the table with a sort of malicious triumph.

"Oh—!" exclaimed Miss Clifford, slightly dismayed. "I don't quite like the sound of that—do you, doctor?"

Without answering her, Sartorius finished his coffee and rose.

"Moi je crois," volunteered Aline with enjoyment, *"que Madame a un peu de fièvre."*

"Oh, I hope not!" The old lady glanced quickly at Roger and then at Esther, who both remained impassive.

"It may be nothing at all," Esther said soothingly, just as she had done on a former occasion. "I shouldn't get upset."

However, within a quarter of an hour, the doctor summoned Esther to Lady Clifford's bedroom. Lady Clifford certainly showed preliminary symptoms of typhoid, he informed her, so that it would be as well to administer the necessary doses of anti-toxin. Taking the thing in time like this was a good chance of warding it off.

"Naturally we won't mention this to Sir Charles," he added. "We'll let him think she's merely suffering from a cold."

The Frenchwoman was lying limp and still in the middle of her low, gilded bed, gazing with unseeing eyes at the rose canopy above. Her hair was pushed back ruthlessly, revealing an unsuspected height of forehead, which somewhat altered her appearance. She was very pale, a pallor with a tinge of yellow in it. She received the injection mechanically, paying scant attention to either the doctor or Esther. She gave a slight nod when the former advised her to remain in bed for a day or so, her manner suggesting the complete exhaustion which follows violent hysteria, but Esther thought the exhaustion was only physical. It seemed to her that Lady Clifford's brain was active, that she was thinking deeply.

As soon as she was free, Esther put on her hat and coat and joined Roger in the car outside. Once alone with him she somewhat reluctantly let him draw out of her exactly what had occurred that morning.

"I can't in the least understand what it was she was so furious about," she ended.

After a short silence Roger said:

"I can. In fact, I was perfectly sure she was going to kick up a hell of a row. Forgive the language! I warned my father she would."

He stopped, deliberating with a frown on his face, as though wondering how much to disclose. At last he went on with sudden resolution:

"There's no reason why I shouldn't tell you. I feel as if I'd known you quite long enough, somehow. . . . You see, my father recently decided to appoint me trustee of all his property. It happens to give me a good deal of power over Thérèse when he dies, or rather not so much power, in actual fact, as knowledge of her movements. She knows it to be a pure formality. I should never interfere with her, but—she hates the idea. That's all."

"Oh!" exclaimed Esther, somewhat blankly.

"You see," he went on with a shrug, "indeed, it's possible you've noticed it, she doesn't find me very sympathetic. She'd hate to have any dealings with me."

"But as much as that? If you'd seen how furious she was—"

"I can imagine it. Yes, quite as much as that. I'm afraid I'm a very sharp thorn in her flesh."

"But you wouldn't try to—to—"

"To restrain her? Lord, no! The position's as detestable to me as to her. I don't want to be compelled to know what she does with her money. However, I'm hoping to have another go at the old man when he's in a more reasonable frame of mind. He's as stubborn as a donkey now."

She nodded with a rueful laugh and said:

"I'm afraid your stepmother is going to hate me most awfully from now on. Still, I couldn't stand by and allow her to go for the poor old man like that. Why, she was like a tigress!"

She stopped, looking as though afraid she had committed an indiscretion.

"Oh, don't apologise; facts are facts. I'm only sorry you had to come up against this unpleasant one. You were absolutely in the right, so you have nothing to worry about."

"I shall be uncomfortable, though. It puts me in an awkward position."

"Never mind. It looks now as if she's made up her mind to be laid up for a bit, so you won't have to see her."

She looked at him curiously.

"What do you mean—made up her mind?"

"Well, isn't that what a hysterical woman usually does when she wants to get sympathy and put other people in the wrong? It's an old trick. What do you think?"

"I don't know," she answered slowly. "Anyhow, the doctor is taking it seriously. He's given her an injection of anti-toxin for typhoid."

"And why not? He must earn his money. Besides, it won't do her any harm."

She smiled doubtfully.

"She really does look ill," she said.

"And so would you if you'd been in a couple of rages like hers within twelve hours," he retorted quickly, then, as though he had committed himself, changed the current of thought suddenly. "What a conscientious child you are, Esther," he said, smiling at her; "you won't let me abuse anyone, will you? I say, will you let me call you by your first name? It seems so—"

He had been regarding her with a closer attention than any driver should give to his companion. The result was a violent swerve to the far side of the road, barely missing a lamp-post.

"Good God! What's the fool about?"

Esther screamed, starting to her feet. They had only just avoided cutting short the life of an ill-starred pedestrian who was in the act of crossing diagonally to a small café. The wayfarer stood in the middle of the road, hurling imprecations in the choicest argot at Roger, while a waiter in a dirty apron and two seedy guests on the sidewalk joined him ardently. Ignoring the abuse with lofty scorn, Roger was proceeding on his way when Esther clutched his arm.

"Stop please, stop! I want to speak to that man. He's a friend of mine!"

She laughed as, completely astonished, Roger obeyed her command and brought the car to a halt.

CHAPTER XX

The man in the road, a short, thickset brigand by the look of him, rushed up to the car, hat in hand, his face beaming.

"*C'est bien, mademoiselle! Ah, mademoiselle, que je suis ravi de vous voir!*"

"Jacques!—it's Jacques, Roger, the doctor's servant."

On hearing this, Roger expressed his regret at having so nearly ended the other's career. The little man's animosity had quite vanished, his black eyes shone with kindly affection which included his late enemy.

"*Ah, ça n'est rien, monsieur, ç'était ma faute, je vous assure!* And how goes everything with you, mademoiselle?"

"Quite all right, thank you, Jacques. And you?"

"Ah, what you call so-so—*comme çi, comme ça.* Now I look after Captain Holliday; he stay at the house, but I think not for long. The Captain he sleep nearly all day; I not have to cook much for him. But I learn to make cocktails," he added, with a twinkle.

"I suppose you'll be glad to get the doctor back?"

The little man looked dubious.

"Yes, but I tell you, mademoiselle, I not feel so sure the doctor means to come back soon, perhaps not for a long time."

"Why, what makes you think that?"

"Ah—" He hesitated, digging the thick toe of his boot in between the cobble stones and gazing at it thoughtfully. "Mademoiselle, the doctor say to me the other day, when the Captain go, I can take a long what-you-call holiday. I can go to my people in Cognac a month, two months, maybe more. He say he not sure what he will do; perhaps he go away from Cannes."

"You mean he might give up his practice?" asked Esther, astonished.

Jacques shrugged expressively.

"I know nothing. He always say he hope one day to stop work again, I cannot tell you. And then he speak yesterday to the Captain and say he think he will—how do you say?—*sous-louer* the house."

"Sub-let the house! Then he does mean to go away. How extraordinary!"

"To you, mademoiselle, not to me. I know the doctor for a long time. *Il fait toujours des bêtises!*"

"Well—I'm glad to have seen you, Jacques. Good-bye and good luck."

She leaned out of the car and shook his hand warmly, an attention which delighted Jacques's soul beyond measure.

"*Au revoir, mademoiselle! Au revoir, monsieur! Bonne santé!*"

When they had gone on again Roger remarked:

"Your Sartorius is a queer card. No one, to look at him, would think he could be so temperamental."

"Yet he's first and foremost a scientist. I believe he would almost starve in order to pursue his work in the laboratory."

The thought in her mind was that the Cliffords must indeed be paying the doctor well if he could afford to drop his practice in this casual fashion. A few weeks was one thing, a matter of months was another. In spite of what Jacques had always told her, she felt there must be some mistake about it. Perhaps it merely meant the doctor was thinking of moving to another part of Cannes; she had more or less wondered why he had chosen the Route de Grasse.

As for Lady Clifford, whether her symptoms were prompted by hysteria or not, she kept her bed for two days, frequently visited by the doctor. On the afternoon of the third she emerged from her room, still pale and wan, but otherwise quite herself. The anti-toxin had done its work, the typhoid was routed. As she went about passive and subdued, with pensive eyes and a pathetic droop to her mouth, it was hard to believe in her insane outburst of only a few days ago. One would not have believed it possible that she could work herself up into such a rage over a trifling matter. Indeed, to Esther at least, the cause of Lady Clifford's fury seemed so inadequate that more than once she found herself turning it over in her mind with a growing sense of bewilderment.

Both the old lady and Dr. Sartorius remained in ignorance of the regrettable happening. Since the patient, miraculous though it appeared, suffered no bad effects from the shock, Esther had deemed it the wise course to say nothing about it. After all, it was not the easiest thing in the world to tell tales on your patient's own wife, and to do so could only increase the latter's dislike. Better let well alone.

Two days more went by uneventfully. About three o'clock on the second afternoon, Esther put on her coat and hat and set out for a walk. Roger had not been home for lunch, but to her surprise she found him in the hall, wearing an old tweed overcoat, and engaged with a somewhat angry air in ramming tobacco down into the bowl of a pipe. It was the first time she had seen him smoke a pipe. It gave him a different sort of look.

"Hello! Going for a walk?"

"Yes, I need exercise."

"So do I. I'll come with you if I may. I was just going to start out alone."

"Wouldn't you rather go alone?"

He looked at her, scorning to reply, then jammed the pipe in his mouth and reached for his hat and a stick. His chin was particularly aggressive, his blue eyes smouldered ominously. She forebore to question him, and they left the house and walked briskly along the road for two hundred yards before either attempted to break the silence. At last, with his pipe-stem between his teeth, he spoke.

"I wish," he said in a hard voice, "that people would not tell lies simply for the sake of lying. A good, thumping lie in the right place is a thing I thoroughly uphold. But pointless untruths irritate me beyond measure."

She stole a look at him.

"Perhaps," she ventured, "the person who has incurred your displeasure believes in the saying of Pudd'nhead Wilson—'Truth is the most valuable thing we have. Let us economise it!'"

His face relaxed for a moment, then stiffened again.

"No, but hang it, Esther, I'm damned annoyed."

"That's quite apparent."

He strode on again in angry silence, then, with a sudden laugh, became more communicative.

"It's nothing much. I might as well tell you. By the way, I suppose as a nurse you are quite in the habit of having people confide in you, aren't you? Though I hope you realise I don't bare my soul to you because of your official position. It's more because you happen to have lashes that turn back in a certain way."

"Many thanks!"

"Well, then, it's about my stepmother—Thérèse. Gad, how that woman does rub me the wrong way!—A little while ago I came back from the courts, earlier than usual; it began to rain. I went up to my room to change, and, what do you think? She was there."

"Lady Clifford in your room? Why?"

"You may well ask. She has never been near it before, to my knowledge; there's no reason why she should, especially as she's not particularly fond of me."

"What was she doing there?"

"I'm blessed if I know. When I threw open the door she was in the middle of the room, I should say on the way out. She looked startled, naturally. Then she smiled and said she hoped I didn't mind, that she had slipped in, thinking I was still away, to get a book out of my bookcase."

"So that was it, was it?"

"Wait till I tell you. I said, certainly, go ahead and help herself, and she kneeled down in front of the bookshelves and took out a book. I should have thought no more about it—only I happened to see the book."

"What was it?"

"You'd never guess. It was *L'Abbé Constantin.*"

"L'Abbé Constantin!"

"Yes. Can you see Thérèse reading a thing like that, a sweet little sentimental tale they give young girls in an elementary French course?"

"Oh, so you think that was an excuse?"

"What do you think? I know it was. The point is, why should she have to invent an excuse for being in my room? No doubt she had a perfectly good reason for being there, why not say so? I daresay she likes to see herself in my mirror; it's in rather a good light. Something of that sort. What exasperates me is that she should think it worth a lie. Now I shall go on bothering my head as to why she really was there. I shall be wondering whether she came to read my letters, or something absurd like that."

He laughed lightly, his good nature restored.

"I suppose," said Esther slowly, "that there are people whose minds work in devious ways, who'd rather not give their reasons for doing things."

"You may be right. It doesn't matter a hoot what she does. Oh, by the way—did you happen to see these items in the Paris *Daily Mail*? They may interest you."

From the depths of a side pocket he fished up a folded newspaper, which he handed to her.

"Read these," he said, pointing to a couple of bits in the social column, juxtaposed.

Following his finger, Esther read aloud:

"Arrivals at Claridge's include Señora Toda and her daughter, Señorita Inez Toda, who, after spending the winter in the Riviera, are now returning to their home in Argentina."

"Captain Arthur Holliday, well known in Paris and in Cannes, is staying at Claridge's before sailing from Marseilles for South America, where he has important interests."

Esther lapsed into the vernacular of her adopted country.

"Well, what do you know about that?" she exclaimed, turning wide eyes on her companion. "So he is going, after all."

"So it appears. His Spanish friends have him in tow. I wish them joy."

Esther was silent, wondering if the thought in her mind had also occurred to Roger, namely that Holliday had at last given up hope that Sir Charles would die. She wondered, too, how the news would affect Lady Clifford. Perhaps, indeed, the latter had known days ago of his departure, in which case her violent emotional burst, as well as her illness, became more comprehensible.

They made a big circuit, and an hour and a half later turned homeward, approaching the house from a different direction. While still a little distance away they caught sight of a small Aberdeen terrier in the act of disappearing around the corner of a leafy avenue. The dog, red collar and all, had a familiar appearance.

"Can that be—why, yes, it is Tony!" cried Esther, recognising Lady Clifford's pet. "He must have slipped out. Here, Tony, Tony!"

The Aberdeen turned and bent upon her an inquiring eye, smiled coyly, dog fashion, wagged his brief tail, then, instead of coming closer, wheeled about and dashed off down the avenue.

"That's not like him," Roger said. "He's always such an obedient dog. Tony, here, Tony!"

Tony, however, had a mind of his own. Paying no heed to Roger's whistle, he ran without stopping until he joined, far in the distance, two figures who were walking slowly in the opposite direction.

"He's evidently with someone," Roger remarked. "A man and a woman. Can your long-sighted eyes see who they are?"

In the growing dusk it was not easy to tell, but there was something familiar in the big, heavy frame of the man.

"It looks like the doctor," Esther said, hesitating. "And I believe the woman is Lady Clifford."

As she spoke the pair separated, the woman went on, the dog following, and the man turned and came back along the avenue. It was the doctor, there was no doubt about it now.

"I have scarcely ever seen Thérèse out walking before. I wonder what has come over her?" Roger said as they quickened their pace again. "What are you in such a hurry for? Don't you want the doctor to see you?"

"It isn't that; I only feel I'd like to be home first," Esther excused herself, not quite sure of her own reasons for trying to escape Sartorius's notice.

"Rubbish. You don't want him to see you with me. Now own up, my dear. Isn't that true?"

"No, it isn't a bit true. That's too absurd!"

"Well, true or not, why should we mind? We are not the conspirators," Roger retorted lightly.

Somehow the word "conspirators," jokingly uttered, gave her a queer, uncomfortable feeling. There had been something about those two sauntering figures, so close together, that had emphasised the dim, instinctive notion she had had before of something between the pair. Yet what was there strange in Lady Clifford's taking a short stroll with her private physician?

"More of my nonsense!" was Esther's mental comment as she put the matter determinedly out of mind.

It was much later in the afternoon, nearly six o'clock, when Lady Clifford returned in the Rolls. Esther heard her come upstairs and go to her room, but she did not see her, being busy making Sir Charles ready for the night. When it came time to take the old man's temperature she discovered her watch had stopped for want of winding. She went into the boudoir to look at the clock on the mantelpiece there, throwing open the door, feeling sure the room was empty.

The next instant she heard herself murmuring "I beg your pardon!" as she retreated hastily, utterly flabbergasted by what she had seen.

Standing bolt upright on the hearthrug was Roger, his arms awkwardly embracing Lady Clifford, who leaned against him, her golden head pressed close to his shoulder, her eyes gazing up at him with every evidence of clinging affection.

What in heaven's name did it mean?

CHAPTER XXI

ONE of the habits of men most annoying to the opposite sex is their reluctance to give explanations.

When one is eager to know the reasons why they did or failed to do a thing, instead of satisfying one's curiosity they go quietly away and say nothing. Women in the same position itch to justify, to excuse, to exonerate. Men keep silent and let one think what one pleases—a form of moral cowardice which remains at once their weakness and their strength.

Why Roger should not immediately hasten to explain the attitude in which he had been discovered with Lady Clifford puzzled Esther and filled her with chagrin. Only a few hours before he had spoken of his stepmother with open dislike, yet here he was with his arms about her, her head against his breast. Perhaps, indeed, it was difficult to explain, yet he might at least try to do so. The evening passed and he said no word.

At dinner Lady Clifford appeared a radiant vision in pale green georgette, a little transparent coat veiling the whiteness of her skin, her lustrous pearls heavy upon her white neck. She had an air of sweetness and frankness. Esther had never seen her so charming. She talked to Roger, asked his advice on various matters, and made herself so agreeable that her sister-in-law noticed it and was pleased. Yet, although an atmosphere of harmony prevailed, Roger did not look at ease. When his eye rested on Esther he withdrew it quickly, and with an air frankly shamefaced. What had happened? Had he experienced a change of heart, and was he feeling apologetic about it? If that was so, he need not, Esther reflected proudly. It was nothing to her. She applied herself to her dinner and refrained from paying the slightest attention to him.

When coffee was brought into the drawing-room, Roger drank his hastily and withdrew. A few minutes later she heard a car start outside and knew that he had taken himself off. In spite of herself she felt hurt. It was a trifling thing to mind about, yet she did mind, and it was with a sense of blankness that she resigned herself to playing piquet with Miss Clifford.

On the chaise-longue in the circle of light from a rose-shaded lamp, Lady Clifford smoked tranquilly, her silver-shod feet in front of her, a fashion magazine spread on her lap. She seemed at peace with the world.

"What a relief, Thérèse, to think Charles is going on so well," the old lady remarked at the finish of a hand. "In a day or so he will have passed the crisis. I feel so much easier in my mind."

"Ah, yes," Lady Clifford replied, looking up. "From now on I should think we have nothing to fear."

Just then the doctor entered from the hall, setting his empty coffee cup on a table.

"You are wrong when you speak of a 'crisis' in typhoid, Miss Clifford," he informed her. "The correct term is 'lysis,' which is quite a different thing from a crisis."

"Oh, well, you know what I mean, anyhow. I've always called it a crisis, all my life, but it shows how ignorant one is. At any rate, in a few days we may consider him out of danger, mayn't we?"

Sartorius shook his head with slight disparagement.

"I certainly trust so, Miss Clifford, but, frankly, no one can be sure. If everything continues to go smoothly—"

"But why shouldn't it, doctor?" Lady Clifford asked quickly.

He shrugged his heavy shoulders in a weary fashion.

"My dear lady, I only want to warn you against over-optimism. One mustn't allow oneself to forget Sir Charles's age and the fact that he has been in bad health for some time. Weakened as he is now, any shock, however slight might do irreparable harm. However, there is no reason for alarm."

Miss Clifford sighed deeply, shuffling the cards over and over.

"I was thinking we were safe out of the woods," she said sadly. "Now you've depressed me again."

"There is no need," the doctor assured her, patting her shoulder with the deliberate kindliness he reserved for her. "Barring accidents, we may hope for good things."

When he uttered the word "accidents" it seemed to Esther that his eyes rested coldly upon her, quite as though she herself might through some piece of carelessness endanger Sir Charles's chance of recovery. Why on earth did he take that suspicious attitude? It had struck her often the past few days that he was over-critical in regard to her, always ready to find fault. Yet she knew that Sir Charles liked her and that as far as she could tell, she had never failed in her duty. She was glad when the doctor withdrew from the room; she felt she could breathe again.

"Don't let him upset you," she could not help saying to the old lady: "I am sure he only wants to be over-conscientious, and—though perhaps I shouldn't venture to say so—it strikes me Sir Charles has really quite a lot of fighting power. Why, if he wasn't any worse the other day—"

The words slipped out before she knew it. She broke off, her face scarlet. Not for words would she have referred to the incident, least of all in Lady Clifford's hearing.

"Why, what happened the other day?" inquired Miss Clifford, placidly dealing.

"Didn't I tell you? I upset a basin of water, almost over him. Wasn't it stupid?"

It was the first thing that came into her mind. She felt the French-woman's eyes upon her full of shrewd understanding.

"Oh! Was that all? That couldn't have been very serious."

"I assure you the doctor thought it was."

Lady Clifford lit a fresh cigarette and fitted it into her long holder, then she spoke.

"I think, Dido, Charles is certainly less feeble than we feared. These past few days I have felt quite sure he is going to get well. Roger thinks so, too."

The final sentence was not lost on Esther, who chid herself indignantly for being annoyed. Wasn't it better that there should be peace in the house instead of an armed neutrality?

At that moment one of those trifling things occurred which lately seemed constantly coming across her path. A movement of Lady Clifford's arm swept her cigarette-case to the floor and it fell with a clatter close to the card-table. Stooping down, Esther picked it up and crossed to restore it to its owner.

"*Merci, mille fois,*" Thérèse murmured mechanically, putting out her hand. She did not look up or she would have seen the sudden dilation of Esther's eyes as she caught sight of the fashion drawings on the two pages open in front of her.

The sketches showed in every detail, and with the greatest possible degree of *chic* and *coquetterie*, the latest mode in widow's garb.

What a curious paradox! It was absurdly unimportant, yet how odd it seemed that Lady Clifford, while speaking with calm confidence of her husband's recovery, should at the same time be regarding with interest the newest ideas in mourning!

"Your play, my dear. Why, what is the matter? Were you bothered about something?"

"No, not in the least, Miss Clifford. I'm rather tired to-night, that's all. Perhaps it's the weather."

She was not sorry to say good-night and withdraw to the solitude of her bedroom. The sense of vague trouble which had so often haunted her since she had entered this house was strong upon her now. It had been an uncomfortable evening; Roger's enigmatic behaviour still disturbed her peace of mind. Now, for an insufficient reason, she felt uneasy about her patient. She could not go to bed without having a look at him, merely to set her fears at rest.

The night-nurse was sitting in an easy chair behind the screen, reading a Tauchnitz edition of a novel by Florence Barclay. She came forward with her elaborately cautious step, smiling with all her false teeth to the fore.

"How is he to-night? Going on as usual?" Esther whispered.

"Oh, quate, quate! Look at him—as peaceful as a baby, poor old thing. I hardly think we need to worry. I hear *she's* down to-night. How's she looking?"

"Quite herself. I don't believe there was much the matter with her really."

"No, they took it in time. Ah, she is a lovely thing and no mistake. Aline's been showing me some of her undies; simply a dream they are—*I* never saw anything like them."

Reassured, Esther proceeded to her own room. Try as she would, she could not dismiss from her mind that matter of Roger and Lady Clifford. It stuck like a burr. Constantly before her mental vision was spread the picture of those two, clasped in an embrace which looked at the very least affectionate. She realised now that probably she had done the wrong thing by bolting out of the room; it would have been wiser to go in as if there were nothing unusual. Only she was so startled she had not time to think. What was the meaning of this sudden reconciliation? An idea came to her. Suppose Roger had all the time been secretly fond of his stepmother—too fond? So often hatred was an inverted form of love. Could it be true, that he subconsciously loved her and despised himself for so doing?

What a hateful thought! There was something particularly humiliating and unpleasant about it, yet now that it had come she could not get rid of it. She seized a brush and attacked her hair angrily, brushing hard to exercise her annoyance.

A knock sounded at the door, a man's voice called softly:

"Have you gone to bed yet?"

With her curls all wild, she dropped the brush and opened the door. Outside was Roger, in his old tweed coat, raindrops standing out on its hairy surface.

"I want to talk to you," he said simply.

CHAPTER XXII

"Oh! Is anything the matter?"

She noticed that he looked embarrassed.

"No, nothing. Come outside for a few minutes; downstairs is best, where we won't disturb anybody. The whole house seems to have turned in, and it's only ten-thirty."

They descended to the floor below and sat on the broad stairs in semi-darkness. Esther waited, curious to know what he was going to say. He lit a cigarette and seemed reluctant to begin.

"I've been driving in the rain for a couple of hours," he volunteered at last. "I've got a beastly head for some reason or other. I thought the air might do it good."

There was a long, awkward pause, then finally he turned and eyed her with the same shamefaced expression she had noticed at dinner.

"Well," he said abruptly, "what do you think of me?"

She returned his gaze with transparent innocence.

"Think of you?" she repeated. "Nothing. Why?"

He drew a deep breath.

"Come now, Esther, you know you've been wondering about what you saw this afternoon. It wouldn't be human not to. What conclusion did you come to in regard to my stepmother and me?"

"Oh," she replied indifferently, "I don't know. What do you want me to think?"

"Poker face! There's nothing to be got out of you, is there?" he said, smiling. "I see I'll have to tell you—and yet I feel such a beast to say anything about it. Besides, there's a bit I can't tell; it wouldn't be decent."

Esther interposed quickly:

"There's no reason why you should say anything. Please don't, if you'd rather not."

"But I'd like to; I couldn't let you get wrong ideas."

He halted again, frowning at the lighted end of his cigarette.

"Oh, well, it was like this. About a week ago I had a sort of a brush-up with Thérèse. She was very angry and so was I, and I laid down the law to her a bit. Since then we've scarcely spoken. . . . I don't believe I had said a word to her until I found her in my room, early this afternoon. Well, this evening I was on my way to dress, and when I passed the sitting-room she was in the doorway. She asked me to come inside, said she wanted to explain something to me."

"Oh! So that was it?"

"She was extraordinarily nice, appealing, and all that. She admitted it was a stupid lie about coming to get a book, that she had tapped on the door and thought she heard me say 'Come in.' Then when she was inside she found out she was mistaken, and was about to go out again, when I appeared, and frightened the life out of her by the suspicious look on my face, so she just said the first thing that came into her head. She made me feel rather a brute. She said, 'You know you always terrify me, Roger, you are so hard, so intolerant. You always think the worst of me.' I have to admit that's true. I may not have given her a chance."

She waited for him to go on. He continued to frown, not looking at her, plainly troubled in his mind.

"I can't tell you all she said, but she told me something about the scene we'd had that put rather a different light on matters. She told me how sorry she was, and I think she meant it. She was quite upset. Do you know, Esther, I felt rather ashamed of myself for—for not having tried to make a friend of her. It makes me out a frightful prig. Looking at things from her point of view, I'm sure it hasn't always been easy."

"No, of course not."

"You see that, don't you, Esther? I mean a young woman married to an old man—I daresay she didn't realise what it was going to be like."

He leaned his head on his hands for a moment, his forehead furrowed. He gave the impression of arguing with himself. Then he looked up suddenly.

"She said to me, 'I don't expect sympathy from you, Roger, but you are a man of the world; you can't go on for ever so completely misjudging me. You had the wrong idea about me six years ago' . . ."

He broke off, evidently regretting his last words, but Esther made no comment, and he went quickly on:

"I didn't know what to say. I was damned uncomfortable. The odd part about it is, Esther, that inside me I don't like her much better than I did before, only she made me see how unfairly I've behaved. I feel I owe it to her to try and be nicer. Can you understand?"

"Of course I can. Why shouldn't you feel like that? She's your father's wife."

"Yes, she's my father's wife. . . . Well, the finish of it was she put her hands on my shoulders, very simply, like a child, and asked if we could be friends. What could I say? And then she put her cheek against me, and—and I put my arms around her; she seemed to expect it, and I didn't know what else to do. And then you came in. Gad, shall I ever forget your eyes!"

Esther laughed in relief, her companion joined her, and for several seconds they were a prey to helpless merriment. The whole affair was so different now; Roger's explanation had taken all the sting out of it. She could understand his guilty look; he had been the battle-ground for one of those fights between reason and prejudice, his sense of justice Striving to overcome a deeply rooted aversion.

"S'sh! We mustn't make a noise! Good-night—I'm off to bed."

He caught hold of her hands, detaining her.

"See here, you don't think me a hopeless fool, do you?"

"Certainly not; why should I?"

"And you don't think now that I was making love to her or anything like that, do you?"

"Well, I'm not quite sure! If you keep protesting—"

She broke off with a teasing smile, looking down on him from the step above.

"Esther, you—"

Chalmers entered the hall with a measured step, on his way to bolt the front door. Esther took advantage of the interruption to tear herself away.

"Good-night," she called softly over her shoulder, and vanished up the stairs.

Roger gazed after her with eyes that shone. Then he put his hand to his head and frowned again.

"Bring me a whisky and soda, will you, Chalmers?" he said. "I'll see if that will do this beastly head any good."

The headache had not gone next morning, though it had subsided into a duller sensation. His aunt at breakfast noticed that he had no appetite, merely trifling with his grapefruit and tasting his coffee. At once she inquired the reason, remarking at the same time that he had not his usual healthy colour.

"Oh, it's nothing, Dido. I do feel a bit rotten."

"Does your head pain you?"

"A bit: I shall be all right presently."

He was annoyed to see apprehension cloud the old lady's eyes.

"My dear, don't begin bothering about me. Can't a person have a little ordinary headache without—"

"I know, Roger, darling, only with your father and then Thérèse . . . Don't you think you'd better see the doctor?"

"I see altogether too much of the doctor, thank you; wherever I go I seem to run into him. He's a depressing brute."

"Don't be childish, Roger, that's only a manner."

"Well, it's a damned bad manner, and I'll look after my own headache if it's just the same to you. It's not the first I've had. Got any aspirin?"

"I've got something much better than aspirin—a new French preparation. If you'll come upstairs I'll get it for you."

A little later, having managed to finish his coffee, he joined his aunt in the boudoir, where he found her ineffectually trying to get a stopper out of a bottle.

"It's a glass stopper, and absolutely refuses to budge. Why will they make bottles that one can't open?"

"Give it to me. I'll put it under the hot tap."

"I've done that; it's no use."

"Then let's see what a lighted match will do."

He struck a match and held it under the neck of the bottle until a ring of smoke appeared on the glass.

"Now, here goes."

He gave the stopper a sharp twist, there was a cracking sound, a cry from Miss Clifford, and a pungent odour filled the room as the contents of the bottle gushed over the carpet. The neck was broken away, and the jagged glass had cut a deep, ugly gash across the base of Roger's thumb. Blood welled up freely from the wound.

"Oh; how dreadful! I'm so distressed! What shall we do?"

The old lady gazed about distractedly, while her nephew regarded the pool of blood forming in his hand.

"Get my handkerchief out of my trousers pocket, will you?"

"Here, take mine. Don't stir—I'll call Miss Rowe; she'll know what to do. That beastly bottle; it's all my fault!"

In her flurry she entered her brother's bedroom without knocking, calling out:

"Miss Rowe, can you come quickly? My nephew has had a horrid accident here."

"Accident?"

"Yes; will you give us a hand?"

Esther was leaning over the bed on the opposite side from the doctor, who had that moment administered an injection to the patient. She straightened up and stared in alarm at Miss Clifford, holding in her hand the hypodermic needle she had just taken mechanically from the doctor.

"Certainly, I'll come at once."

She hastened after the older woman, leaving the doctor to draw up the cover over the old man.

"Nurse!"

There was a note of slight annoyance in the doctor's voice as he viewed her abrupt departure.

"I won't be a second, doctor. . . . Oh, what has he done to his hand?"

She was already beside Roger. He was endeavouring to staunch the flow of blood with his aunt's handkerchief, which was already sopping.

"My dear girl, it's merely a cut. If you can get me a towel or something—"

"Let me look."

Gently she examined the deep and jagged wound.

"Ugh! What a horrid affair! It must be seen to properly. Will you hold your hand over this newspaper while I fetch some water and bandages?"

For an instant she stuck her head into the bedroom door, to say reassuringly to her patient:

"It's only a cut, Sir Charles, nothing serious."

Then she dashed off in search of her little first-aid box, returning a moment later with it and a basin of water. Miss Clifford cleared the table for her paraphernalia.

"What a comfort you are. Miss Rowe! Do you think it will want stitching up?"

"Oh, no! But he must keep it bandaged. It's in such an awkward place, the right hand, too."

"Good-bye to tennis, also golf, for the rest of my stay," was Roger's rueful comment. "What rotten luck!"

Esther worked skilfully and quickly: soon the injured hand was swathed in a neat and snowy bandage that smelled of iodine. She was aware that Roger's eyes not only followed the movements of her fingers, but dwelt as well on her cheek, her mouth, the downward sweep of her lashes. It was a pleasant moment, fraught with potentialities.

"Can I be of any assistance?"

The question came in a somewhat laboured manner from the door behind. Over her shoulder Esther saw the doctor, his bald head lowered, his small eyes regarding them in a sort of dull, tentative way.

"No, thanks, doctor, I've just finished. . . . You didn't want me for anything, did you?"

It struck her he had something on his mind.

"Not at the moment."

He came into the room slowly, his eyes roving about as if in search of something, now dwelling on the table, now on the mantelpiece, now on the Louis XV commode. Then in the same preoccupied manner he went out again.

"What an odd man!" Miss Clifford remarked with a smile. "You'd have thought it natural to ask how Roger came to cut his hand, wouldn't you?"

But Esther knew how little the insignificant detail of life interested Sartorius; his indifference no longer struck her as strange. Firmly she tied the last knot about Roger's wrist.

"You'll have to keep that on and try not to get it wet," she cautioned him.

"And how do you suggest I'm going to take a bath?"

"You'll have to manage with a shower, or else get Chalmers to rub you down like a horse," she told him gaily.

As she began putting away her rolls of gauze a thoughtful look came over her face.

"You know, I wonder if the doctor did want something? I shouldn't like to offend him."

"See here," said Roger decidedly, "you waste a good deal too much energy bothering about that man's opinion. Tell him to go to hell."

"And where should I be?" she laughed spontaneously. "Catching the first train out of Cannes, I suppose."

"No, I'm dashed if you would! Not if I had any say."

She looked up, thrilled by his warmth, and saw his laughing eyes grow serious as they dwelt on her. In that instant she had a certain knowledge that only his aunt's presence in the room prevented his kissing her.

There was a mist before her eyes and her breath came quickly as she went about her tasks. She recalled the odour of Roger's tweed clothing mingled with the indescribable masculine scent of his skin, and the memory caused her a thrill of joyous excitement. She began to believe that he did care for her. Oh, if only he really cared, if it wasn't the light sort of thing a man so easily feels and so readily forgets!

When she returned to the bedroom she noticed the doctor, with his back turned to her, standing by the window and rummaging through his black leather bag. At once she got a feeling of something wrong. The very lines of his figure suggested tension. Was he disturbed about something? If so, she couldn't imagine what it was. He said nothing, but presently followed her into the bathroom when she went there to replace the enamelled basin she had used for Roger's hand.

"Oh, Miss Rowe!" he said, speaking casually enough, yet with a sub-current of something indefinable which made her turn and look at him.

"Yes, doctor?"

He had the hypodermic case open in his hand.

"What have you done with that needle I was using just now?"

She wrinkled her brow for a moment.

"The needle?" she repeated, and gazed at him blankly.

CHAPTER XXIII

It took her a moment to collect her thoughts.

"Oh, the needle! Did I have it?"

"Certainly. I handed it to you as I usually do."

She rubbed her forehead in the effort to recall.

"Did you?" she murmured in perplexity. "I don't remember."

"But I remember. I want to replace it. What have you done with it?"

Her memory was a complete void; the business of Roger's thumb had routed everything else.

"Are you quite sure—" she faltered.

"Sure!" he repeated sharply, and with a gesture of annoyance. "I tell you you had it in your hand when you bolted out of the room. There is no question about it."

"Then I must have laid it down somewhere. I'll look for it in just a moment."

She was washing the basin at the bath.

"You'll look now."

She glanced quickly at him, amazed at his peremptory manner. Never before had any doctor spoken to her in that fashion. Besides, how could he be angry over such a trifle?

"Certainly, doctor."

She spoke calmly, hiding her wounded dignity, and without more ado hastened back to the boudoir, now empty. Where could she have put the wretched thing? It was true she had had it in her hand, she recollected that much now, but nothing more. She made a thorough search, disagreeably aware that the doctor kept coming to the doorway and watching her.

"There's no sign of it here, doctor. I'll look in my bedroom. I went there to get my first-aid."

"Do so."

She would rather not have done so when addressed in that manner. The blood rushed to her cheeks, but she stifled her resentment and continued to search in every likely and unlikely place. It couldn't be lost, that was impossible. Yet in ten minutes she returned empty-handed.

"I'm so sorry, doctor. I've looked everywhere. It's simply disappeared."

"Disappeared!"

There was no describing the sudden look of rage with which he turned on her. His face grew a mottled red, his clenched fist made an abortive gesture as though he would have liked to strike her.

"Disappeared!" he reiterated. "Have you the face to stand there and confess to such a piece of flagrant carelessness?"

She bit her lip.

"I suppose it was careless of me, doctor, but I didn't think—"

"That's the whole trouble; you never think—except about frivolity, men, anything but your work! There is no excuse for your conduct—none."

The attack was so unwarranted that, although she felt her face burn with indignation, she was able to regard him with sudden calm detachment, noting curiously his twitching mouth, his laboured breathing. He seemed in a few minutes to have become quite a different person. She had never seen him violently angry before.

"I was only going to say that although I was no doubt to blame, I certainly had no idea that you could possibly consider the matter so important."

He seemed suddenly to rein himself in for a second or two, during which he glared at her fixedly. Then he burst out again with scathing venom, the more concentrated because he kept his voice low.

"*You* didn't consider it important! That's what you mean to say. Let me tell you that any nurse worth her salt does not rush off and leave her patient as you did just now in that cavalier fashion. It was your duty to ask my permission, to find out if I was ready for you to go. Your behaviour was undisciplined, un—"

"Oh, I see. Then it was my running off to help Mr. Clifford that was wrong, not losing the needle?"

She tried to keep sarcasm from her voice, realising that it was the first time in her career she had ever given anything approaching a "back answer," yet unable to resist making some retort. She saw an odd gleam come into the doctor's deepset eyes, an expression she did not understand. For the moment the cold scientist was non-existent.

"Find that needle," he commanded, his whole huge frame tense with suppressed fury. "It is the principle that matters. I have no use for careless people."

Then, as though maddened by the passivity of her regard, he lashed out at her once more, blindly cutting her with abuse that stung, even though it was entirely undeserved. A certain crude coarseness crept into his phrases, perhaps something long repressed had found vent. The cold, inert mass of him had turned into a volcano of vituperation.

Shaken and outraged, she felt that a few words more, and she would be compelled to say, "Very well, if that's what you think of me I'd better go at once and let you get another nurse." The sentence trembled on her lips, but she did not speak it. In her heart she knew why. The truth was she did not want to go. She was interested in her case; these people had been kind to her, and then—perhaps it was the real reason—there was Roger. . . .

When at last the man paused for breath, she bowed her head slightly.

"I can only say again that I am sorry," she replied, and left the room.

Trembling with anger, she went straight to her room and stood by the window, clutching the curtain and staring out unseeingly. Ten minutes passed before she was able to subdue her pounding heart, which seemed with every beat to choke her. For a time she was quite incapable of seeing anything clearly, so bewildered was she and shaken by indignation.

At last she tried to arraign her chaotic thoughts and reason the affair out. Was the mislaying of a hypodermic needle such a heinous offence? Impossible! There was no sense in it. Was it then that the doctor had a sort of fixation on the subject of precision, that she had unknowingly offended him in a vulnerable spot? That explanation was more likely, yet not quite satisfying. Something else occurred to her. Perhaps he had been made angry by another person, and had tented his rage on her. That sort of thing was easy to understand. Or else—and now she felt she had hit upon something at last!—he might have some reason of his own for wishing to be rid of her, and had taken this method of driving her to give notice. She could not conceive in what way she could have caused him so to dislike her, but he was a strange man, there was no knowing what his prejudices were like. Perhaps, indeed, he was acting for Lady Clifford, who might easily have reason to wish her away. . . . Yes, that was distinctly possible.

The very thought aroused all her fighting instinct. She squared her jaw firmly, determined to stand her ground.

"No," she said positively to herself, "I'm not going to leave this case unless they put me out. Sir Charles is my patient as much as his, and I'm jolly well going to look after him."

She knew how hard it was going to be to face Sartorius after the recent scene—she would even find it unpleasant to sit opposite him at table. Still, there was no help for it; she must simply cultivate a thick skin and not let anyone suspect there was anything amiss. At any rate, her conscience was clear. So thinking, she set her cap straight before the mirror, and, with eyes brighter than usual and head held high, went back to her duties.

To her relief her late assailant made brief work of his lunch that day and left the dining-room before the end of the meal.

"So unlike him," was Miss Clifford's mild comment. "He usually has such a good appetite. But no one seems hungry to-day. Roger, my dear, you are not eating at all. Is your head still bad?"

Her nephew eyed his *crêpes Suzettes* with disfavour.

"Yes, it's rather tiresome. Can't think what causes it. I've had it since last night."

Esther shot him a speculative glance. Up till now she had been too deeply absorbed in her own thoughts to observe how heavy-eyed he was, listless and unlike his usual self. He caught her eyes and laughed in protest.

"Don't *you* begin on me. I refuse to be doctored. The last attempt to cure my headache resulted in this—" and he held up his injured hand.

"Then I'd better not suggest an aspirin for fear you'd go and break your leg?"

"No, don't. It's a gorgeous day, though, simply a crime to stay indoors. Will you chance left-handed driving and come for a spin?"

"I will not," she refused decidedly. "The man who drives me will want two hands."

"Ah—*formidable*, as these French say. Then you don't trust me?"

"No, I don't. That's a very nasty cut you've got; it will be every bit of ten days before you can take a car out. You must give the thing a chance to heal properly."

She finished her lunch in a more agreeable frame of mind than she had begun it, then, excusing herself, went up to settle her patient for his afternoon nap. Something restless and fretful in Sir Charles's manner caught her attention for a moment, but when she had sat with him a little he quieted down so that she was sure when she left him he was about to doze off. She was glad not to encounter the doctor, although the flame of her anger had died down, leaving only the cold ashes of resentment.

She could not explain why it was that after a short brisk walk through the streets of La Californie she should suddenly feel impelled to return to the house. It seemed as though she were being literally drawn back to her patient. She had never had such a thing happen before. She raced home and ran upstairs, slipping quietly into the darkened bedroom. She hoped to find the old man asleep, but his feeble voice greeted her at once.

"Is that you, nurse?"

"Yes, Sir Charles. Haven't you had your nap?"

"No—no. I feel uncomfortable. Queer . . ."

She drew aside the curtains and went to the bed.

"Do you?" she asked soothingly. "How's that, I wonder? Let's have a look at you."

A dingy crimson flush underlay his dried skin, his head turned restlessly from side to side. At once she suspected that his temperature was up again.

"I'm devilish hot; burning up . . . fever . . . I thought I'd finished with it."

"So you have; you're getting on famously."

She gave no sign of the sudden fear that darted through her. Why should his temperature go up like that? She did not like the look in his eyes.

"Well, let's see what you've been up to," she cajoled him gently and, having made the bed more comfortable, reached for the thermometer.

As she suspected, the mercury rose high into the danger zone. When she examined the little tube, her heart stood still in sickening alarm. What had brought about this change for the worse in such a short space of time? She racked her brain, but could not account for it. She glanced searchingly at the old man, who had abandoned interest in his condition, and lay absolutely still, save for the faint movements of his bony fingers upon the coverlet.

She was too disturbed even to shrink from the duty of informing Sartorius; there was no room in her mind now for personal animus. She found the doctor in his own room, a medical journal on his knee and an untidy ash-tray beside him, together with a cup of strong Indian tea.

He received her information stolidly, only his small eyes quickened to attention as, without comment, he rose and followed her.

The ill man submitted almost without noticing to the doctor's examination. There was not the slightest doubt that he had taken a serious turn for the worse. Presently, when the doctor had completed his investigation, he summoned Esther to the other end of the room with a brusque movement of the head.

"Have you any idea of what may have caused this?" asked in a low voice.

"Not the slightest, doctor: I simply can't imagine!"

"Then I can."

She looked up at him, puzzled. What did he mean?

"You know what I said to you this morning," he continued deliberately, but looking away from her, "on the subject of your unprofessional behaviour. Perhaps this will be a proof to you of how serious the matter was."

She could not believe she had heard aright.

"What on earth do you mean?"

"I mean that in shouting out the word 'accident' as you did and then dashing out of the room, you may easily have caused Sir Charles a shock which in his condition was sufficient to bring on this relapse. From your manner he may have thought some really grave catastrophe had overtaken his son. It is quite possible that you are directly responsible for his state now."

She stared at him, speechless. How could he wilfully distort facts in this barefaced way? It seemed a revelation of some incredible pettiness of character hitherto unsuspected in him. When she found her voice she spoke evenly, with perfect self-control.

"I think, doctor, you will have a hard job of it trying to pin this on *me*," she replied, and left him.

She knew that his eyes followed her, and that during the rest of the afternoon he glanced at her often, as if he did not know how to construe her momentary defiance, but she was indifferent to what he thought. She knew that at this late date he would not risk a change of nurses, and that was enough for her. Her only concern was for her patient.

Before evening everyone was aware that Sir Charles, whom they had believed to be out of danger, had suffered a severe relapse. Depression lay like a pall on the household. Lady Clifford fidgeted about from one room to another aimlessly. Roger smoked endless cigarettes.

"Do you think the doctor could have foreseen this?" Miss Clifford inquired of Esther about night-fall. "You remember how he warned us last night against being too hopeful."

"He couldn't possibly have guessed it! No one could. The whole thing has come out of the blue. I can't think how to account for it. If he had been given anything to eat, solid food, or—but no, that is simply out of the question."

The more Esther thought of it the more utterly she was mystified. The affair was inexplicable. She scorned to consider for a moment the doctor's absurd attempt to accuse her, having seen the old man weather a storm infinitely worse.

When, tired and dispirited, she went to her room that night, she fancied, on opening the door, that a faint odour of tobacco greeted her—the doctor's strong Algerian tobacco.

"That wretched man is getting on my nerves," she murmured under her breath. "I couldn't possibly smell cigarette smoke here, the door has been closed all day."

A moment later she stood still in front of the dressing-table, her eyes running over its contents. Was everything as she had left it? The maid never touched anything after she did the room in the morning, yet somehow the various boxes and bottles, trays, and so on, had an altered appearance. Her quick eye roamed around. On the table was her first-aid case, where she had put it down that morning. She opened it and looked inside. She could not absolutely swear things were different and yet . . . She turned and surveyed the whole room, then one by one pulled open the drawers in the commode. Here and there she felt sure some object had been touched and disarranged. If she had not been an orderly person she might not have noticed. Last she opened her shopping bag. She found the metal cover of her lip-stick off, and a streak of red on the lining of the bag. Then she felt certain: there was nothing missing, yet she was convinced that someone had been ransacking her belongings pretty thoroughly. One of the maids, perhaps, out of idle curiosity. It didn't interest her much.

"What on earth does it matter?" She sighed indifferently, and then she remembered the tobacco smoke. Could it possibly have been . . .

She remained motionless for a full minute, her brow knitted in puzzled thought. Then, with a shake of the head, she slowly undressed.

CHAPTER XXIV

WITHIN twenty-four hours Sir Charles was in a condition bordering on coma. Arrangements were hurriedly made for a consultation of physicians to be held the following day, it being Lady Clifford's wish that no stone should be left unturned in the effort to save her husband. However, everyone realised that the consultation would be a mere formality: there was scarcely any possibility of stemming the tide. Yet Thérèse's zeal was not without its effect on both her sister-in-law and her stepson.

"No one can say she hasn't done her best for the poor old boy," Roger confided in subdued tones to Esther. "He's had every chance. I suppose there's no hope whatever?"

Reluctantly she shook her head.

"It would be wrong for me to tell you there was. You know what happens at this stage of typhoid—" And she went on to describe the condition now prevailing.

"It's the suddenness I can't get over," Roger said for the fourth time. "Nor I."

In fact, she felt still dazed. Her eyes dwelt with compassion on Roger's face until she saw him pass his hand heavily over his forehead with a suggestion of pain. Then she spoke impulsively:

"Roger—do you mind? I'd like to take your temperature."

"Mine? What for?"

"Don't be cross, I really think I'd better."

"Oh, all right, go ahead."

A moment later, when she was in the act of counting his pulse and while the thermometer was sticking out of his mouth, Lady Clifford entered, followed by her sister-in-law, the latter looking tired and much older. Both women looked on with interest and concern.

"Miss Rowe—you don't think—?"

"It is up a little," Esther admitted, holding the thermometer to the light. "Just a hundred. I thought so last night. It isn't much, of course."

"So did I. You see, Roger! You wouldn't believe me."

"Well, what if it is? It's nothing worth mentioning."

Miss Clifford glanced helplessly at the others, and Thérèse gave a pathetic shrug. She looked fragile and wan, all life gone out of her.

"My dear," she said gently to Roger, going up to him and putting her hand on his shoulder, "I had the same symptoms that you have— the same that poor Charles had. This is a dreadful epidemic; no one is safe. But look at me—I escaped it, I am perfectly well. Why? Because I took the anti-toxin."

"Of course, Roger," his aunt urged eagerly. "You must let the doctor see you at once; you mustn't waste a minute!"

"You think I ought to have typhoid anti-toxin, do you?"

Thérèse shrugged her shoulders again very slightly before replying, "I think so, naturally. But I should leave it to the doctor. He'll advise you."

Roger turned to Esther.

"What do you think about it, Miss Rowe?" he asked. "Would you have it if you were I?"

"The anti-toxin? Oh—that is something you must decide."

Why on earth did she make such an inane reply? She saw Lady Clifford smile a little and raise her eyebrows, as if amused by what she considered a stupid conversation. The old lady merely looked troubled.

"Well," remarked Roger, rising, "you women may think what you like, but there's one thing I never have been able to stand the thought of, and that is having a needle stuck into me."

"My dear, that's simply childish," his aunt chid him mildly. "It's only a tiny prick."

"Yes and it's just that tiny prick that is worse for me than going over the top ever was. You'll think me no end of a fool, but I mean it."

He left the room to avoid argument. Miss Clifford turned to Esther for sympathy.

"Miss Rowe, did you ever know anyone so stupid?"

"Yes, Miss Clifford. He's not the first man I've met who felt like that."

"You don't mean it! What cowards men are! I wonder what we ought to do? Of course I'll manage to persuade him."

"Of course you will," Lady Clifford assured her. "When such a small, small thing can prevent a bad illness, one must try to find a way of removing a silly prejudice."

"Oh, leave him to me, I'll talk him round."

"Only, don't let him wait too long—stupid boy! It might be too late to do any good. Persuade him to let the doctor examine him now."

"I will. I'll go after him this minute. He mustn't be allowed to trifle with his health in this way," and the elder woman left the room, glad of the relief of action.

As Esther rose to go back into the bedroom. Lady Clifford inquired wearily:

"Is there any change, nurse?"

"I'm afraid not, Lady Clifford. He's barely conscious, that's all."

The Frenchwoman sighed slightly as she turned away.

"It only there were something one could do," she murmured. "If one didn't feel so helpless!"

The afternoon dragged by, the invalid drifting surely towards the other world in spite of all the efforts made to anchor him to this one. Esther stayed close beside the bed, even though there was little she could do, mildly saddened because of sympathy for at least two members of the old man's family who would mourn his loss. The "case," now so nearly finished, appeared, as she reviewed it, quite an ordinary one, all the tiny things that had struck her as odd or arresting seemed trivial in retrospect, unworthy of the attention she had bestowed on them. No doubt everything had grown out of the rather peculiar personality of Sartorius from whom she would soon be dissociated—without regret. She would certainly not continue to work for him, even if he wanted her, and of course he would not want her. No, if nothing prevented her, she would probably spend a few free weeks in Cannes, then take passage back to America.

If nothing prevented: would Roger try to stop her going? Or had his feeling for her not risen above the plane of mild flirtation? He had said nothing, there was nothing for her to go on beyond the look in his eyes. She was ashamed to confess to herself how much she hoped that he really cared. Thank goodness she had not committed herself in any way; that was one good thing.

That evening there was a dreadful feeling of low ebb about everything. In addition to Sir Charles, who was steadily sinking, there was now Roger to worry about. He had apparently allowed the doctor to examine him, but continued to hold firm against the anti-toxin, out of sheer obstinacy, it seemed. His aunt could not understand his stubbornness, and began to be filled with anxiety, particularly as he had gone off to bed with the headache unabated and a temperature still upon him.

"As if one didn't have enough to make one unhappy," the old lady sighed to Esther. "Now if Roger is going to be ill, it will be too utterly dreadful!"

Esther comforted her as well as she could, but she herself felt a load of apprehension upon her. Of course Roger was a young, vigorous man, there was no special reason to fear for him, and yet until two days ago they had felt such confidence in Sir Charles's recovery. What if the same sudden thing should happen again? It was perhaps stupid to entertain such fancies, but she was shaken, unnerved.

Ten o'clock found her alone in the drawing-room, tired, but not ready for bed, so restless she was unable to pin her attention to a book. How could she occupy her mind for a little? She looked vaguely about, and was about to pick up some cards for a game of patience when her eye fell on a large portfolio of colour-prints, reproductions of the work of modern Russian painters. The cover, reminiscent of the Chauve-Souris, attracted her, she recalled having noticed it upstairs in the boudoir several days ago. She had meant then to look at the book, but it had disappeared and she had forgotten it till now. She lifted it to her lap and opened it—or rather, to be exact, it fell open, by reason of some obstruction wedged in the crutch. A pencil, perhaps. . . .

It was the hypodermic needle!

Dumbfounded, she stared at it. How on earth did it get there? Then all at once the whole thing flashed on her. The book had lain open on the table in the boudoir; she had put the needle down upon it when she first began to minister to Roger. His aunt had cleared the table to make room for the basin of water and bandages, closed the book hastily, no doubt, and pushed it aside. Then at some time later one of the servants had removed it, with others in the same pile, to this room. She had not seen the book when she had searched for the needle, else she would have recalled the whole thing, and this suggested that the book had been taken away within the next half-hour or so. Of course! How plain it all was now!

Well, there was nothing to do but to restore it to the doctor and finish up that unfortunate episode. She would do so at once. . . . And yet—why reopen the matter? She had taken her scolding, why should she give him the satisfaction of . . . Stay! Was it possible, after all her theorising, that what the doctor had been so disturbed about was this actual needle itself? She had rejected that explanation as wholly absurd, but now that she held the concrete object in her hand, she began to wonder. Certainly he had made strong efforts to recover it, had even joined in the search. For that matter—why, what about that smell of tobacco in her room? What about her conviction that someone had gone through her things? Suppose, incredible as it seemed, the doctor had really been there while she was out of the house, turning everything over in the hope of finding his lost property? Odd that she had never thought of that possibility until now.

She turned the little instrument over, looking at it thoughtfully. If what she had been thinking was really true, why was it that he wanted this particular needle back? what was there about it? . . . All at once it came upon her like a thunderbolt that it was soon after the last injection, only a few hours, that she had noticed the change in Sir Charles. Iron and arsenic, that could have no bad effect—on the contrary, it put strength into one. With an idea forming in her mind, she furtively raised the needle to the light and examined it closely. A trace of palish liquid remained. Was it the exact hue of the familiar mixture? She could almost think it was slightly different in colour, but it was impossible to be sure. Fixedly she regarded it, recalling meantime the mottled red of the doctor's face, his unreasoning fury. If he had been only a little less enraged!

There was a tightness in her chest. The suspicion, monstrous, unthinkable, seemed likely to burst her head asunder. She heard within her two voices arguing. The first said, "What utter nonsense! Such things don't happen, at least, not to you, not in this atmosphere of safety." The second retorted promptly, "Why should it be nonsense? Such things do happen, why not to you?"

Chalmers entered softly, removed the coffee things and placed whisky and soda, although there was no one to want it. His quiet step, the ticking of the buhl clock, the very roses on the Aubusson carpet gave her gross suspicions the lie. And yet . . .

Now, to think clearly, she mustn't let the thing run away with her. What was it she had often heard? That the motive was everything. That was it, one must look for a motive. In this instance, was there a motive? *She knew there was.* Or at least it might be construed into one. But, after all, was she sure even of this? The young man Holliday had departed on his way to South America, Lady Clifford had let him go. Didn't that rather knock the bottom out of this dreadful idea? For a moment she felt confused, then came a revulsion. Of course, the whole thing was perfectly ridiculous; how could she ever have thought it for a moment? In this day and time, in this house! She was filled with unutterable relief, ready to laugh hysterically at her own mad notion.

A heavy step in the doorway, and she realised that the doctor was on the point of entering. Now was the opportunity to give him back his needle, get it over quickly. Her hand closed over it; the next instant Sartorius came and stood just inside the room.

"The consultation, nurse, is arranged for three o'clock to-morrow afternoon. I thought you might like to know."

"Yes, doctor. Thank you."

Why he should take the trouble to inform her she had no idea. It wasn't exactly like him. Moreover, he continued to stand in the doorway, looking at her, as if there were something on his mind. She was screwing up her courage to tell him of her find when he spoke again, as an afterthought, in a casual manner.

"By the way, I suppose you've never come across that needle you mislaid?"

Now was the moment. She opened her lips to speak, then heard herself saying quietly:

"No, doctor, isn't it odd? I can only think it must have got thrown into the fire."

CHAPTER XXV

THERE was little sleep for her that night. The most serious problem she had ever had to face presented itself, demanding a speedy solution. What course ought she to pursue? Hours passed and she had not found the answer.

Here was the difficulty: if she confided her dreadful suspicion to some member of the family and it was proved to be correct, then a criminal investigation would follow and her own position would be unassailable. But if, on the other hand, it were found to be false—and it seemed far more likely that this should be the case—then her career as a nurse would be absolutely, irrevocably dished. To bring an unfounded accusation against the doctor one worked for was an unpardonable offence. No physician would think of employing her again. She might have the purest motives for her action, they would not help her one particle. Henceforward she would be branded as flighty, irrational, not to be depended upon. Her living would be taken away, but something even worse might happen. She stood the chance of landing herself in a libel action, she might indeed be accused of having the intent to blackmail. She knew one case of the kind—the woman in question had been utterly disgraced.

No, only too obviously she could not afford the risk of sharing her secret doubts, or at least not yet. It was not as if by any possible knowledge or means she could save the old man, who was now doomed, beyond the shadow of a doubt. His symptoms were already those of the last, fatal stage of the disease. It was too late to hope for any change, had been too late for at least two days. No, whatever she did could only be in the interests of justice, unless . . .

Suddenly she thought of Roget. For the past few days he had shown definite signs of typhoid, mild, it is true, but unmistakable. She recalled the fact that the father, too, had suffered from a light form of the disease in the beginning. Roger's case was extraordinarily similar, allowing for his being a younger, more vigorous man. Of course, she reflected, veering round, typhoid was rampant in and about Cannes; it was not strange that two members of a household should succumb—no, more than two in this case, for first of all there had been the housemaid, then, later, Lady Clifford, only she had staved it off. There might well be someone in the house who was an unconscious carrier of germs, like the famous "Typhoid Mary," in America, some years ago. No, it might all be perfectly natural, and yet . . . there remained the poisonous doubt in her mind. It was just possible there was something wrong. What in heaven's name ought she to do?

It was not till early morning that she reached a decision. There *was* a thing she could and would do, to-morrow, without waste of time. Having made up her mind upon this point, she drifted off into a light and troubled sleep, so unlike sleep indeed that she could hardly believe she had lost consciousness when sounds in the hall roused her. She slid out of bed and into her dressing-gown. It was four o'clock. She knew by instinct what had happened.

Lights were on in the hall; she met the night-nurse coming softly out of Sir Charles's bedroom. It was true, the old man had breathed his last about a quarter of an hour ago.

"Sooner than I expected even. I gave him another twenty-four hours. No need to wake anyone, let them sleep, I say. But as you're already up, you may care to lend a hand."

Esther nodded and the woman hurried away. A door opened quietly and Roger appeared, heavy-eyed, flushed, his dark-blue dressing-gown wrapped around him. She turned to him with eyes of compassion.

"Is it—?" he asked.

"Yes, a little while ago," she told him gently.

He came and stood beside her without speaking. Almost instinctively his hand closed over hers and held it fast. She felt the dry heat of his skin, the hard throbbing of a pulse.

A sudden panic seized her; the very name of Typhoid had become a shapeless dread, a horror creeping unseen, singling out its victims, playing with them as a cat does with a mouse, letting them go, then springing . . . She wanted to cry out, to warn the man beside her of approaching danger.

Warn him? Of what? What was she able to say, what dared she say? She took a firmer grip on herself. She must remember there was about one chance in a hundred of there being anything in her mad idea; she must say nothing till she knew for certain. There could be no immediate peril, unless, of course. . . . The needle again! Those injections, of anti-toxin they kept talking about . . . if only she knew, could be sure! Fresh terror assailed her, she felt herself caught in a trap. . . .

What was this Roger was saying?

"Esther, I wasn't joking when I said I couldn't bear to have things jabbed into me. I'm not bothered a hang about myself, but I can't have poor Dido worried unnecessarily, at this time and all. Tell me—since she keeps on about that anti-toxin stuff—would you have it, or wouldn't you?"

Why did he ask her that? Her tongue felt dry, she hesitated a long moment before replying.

"I wouldn't be forced into anything," she said as naturally as she could. "As you've already got the symptoms considerably developed, it wouldn't be absolutely infallible, anyhow."

"That settles it. I won't have it at all."

She felt she ought to say something more, but was not sure how to set about it.

"Still, Roger, you are ill, you know, and you certainly ought to be in bed. There's no good that can come of walking about with a temperature."

"Well, once this is over"—she knew he meant the funeral—"if I don't feel any better, I'll take your advice. Only, somehow, I don't awfully like the idea of . . ."—he did not finish, but instead looked about him with a slight gesture of distaste.

"Why do you stay here?" she whispered quickly. "Why not go to a nursing-home."

His eyes met hers in a flash of sympathetic understanding.

"Would you come and see me there?" he asked seriously.

"Of course. I'd even nurse you, if you wanted me to," she answered simply.

"If you really mean that," he returned, frowning earnestly down at her, "I've half a mind to do it."

They moved apart as the night-nurse returned up the stairs. Esther felt slightly easier in her mind about him now. There was another thing, though. As he turned to go, she noticed that the bandage was off his right hand, and that the wound was open and bleeding again.

"That won't do," she chid him gently. "I must attend to it again before you get it infected. You really are stubborn, you know! Leave it till break-fast-time, though. Go back to bed and rest; you need it."

The day, begun so early, seemed interminable, yet there were so many things to see to that it was afternoon before she found an opportunity of carrying out her secret intention.

At last, about four o'clock, she set out in a taxi-cab to execute a number of small commissions for Miss Clifford, at whose desire she was to remain on in the house till after the funeral. The other nurse had already gone. Her errands finished, she stopped the taxi at a small chemist's shop which she had noticed before, not the one usually patronised by the Cliffords, but a smaller one about a mile away. It was neat and old-fashioned in appearance, with a row of majolica jars in the window. She went in briskly, resolved to show no nervousness and to state her request with perfect sang-froid. At any cost she must avoid the suspicion of anything out of the ordinary.

"What can I do for you, mademoiselle?"

She was relieved to find the assistant spoke English, it made it easier to explain what she wanted done. The man was a blond, pink-skinned Frenchman with half his face hidden by a curly fair beard. He eyed her indifferently while she undid the tissue-paper wrappings of her little parcel and displayed the hypodermic needle.

"I wonder if you could get this analysed for me?" she said, looking straight into his eyes with great frankness of manner. "You see there is a tiny drop of the stuff left. The doctor I am working with has reason to believe the mixture may not be quite the same he is accustomed to using."

She had prepared her speech carefully, but now she trembled within for fear it had not sounded plausible. However, the blond young man took the instrument and turned it about, examining it casually enough.

"Ah, yes, I understand. We do not ourselves make these analyses, mademoiselle, but we can of course have it done for you."

"How long will it take?"

He shrugged his shoulders expressively.

"That I cannot tell you, but I will try to get it for you soon as possible. What is your address?"

She told him, being careful to give her own name, not the doctor's. Then she thought that it might not be wise to have the report sent to the house at all. One never knew.

"If you can give me some idea of when it will be done, I will call for it myself."

"Shall we say, then, five o'clock to-morrow afternoon, mademoiselle? Although, of course, I cannot promise."

With a sigh of relief to have this particular ordeal safely over, she walked out of the shop door—and straight into the arms of Captain Holliday! She pulled herself up abruptly, almost speechless with astonishment.

"Why—you!" was all she could ejaculate.

The sudden encounter with him, when she had confidently believed him miles away, took the wind out of her sails, upsetting her calculations completely. She continued to stare at him so stupidly that she could see he was beginning to wonder what was the matter. His car, travel-stained and looking as though it had seen hard service, stood close to the curb. He had been in the act of entering a tobacconist's next door to the chemist's shop.

"I'm not quite a ghost," he informed her with a short laugh, "although I admit I feel rather like one."

He paused uncertainly, rubbing his hand over a day's growth of beard.

"But I—we—thought you'd gone to South America," she blurted out, then was sorry she had said it. "That is, we saw it in the Paris paper."

"Not yet; my boat sails in a few days. As a matter of fact"—here he shifted his gaze and glanced about in every direction except at her—"I felt I ought to come back here for the funeral, even though it made a bit of a rush. Old friend of the family and all that."

"Funeral!"

She could not keep her amazement out of her voice.

"But I don't understand. How did you find out. . . ."

She broke off, colouring up to the edge of her nurse's veil. To tell the truth, she could not see how, since Sir Charles only died at four o'clock this morning, Holliday had received the news in time to be here in Cannes now, by car, too, all the way from Paris. It seemed incredible; if he had flown he couldn't have done it.

He shot her a shrewd glance, surmising her reason for being astonished.

"How did I find out Sir Charles was dead? I didn't, at least, not till a little while ago when I arrived in Cannes and rang up the house. But I knew he wasn't expected to live more than a day or two. You see, I've been in communication with—Chalmers more or less during the past few days. I asked him to keep me posted in case the old man got worse or anything. Yesterday he telephoned me that there was absolutely no hope. I hopped into the car and burnt up the road a bit."

He cast an approving glance at his somewhat battered Fiat.

"Fourteen hours from door to door," he remarked with satisfaction. "I didn't believe she could do it. By the way, I hear the funeral is arranged for the day after to-morrow. Is that right?"

"I believe so."

"I needn't have broken my neck to get here, after all. Still, there may be something I can do for the family, as I hear Clifford is on the sick list. . . . Is Sartorius still at the house?"

She replied that he was and, bidding a hasty good-bye, got into her waiting taxi. Once alone, the thoughts stirred up by the young man's unexpected appearance on the scene buzzed turbulently inside her brain. She could not get over the surprise of seeing him, nor could she help remarking how remarkably jovial and carefree he appeared, in spite of his lowered voice and studious air of reverence when speaking of the dead man. Moreover, there seemed to her something almost indecent in the haste with which he had arrived on the spot. It had less the appearance of solicitude for the sorrowing relatives than the eagerness of a vulture swooping down upon a good square meal it had long been hoping for. Had Chalmers really telephoned him? Somehow she could not believe it, apart from Holliday's very slight hesitation before pronouncing the butler's name. Whoever it was who gave the information must have been quite confident of Sir Charles's death, had indeed timed it with extraordinary accuracy—or so it seemed to her somewhat stimulated imagination.

Another disturbing idea now occurred to her. Would Holliday by any chance mention to the doctor that he had run into her coming out of a chemist's shop? It did not seem at all likely, and, of course, if her suspicions were wrong and she was doing the doctor a gross injustice, then the information would mean nothing at all. Still, if she was not mistaken . . .

"Oh, I must be mistaken!" she exclaimed vehemently in the seclusion of her taxi. "It is utterly absurd! I have made up the whole story out of whole cloth. In all that household no one but me has a thought of anything wrong. How ashamed I should be if they knew!"

Still, when on arriving at the house Chalmers opened the door for her, she could not resist saying to him:

"Chalmers, I ran into Captain Holliday in the town—such a surprise. He's hurried back to be here for Sir Charles's funeral. He says you telephoned him yesterday that Sir Charles was sinking very fast."

There was no mistaking the blank look on the old butler's face.

"Me telephone the Captain, miss? Oh, you must have misunderstood him! I never even knew where he was stopping in Paris, miss."

So it was Lady Clifford herself who had done it! She felt sure on that point. Not that it meant anything in itself. Yet all the rest of that day and the next as well Esther found herself watching faces covertly, most of all the doctor's. In the midst of all the subdued but busy preparations for the funeral—undertakers coming and going, messengers with flowers and telegrams, strangers arriving on this errand and that—she was acutely aware of the heavy, silent man who, without doing anything in particular, gave her the almost morbid impression of dominating the scene. As an actual fact he almost effaced himself, but to her excited fancy he was omnipresent, overpowering. She thought of him now not so much as a python as in the form of a huge bloated spider in the middle of an invisible web, spinning, watching, closing in. She was ready to believe he was always watching her, spying on her movements, reading her secret thoughts. There were moments when she had a wild desire to scream aloud, so tense had her nerves become with the strain put upon them.

Then common sense came to the rescue, she realised the calm normality of the household life about her and, with an effort, was able to pull herself together. She had not long to wait, she told herself, before knowing the truth. Until then, she must remain perfectly cool.

At five o'clock in the afternoon she managed to slip out of the house and hasten to the chemist's shop, where a disappointment awaited her.

"I am extremely sorry, mademoiselle," the blond assistant made apology, "but the report has not yet come in. I am afraid now we shall not get it before to-morrow."

CHAPTER XXVI

TWENTY-FOUR hours after this Esther slammed down the lid of her steamer trunk and sat upon it. If her breath came quickly it was less from her exertions than from the stinging memory of her curt dismissal half an hour agone. Whenever her thoughts recurred to it her eyes flashed and her lips tightened into a thin line. It was the second time since she had entered this house that she had been extremely angry, although perhaps in the present instance it might be foolish of her to be so sensitive. She knew she ought to consider the source of the affront, yet all she could think of was the fact that never before had she been treated with such scant courtesy.

The funeral was over. The family, including the doctor, the old butler and herself, as well as Captain Holliday, had followed the body to its interment in the British Cemetery, and had then returned to the house for a late lunch. Immediately after this Miss Clifford, in the presence of Lady Clifford, had taken her hand very simply and said, "Thank goodness, my dear, you don't have to leave us at once. I am afraid now my poor nephew is going to want looking after, and it will be such a comfort having you." This had touched and pleased Esther, who had nodded understandingly, more than glad to be of use. She recalled later that Lady Clifford had not spoken, but at the time she had not thought of it. As far as Esther was concerned, it was in no way a question of money, she would have been delighted to remain as a friend as long as the family needed her. She felt decidedly troubled about Roger. He still refused to give up, but his temperature rose regularly each afternoon towards nightfall—not very high, yet high enough to cause alarm. He undoubtedly had "walking typhoid," which, though apparently mild, had sometimes disastrous results. She wanted to have a word with him about himself, but there was no opportunity. He had disappeared directly after lunch, she suspected because he resented the presence of Holliday. Thinking she was sure to see him later in the day, she busied herself in a variety of ways, doing all she could to be useful.

About half-past four she went to her own room to put herself tidy for tea. As she was in the act of brushing her hair before the mirror, Lady

Clifford's maid, Aline, entered after a perfunctory knock and informed her briefly that her ladyship wished to speak with her in the boudoir.

"Certainly, I'll come at once," she replied, laying down the brush, and not altogether liking the sidelong glance the woman bestowed upon her out of her close-set eyes, nor the way she lingered unnecessarily inside the door.

Entering the boudoir, she sensed at once an altered atmosphere, something not easy to describe, yet part of the general, rapid, business-like readjustment she had observed going on for the past two days. Next her attention was riveted by the chic, black-clad figure of her employer, standing in the centre of the pale grey carpet, minus her voluminous, inky veil which, during the early half of the day, had transformed her into a creature of mystery. Her mourning was exceedingly elegant and smart. Esther, gazing fascinated, wondered in spite of herself how long before Sir Charles's death it had been planned. She had never been able to rid her memory of the fashion-book incident.

The veil shed, Lady Clifford stood revealed as a figure electric with renewed energy. Her eyes shone like grey stars, her hair, freshly waved, was glossily golden, one foot in its well-cut suede shoe tapped the floor with nervous impatience. Her hands, milky-white against the dead black of her dress, waved in the air a cheque upon which the ink was still wet. Esther caught a glimpse of the almost crimson enamelled nails, while a breath of the characteristic perfume wafted towards her.

The next instant she drew in her breath sharply, for, in a metallic voice, the Frenchwoman had informed her that her services were no longer required and that she was at liberty to leave at once.

"Yes, certainly, Lady Clifford, I will go immediately," Esther heard herself saying in a collected tone, though the blood was singing in her ears.

What was it all about? What had happened?

"I have made the cheque out for an extra week," the ringing voice continued carelessly, "since in all probability your engagement here terminated rather sooner than you expected."

"Oh, no, please, Lady Clifford, I couldn't take it, really! Will you alter the amount? I haven't earned it, you know."

"Certainly not. I must ask you to take it as it is."

"Oh, but really, I can't . . ." Esther continued in earnest protest, really meaning it, feeling it impossible to accept favours from this woman.

She was rudely cut short.

"Will you kindly leave me now? I have a great many things to attend to. Good-bye."

That was all. Hot to the roots of her hair, Esther had left the room, blindly colliding with Chalmers as she did so.

"I beg pardon, miss!" he apologized with his invariable courtesy. "I hope I haven't hurt you?"

"Not at all, Chalmers, it was all my fault."

Then before she was out of earshot, she had heard him saying to his mistress:

"I was going to ask, my lady, as I hear the nurse is about to leave, whether you'd care to have Thompson drive her down to her hotel. He's waiting to know."

The reply came crisp and uncompromising:

"Not at all; let her get herself a taxi."

It was the crowning touch to an exhibition of rudeness unparalleled in her experience. Never before, happily, had she felt herself pushed out of a house where she was neither needed nor wanted. She had served her purpose, she could get herself a taxi and quit the premises.

Burning with indignation she returned forthwith to her room and began throwing things into her trunk, anxious not to lose a minute in getting away. Since the occasion when she had been forced to intervene between Sir Charles and his wife, Esther had been afraid that the latter must cherish resentment towards her, but till now there had been no open sign of it. During the past ten days, indeed, Lady Clifford had spoken very little to either of the nurses, but that little had been polite. This abrupt change of attitude indicated plainly that tact was no longer necessary. There was something superbly arrogant in the way in which she washed her hands of Esther, lost no time about getting her out of the house.

Stay—was it because of Roger's evident liking for her? Did Lady Clifford resent that? Or could it be that she definitely wanted Esther out of the way?

She was too deeply humiliated to think very clearly, and yet, sitting there on her trunk, she felt her attention drawn by this new idea. What if it was true that Lady Clifford was *afraid* to have her in the house? She had not had time properly to consider this fresh possibility when a knock came at the door.

"Who is it? Come in," she called indifferently.

She expected one of the servants, come to inquire about taking her luggage down, and, consequently, she was unprepared when the door opened to reveal the big, stolid bulk of the doctor. His slow-moving eyes glanced about the little room, taking in her preparations for departure. When he spoke it was in a tone unexpectedly agreeable.

"I thought of inquiring, Miss Rowe, what plans you have for the immediate future? Is it your intention to go back at once to New York?"

"I don't think so, doctor, but really I don't quite know what I'm going to do."

He nodded and cleared his throat slightly.

"I think I have mentioned to you that for the present I do not intend to resume my practice. I mean to take a short holiday instead, so you of course understand that I shall not require your services."

"Oh, perfectly, doctor," she replied quickly, sure that her voice must betray the irony she felt. As if she cared, indeed, whether he wanted her or not!

"I take it, then, that you may remain in Cannes for some time. Have you any friends here?"

Really! She had never before discovered his taking any interest in anyone's personal affairs. What had come over him? She replied with a certain reserve:

"No, none at all. I shall go for a few days to a pension Miss Clifford told me about. After that I have no idea what I shall do."

He appeared to ponder this information, though for the life of her she could not see how it could interest him. At last, eyeing her trunk absently and tapping his chin as if in thought, he spoke again.

"In that case I may as well drive you down to your pension. Let me know when you are ready to go."

Completely taken aback, she hastened, perhaps overhurriedly, to disclaim the proffered civility.

"Oh, no, thank you, doctor, I'll just take a taxi. I couldn't think of troubling you."

"It is no trouble," he returned firmly and in a manner that brooked no dispute. "I should prefer to see you safely to your destination. In any case, I am going that way myself."

Much as she shrank from the thought of half an hour in his company, she did not well see how she could refuse, particularly as it seemed as though he were making an awkward effort to atone for his past rudeness to her. Accordingly she resolved to put a cheerful face on it.

"All right, then, doctor, if you're quite sure it's not putting you out. I'll be ready in a quarter of an hour."

Not till after he had gone did she recall his words, "I am going that way myself." Why, she had not told him where the pension was! Never mind, perhaps he was sorry for his behaviour to her; she would give him the benefit of the doubt. It was surely unlike him to be so gracious. She shook her head over the puzzle he presented.

Her packing done, she put on the coat of her costume over her marron crêpe-de-Chine jumper—the one she had bought in the Croisette—and going to the mirror adjusted her little felt hat carefully. She recalled the fact that, except for the blouse, these were the same clothes she had worn that day she first called to interview the doctor, and later had gone on for tea at the Ambassadeurs. How long ago it seemed! The costume and hat looked as new and smart as ever, she had a indeed scarcely worn them since she went on the case. She could hardly realise it was less than two months since she had answered that advertisement.

She sighed as, mechanically, she tucked a fresh handkerchief into her breast pocket, and started for Miss Clifford's room to say good-bye to the old lady. She hoped she would see Roger, but she did not like to ask where he was.

On her way through the hall she met Holliday. His appearance was decorous and subdued, as befitted the occasion, yet as he came up the stairs in his dark, inconspicuously correct attire, she felt in his manner something assured, almost proprietary, as if he considered himself already master here. She inclined her head slightly and was hurrying past when, to her surprise, he grasped her by the arm and pulled her around facing him.

"I beg your pardon?" she said, a little offended by casual insolence, and drew her arm away.

"Hello," he murmured softly, still detaining her by sleeve. "Stand as you are; let me look at you."

His shallow eyes ran over her carefully, taking in every detail of her appearance. Then he slapped his leg and gave a noiseless chuckle.

"By Jove!" he whispered deliberately, "by Jove!"

"Well, what's the matter?"

"Oh, nothing—only I've got it now."

"Got what?"

"Where it was I first saw you. Of course—fool that I was!"

He continued to stare, and then she saw his smile fade and a curious reminiscent look take its place. She knew what the look meant. He was trying to recall more of the occasion, and wondering how much of his conversation with Lady Clifford she had overheard.

"I thought it would come back to you one day," she remarked easily.

"It's the hat that made the difference, you know."

She left him standing there motionless, looking after her, his eyes narrowed in thought. She was careless now as to what he recalled or didn't recall. What difference could it make?

"Come in, my dear. I'm trying to write some of my many letters—such a trying task!"

The old lady was sitting up in bed with her writing materials before her on a little bed-table. She smiled at Esther, but her face looked weary and old, with lines of grief that had not been there a month ago.

"Are you going out?"

"I'm leaving, Miss Clifford. I came to say good-bye."

Miss Clifford's jaw dropped; she laid down her pen and stared.

"Good-bye? Not now, surely! I thought—"

"So did I, but it was a mistake. Lady Clifford doesn't need me any more."

There was no doubt that the old lady was as much astonished as she was distressed.

"But, I don't understand! I thought, of course, that you were going to stay on a bit, at least until we know about Roger!"

Esther felt awkward, uncertain what to say.

"It's quite all right, Miss Clifford. Your sister-in-law doesn't think there's any good keeping me on. She told me half an hour ago."

In spite of her efforts her eyes met the old lady's honest ones for a second. Then the old lady shook her head helplessly, looking both embarrassed and regretful.

"If only it were my house, my dear," she faltered uncomfortably. "Of course you know how I felt about it. I took it for granted . . . besides, we looked upon you more as a friend than as a mere nurse, you know that. Roger will be dreadfully upset when he hears."

"Never mind, I shall hope to see you very soon. I'm not leaving Cannes just yet. I shall ring up to-morrow to inquire how you all are."

"Yes, please do!"

Miss Clifford took her hand and gave it a squeeze, troubled frown wrinkling her forehead.

"I wish I knew what to do about Roger. I am sure he has kept going by sheer will power and obstinacy. I am so afraid I shall have all the same dreadful uncertainty over again, just as I did with poor Charles."

"Oh, no, he's a young man, remember," Esther reassured her quickly.

"He will be all right, only you must make him go to bed."

"I persuaded him to lie down after lunch, and he's sound asleep now, so Chalmers tells me. I wonder if I ought to tell him you're going? He'll be so cross when he finds out."

"Not on any account," Esther forbade her firmly. "It would be wrong to disturb him."

"He is really very difficult," went on the old lady confidentially. "Between ourselves, I don't know what my sister-in-law is going to think of his behaving in this way, refusing to take the doctor's advice. She's doing all she can for the boy, and if he continues as he is doing he is almost sure to offend her. She's extremely sensitive!"

Esther was silent, hoping Roger would follow her advice about the nursing-home.

"Well, au revoir, my dear! I'm very sorry indeed, and I shall miss you. I shall never forget how kind you were to my brother."

Her brown eyes filled with tears as she kissed Esther's cheek.

There was no sign of the doctor when Esther slowly descended to the entrance hall. She would have liked to slip away by herself, but it was too late, Chalmers had just placed her luggage on the back of the doctor's car; she met him coming back. Moreover, she had intended to stop at the chemist's on her way down; now of course she dared not do it. What Miss Clifford had said about Roger's symptoms and the dreadful uncertainty had intensified all her vague fears, so that suddenly she felt she must end the suspense at once—if possible, before she quitted the house. Who could say what might happen once she got away?

Was there anything she could do? It would be late, perhaps too late before she would have a chance of reaching the chemist; the shop might be closed. Her eye fell on the little cloak-room at the back of the stairs, where the telephone was kept. Of course—she had a minute to spare now. What was to prevent her telephoning? The chemist spoke English—she could make him understand.

She cast a swift glance around; there was no one in sight. Then she slipped into the little room and rapidly searched in the telephone book for the name—Cailler, it was; she remembered because it was the name of a milk chocolate. Ah, here it was! With gratifying dispatch she got the connection, heard a voice which she recognised as belonging with the curly blond beard.

"*Allo, allo! Oui, c'est bien*—ah, yes, it is the Pharmacie Cailler, yes, yes. . . . What is it you say? I do not understand . . . report? Report of what? . . . Needle? Hypodermic needle? . . . But yes, yes, mademoiselle, it has been sent already to your address; it came this afternoon, so we have sent it to you."

"Sent it! But I haven't received it. Are you quite sure?"

"But yes, certainly, one hour ago, to Mademoiselle Rowe, the Villa Firenze."

What was this? A suspicion crept into her mind.

"Yes, yes, monsieur. I'm afraid it must have gone astray. Could you possibly look it up and tell me over the telephone what the report was? It is rather important. . . ."

Gripping the receiver hard, she held her breath, straining her ears for the reply. It followed without hesitation, distinct and clear:

"But certainly, mademoiselle, I can tell you. The needle contained, *tout simplement,* what one calls in English the pure toxin of typhoid!"

"Toxin of typh. . . ."

The words died in her throat, the receiver dropped clattering down. For an instant she sat as though paralysed, her dry lips parted, her eyes staring in front of her. Then with a sudden rush the horrible truth swept upon her, overwhelming her utterly. Curiously enough, it seemed as though she had always known it from the first. How could she have shut her eyes to the facts? Incidents, motives, all suddenly fitted together like parts of a puzzle moved into place. It was all clear now; she saw the entire plan, so simple, so natural, so diabolically clever—the unsuspecting old man being done to death by a natural disease that was prevalent at the time, while every effort was made to save him, all the world looking on—"see, just to show you there's no deception"—"all open and above board"—only the one flaw which she, by accident, had hit upon. Yes, she alone of all the household had held the clue in her hand, and had not had the wit to use it, to follow it up! Fool, fool, that she was! Yet, no—not quite that. The first injections were iron and arsenic, just what they pretended to be; only the last one was the pure toxin, renewing and intensifying the disease beyond hope of salvation. Even if she had known then, it would still have been too late to rescue Sir Charles. . . .

But then, there was Roger! Was he, too, an intended victim? Was another murder in progress?

She jumped to her feet, pushed open the door blindly, ready to fly up the stairs and warn him of his danger, tell him all she knew. It was no time to mince matters, she must act and act quickly. If they persuaded him to submit to those injections of so-called anti-toxin. . . .

"Oh—Chalmers!"

For the second time that day she ran bolt into the dignified person of the butler, who was crossing on his way to the stairs. She pulled herself up and spoke to him in a choking voice:

"Chalmers, for God's sake wake Mr. Roger at once! Tell him I have something to say to him. Tell him it's very important!"

"Yes, miss, certainly!"

Without betraying the least amazement at her husky voice and trembling hands, the butler mounted the stairs steadily to do her bidding. She remained where she was, clutching the back of one of the tall Stuart chairs, listening to the man's measured tread and her own hammering heartbeats. Oh, why wouldn't he hurry? Still, it would be all right now, she had found out in time. Thank God, she had telephoned, thank God, she knew . . .

There was a slight movement behind her; she jumped apprehensively, suddenly suspecting that someone was behind the cloak-room door she had so rapidly thrown open.

She turned to see who it could be, but she was not quick enough. In that instant a thick hand closed over her mouth, completely gagging her, while a huge arm that seemed like the limb of a tree or the python of her dream coiled around her with powerful force. She squirmed, panted, choked; a horrible panic seized her. Then in the upper part of her left arm she felt a sharp stab, piercing through her clothing deep into her flesh.

Immediately, it seemed, her head swam round, consciousness melted in a black mist. She knew nothing more.

CHAPTER XXVII

FIVE minutes later Roger, hastily attired in his shirt, trousers and dressing-gown, his eyes heavy with sleep and fever, descended the stairs and looked inquiringly about. The hall was empty.

"Why, where has she got to?" he murmured in perplexity, then rang the bell and called for Chalmers at the same time.

The butler appeared without delay.

"Where is Miss Rowe, Chalmers?"

The old man looked surprised.

"I'm sure I've no idea, sir. I left her here a short time ago. She was waiting to speak to you, sir."

"Was she still here when you came downstairs?"

"I can't say, sir. I went down the back way. Perhaps she's with Miss Clifford, sir. Shall I see, sir?"

"Never mind, I'll go."

He found his aunt lying back on her pillows with her closed.

"Dido, have you seen Miss Rowe?" he asked without preliminaries.

"Yes, dear, about a quarter of an hour ago. She came to say good-bye."

"Good-bye! You don't mean she's left us? Why, what does this mean?"

"Well, my dear, I was as much astonished as you. It seems that Thérèse dismissed her at about tea-time; simply said she didn't need her any longer."

Roger gave a sharp exclamation of annoyance.

"Dismissed her! See here, Dido, do you think Thérèse was rude or anything?"

"I'm sure I don't know. I didn't like to ask, naturally. Miss Rowe didn't say anything, she simply seemed in rather a hurry to get away."

"And you let her go without seeing me?"

"You were asleep, dear. We neither of us thought we ought to disturb you. Besides it isn't as if she were leaving Cannes, we shall soon see her again."

He frowned, dissatisfied.

"That's not the point. A moment ago she sent me a message by Chalmers saying she wanted to speak to me about something important. I dashed into my clothes expecting to find her downstairs, but she'd disappeared."

"It is odd. Still, I should find out if the doctor is about. I hear he was going to drive her into Cannes."

"Oh, was he? I'll look for him."

He discovered Sartorius in his own bedroom, sorting out the contents of his black leather bag.

"Have you seen Miss Rowe, doctor?" he demanded rather abruptly.

With a visible effort the big man tore his attention away from his occupation.

"Miss Rowe?" he repeated vaguely. "Oh, yes, I believe she left the house a little while ago."

"But wasn't she going with you?"

"I offered to drive her, but as I was not ready as soon as she was Captain Holliday gave her a lift instead."

"Holliday!" exclaimed Roger, puzzled. "Are you sure?"

He noticed that the doctor had the air of being slightly bored by his importunities, but he was indifferent, merely determined to get to the bottom of the matter.

"Oh, quite, Mr. Clifford. I helped the Captain transfer her luggage from my car to his, and I saw them start off."

It seemed conclusive enough; there was no question as to her being gone. Roger thanked the doctor briefly and left him, feeling perplexed and exasperated. Why had she sent him that urgent message, only to hurry away before he could possibly get downstairs to see her? Why, for that matter, was she in such a rush to be off that she had accepted Holliday's offer of a lift? Not that she had any reason for disliking Arthur, only the whole affair struck him as decidedly odd, unlike Esther. He resolved to wait a quarter of an hour and then telephone the Pension Martel, which was where he knew she had intended to go: he had heard her say so several days before.

On the telephone the proprietress of the pension informed him that no person of the name of Rowe had arrived, in fact there had been no new arrivals to-day. This did not altogether surprise him, because the pension was some distance away. Esther might not have had sufficient time to reach there. He tried again considerably later, but the answer was the same. She must have changed her mind and gone somewhere else. No doubt she would ring up in a day or two, but he was impatient to find out what had happened, why she had been so anxious to see him; he could not let the matter wait. Somewhat reluctantly he sought out Thérèse, whom he found in her bedroom surrounded by decorative hat-boxes and mounds of tissue-paper, engaged in trying small black hats with the aid of Aline.

"I'm sorry to trouble you, Thérèse, but can you tell where Arthur Holliday is staying?"

Her grey eyes regarded him with a look of instant suspicion, but he allayed her fears by adding amicably:

"I only want to ask him where he left Miss Rowe. He drove her down into town just now."

"Oh, did he?" she inquired thoughtfully, "I didn't know. I think he told me he was staying at the Carlton."

"Thanks. That's all I wanted to know."

As he turned on his heel she took a quick step towards him and put both hands on his shoulders.

"Roger, dear, why will you persist in wandering about in this stupid fashion? Why won't you go to bed and stay there till you're better? You know you are running such a frightful risk!"

He shook her off a little impatiently.

"Oh, don't bother about me, Thérèse. I'm not so very ill, not enough for you to worry about."

He hoped he did not seem rude, but the fact was he felt anxious to get away. He was unpleasantly aware of the black, gimlet eyes of the maid fixed upon him from the background; he knew that both she and Thérèse were inwardly commenting upon the interest he took in Esther, that they would speak of it the moment he was gone. Since his father's death he had known himself an alien in this house, in spite of Thérèse's protestations regarding his health. Never mind, he would not remain here much longer.

Back at the telephone he rang through to the Carlton Hotel. Yes, he was told, Captain Holliday was staying there, but he had not been in since the morning. Roger dropped the receiver angrily. There was nothing to do, then, but to wait for Esther to telephone him. She would surely do so soon if what she wished to tell him was really important. What could it have been? He had no idea.

Still, the day passed and no message came. In all likelihood she had decided that the matter could wait after all, but in his present restless mood Roger did not find this explanation satisfactory. Besides, he was unreasonably displeased by the fact that Holliday had given Esther a lift when she left. There was no reason why he shouldn't have done so, yet the fact remained that to Roger the mere suggestion seemed a piece of impudent effrontery. What was the fellow up to? Roger bitterly resented Arthur Holliday. He resented his dashing back post-haste for the funeral, it was too officious. Thérèse had said during that memorable interview which Esther had interrupted that her lover was gone, that she had sent him away. Yet here he was back again, walking about as if he owned the place, almost before the old man's body was cold. And now he had taken Esther away, no one could say where! It was too much for human endurance.

When at eight o'clock Chalmers came up bringing him some dinner on a tray, Roger questioned him closely. What exactly had Miss Rowe said?

"Only that I was to wake you at once, sir, and tell you wanted to see you—that it was very important."

"How did she seem to you?"

"Why, sir, very excited, as if she was upset about something. She was just coming out of the cloak-room, sir, which made me think perhaps she had been telephoning, but I may be wrong."

Roger pondered this information, but could make nothing of it. He resumed frowningly:

"I suppose you have no idea why she went off so suddenly, have you, Chalmers?"

"Why, no, sir, I was very much surprised myself. Almost as surprised as I was when I heard . . ."

He did not finish the sentence, and looked sorry he spoken.

"Go on, Chalmers, what were you about to say?"

"Oh, it was nothing, sir, not of the least consequence," returned the old man, embarrassed. "Only women's gossip, sir, and Frenchwomen's gossip at that."

Roger looked at him keenly.

"Never mind, I must insist on your telling me what it was you heard, if it has the least bearing on Miss Rowe."

"I'd rather not, sir. I'm extremely sorry I mentioned it. It was a slip, sir."

"Chalmers, you can't say that much without telling me the rest, so go ahead."

"Very good, sir, though I hope you won't attach any importance to it, sir. It seems that one of the maids—Marie it was, sir—went out to post a letter at about half-past five. Coming back she met the Captain's car . . ."

"Yes, go on."

"She says the car was going fast, but as it passed her she could see inside very plainly, and the nurse was sitting quite close to the Captain, with her head resting on his shoulder. That's all, sir, and it's not the kind of thing I care to repeat, though of course there may be nothing in it, sir."

"No, certainly not, Chalmers, nor does it explain what I'm trying to find out. Thank you."

He had preserved an indifferent air, but what the butler had told him was in the nature of a great shock. He felt suddenly quite sick with disillusionment. Had he been a fool all along, completely wrong in his estimate of this girl? Was she simply like so many others, possessed of two sides, one which she kept for him, and the other, perhaps, not quite so restrained? But for this story he would not have believed it possible. . . . After all, why attach so much importance to the tale of an idle servant? What if she had made a mistake, what if she had invented it out of mischief? Surely he knew Esther too well to be deceived in her. Impatiently he strove to thrust the suspicion aside.

Yet in his unhappy brain, buzzing now with fever, a voice sardonically demanded, "What man ever does really know a girl?" Particularly—he winced at the thought—what man who has money? Isn't it a common sight, that of a woman making herself attractive to a man because of what he can give her, while all the time she is secretly drawn towards someone else? For that matter Esther herself had admitted to him that she found Holliday attractive. Then what about that occasion, a trifling incident enough, when he had come upon the two of them standing so close together, gazing into each other's eyes? He had thought at the time that the moment held at least the germ of a flirtation. Why should Esther be immune from suspicion? Wasn't it possible that from the beginning she had cherished a hidden penchant for the callous Arthur? She would not be the first victim by a long shot.

Yet—Esther! He could picture her now, her clear, frank eyes looking straight into his with an expression of boyish simplicity. How could one suspect her? Surely she was incapable of intrigue; why, he had believed in her so! She was the one girl he felt he wanted for his wife, if she would have him. Only a little North Country streak of caution had held him back from asking her the actual question—or at least it was partly due to caution and partly to the circumstances of his father's death and his own illness. He had meant to as soon as this business was over. Good God! Suppose he had proposed and she had accepted him, but without caring for him—suppose without any love in her heart she had married him! He might not have found out the truth until too late. The very idea revolted him; he clenched his fists so violently that the nails of his right hand dug deep into his injured thumb. Feeling the pain and seeing the red ooze up through the bandage, he struggled briefly with unwelcome recollections, then on a sudden impulse tore off the enfolding gauze and flung it angrily into the fireplace. He had broken open the plagued wound again, but he did not care.

If only he could know for certain whether to believe that maid's story or not! Was Esther in plain language "that kind of girl"? The thought that he might never know the truth goaded him to fury. If she was all he wanted to believe her, how could one account for that detestable picture of her nestling close to Holliday, her head on his shoulder? How explain her disappearance? For that is what he began to call it. During the course of the evening he rang up every hotel and pension in Cannes and the neighbourhood without finding any news of her. Moreover, the one person who could give him any information about her movements—Holliday himself—had at midnight not returned to the Carlton. What was one to make of that fact? It seemed to indicate that the pair of them were off somewhere together dining—and after that, what?

There was no real sleep for him that night, and the morning found him decidedly worse. He did not even demur when the doctor came with Dido and quietly laid down the law about rest and diet. He agreed listlessly, unwilling to cause poor Dido additional anxiety. After all, why not give in to them? They were only giving him good advice; he had been stupid.

An hour later, however, he was not too ill to crawl to the telephone when no one was about. Once again he rang up the Carlton in quest of Holliday, only to be told that the Captain had not returned all night, was still away.

The inference of this, acting upon his present state of mind, was like pouring petrol on a smouldering fire. So she had gone off with the fellow, had spent the night with him somewhere! The thing was true; there was no good trying to shut one's eyes to it any longer. A dozen tiny incidents recurred to him, each magnified a hundredfold, together bearing incontrovertible evidence against Esther. What a good thing he had found her out in time! He ought to be thankful. Why wasn't he thankful? He was only furious, sick at heart, utterly miserable . . .

He must have sat for an hour on the side of his bed, huddled in his dressing-gown, shivering and moistening his dry lips. He was like that when Thérèse came in to inquire how he was feeling. He saw her face alter as she caught sight of him, and he dully surmised that he must look pretty queer. He submitted without protest when she urged him to get back into bed.

"Is anything the matter?" she inquired gently, smoothing the covers over him with her white, well-manicured hands.

"I'm devilish thirsty," he told her with a laugh.

"Ah, I will get you some water!" she cried quickly, and going into the bathroom brought him a bottle of Evian water and a glass. He drank greedily, finished what was left in the bottle.

"You'd like some more, wouldn't you?" he heard her say, and started to utter a protest, but she was already gone. He hated to have Thérèse waiting on him; but if she would she would, he couldn't stop her. She was trying to be decent; after all, he mustn't behave like a bear.

She was back almost at once with a full bottle of mineral water, and he drank another glassful thirstily.

"I really think, my dear, we shall have to have a nurse for you," she remarked softly, studying his face.

"Nurse!" he exclaimed, starting up in a rage. "No, I won't have a nurse. I tell you it's no good. I'm not going to be ill—but if I am I'm going to . . ."

When it came to the point he couldn't bring himself to mention the nursing-home idea. In the face of Thérèse's kindness it seemed so ungrateful. He lay back and closed his eyes with a frown, conscious that she was watching him curiously.

"Thérèse," he said after a pause, "I suppose you haven't had any word from Arthur Holliday, have you?"

"From Arthur? But yes, certainly; he telephoned me a little while ago."

Roger sat up again, galvanising into life.

"He telephoned you? What did he say? About Miss Rowe, I mean."

"I asked him. He said after they left here he had a breakdown; I forgot what he said went wrong. The nurse was in a hurry, so he got her a taxi, put her into it with her luggage, and she drove off. That's all he knows."

"Oh! Did he happen to mention why he didn't go back to his hotel last night?"

She smiled shrewdly, as if she guessed his thoughts.

"Yes; he said he dined at the Casino with a man he ran into, took a bank at baccarat, and as he was winning he didn't like to leave off until the room closed. After that he went to a Turkish bath."

It furnished an excellent, complete alibi, if one could believe it.

After all, why not? It could easily be true.

"He's catching the night train back to Paris," she went on. "He only came for the funeral. You know he was so fond of poor Charles."

"So he's going to South America, after all," mused Roger. "I thought he'd given it up."

"Why should you think that?" she demanded quickly. "He must do something to make a living."

He was not listening, his thoughts busy again with the question of why, if Esther had not gone off with Holliday, she had failed to communicate with him? In one way he felt slightly relieved, yet the business was as mysterious as ever.

"Roger," Thérèse said suddenly, sitting down on the side of the bed, "I believe you are still worrying about that nurse. Isn't that so?"

He was silent, unwilling to discuss the matter with Thérèse. Yet, in spite of himself, something in her tone made him look at her attentively.

"If I were you," she continued slowly, "I shouldn't think too much about her. I feel I ought to tell you that."

His eyes flashed at her a belligerent glance.

"Just what do you mean by that?" he demanded.

"I hadn't meant to tell you," she went on with slight hesitation. "But you know I had a reason for sending her away yesterday. If it hadn't been for the fact that your father seemed to like her so much the doctor would have made a change some little time ago. He wasn't altogether . . . pleased with her."

"Pleased with her! What are you getting at?"

"Roger, don't upset yourself; lie down quietly, or I won't tell you."

"Very well, I'm perfectly quiet; now tell me. This is something I want to hear. What did he think was wrong about Miss Rowe?"

The hardness in his voice was a challenge. Thérèse examined the nails of her right hand and lightly polished them on the palm of her left. Then she replied carefully:

"Well, you know soon after she came here she began to behave just a little oddly at times. At first the doctor did not think it serious, but towards the end he was afraid that she was a little—a little—"

"A little what?"

"Well—unbalanced. Have you ever heard of anyone having 'confusional attacks'?"

"I don't know. Yes, perhaps. What about it?"

"That is what the doctor thinks she has."

"Utter rubbish! Miss Rowe is one of the most normal people I have ever known."

"So she impressed me, at least most of the time. Indeed the doctor says that a person who has those attacks may be quite normal part of the time, only sometimes they get strange ideas into their heads and behave queerly. That was what Miss Rowe was doing. It didn't seem altogether wise to have her here."

There was an ominous glitter in the ill man's eyes, the muscles in his cheeks twitched as his lips tightened.

"What do you mean by 'not altogether wise'?" he inquired coldly.

"I see you don't believe me, Roger. I don't suppose you noticed anything wrong with her. I don't know that I should have done so, if the doctor hadn't told me certain things. But the fact is, she wasn't always quite to be trusted in emergencies. She was a little—what do you call it?—erratic, that's the word. The doctor is even convinced that she was largely responsible for your father's relapse. There! I had not meant to speak of it!"

"That at least is a lie, a barefaced attempt to injure her!" cried Roger, unable to bear any more.

"My dear! How can you!" murmured Thérèse so incredulously that he felt slightly ashamed.

"I don't say you invented it, Thérèse, but it's a lie for all that."

"I heard, too, from Dido about her sending you an excited message and then going off without seeing you," continued his stepmother calmly. "That is quite typical behaviour, so the doctor says. It is just the sort of thing she would do; it is really a mild mental case."

He made a gesture of weariness, suddenly feeling he must get rid of her.

"It may all be true, Thérèse; I'm sure I don't know. At any rate I think I'll try to get a nap, if you'll leave me. I didn't sleep well last night."

"Of course, dear! Thank Heaven you are going to be sensible. Perhaps, too, you'll let the doctor advise you about that anti-toxin? I should, if I were you."

"Yes, I'll let him talk to me, if you like."

Anything to get rid of her, he thought. He kept his eyes tight closed until she was well out of the room and the door shut behind her. Then he sprang out of bed and with trembling haste put on his clothes. When he was completely dressed he rang for Chalmers and demanded a taxi.

"But you're not going out, Mr. Roger! I don't know what the doctor or your aunt will say, sir!"

"Look here, Chalmers, you're not going to mention this to anyone, do you hear? I'm absolutely all right; I know what I'm about. Just you get me that taxi and be quick about it."

Five minutes later he slipped quietly out of the house and with a whirling head fell into the waiting taxi. He might or might not be doing a foolish thing, but no matter what happened he intended to scour Cannes in search of Esther.

CHAPTER XXVIII

OUT of what seemed a long dark night, filled with shapeless images, Esther woke at last. She believed herself in her comfortable bed at the Villa Firenze, and for a brief moment she wondered at the hardness of the mattress beneath her. Next she was aware that her head throbbed dully and that her mouth felt dry and harsh. She swallowed several times. Was she ill? Had anything happened? Then followed the discovery that she was fully dressed, even to her coat and shoes. How could that be? It was vaguely disquieting.

She opened her eyes wider and let them roam slowly around. The light was failing; it was almost dusk. She saw on one side of her, close, a bare, blank wall, on the other a wide opening, more than a doorway, hung at the sides with heavy, dusty curtains of a dingy red material. The curtains looked familiar. Where had she seen them before? She lay perfectly motionless, pondering the matter idly, not deeply interested. All at once it came to her: they were the portières of the doctor's laboratory; she was in the alcove of the room; this bed that felt so hard and unyielding was Sartorius's bed. . . .

Instantly memory flooded back upon her in a vast wave. She sat up, sick with terror, and clapped her hand over her mouth to keep from screaming aloud. Her hand itself trembled, her whole body shook as though with ague, but she made no sound. Instead she leaned against the wall for support and with her heart beating like a trip-hammer continued to stare about her, listening acutely. All around was dead stillness; she could hear nothing except the steady drip-drip of water from a leaky tap. The room was empty but for herself, perhaps there was no one in the whole house. Beside her was an old bedside table with two or three dusty paper-bound books on it. Through the curtains she could just see the end of the long work-table and one of the cupboards.

The time puzzled her. It had just been getting dark when she last remembered anything; it was getting dark now. Yet surely she had been here more than, say, half an hour? She thought of her wrist-watch. It had stopped, the hands pointing to a quarter to one. That meant it had run down, for she had wound it at a quarter to one—was it yesterday? How could she tell? She caught herself yawning heavily, overcome with fatigue and drowsiness. The one thing she instinctively desired with her whole being was to lie down again and drift off to sleep.

"Good God, I can't do that!" she muttered, shaking herself. "I've got to think, to think hard. I've got to find a way out of this!"

There was no doubt in her mind as to why she was here. She was dangerous to the doctor; she possessed information which would ruin him. He had overheard her conversation on the telephone; more than that he had probably received and opened the chemist's report when it came to the villa. Without doubt he had had something of this sort in mind when he came and suggested driving her to her pension. He hadn't meant to let her out of his sight; he had even inquired about what friends she had to ascertain whether there was much danger of her being traced. He had meant to get her alone in his car, then stupefy her in some way and bring her here. Her telephoning to the chemist had precipitated matters, made him take a desperate chance and act quickly. At least that was how she construed things. How he had managed to get her out and into his car was a mystery. She had just sent that message to Roger, she recalled. Two minutes, one minute's delay, and the bold plan would have miscarried. Would they miss her at the villa—Miss Clifford or Roger? With a sinking heart she knew they were not likely to for some days. She had said good-bye to the former. Roger indeed might think it a little odd, her sending for him and then going away, but he would hardly imagine anything seriously wrong. No, there was no chance at all of her being sought for, at any rate not here. No one would ever think of looking here.

How had she lost consciousness so completely, so instantaneously? Ah, of course! That stab in her arm, it had been the wound of a hypodermic needle, that weapon she now so closely associated with the doctor. Her arm felt sore to the touch, a spot near the shoulder. She had been doped, kept stupefied—she had no idea for how long. What a risk the man had taken! That proved conclusively how much he feared her. She knew him for a murderer, she alone. His own life was in peril, as well as all his hopes for reaping the benefit of his crime, as long as she was free to tell what she knew. There was no one but herself to give him away, no one else to say how he had cold-bloodedly done away with one victim and now was laying a trap for another one . . . for Roger. . . .

Roger! As the thought struck her she almost leapt to her feet in consternation. He was in danger now; he had no suspicion to protect him. Unless he held firm against that anti-toxin he was already doomed. How could she tell if they had already overcome his prejudice? Perhaps he had by now had the injections, one, two even. If he had, nothing could save him, she knew that. Her heart grew cold with fear.

Still, there was a loophole of hope. He had distinctly assured her he had made up his mind against the anti-toxin. If only he could be depended upon to remain obstinate! The danger was that he might at any moment yield to the persuasions of his aunt. He hated to distress her needlessly. After all, his resistance was only a caprice; it could not be depended on as a safeguard. It came to her with dreadful certainty that there was no one who could warn him but herself—and she was a prisoner, several miles away. For the moment her own possible fate scarcely concerned her at all. It was the thought of Roger's position which drove her nearly frantic, impelled her to rise with tottering, cautious steps and investigate her prison.

She crept, trembling, to the door and tried the handle. It was locked, of course; she had known it would be. She clung to the knob and looked around. The room, built for a studio, had no window, only a sloping skylight, which was firmly fastened. The atmosphere was close, that of a room long shut up, flavoured with tobacco-smoke and the clean, pungent odour of carbolic. Dust lay on the furniture, but here and there it was disturbed in streaks, showing that someone had been there recently. She wondered if she was all alone in the house. She remembered that Jacques was away on holiday. Yet it scarcely seemed likely that Sartorius would care to risk leaving her completely unguarded. Again she listened, leaning against the door, conscious of extreme weakness and trying hard to keep her teeth from chattering. No sound whatever came from the rooms below; the silence somewhat reassured her. She resolved at once to see if there was any possible way of escaping. Yet as she left the door and took a cautious step towards the centre of the room, perspiration broke out all over her body and ran in streams down her back, her limbs, her face. She felt her knees give under her. Whether all this was due to pure weakness or in part to fright she could not tell, but it occurred to her as possible that she had been here several days without food and repeatedly drugged. How she came to be conscious now caused her a fleeting wonder.

If only there were a telephone in the room—but the one instrument was on the ground-floor. There seemed no possible means of communication with the outside world. She could scream, of course, but that would only serve to alarm anyone who happened to be in the house, or even if the house was empty she could scarcely hope that her voice would be heard far below in the street. The one chance that suggested itself to her was the skylight. It seemed just faintly possible that she might be able to get through it and somehow down to the ground. It presented decided elements of danger, undoubtedly, but there was no choice. She knew too well what it would mean if she stayed here. No, it was the skylight or nothing; she must think how the attempt could be managed.

Clutching on to the back of a chair for support, she eyed the sloping glass above her and made certain rough calculations. If she mounted upon a chair placed on the table she might fairly easily unfasten the big central group of panes, which was the part that opened outward. She even thought she could contrive to climb up to the opening and get outside, but after that came the rub. She would have to slide off the side of the roof and drop to the ground, and common sense told here there was not a chance of her reaching the ground without a broken leg or arm, even if she was not killed outright. The distance was too great; there was nothing to break her fall. There was no use whatever in getting outside the house if she was going to be too disabled to go farther. She must try to find something she could turn into a sort of rope to cling to. Her eyes sought rapidly about and fell upon the long red curtains. The stuff seemed thick and strong; she could perhaps tear them up into strips, knot the lengths together and so make something that would serve for part of the distance, at any rate. If it didn't reach to the ground, she must chance it. She would have to be quick about it, too, for something warned her she was not likely to be left very long alone. Indeed, she was sure within her that the doctor had meant for her to remain unconscious, never wake up again. The idea filled her with a sickening horror, so that she had to set her teeth hard together to stop their chattering.

Standing upon the chair she began with shaking fingers and as hurriedly as she could to undo the rusted curtain-hooks from their big wooden rings. She had managed only the first one when a sound from the street below made her stop and listen, petrified. A car had stopped. She waited, breathless, and an instant later heard the loud bang of the street door. Like a flash she was down again on the floor, and in one panic-stricken movement had slithered back on the camp-bed and drawn up the army blanket over her, as it had been when she came to. As far as she could remember it she arranged herself in her former position, half turned towards the wall on her right side. Thank Heaven it was darker now. She recalled with gratitude the fact that there was no electric fixture in the alcove. If anyone came, she must do her utmost to appear unconscious, and trust to the sheltering gloom to aid her in the deception.

She waited and waited. Long minutes went by; it might have been half an hour, but it was probably not nearly so long. Her body began to be so cramped she felt she must move or die; moreover, it was some time before her heart ceased beating so violently as to lift the blanket. At last when she thought she could bear no more the footsteps of two persons mounted the steps to the laboratory. The key grated in the lock of the door. With an inward desperate prayer she closed her eyes and relaxed the muscles of her face, just as the door swung open and the light flashed in her face from the larger part of the room. It was only a dim light in here, though. She knew that the lamp, a high-powered one with a green shade, shed its rays straight down on the work-table.

Heavy steps at once crossed the floor and paused beside her. She heard the doctor's breathing as he bent over her, she smelled the tobacco odour of his clothing, and felt her cheek burn as though seared beneath his scrutiny. Presently he spoke, in her ear, it seemed.

"I suppose you gave her the injection at the time I told you to?"

"Oh, God, yes; I gave it to her all right!"

Esther experienced a sharp shock. The second voice was that of Captain Holliday. How on earth did he come into this? Or had he been in it from the first? Somehow from his tone of frightened tension she thought he had not, yet she could not imagine what he was doing here now. Instinctively she knew that the doctor was still studying her closely, and she felt that if he kept it up much longer she would give herself away. Already she feared that in some way she had betrayed her astonishment of a moment ago. Had he noticed anything? She was ignorant of how to simulate a drugged sleep; she might be doing it all wrong.

Suddenly, without the least warning, she felt a cruel pinch on her shoulder. The doctor, to satisfy himself, had resorted to this crude but effectual method of finding out if she was quite unconscious or not. At least it might easily have proved effectual, only Providence intervened. She never knew how it was she did not shriek aloud, but instead managed to remain perfectly quiescent, unresisting. A second later she had her reward. She heard the huge man move away, his step creaking across the bare boards out into the main room. She breathed again, and listened.

For about two minutes there was silence, then Holliday spoke, bursting out with a sort of defiance that had terror in it, she thought.

"See here, Sartorius, I'm going to clear out. I've had enough. I didn't know what I was letting myself in for the other day, or I wouldn't have helped you out."

"You'll stay here."

This bald statement, uttered with peculiar emphasis, caused a shudder to run through Esther. There was something ominous in it, crushing. The young man may have thought so too, to judge by the nervous, uncertain fashion in which he strove to combat the command.

"The hell I shall! Who'll keep me if I want to go?"

There was no response, and after a second Holliday continued argumentatively:

"You know I've had nothing to do with this business—nothing! It's true I told Thérèse, long ago, the things that people said about you in Algeria. I never knew if they were true or not; I didn't want to know. It was nothing to me how you got money to live on. You saved my life, that was enough for me. Good God, the past few days must prove I'm not ungrateful! Still, there's a limit to everything, and this thing's too damned risky for me; I don't want anything to do with it."

"Listen to me."

The doctor's voice was level, his words dropping like a heavy weight across the young man's nervous protest.

"Well, I'm listening."

"You appear to have got the idea that you are sacrificing yourself for me. That is not quite true. By doing as I tell you and remaining here you are saving yourself."

"How do you make that out?"

"It is perfectly simple. You realise of course that that woman in there is the only person who has the knowledge necessary to bring a charge; no one else has even a slight suspicion. Therefore it is hardly worth while to emphasise the reasons for keeping watch over her closely until such time as I am able to dispose of her satisfactorily. These things take time and thought. One can't rush into them without running risks."

A shiver shook Esther from head to foot. She knew now, if she had had any doubts before, what was going to happen to her. The cold-blooded statement had an effect on Holliday also, for his voice sounded high-pitched and oddly rough as he replied:

"I suppose one has to admit all that, but why in hell's name have I got to be her jailor? If she's unconscious, why can't she be left alone?"

"Simply because I refuse to take the risk. There is no knowing what might happen; one can't be sure of anything."

There followed the scratch of a match and the smell of cigarette smoke; then, as if reading his friend's thoughts, Sartorius continued:

"And in case you have any secret intention of giving me the slip, just bear this in mind: If the detention of this girl ever comes out, the fat will be in the fire, for you just as much as for me. Dead or alive, it will make little difference; you are bound to be implicated. How good a chance do you think you'd have of proving your innocence? You'd be held as an accessory both before and after the act, if you were lucky enough to escape a more serious charge. You are in it now; it's to your own interest to help me by staying in it."

"Good God!" groaned the young man, as though caught in a trap.

"I thought you'd see my point. You know me. You I never exaggerate."

"But is it essential to get rid of the girl entirely?" Holliday asked in a jerky fashion. "Isn't there any other means of keeping her quiet?"

"Oh, yes, but nothing that can really be depended on. I could, of course, by means of a simple operation, destroy certain areas in the brain which would deprive her of memory and speech, but these faculties sometimes have a tiresome tendency to restore themselves or to delegate their functions to other areas. No, there is only one safe plan, and even that wants thinking out. There must be no trace left."

"God!" exploded Holliday weakly, yet with a kind of loathing. "Why don't I go straight to the police and give the whole show away? I've half a mind to."

"Oh, no, I think you won't do that. There is too good a reason for not giving the show away, as you call it."

"What reason do you mean?"

"If you did go to the police you would deprive yourself of a large fortune. By sitting tight and saying nothing you will quite soon be able to marry Lady Clifford. In the circumstances, you will hardly persist in attaching a purely fictitious value to two insignificant lives."

"Two!" gasped the younger man in a whisper. "Then you really mean to go on with Clifford?"

"I have no choice in the matter; it has become imperative to remove him. Since his father appointed him trustee of the estate, Lady Clifford is powerless to draw any large sums of money without his knowledge and consent. Consequently she would not be able to remunerate me for my services to her with regard to her husband."

"You mean it would rouse his suspicions if she kept paying out money to you?"

"Exactly. Of course to take on another case was more than I bargained for, but the thing was practically forced on me. It was Lady Clifford herself who began it without consulting me. She had kept back some of the typhoid culture, having sworn to me that she had thrown it all away. She started putting it into his bottled mineral water—she would keep the water a day or two in her own dressing-room, then carry it into his room and exchange it for the bottle that was there already. A fool's game—at any moment she might have been caught at it. However, there you are, she took the risk, then came to me and told me what she had done and why."

"I see. Then you only have to leave Clifford alone and let the disease take its course, I suppose?"

"Not at all. Typhoid, artificially given, seldom is severe enough to kill, particularly in the case of a young and vigorous subject. No, we should have to find some excuse for administering the pure toxin. It would do the trick at once, and without the least fear of detection. However, that is my difficulty; the man refuses utterly to submit to any sort of injection. Idiotic prejudices!"

Esther's heart gave a leap. Roger was still safe; he had not given in. She was so relieved that for the moment she almost forgot her own situation. The doctor continued thoughtfully:

"He is not sufficiently ill to be given anything without his consent, and as things are I daren't press him too much; he might think it peculiar. . . . No, it is no good; there has got to be some other way, something altogether different. Quickly too. To postpone it now would be the greatest risk of all. . . . It would have been very natural to have two members of a family fall ill with the same disease, but it can't be helped now. I happen to have some stuff here which will accomplish my purpose just as satisfactorily. That's why I came back this afternoon; I don't want to waste any time."

Esther's brief elation vanished like a bubble into the air. Some fresh horror was afoot. What was this man plotting now? She held her breath and listened painfully. She heard the doors of the oak armoire creak on their hinges as they swung open, then came the click of a glass jar. Holliday spoke, a tinge of fascinated curiosity in his tone.

"What sort of stuff do you mean? Not any kind of poison?"

"Good Lord, no! That would be asking for trouble. This must be a natural death; there's no good attempting anything else. Here's the thing I propose to use."

"What is it? It looks harmless."

"Simply tetanus."

She thought that her heart entirely stopped beating. Tetanus! Gripped by a sickening fear she forced herself to lie quite still, while waves of horror passed over. She heard as in a dream the stifled ejaculation of the young man.

"Tetanus . . . why, God in heaven, that's lock-jaw!"

"Quite. The anti-toxin for it has been discovered, as a matter of fact. I have discovered it. However, that is not known to the public yet; it was very recent."

There was the sound of a long-drawn, shuddering gasp.

"But how do you mean to . . . won't it be dangerous?" Holliday faltered.

"As it happens it is quite simple—a piece of luck. In fact that is why I thought of tetanus. It seems Clifford has been going about for nearly a week with an open cut on his thumb. Half the time there's no bandage on it, although I've warned him more than once of the risk of infection. This morning his aunt persuaded him to let me disinfect it properly and bandage it. So that is what I am going to do when I get back this evening."

There was a choking sound, as if Holliday were in danger of being sick.

A chair scraped on the floor; there was the clink of glass.

"Here, pull yourself together; this will fix you. Sit there. . . . I did not know you were so sensitive."

A gulp, followed by another shuddering sound. Then, weakly, with a sort of loathing, "I don't know. I never liked the fellow . . . but this . . . Besides, it's damned risky; you can't pretend it isn't."

"Why? Think of it calmly. Who can prove how he got the infection? It's a thing that can never be proved, one way or the other. Everyone knows he's laid himself open to it, that I have warned him. . . . No, no. You will see. As for any other feeling you may have, you must settle with your own squeamishness; that is no concern of mine."

There was a short pause, while upon her hard couch Esther set her teeth together and clenched her hands with all her remaining strength. She wondered if she was going to faint. She felt she must listen, listen, not miss one word. Like something in a nightmare the cold, phlegmatic voice continued slowly:

"I look upon things as they are, simply, without prejudice. With all life, human or otherwise, one creature preys upon another. One has to decide, Am I worth the sacrifice of another human being? I do not know that I should consider you worth it, my good friend, to be quite frank, but in my own case I venture to think that I am. Having made my mind clear on this point, I go ahead, merely observing certain precautions which will be necessary as long as the exceptional individual is so far in advance of the mass. I do not hesitate to declare that the work I can do for science is worth many hundreds—or shall I say thousands?—of Cliffords, young and old. To think for one moment of putting my labours for the next twenty years in the balance against a couple of cotton-manufacturers is ludicrous, that is all."

"Ha, ha, ha, ha! Yes, if you look at it that way, I suppose it's a devil of a joke!"

Holliday was becoming hysterical.

"Also one must not lose sight of the fact that when the young one is out of the way, you and I will both benefit considerably more than we first expected. Lady Clifford will inherit three to four times as much. I look forward to being quite unhampered; I shall be able to devote myself to research for the rest of my life."

Somewhere far below a clock struck a single mellow clang. It was the same clock that had ticked so loudly that day when Esther first came to the house. She could see it now, its wide white face crossed by its thin hands of decorated bronze.

"Six-thirty. I must be off to catch Clifford when he gets home. The imbecile has been out and about the town for two days with a temperature of over a hundred and one—searching everywhere for this girl. I believe he was going to the police to-day. That is another reason for not losing time. There is little likelihood of anyone's coming here, but one never knows."

In the midst of her almost paralysing fear a thrill shot through Esther when she heard that Roger was concerned over her disappearance. Then it had mattered to him when she didn't telephone! She also knew now how long she had been here. If only these two would go, would leave her alone, she might possibly be able to carry out her plan of escape; she would risk it, anyway, desperate though it seemed. Once she got clear of the house she could find a telephone and ring Roger up. That would be sufficient. If only they would go! Why were they still lingering here?

At last the floor creaked with the heavy tread. A wild hope rose in her breast. A second later and it perished miserably, as she heard the doctor say:

"I'll just give her another shot before I leave. Then she'll be safe for some time. Where is the syringe?"

"Here, on the table."

A silence, then Sartorius's voice, reflectively:

"Humph, you didn't give her quite all of it, did you? There's a bit left."

That, perhaps, explained her being conscious now. What an irony! To think that Holliday's inexpertness should have brought about the agony of the past half-hour! But for him she would have remained in peaceful oblivion, out of which she would have passed imperceptibly to her final sleep. These terrible moments were her last glimpses of life. In a few seconds would come utter blankness again; her last chance would be gone for saving Roger and herself. Should she make a struggle for it and die fighting? Or was it better to continue her supine pretence and quietly allow the needle to reduce her once more to a merciful torpor?

"Hand me that tumbler, will you?"

Water splashed from the tap into the basin. She could have burst out laughing at the precise habits of the man which remained with him now when they mattered not at all. She could almost see him wash the needle, could follow every movement up to the setting down of the glass beside her on the little *table de nuit.*

It was coming, now, the stab that marked the end of conscious life, the ruin of her one hope of rescuing the man she loved from a horrible death. It was all over now. . . . She felt the doctor's breath stir her hair, she smelled again the hot odour of strong tobacco, was conscious of the wave of animal heat emanating from his body as he bent over her. Now . . . her lovely chestnut-coloured blouse must be peppered with holes. What a pity! . . . not that it mattered now—how absurd to think of that! . . .

CHAPTER XXIX

WHAT sound was that? The noise of ringing. Was it within her own brain? No, surely not; it was the bell downstairs, a loud, persistent peal. Not the telephone; no, it must be the front-door bell.

An annoyed exclamation came from the doctor.

"I'll have to answer that; it won't do to leave it."

A little click as the needle was laid down, then the retreating steps of both men, out of the room. The door closed, the key turned mechanically. She could hear the doctor's heavy steps lumbering all the way down to the bottom floor, while she fancied Holliday remained on the stairs. Was this a providential respite, or only another tantalising false hope?

Cautiously she opened her eyes and moved her cramped limbs a little. What difference could it make now if they knew she had been awake? On the table at her side she saw the hypodermic syringe, fully charged, lying beside a glass of water. She stared at them fascinated.

Suddenly an idea came to her, the wildest idea conceivable, not one chance in a million of its succeeding, yet now, in the face of extinction, anything was worth trying. She had nothing to lose. Quick as lightning she seized the needle, squirted its contents on the floor back of the bed, then with the same speed refilled it from the tumbler. She laid it down again exactly where it had been before, looked to see that there were no drops spilled. Then once more she lay down, trying with meticulous care to resume her old posture. Was this right? No, her head must have been a little lower. Oh, what hope was there of deceiving those keen little python's eyes? The man would surely detect the smallest variation in her attitude. No, it was a pathetic ruse, foredoomed to failure. If he suspected she had moved he would examine the needle, he would see the difference in colour. Her one hope lay in the gloom of the alcove. A few minutes more and she would know the worst.

She lay still and counted to keep from going mad. One, two, three, four, five—slowly, more slowly still, so as to make sixty counts equal a minute. One never could do that, one always went too fast. She had counted three sixties when the front door closed below and returning footsteps mounted the stairs. One flight, two flights . . . the key rasped, the boards creaked, she heard Sartorius saying:

"You see now, that is the sort of thing one must be prepared for. Suppose no one had been here? Those asses would have gone back to the agent's and got a key, or else some fellow from the office would have come back with them to show them the house. Just the same, I want you to telephone the estate office that I've changed my mind about sub-letting."

He was now at her side. Would he notice anything wrong?

"She's about to come to. I thought that dose wouldn't last long."

She heard him pick up the needle. Now . . . what was happening? Was he examining it? . . . An agonising pain in her upper arm reassured her. She was prepared for it to hurt worse than an ordinary injection, plain water did. She bore the torture without a quiver, holding her breath until she heard the doctor move away.

Suddenly Holliday burst out again with an edge of nervous apprehension in his voice.

"See here, Sartorius. What about that chemist? He knows. What if he goes to the police?"

The doctor gave a disparaging grunt.

"What does he know? Merely that an American nurse brought him a needle to be analysed and gave the Villa Firenze as her address. Very likely he would never think of doing anything; it is no business of his. But if he did, what could he prove? Why, nothing at all. There is no evidence whatever. If this thing ever got into court, I could suggest that the woman was mentally unbalanced, suffering from the delusions which cause intent to injure. I can prove that the nurse had access to the laboratory; it would be easy to make a jury believe that she put the toxin in the syringe herself, with the insane idea of making trouble for me. If she's not to be found, I should not have much difficulty in getting away with that theory. But it will never come to that."

"You seem devilish sure, but all the same—"

"Rubbish—if both Clifford and the girl are dead, who remains to bring a charge? Assuming the worst, I do not know that I'd have much to fear from a French jury with Thérèse Clifford facing them. No, the girl here is our one weak spot, and by the day after to-morrow at the latest I expect to be able to deal with her. No good rushing the business, though—it's fools who get into trouble because they won't lay their plans carefully."

The indescribably casual manner in which he referred to his coming crimes struck a chill to the listener's bones. He had apparently allowed for everything; any possible effort she might make to escape from his clutches seemed vain and bootless. She would have lost heart entirely, only there was the knowledge within her that on one point at least she had succeeded in foiling him.

"Give me that smallest phial from the rack, will you? I shall want only the merest trace of this. The rest can go down the drain."

The tap ran again; Esther knew that he was methodically washing out the bottle that contained the deadly culture. Another hour, perhaps less, and no power could save Roger from a torturing death, not even the certainty of what had caused it. Once an invisible touch of the villainous stuff penetrated the raw tissues of the wound, it would work its way straight into the blood-stream. Soon, very soon afterwards the jaw muscles would begin to stiffen. . . . Oh, if there were any sort of weapon in reach, knife, pistol, anything! She knew she would have thrown herself, weak as she was, upon that insensate, deliberate machine in the furious attempt to wreck it, careless of what might happen to herself.

"Come, I have no time to lose. Lock the door behind you."

The light was switched off, the door closed, she was alone once more, this time in almost complete darkness. Again she strained her ears upon the retreating steps, afraid yet to move her cramped muscles. The punctured arm throbbed and smarted painfully; every nerve in her body was stretched like a fiddle-string. Finally, far below, sounded the door's slam; a moment later, in front of the house, the whir of a starting engine vibrated upon the still air. The doctor was gone. Now or never, quick, not an instant to waste, every second lost lessened her slender chance of reaching the villa in time, even by telephone. Her plan was laid, she had no need of further deliberation.

First, crossing the floor on tip-toe, she turned on the light. She was afraid to do this, but it was necessary, and the chances were that Holliday could not spy the tell-tale crack of light that would show under the door without coming to the enclosed well of the staircase. Next she climbed upon her chair again and unpinned the curtains. Her fingers shook uncontrollably; never in her life had she known such a devastating weakness—at a time, too, when she needed far more than her normal strength! Towards the end of her task it was as much as she could do to keep from sliding off the chair into a heap on the floor. When the curtains lay in a dusty pile she was forced to rest a moment on top of them before attempting to continue. Her condition frightened her. At this rate she would not get far.

Wasn't there a brandy-bottle somewhere? Surely she had heard the doctor give Holliday something to drink. Rising cautiously, she looked about and discovered it on the long table, uncorked it, drank from the bottle. Only two fiery mouthfuls, however. She dared not take more in her present state of weakness and emptiness. The drink warmed her slightly, gave her back just enough strength to go on. Her project began to look less hopeless.

She found a knife and slit the tough fabric into strips, five lengths each, then tied the ends together, tightening the knots as well as she could. She had little idea of how far the improvised rope would reach, but it seemed fairly long when it was done. She began to think it would mean everything to get outside the house, whether she was injured or not. She had at least the chance of attracting some passer-by's attention before Holliday could discover she was gone and drag her back to her prison. Gathering up her load of rope she listened again. No sound whatever save the drip-drip of the tap in the corner. Laboriously she climbed to the top of the table, pulled the nearest chair up after her, planted it firmly beside her. Then she examined the skylight once more, deciding that if it were open she could manage to get her body through the central section, provided she had the strength to hoist herself up that high.

With infinite caution she undid the hasp and pushed open the casement, terrified lest the rusty, scrunching sound should penetrate to the lower floors. She shot out the iron rod to its full extent and fastened it, then started to search for something to which she could secure the end of her rope. There was a wooden shelf against the wall supported by iron brackets. Perhaps one of these brackets would serve, though she was afraid that her weight pulling suddenly upon it would tear out the screws from the plaster. There was nothing else close enough; she must trust to its holding firm. She made fast the rope's end, then with haste, but noiselessly began removing the row of bottles from the shelf and setting them down on the table beneath. She must get them out of the way for it would be necessary for her to step upon the shelf in order to climb up to the opening, there being nowhere else to set her foot. Five, six, seven bottles she put down. The eighth, a small one, had an uneven bottom. Before she knew what had happened it overbalanced, rolling over and over towards the table's edge. She tried to stop it, but could not reach it in time. Before her agonised eyes it fell to the floor with a loud, clear "ping."

Her heart in her mouth, she stood for one petrified moment rooted to the spot. Would Holliday hear? The answer came immediately. There was a sudden, loud clatter of footsteps, leaping headlong towards the laboratory stairs, charging full upon her. Like a flash it came to her that, discovered or not, she must get out of the skylight now, now, or it would be too late, she must stop for nothing. She mounted her chair, hurled the rope from the opening, and had just set foot upon the shelf ready for the final hoist when the door burst open and Holliday, wild-eyed, confronted her.

"Stop!"

There was a revolver in his hand, but she took no account of that. Urged by terror she strained with every ounce of force in her body to draw herself up to the skylight. The single glimpse she had of the young man's face showed it to be pale with anger and fright, the eyes glaring, the mouth parted to show snarling teeth. He raised his arm full-length, the revolver glittered in the greenish light.

"Drop it, damn you!"

He made a sort of rush at her, grabbing at the chair.

"Keep away!"

With both hands she seized the only available object, a huge jar which remained upon the shelf, lifted it on high, aimed it at his head. Simultaneously a revolver shot deafened her and choked her with smoke, there was a crash and falling glass splintered in a rain. The room was plunged in darkness. Half dazed, she still realised that amid the confusion she had completed her intention, had with a terrific effort launched the big jar as she had meant to do. Smothered curses followed and a second, duller smash, then, though she could see nothing, she smelled the strong, acrid fumes of ammonia rising, mingling with the stench of the powder. Had she hit him? She must not stop to inquire. During the ensuing instant of silence she tugged at the ledge above with a fresh, despairing effort, dragged herself up to the brink, felt the pure night air upon her face. The next second, clutching her rope in a mad grip, she let herself go, hurtling head first, then feet first, down the tiled slope of the roof, then into space over the sheer drop of the house's side.

Bumping, thumping, scraping her knuckles and shins, somehow, anyhow, down she slid, reached the end of the swaying rope, hung for one frightful moment kicking in mid-air, then dropped, plunk, like a lead in water. She landed, shaken and stunned, but not injured, upon the damp soft earth of a flower-bed. The rope dangled above her, only a few feet away. For a whirling space she feared she was going to faint, and with her whole will she fought off the engulfing fog, knowing she must not stay here a minute. She was out of the house, true, but still in imminent peril. At any moment Holliday might dash out and seize her, and as she was now she had no resistance whatever, scarcely power to scream.

Even as this thought matured in her brain, there came from within the walls the drunken sound of steps careering down the upper flight of stairs. Holliday! He might be slightly stunned, but he was recovered sufficiently to come in pursuit. A second and he would reach the door, only a few yards away from where she huddled. Quick—where could she hide?

Struggling to her feet she staggered across the little strip of garden and out the gate. If only there were someone in sight, anyone she could appeal to for protection! But no, for once the Route de Grasse stretched for a hundred yards in both directions empty as a desert. Turning blindly to the left she ran crazily, swaying from weakness, past the next two villas. At the gate of the third house she stopped, afraid to venture farther. Inside the garden a low, square-cut hedge offered a hope of shelter, if she could reach it in time. Already behind her she heard the doctor's door flung open, saw a bar of light stream into the dark street.

Like a shot partridge she dropped to the ground and wormed her way on her stomach through the gateway into the shadow of the hedge, crept close, lay still, afraid to breathe. Less than twenty yards away loud steps resounded on the flagstones. They came in her direction.

CHAPTER XXX

FOR a short space Esther believed herself lost. If Holliday found her, which seemed almost inevitable, she knew she would be powerless to put up a defence. It would be a simple matter for him to gag her and drag her back over the few yards of intervening side-walk before anyone could know what was happening. It was not as though there were many people about. She had never seen the street so deserted. An occasional motor passed, but she could detect no footstep save that of the man pursuing her.

She rolled over and lay prone on the damp mould, as close under the hedge as she could squeeze. The hedge itself was barely four feet high, but it presented a certain amount of cover now that it had gone dark. Perhaps if she knew in time that she had been discovered she might manage to dash to the door of the house and ring the bell violently. She gathered her strength for the attempt, then for the first time noticed a sign, "*À louer,*" across the front windows. The place was vacant.

Her one hope lay in remaining stock-still, trusting to the shadows to hide her. This she did, and listening heard Holliday run around the side of the doctor's villa to the spot where she had fallen, then back again and once more out into the street. Here he paused, and she could picture him reconnoitring in every direction. He would know that she could not have gone far, that she must be concealed within a short radius. Unless someone came along the street discovery was merely a matter of minutes.

Her head still ringing from the bumps she had recently received, she felt herself rapidly relaxing, in spite of her danger. The thought of complete abandonment to repose stole over her like a powerful narcotic. It would have been heavenly to let herself go, to fall asleep here or lapse into a faint; she didn't know which it would be. For several seconds she saw the dark garden through a veil of black gauze. Then a voice inside her brain roused her; she braced herself and set her teeth fiercely to dam back the treacherous tide that threatened to swamp her senses. Whatever happened, she must hold on a little longer; she must, she must! ... She heard Holliday go down the street in the opposite direction, stop, then after another minute return, more slowly, towards her hiding-place. Another two seconds and he would be on a line with her. Now, through a rift in the hedge she could see his feet, moving undecidedly. Oh, why did no one come? The feet came towards her more and more slowly. Why was he hanging about in that way? At last, at a distance of six feet away from her, he stopped altogether. She could no longer see him, but she felt his presence. She almost knew that he was silently peering through the wall of foliage, endeavouring to probe into the shadows. The suspense grew unbearable, she felt she must scream out, "Here I am! What are you going to do about me?"

Suddenly other steps approached, those of two or three people. She listened eagerly: then she heard voices talking in quite unintelligible French, interspersed with laughter. She visualised a group of returning workmen. Just opposite her one of them spat on the pavement and broke into a snatch of song. Hardly had they passed by when others came—the desert was populated once more. She felt a merciful degree of security. At any rate Holliday would not dare now to come and seize her, or even if he did she had a better chance of creating an effectual disturbance. But where was Holliday? Had he departed, or was he still standing there, searching for her? She could not tell, and she was afraid to move to see better. What seemed an infinitude of time went by; then at last, realising how late it was growing and that she must not waste the precious minutes, she raised her head and took a cautious look through an open patch in the leaves towards the doctor's door. A few minutes ago it had stood open, emitting a bar of yellow light. Now the place was in complete darkness. That argued that Holliday had gone back whence he had come.

Dare she rise to her feet and hasten on her way? She knew that she must dare; to stop here longer might easily be fatal to her project.

Yes, he was nowhere in sight, had apparently relinquished the pursuit. She did not stop to wonder why, or if he had anything up his sleeve. Instead she turned out of the gate to the side-walk, her clothing damp and clinging to her, her limbs trembling. She had passed one terror, but she was faced with a second almost as bad. Had the doctor already reached the Villa Firenze? Could she possibly contrive to forestall him? She must at once get to a telephone; it was her one chance.

A telephone—there must be one in this next villa; she would ring the bell and ask. With her knees giving under her at every step she hurried up the walk of a gingerbread pseudo-chalet, vilely prosperous-looking, and pressed her finger firmly on the electric button. There was a shrill peal, echoing throughout the house, but no one came. She rang again and yet again, holding her finger glued to the bell at last and stamping her feet with impatience. At last, after an endless interval, someone approached with a deliberate, shuffling tread, the door was unbarred— there seemed several bolts—and opened half-way to reveal a gim-crack interior in execrable taste and the figure of an old woman with a hard wrinkled face and grey hair smoothly banded under a black cap.

"*S'il vous plait, madame,*" began Esther, half crying with agitation, "*Est-ce qu'on peut téléphoner? C'est très important, madame.*"

The old face, unsmiling, critical, looked her over from head to foot. Esther for the first time realised her dishevelled appearance, her hatless head. She saw the hard eyes fix themselves in a suspicious stare on a point upon her cheek under the left eye. Mechanically she put up her hand and discovered a needle-like splinter of glass sticking into her face. She had not felt it before: it must have come from the electric-bulb which Holliday's revolver had shattered. There must be a good deal of blood on her cheek. . . .

"*Un accident,*" she murmured apologetically, trying to smile, then repeated desperately, beseechingly: "*Le téléphone, madame—? Je suis très pressé—*"

The old woman spoke at last:

"*On n'a pas de téléphone ici,*" she replied with a Belgian accent, and pushed the door to in Esther's face.

Outraged and disappointed, the more so as she had caught sight of the telephone-instrument in the hall, Esther stumbled down the steps and out again to the street, sick at heart over the waste of time and strength, both priceless now. The old witch, the iron-faced creature, eyeing her as if she wanted to steal something! Never mind, she must simply try the house next door.

This proved to be an imposing edifice where one would expect to find several well-trained servants. Yet she rang the bell for three minutes at least without eliciting any response. At length she was on the point of departure, maddened by her fruitless efforts, when she was rewarded by a sound above her head. Looking up she saw that a casement had been thrown open and that a gentleman with his face covered in lather was gazing down upon her—at first angrily, then archly. Quite desperate now she framed her request in what French she could command, scarcely able to wait for the reply. The result was disconcerting. The shaving gentleman became excessively gallant, entreated his fair visitor to remain where she was for a tiny instant until he could descend and admit her, implored her with expansive gestures not on any account to go away and blight his life. As the sweep of the arm and the shrug of the shoulders betrayed only too plainly the fact that the hospitable gentleman was very much in a state of nature, except for the lather on his face, Esther took fright and bolted out of the gate, inwardly execrating the Gallic race and their amorous propensities. One more chance gone, she thought in a panic of dread, five minutes more wasted. Oh! to think a simple matter like finding a telephone should present so many difficulties!

Diagonally across the street loomed a large, modern apartment house of familiar design. Without doubt there would be a telephone there, in the loge of the concierge. Precipitately she darted across the street, narrowly escaping a motor-cycle, and plunged into the court. She could see the loge at the far end, up a flight of three shallow steps. Light streamed out of the wide glass double doors so frequently seen in this type of building; she aimed her faltering steps towards it as to a beacon. Within the doors she saw a brightly lit, stuffy room overcrowded with machine-carved furniture, the central table covered with a red chenille cloth, on which lay a string-bag bursting with vegetables and parcels. No soul was visible, but she spied the telephone against the back wall. She opened the doors and went in, a bell tinkling as she did so. From an inner room issued the sound of voices laughing and gossiping. The door was shut, and no one troubled at all to answer the summons.

She crossed hurriedly to the other door and opened it, disclosing a domestic group, fit subject for one of the Dutch school paintings. There was a neat, compact, black-clad woman with shining, immaculate coiffure, an old, florid, bald-headed man sluggishly fat, and a youth, long-limbed and pale, with the face of an apache and a dank lock of black hair dipping into his eyes. The woman was peeling potatoes and recounting a history, the old man smoked, and fondled a cat, the apache lounged against the chimney with a cigarette dangling from his thin lips. A dog slept on the hearth; there were two love-birds in a green cage upon the wall.

"S'il vous plait, madame—"

The three turned instantly and regarded her, all merriment gone, their eyes shrewd, alien, inquisitorial. She began to feel like a criminal, and struggled stammering in the effort to make her desire known, urgent though it was.

"Bien, mademoiselle, qu'est-ce que vous désirez?" the woman rapped out in staccato accents.

"Madame, s'il vous plait, je veux bien téléphoner. Je regrette de vous déranger, mais c'est tellement important."

She saw the woman's gaze, hard and curious, take in the details of her appearance, from her muddy shoes up to her blood-stained cheek.

"I've had an accident—*je viens d'avoir un petit accident,*" she explained hurriedly. *"Il faut que je téléphone immédiatement."*

The concierge's face cleared slightly.

"Pour chercher un médecin, sans doute?" she suggested. *"Bien— voici le téléphone."*

Gratefully Esther thanked her and took down the receiver in her trembling hand. The operator failed to understand her accent; she repeated the number three or four times without success, and was on the point of bursting into tears when the concierge possessed herself of the receiver and delivered the number for her, crisply and precisely.

"Voilà, mademoiselle," she announced in triumph, and returned to her potatoes.

There followed a long wait. From the other room Esther could hear the family group discussing her in subdued voices, her strange aspect, her evident weakness. They hazarded guesses as to how she had received her injuries. The old man was positive that the lady's lover had been chasing her with a knife; the wound on her face was a proof of it, in his opinion.

A series of buzzings, tappings and clinkings came over the wire, with hints of far-distant unintelligible conversation. This continued while with agonised eyes Esther watched the hands of the big clock on the wall creep from five minutes past seven to eleven past. Still no connection. At last the operator, remote and chill as the top of the Tour Eiffel, informed her that there was no reply. With French born of desperation Esther cried, *"Sonnez encore! Sonnez toujours! Je suis sûre qu'il y a quelqu'un là!"* Then recommenced the mysterious commotion on the line, which, before, led to nothing.

"Oh, God! oh, God!" she breathed hysterically. "It will be too late, it may already be too late! Oh, God, help me, make them answer!"

She was dimly aware that the apache was lounging in the doorway, using a toothpick and examining her with interest. The voices from the inner room had ceased; everyone was listening, but she did not care. All at once a click louder than those preceding told her she had been put through at last. Hope leapt within her. Alas! It suffered an immediate extinction, when she found herself *au courant* of a conversation between two people of opposite sexes, a dalliance flirtatious in character, interspersed with laughter and snatches of song. Three times she lowered the hook, three times she raised it to find herself still listening to the idiotic babble—*"Tu ne m'aimes pas? Hein? Pourquoi pas?"*—laughter—*"Quand j'ai regardé le couleur de ton nez l'autre soir, j'étais complètement bouleversé, j' t'assure!"*—*"Ah, formidable!"* then another shrill cackle. It was beyond endurance.

There was no use trying further. The clock hands touched twenty minutes past, she had thrown away over a quarter of an hour here while at the villa death was closing in surely upon its unsuspecting victim. She dropped the receiver with a groan, turning to the woman, who had just come out.

"Madame, c'est inutile. Je vous remercie."

The woman looked her over again with a softened glance, touched, perhaps, by the tremor that shook her visitor's voice.

"Mademoiselle est souffrante?"

"Non, madame, pas trop, ce n'est pas ça—mais il y a quelqu'un qui est en danger—quelqu'un qu'il faut prévenir. Si je peux trouver un taxi—"

"Gaston! Vite! Cherche un taxi pour mademoiselle. Va!"

With a warmed feeling that these were kindly people after all, Esther watched the young man's long figure slink out of the door like an otter around the bend of a stream.

"Asseyez-vous, mademoiselle," the woman bade her, and pushed forward a chair.

But she could not sit down. She was in a fever of excitement, quivering all over. With one section of her mind she thanked the woman again, with another she looked for the young man's return, with still another she said to herself, "How long will it take me to get to La Californie from here? Has Roger come back? Is the doctor getting the bandage ready for his hand? Oh, if it should already be too late!"

A torturing interval ensued. She left the loge and wandered out to the entrance. Rain had begun to fall, that would make it harder to find a taxi. It would happen, now of all times! Ten minutes passed, then up the street chug-chugged a somewhat battered motor-vehicle with the apache hanging on the step. Yes, it was a taxi, an antediluvian one, but she must not be critical. If a chariot offered one a lift out of hell, one would not stop to inquire its horse-power. The apache helped her in and closed the door. She turned grateful eyes on him through the open window and with an expressive gesture showed him she had no purse.

"Pas de quoi, mademoiselle," he responded gruffly, and her opinion of the French rose several points.

The chauffeur, a septuagenarian who smelled of wine, had a bulbous nose and was so deaf that it took her several seconds to make him understand where she wanted to go. When finally he grasped the address, he tapped his most conspicuous feature with a horny finger, and, his engine having by this time stopped, descended with creaks and groans to crank it up. He was so long over the operation that she began to be alarmed. However, he was not drunk, only senile. Of the two, his taxi was far worse—rickety, spavined, with every evidence of decrepitude. It started with a jerk which threw its occupant off her seat.

"At any rate I'm moving," she told herself with real relief. "I'm getting there at last. That's something."

Any sort of motion might be better than none, yet when she realised the pace at which she must crawl she suffered strong misgivings. To jog along like this when speed was a prime essential! Moreover they did not always jog, frequently they stopped dead still, while the ancient driver fumbled with the gear and eventually hit upon something which sent them forward again with a fresh spasm. It was so completely maddening that after the fifth attack she could bear it no longer. Thrusting her head out of the window she shouted shrilly:

"Vite! Vite! Je suis très pressé! Vite!"

She regretted her lack of expletives, but she need not have done so. The sole result, amid mumblings and grumblings, was an abortive spurt which ended in a breakdown more disastrous than any preceding. Minutes were lost while the septuagenarian got down for another cranking up, and then in the old fashion they chugged on again. At this rate it would take them more than half an hour to reach the villa, during which time anything might happen—would happen, in all probability. Still, she resolved not to risk another exhortation to speed, but to trust to luck to send another taxi in her way. She had no money to pay for this one if she abandoned it, but she reflected that she could give the old man her wrist-watch. It was a problem which need not have concerned her. Many taxis whizzed by, but not one was disengaged.

When they mounted the steeper part of the incline the unhappy engine so laboured that each revolution of the wheels threatened to be the last. Still they moved onward with a sort of grim persistence, and it occurred to Esther that if she did not go altogether mad in the interval there might just possibly be a glimmer of hope. They had passed many familiar landmarks; in a sort of fashion they were getting there. She sat on the edge of the lumpy seat, alternately praying and gibbering, her hands clenched, her head throbbing with the sharp pain born of fear.

"Oh, God," she murmured for the twentieth time, "don't let it happen, make him wait till I get there! Oh, God—"

The taxi slowed down with an ominous finality. Again the driver climbed down, fiddled about for several seconds, then with immense deliberation approached and opened the door. "What's the matter? Can't you get on? *Qu'est-ce qu'il y a?*" she cried, ready to shake him.

He shrugged his shoulders and blew his red nose on a huge filthy handkerchief. Then with an air of great philosophy he replied:

"*Ça marche plus.*"

"*Comment?*" she screamed at him, although she had heard only too well.

"*Plus d'essence,*" he explained briefly, spitting into a puddle. "*C'est fini.*"

There it was concisely; she could take it or leave it. No more petrol, and still at least a mile away from the Villa Firenze. As well write "finis" to her whole desperate attempt. How she had got this far without fainting was almost a miracle; if she tried to walk the remaining distance she was quite certain to fall by the wayside. At the moment the one thing that would have brought her some slight relief would have been to slay this old man—and she had no weapon.

Slowly she got out of the mouldy cab and began automatically to unfasten the strap of her watch. At least she must pay her debts. . . .

"*Plus d'essence . . . C'est fini. . . .*"

The words rang in her brain like a knell.

CHAPTER XXXI

"Chalmers, was that Mr. Roger who came in? I thought I heard him."

"Yes, miss, he's in his room, but I fancy he's on his way to you. He asked where you were."

Chalmers came a step farther into the room, rubbing his grey chin in an undecided fashion. There was plainly something on his mind.

"I wish, miss, we could manage to keep Mr. Roger from going about in all weathers the way he's doing. With this fever on him I'm afraid he'll come to harm. It fair frightens me to see him looking as he does and taking no care of himself."

The old lady shook her head in despair.

"I know, Chalmers; you are perfectly right—but no matter what I say it does no good. He is worried for fear something has happened to Miss Rowe, and he insists on making efforts to trace her. I'm sure I don't know what to do with him—and he really is ill."

The butler looked at the carpet and cleared his throat slightly, the action constituting a tactful but unequivocal indication that in his own opinion the search for the missing person was a complete waste of energy. Miss Clifford understood the cough, and agreed with its main contention that her nephew was not in a fit condition to be wandering about the streets.

"If you'll pardon the suggestion, miss, hoping you'll not think it's an impertinence, it strikes me the thing to do is first to get Mr. Roger into bed and then to give him a good strong sleeping draught. If he still is bent on going out to-morrow, miss, with your permission I'd take away his clothes."

"It's not a bad idea, Chalmers," replied Miss Clifford, smiling in spite of herself. "But I hope it won't be necessary. He's half promised me to give up the search after to-day—it really seems quite useless—and let us look after him properly. I'm waiting now to hear what news he has; then I shall try to persuade him to go to bed."

"Here is Mr. Roger, now, miss."

He stood aside to admit the young man, who entered with a dragging step, then after a single searching glance at the drawn and haggard face he quietly withdrew. Miss Clifford also scrutinised her nephew closely through her spectacles. He seemed to her appreciably thinner, and there was a feverish glitter in his blue eyes that filled her with alarm.

"Roger, my darling, do please undress and get into bed at once. I will come and talk to you there."

He shook his head obstinately, and sat down on the chaise-longue beside her, deeply dispirited, yet with a look of concentrated purpose.

"I'm not ready to give up," he said slowly. "Not just yet, there's too much to do. However, if it's any satisfaction to you to know, I took my temperature just now to make sure, and as I thought it was a bit lower than it was this time yesterday, I am inclined to think I'm over the worst of this."

"I don't see how you can be; you look very ill indeed," sighed his aunt. "You are only keeping about from sheer will power, and I'm afraid you'll pay for your stubbornness later on. Tell me, though," she went on, slightly lowering her voice. "Is there any news of her?"

He shook his head and drew a long discouraged breath.

"None whatever; not a word, not a sign. It is most mysterious. I've done everything I could think of. There may possibly be a pension or two I haven't discovered, but even so it's very odd that not one of the taxi-drivers in Cannes can recall taking a fare on Tuesday afternoon that answers her description. I've investigated it thoroughly."

"Don't you think the driver may have forgotten?"

"Most unlikely. It was sufficiently odd picking up an American girl in the street with her luggage, to say nothing of the broken-down car; the circumstances were unusual enough to impress themselves on a man's memory for a couple of days at any rate. I have even looked up two chauffeurs who were home ill, but it was no good."

"It is indeed most odd! Have you done anything else?"

"Yes. I've seen the police and reported her as missing."

"Oh!"—in a shocked tone—"Do you consider it as serious as that?"

"What do *you* think? If Esther were my sister and went off like that, leaving no trace, wouldn't you consider it serious? Here is a young girl in a strange country, without friends. If we don't take an interest in finding her, who will? All sorts of things may have happened to her, things one doesn't like to think about." He moistened his lips, continuing with difficulty. "She may have been decoyed and robbed, or—or even something much worse. It's no good shutting one's eyes to the possibility of it."

His face betrayed the serious disturbance of his thoughts. For several seconds his aunt went on with her knitting. Then laying down her work she said in a guarded tone, glancing at Lady Clifford's door:

"Of course there's one thing that would alter all that. Suppose what Arthur Holliday told Thérèse wasn't true."

"You mean he may have invented that story of the breakdown? Yes, it's quite possible. Only in that case . . ."

"Don't misunderstand me, Roger," interrupted the old lady quickly. "I could never bring myself to believe anything wrong of that nice girl, I simply couldn't—that is if she were quite herself, responsible, and all that. Only I can't help wondering if you have heard what the doctor hinted to Thérèse about Miss Rowe, about his thinking that sometimes she was—was not quite—"

"Has Thérèse repeated that nonsense to you too?" he demanded angrily.

"Well, I—I admit it startled me very much. I could scarcely believe there was anything in it. I'm sure I never noticed anything the least bit odd about her, and I was amazed to hear that anyone had done so. Yet the doctor is so positive about it, although he hasn't said much. And when a man like that makes a statement, one is almost forced to believe there must be something in it. In any case it occurred to me that if his theory is true she might have left Cannes and gone away, quite forgetting for the moment that she was going to communicate with us. She may even have lost her memory, you know."

"Then if she has," declared Roger firmly, getting to his feet, "there's all the more reason for my making every effort to find her. Although, Dido, I may as well tell you I don't take very much stock in that idea of the doctor's. Oh, I've had a talk with him; he was very scientific, very convincing. He assured me there are a great many people walking about with the same complaint who regard themselves and are generally regarded as perfectly normal. He says they unconsciously invent and believe all sorts of preposterous things. He says no one could predict at what moment they might suddenly go off the handle and behave quite irrationally. No doubt what he says is entirely true, only I can't see it applying to Esther. Why, if I'd been asked to pick a thoroughly normal, well-balanced woman—"

"Yes, yes, I know. I should have said so too."

"He made a good deal out of a trifling incident that I shouldn't have bothered to repeat at all—something about dropping a basin of water. Utter nonsense, I call it. Then he said that she had taken a marked antipathy to him without any reason, and behaved queerly towards him. I'm sure I didn't notice it."

"Of course, Roger, there was one odd thing that appears to bear out his theory. You know how just as she was leaving she sent you that message? Chalmers tells me she was terribly agitated, quite beside herself. Yet before you could get downstairs . . ."

"I know, I know," he interrupted her, as if the subject were painful to him. "It does seem to fit in with what he says, and yet . . ."

He lit a cigarette thoughtfully and after a few puffs threw it away. Then, walking to the nearest window, he parted the curtains and stared out into the cloudy darkness.

"There's no use talking, Dido, I'm frightfully worried. I can't throw this thing off at all. I've got a feeling there's something not quite right, but I'm damned if I can put my finger on the trouble. If someone could have lied to her, if she has some grudge against us for any reason so that she doesn't want to see us again . . . oh, God knows what it is, but the whole atmosphere here has got on my nerves to such an extent that I am anxious to get away. I feel I'll get better, too, once I'm out of the house."

She nodded sympathetically, though with an eye on Thérèse's door.

"I should like to leave, too, my dear. Somehow I can't bear the house since your father's death. I'd like to go back to England, though it's a little early."

"I'll tell you. If there's no news of Esther in a couple of days, why not pack up your things and we'll move along to some other spot—Antibes, perhaps."

"But, Roger, you're not fit to travel at all. It would be madness! I couldn't permit it."

"Oh, well, let's leave La Californie and go to an hotel in Cannes. If you insisted, I'd send for a doctor—another one," he added, looking rather shamefaced.

The old lady gazed at him in frank amazement.

"My dear, you couldn't do that! Why, it would offend poor Thérèse terribly. I doubt if she'd ever get over it." She paused and lowered her voice confidentially. "Perhaps you don't realise that she is keeping Dr. Sartorius here entirely on your account."

Her nephew turned brusquely and stared at her, his brows knit with annoyance.

"Are you sure of that?" he demanded.

"Why, of course! Why else should she go on having him here? It must be a great expense. Besides, she told me so herself; she said your father would have wished you to have the very best attention."

"Best fiddlesticks!" he retorted sharply. "Good Lord, why should I have a private physician? I'm not the King. Thank heaven you told me this. I shall let her know at once that I don't intend to make use of him. She must let him go."

"My dear, do be careful!" his aunt implored him. "You know how dreadfully sensitive she is; don't risk hurting her feelings! It would be such a poor return for all her kindness."

"Leave it to me; I'll do it very tactfully. Really, it's too much! If I'm going to be ill, I must be allowed to choose my own physician and pay the bill myself. It's not that I haven't confidence in this man, but somehow I can't bear his personality."

They fell into silence, each busy with disturbing thoughts. Even Miss Clifford did not know to what an extent Roger was concerned over this matter of Esther's whereabouts. The complete uncertainty, linked as it was with the doctor's guarded implications, had strung him up to a pitch of nerve-racking apprehension. Moreover, not until this had happened did he fully realise what Esther meant to him, how differently he regarded her from any other girl he had ever known. Could it possibly be true that she was in some obscure way slightly unbalanced? If he shut out the thought from his mind, he felt himself at once faced with another equally unpleasant—that never-annihilated possibility that she had gone off with Holliday somewhere. Perhaps she was with him now, in Monte Carlo, or Nice, Paris even. Thérèse would not know, of course. Arthur would be careful to keep it from her. The mere idea of it made him writhe, while he felt his skin flush all over as though a fire flared up inside him.

The door behind him opened quietly, and Thérèse came in, dressed for dinner.

"How damp it is this evening!" she said, shivering slightly. "Chalmers must bring up some more wood for the fire. I am glad you are in, Roger; I have been so unhappy about you. Are you feeling better?"

"Yes, thank you, Thérèse, I rather think this bout isn't going to amount to much after all. It looks like a false alarm."

"Ah, that would be too marvellous! Perhaps you have a very strong—what do you call it?—constitution. Dido, darling, will you be an angel and fasten this strap for me? Aline is out on an errand."

She leant over so that her sister-in-law need not rise. Her dead-black, filmy gown had wide transparent sleeves that fell back to show her white arms, she wore no ornaments except her row of lustrous pearls. She looked fragile and lovely, her hair loosely waved with the artlessness of a child's, her grey eyes with their flecks of gold wide and clear, like the eyes of a beautiful Persian cat.

"Thérèse," Roger said abruptly. "Sit down, I want to suggest something to you."

She patted the old lady's shoulder for thanks and sat down in the blue damask *bergère* beside the fire, looking up at him expectantly.

"Yes, certainly; what is it?"

"Thérèse, you mustn't misunderstand what I am going to say. It's awfully difficult. The fact is, I've only just realised you are keeping Sartorius here on my account. You'll think me incredibly stupid, but I supposed he was staying on as a—a guest."

"Well?" she returned, quite tranquilly, though watching him closely, he thought.

Mechanically she put out her hand to take a cigarette from the table, keeping her eyes on his. He bent forward with a match for her, and the perfume from her hair, her skin, her dress met him in a cloying wave. Why, in spite of all, did he shrink from that scent? He couldn't explain it, it wasn't exactly unpleasant. . . .

"Well," he replied, finding it hard to proceed, "now that I do understand, I must really beg you to get rid of him. I'm not ill enough to need any physician's undivided attention, and besides"—he hesitated, then took the plunge—"I feel I've got to get away. Since Father's funeral this house seems to get on my nerves. I'm horribly depressed. Do you know what I mean?"

Expecting to see her face cloud with the look of resentful suspicion he knew so well he was agreeably surprised when she merely smiled faintly and replied:

"My dear, of course I know! It is most natural. I too would like to get away. Why don't you go to a nursing-home for a bit?"

Both he and his aunt could hardly believe their ears. Thérèse was surely becoming much more reasonable than formerly.

"Perhaps, it depends on how I feel. It's jolly decent of you to understand. Of course it's nothing but nerves—"

"Oh, my dear, don't trouble to explain! As if I didn't know what nerves are! I don't suppose, in that case, you will want Sartorius?"

"Well, I—" He broke off, embarrassed, scarcely able to keep the amazement out of his voice.

"Because I think he wants to run down to Algiers for a little rest. He's only staying to please me."

The matter had cleared up in the simplest fashion. Roger felt a rush of slightly ashamed gratitude towards his step-mother, feeling a little reluctantly, as he had done once before, that he had misjudged her. Confused by her kindly impulses he stooped to pick up the wisp of a handkerchief she had let fall to the floor. As he laid it in her lap she uttered a sharp little cry.

"Roger—your hand! Let me see, please. Why, it's bleeding again! Aren't you doing anything for it?"

He allowed her to examine it, while his aunt adjusted her spectacles and moved nearer to see.

"My dear, that is bad! I'd almost forgotten it, but it isn't healing at all, it looks quite inflamed."

"It's a beastly nuisance, it keeps catching in things and tearing open again. I haven't had a bandage on it since—" He left the sentence unfinished, for it had brought up memories of Esther. "Oh, well, it's nothing serious. Still, I had better let Sartorius attend to it, I suppose—sterilise it and so forth. Don't you think? He was after me this morning about the risk I was running of getting it infected, but I wouldn't wait."

He was pleased to have thought of this; he felt it made a sort of amends to Thérèse for the blow he had dealt her—if it was a blow. He was glad to see that she looked slightly gratified, it mitigated his guilty feeling.

"It is just as well to look after that sort of thing," Miss Clifford remarked placidly. "I can't help recalling poor Smithers, one of your father's foremen, who got a scratch from a bit of wire on one of the looms and died two weeks later of blood-poisoning."

As she spoke the door to the hall opened and the doctor came in, greeting the three with his usual phlegmatic calm. His presence put an immediate pall on the conversation which Miss Clifford made an effort to lift.

"Any news?" she inquired. "I suppose you have had no word from our Miss Rowe?"

He turned a speculative eye upon her, pausing a moment as if trying to recall who Miss Rowe could be.

"Miss Rowe!" he repeated vaguely, moving towards the fire. "No, I have heard nothing. But then I have no reason to believe she will take the trouble to communicate with me."

The slight emphasis on the final word annoyed Roger, who glanced at the doctor keenly, wondering what was in the man's methodical, unemotional mind. Was he keeping something back? Did he know more of Esther than he was willing to say? It had not occurred to him until now.

Thérèse made a sudden graceful and impulsive movement.

"Doctor—will you be good enough to look at Mr. Clifford's hand? I am sure his thumb should be attended to at once: it really is in a shocking state."

Roger held out his injured hand for inspection. Very deliberately the big man adjusted the nearest lamp so that its rays shone where he wished them, then he bent his head and frowningly examined the wound. He took so long about the matter that Miss Clifford put down her knitting to watch. Could anything be wrong? Roger himself began at last to wonder. He submitted quietly while Sartorius felt his arm at intervals exploringly up to the shoulder, but he began to feel a little impatient when the examiner took hold of his face to turn it to the light and with a tentative finger commenced to prod his jaw.

"No peculiar sensation there, I suppose?" the doctor asked as he touched the muscles just in front of the ears.

"No, certainly not."

What was the man getting at? It was exceedingly tiresome. At last the inquisition ended; the doctor straightened his tall bulk and spoke, non-committally, but with raised eyebrows.

"I must certainly disinfect it at once. That at least one can do."

This remark and the tone in which it was uttered were both so far from reassuring that Miss Clifford hastened to inquire: "Has it become infected in any way, do you think?"

"I trust not. I trust not. I fancy some dirt or grit has got into it, and no wonder; still . . . will there be time to see to it before dinner? It really shouldn't be left."

"Oh, it is only ten minutes past eight," replied Thérèse, glancing at the clock, "and I ordered dinner for half-past."

"Very well, I will attend to it now."

When the doctor was out of the room Roger laughed a little, examining the raw, inflamed fissure on his thumb.

"He's not the most cheery person in the world, is he? I've begun to imagine I've caught some terrible germ or other."

Thérèse smiled as she rose from her chair.

"I shouldn't worry, that is simply his way. I am sure he didn't mean to alarm you. I am just going to scribble a note before dinner, while that is being done," she added, and went into her own room, closing the door.

"That was a stroke of luck," whispered Roger. "She wasn't in the least offended, was she? She positively met me half-way."

"She really is a good sort, Roger," returned the old lady cautiously.

"I only wish we . . ."

She was unable to complete the sentence because of the doctor's re-entry. He approached the table near the fire and laid his leather case upon it, then carefully began to spread out various things—cotton-wool, gauze, scissors, a bottle of iodine. With mechanical precision he prepared a long strip of gauze, plodding steadily ahead, entirely concentrated on his occupation. His broad back was turned to Roger and also to the hall door. He did not even trouble to turn around when the door opened rather suddenly, and the voice of Chalmers, sounding somewhat strained, spoke.

"Beg pardon, miss, but here is Miss . . ."

He did not finish, for just then an apparition, startling in the extreme, pushed violently past him and into the room. It was a girl's figure, hatless, bedraggled, mudstained, her hair wild and drenched with rain, her eyes staring strangely, while one lividly pale cheek was defaced by a long smear of blood. Her breath came in gasps, laboured, terrible to hear, as though her heart threatened to burst its walls. She cast one swift, penetrating glance at the three occupants of the room, then a sort of hoarse scream came from her lips.

"Roger—!"

Almost speechless with incredulity, Roger leapt to his feet.

"Esther! You—where have you come from?"

"Roger! Roger!" came the odd, croaking voice again. "Stop him—don't let him touch you—for God's sake don't let him touch your hand!"

Utterly astonished, the sickening suspicion rushed upon him that the doctor was right. She was in the grip of some dreadful delusion. At the same moment he was poignantly aware of her slenderness and fragility, the trembling of her hands. He reached her side, put out his hand to her to find her still staring at him, wild-eyed, panting for breath.

"Don't touch that bandage, he wants to kill you. He killed your father, he and Lady Clifford between them, now he's trying to get you, too. Oh, oh! thank God I reached you in time!"

Something seemed to snap, she wavered an instant like a drunken person, then all at once crumpled into a heap on the floor, where she lay shivering and sobbing.

CHAPTER XXXII

FOR a full second all the onlookers merely gazed, completely dumbfounded. Miss Clifford seemed unable to make a move, the doctor stood rooted to the spot by the table, his face expressionless, his fingers holding the long strip of gauze, which fluttered in the draught from the open door. The first to stir was Roger, who knelt beside the sobbing girl, and putting his arms around her body tried to lift her a little. The startling denunciation she had given voice to had hardly registered upon his brain, meaning to him only a confirmation of the deplorable truth which Sartorius had foreseen. She was, almost without doubt, unhinged: her whole appearance and manner went to prove it. In an agony of mind Roger took in the details of her sodden clothing, her wet, tangled hair, her dreadful pallor. His imagination flashed a swift vision of the poor girl wandering alone in the streets of Cannes for two days and nights. What was this terrible idea that obsessed her? how had she come by it? He spoke to her as to a child, with extreme gentleness.

"Esther, you poor little thing, what on earth is this all about? Try to tell me where you've been since you left here."

Her eyes, which were falling shut from exhaustion, tried to open for a moment. She made an effort to speak, but could not manage it, convulsive sobs still shaking her like a storm. The doctor and Miss Clifford had now come up and were bending over her.

"Oh, oh, so he was right, after all!" the old lady murmured in deep pity and consternation. "Poor girl; what a dreadful condition! What on earth can we do for her?"

Less moved than the others Sartorius motioned to Roger with his head, at the same time putting a firm hand on Esther's trembling shoulder.

"I will attend to her, Mr. Clifford, leave her to me. I have dealt with these cases often. It is a mistake to sympathise too much; what they are playing for is sympathy. Just help me to get her to that sofa."

Right or wrong the cold-bloodedness of his attitude repelled Roger strongly. He could not believe that Esther was playing for sympathy, but before he was able to voice any objection a fresh alarm came from his half-fainting charge. As though galvanised into life by the doctor's touch, she uttered a shriek and cowered away from him.

"No! No! Not again! If he does that again I'm finished!"

The note of abject terror in the appeal struck a chill to Roger's heart. Whatever this delusion was, it had reduced Esther to a serious state. Trembling violently she clung to him, her face buried in his neck. Miss Clifford, who had hastened to arrange the cushions on the high-backed canapé that was set against the wall at the right of the room, looked on nonplussed, then after a moment approached and spoke soothingly.

"My dear, my dear, it's quite all right, the doctor won't hurt you. There's nothing to be afraid of."

"But there is, there is!" Roger heard a low whisper between chattering teeth. "For God's sake protect me, don't let him come near me!"

Sartorius straightened up slowly and shook his head in a disparaging fashion.

"I was afraid of this," he commented coldly. "It is going to be a little difficult to deal with her, unless—"

"Leave her to me, doctor," Roger said in a low tone. "It's no good exciting her."

He picked her up and carried her to the canapé, where very gently he laid her down. Even in that disturbed moment the touch of her damp curls and the faint odour of her skin moved him strangely. She might be demented, but it was not easy for him to forget that she was Esther.

"Don't be afraid," he whispered in her ear. "I promise you he sha'n't come near you."

She sank back with a quivering sigh; only the faintest pressure of her hand on his showed him she understood. He looked about with the idea of discovering some cover to put over her, for she seemed on the verge of a chill. As he did so he discovered Thérèse standing motionless in her doorway, a silent spectator. His eyes caught hers, and the expression on her face made him stare fixedly at her. Why was she gazing in that way at him and at Esther? He felt he had caught something in her eyes which she had not meant to be seen. What was it? It looked like fear—sudden, abject fear. Why were her eyes widened in that fashion? He found himself examining her curiously. . . .

All at once an impossible idea shot across his brain, searing it like a red-hot iron. Could there, after all, be some underlying grain of truth in that wild accusation Esther had uttered a moment ago? At least some deceptive semblance of fact in it? It was nonsense, of course, to consider such a thing, yet . . . The expression in the grey eyes altered completely, the look he had seen was gone. Lady Clifford came forward with an exclamation of concern.

"*Mon Dieu*, what is all this? How did that poor creature get here, and in such a state? Why, look—her clothes are soaking! She must have been in the rain for hours! And blood here on her face!"

The old lady whispered an explanation.

"She rushed in here a moment ago, Thérèse, you must have heard her. She seems so queer and upset, and has been saying the wildest things! And, isn't it odd, she refuses to allow the doctor to come near her at all!"

"Does she? Very odd, indeed!"

With another glance at the *canapé*, Lady Clifford turned towards the doctor.

"What do you think one ought to do, doctor?" she inquired. "She can't stay here, naturally. Don't you think one should try to get her into some really safe place, where she could be properly looked after?"

Something a little tense and sharp in the tone riveted Roger's attention. With his arm still about Esther he turned his head and listened. He heard the heavy tones of Sartorius make answer evenly, without emotion of any kind:

"She is still raving; we must simply let her be for the moment till she quiets down. I will see what can be done. There is a mental home near Grasse where I believe they would take her; I can telephone and find out. They would keep her under observation until we can get in touch with her people."

"Oh, doctor, do you really think that will be necessary?" asked Miss Clifford regretfully.

She had just come out of Thérèse's room bringing a rose taffeta quilt to throw over the shivering girl. Roger made an impatient sign to the others to be careful what they said, but to his relief Esther appeared not to hear. He himself was peculiarly upset by the doctor's matter-of-fact reference to the mental home, and on the spot he resolved firmly to defeat any arrangements that might be made for placing the girl where she could be kept "under observation." Yet what ought one to do? She was clearly in need of medical attention. She seemed now to be delirious, babbling incoherently, repeating in an undertone and in that strange hoarse voice fragments of words and phrases that in spite of their wildness arrested his attention. Listening closely to her he thought that all the happenings of the past two months of her life had become interwoven into the fabric of her delusion. Such words as "typhoid," "toxin," "hypodermic," "bandage," recurred again and again, then "culture"—she was back in the doctor's laboratory now, without doubt, watching his experiments. Suddenly a name caught his ear, he bent closer. What was this she was saying about Holliday? Holliday? How did he come into it? A low, frightened whisper followed; he had to strain his ears to catch it: *"She wanted the money now, you know, so she could keep him with her!"*

He stared at the girl searchingly. Her eyes were closed, she had the look of complete exhaustion. He could almost not believe she had spoken those significant words. Did she know what she was saying? Was it mere accident that her last sentence had sounded so astonishingly rational?

Still keeping one arm beneath her shoulders he once more looked around and took a cautious survey of the other end of the room. Thérèse was no longer to be seen; she must have slipped out, but his aunt was saying something in an anxious undertone to the doctor, who at that moment had moved nearer the fireplace. Watching narrowly Roger noticed the big man put out his hand towards the blazing logs, then saw a small scrap of something flimsy and white—it might have been paper, or perhaps a tiny piece of the medical gauze he had been using—flutter into the flames. The gesture was so negligent that in the ordinary way one would not have given it a second thought, yet now, because of Esther's unintelligible reference to a bandage, it awoke in Roger a vague uneasiness. Again the incredible suspicion crossed his mind; he caught himself wondering if just possibly there were more in this than met the eye.

Studying the white, bloodstained face lying against the blue cushion, he asked himself if Esther did really possess some terrible knowledge of which he was completely ignorant. Could her jumbled utterances be linked together into any sort of meaning? As if conscious of his unspoken question she stirred restlessly, muttering words he could not catch, then turned a little away from him on to her right side. As she did so his gaze fell upon her left coat sleeve. There was a spot near the shoulder, no bigger than a half-crown, where the material was oddly frayed and roughened. He examined it closely, then as gently as possible unfastened the coat and slipped it down from the shoulder. . . . What was this? The heavy crêpe-de-Chine blouse underneath, in the spot that corresponded, was punctured with tiny, round holes, a little constellation, thickly grouped. What did it mean? He laid his finger on the spot, but at the touch she recoiled from him with a shudder that shook her from head to foot.

"No, no, not again!" she cried out in her former accents of terror.

He soothed her, gripped by a sudden fear.

"Esther, darling, it's only me, Roger. I won't hurt you," he whispered softly. "Listen to me, dear. I want to know what these marks are on your arm. Try to tell me. Try to tell me where you have spent these past two days."

She opened her lips and moistened them painfully; then as he thought she was going to speak he saw her eyes fix themselves upon a spot above his shoulder, while her whole face became contorted with fright. Glancing behind him he saw that the doctor had quietly come near them again and was standing, a silent, bulky figure, at the foot of the canapé. Filled with annoyance Roger motioned to him to withdraw from the girl's sight, but already it was too late. With a tremor more violent than those preceding she buried her face in the cushion, then lay completely still, so still that Roger became seriously alarmed.

"Here, will someone fetch some brandy?" he demanded abruptly, looking around. "She's fainted. There's a bottle in the cupboard in my bathroom."

The voice of Chalmers answered quickly from the door-way, "Yes, sir, I'll get it, sir."

Anxiously Roger fell to chafing the girl's cold hands then became unpleasantly aware that Sartorius was regarding him with a faintly sardonic expression on his sallow face.

"I suppose you have realised what those marks mean," the doctor said with a slight movement of his head towards the punctured sleeve.

"Well, what do they mean?" returned Roger aggressively.

"Simply what I ought to have guessed all along—that the unfortunate woman is the victim of a drug-habit."

He turned on his heel and walked away, leaving Roger to swallow his rage at what seemed to him an insulting suggestion. Drug-victim! Esther! What an absurdity! Besides, would anyone give herself injections through her sleeves? Preposterous! . . . He continued to slap the limp hands. Why did she show no sign of reviving? It seemed to him that her heart scarcely beat at all. The awful idea came to him that she might be dead from shock and weakness. . . . Why was Chalmers so long over getting the brandy? Becoming desperate with impatience he decided to go himself; perhaps the old man could not find the bottle.

"Dido," he said as his aunt approached with smelling-salts in her hand, "stay with her, don't leave her, do what you can. I'll not be gone a minute."

As the old lady took his place he quickly ran out and along the hall to his room. Reaching the open door he heard a curious sound which came from the lighted bathroom beyond. What was it? It seemed like strained and heavy breathing; then he caught muttered, angry words in French, an expletive that reeked of the gutter. What on earth did it mean? He strove to the door, then halted on the threshold, completely petrified. Speech deserted him, he could only stare, hardly able to credit what he saw.

Facing him, her back against the wall, was Thérèse, struggling with every ounce of strength she possessed to escape from a man who gripped her firmly by the wrists. Transformed into a tigress, her cheeks burning with passion, she writhed and pushed and panted in her efforts to free herself. Her captor's breath came hard; he was barely more than a match for her, yet he never relaxed his hold.

"Thérèse! What is the meaning of this?"

The man, whom he now saw to be old and grey-haired, turned and looked over his spare shoulder. It was Chalmers.

CHAPTER XXXIII

At sight of Roger the Frenchwoman uttered a cry and redoubled her efforts to get away.

"Roger, make him let go, the old swine, the beast, *le sale chameau*! I dismiss him here, now; he must leave my house. I will have him arrested for attacking me. I . . . Take him away, Roger, do you hear, do you see what he is doing?"

Before Roger could reply or adjust his confused impressions the old butler panted out:

"Just pick up that bottle from the floor, sir, if you don't mind, and put it in a safe place. Then I'll let her ladyship go."

Speechless from amazement, yet forcibly impressed by the old man's words and serious manner, Roger looked and discovered a bottle of Evian water standing on the tiled floor a few feet away. He picked it up and set it high on a shelf over the basin, then quickly closed the door and stood with his back against it.

"Release her ladyship, Chalmers," he ordered sternly, "and let me hear the reason of this extraordinary behaviour."

Like a steel spring unloosed Thérèse broke from the butler's grasp and hurled herself against the door.

"Let me out, let me out! Roger, I shall faint, I shall die!"

He looked at her curiously and stood firm as a rock, Chalmers mopped his brow with a handkerchief, still breathing with difficulty. Roger looked from him to Thérèse, who, half-sobbing now, threw herself again at the door, appealing to him desperately:

"I can't bear it, Roger; I can't breathe the same air with this horrible creature! Didn't you see how he had hold of me, how he—"

A glint came into Roger's eye; he held her off with one arm.

"Yes, Thérèse, I saw. Now I intend to know why he did it. Tell me the truth, Chalmers."

The old man, who was recovering his poise, coughed apologetically.

"I know how it must have looked to you, sir, but believe me I had a good reason. Perhaps you can persuade her ladyship to tell you what she was about to do with that bottle of mineral water when I came in and caught her at it."

The cry that burst from Thérèse's lips was like an angry snarl.

"Mineral water! What is the creature talking about I should like to know?"

Unmoved, the butler continued in reply to Roger's unspoken question.

"If her ladyship won't tell you sir, then I will. When I came in here to get the brandy, she had that bottle in her hand. She was just going to pour it down the bath, sir, when I managed to stop her."

"Pour it down the bath!"

"Yes, sir. You may believe it or not, sir, but I should say there was something in that water her ladyship would like get rid of."

Almost overwhelmed by the tumult of suspicion that rose within him, Roger found it hard to keep his head. Mastering himself with an effort and still holding Thérèse off with one arm he managed to ask evenly:

"What gave you this idea, Chalmers?"

"The nurse, sir," was the prompt reply. "There's something serious behind all this business, and it's my opinion the nurse knows."

Deeply shaken, Roger gazed into the old servant's eyes. What he saw convinced him that Chalmers had not spoken idly. For that matter he knew what a degree of certainty it must have required to make the man attempt such an unheard-of thing as to lay his hands on his mistress. The inference was staggering. . . . With a great effort he pulled himself together, remembering Esther.

"Take the brandy to Miss Clifford, Chalmers. I will stay here a moment."

He stood aside to allow the butler to pass, then shutting the door again turned resolutely to Thérèse, trying to conceal from her the quandary in which he found himself.

"I'm afraid this requires an explanation," he said to her coldly.

"Please tell me what you were going to do with that water."

She bit her lips and faced him defiantly.

"I shall not answer any question that is put in such a way," she retorted. "Let me pass; I insist on leaving this room."

"Listen to me, Thérèse. A little while ago Miss Rowe made a terrible accusation concerning you and Sartorius. I begin to think her statement has got to be investigated. I am giving you a chance now to explain matters."

"Investigated! Are you serious? Surely you saw for yourself that the girl is out of her senses?"

"In view of what Chalmers has just told me I am not entirely sure."

"Absurd! Why, the doctor said before she left that he considered her abnormal. I am sure I have no idea what mad story she has invented, but as for taking her seriously—!"

"Very well, then, tell me what you were going to do with that water. Why were you trying to throw it away?"

As he spoke it flashed upon him that on another occasion she had been in his room. He recalled her flimsy excuse, which she had later on contradicted.

She began to laugh, cajolingly.

"Don't be ridiculous, Roger; where is your sense of humour? I wasn't trying to throw anything away, I was fetching that water for Miss Rowe. I remembered there was none in my room—"

"And why were you sure there was some here? No, Thérèse, that's not good enough. Here, we can't go into the matter now while Miss Rowe's life is in danger, but for all that the thing has got to be talked out. Listen to me: I want you to go to your room and remain there quietly until that girl is sufficiently recovered to tell me what she knows. Until then no one can decide whether it is all nonsense or not. Come, please. I insist on it."

Anger flamed in her eyes.

"I am to remain a prisoner in my own house! You are raving!"

"I am perfectly serious, Thérèse; you have brought it on yourself. Don't argue. If you refuse you will force me to communicate with . . . the police."

She looked at him as she had done once before, all the venom of her hate concentrated in her eyes.

"Do you know what you are saying to me?" she whispered between dry lips. "Do you realise what this means?"

"I do. I have no wish to make this affair public, any more than you have. Just as long as there remains the possibility of all this originating in Miss Rowe's imagination, I shall do nothing unless you compel me to. Come now, what I suggest is in your own interests. If there's nothing in all this, you are at liberty to bring a suit against me for libel or anything else you can think of."

After a moment's thought she bowed her head very slightly. He moved away from the door and let her precede him. As he passed through his bedroom he put his hand inside the top drawer of his dressing-table and, feeling half ashamed, slipped something he had not used since the war into his pocket. . . . Was the whole thing a monstrous mare's nest? Was he going to despise himself later on?

With a mind full of doubt he followed the slender black-clad figure out into the hall.

"The other door, please," he ordered, feeling uncomfortably a brute, as she was about to go through the boudoir.

With a slight shrug she walked on and entered her own bedroom, closing the door behind her. He hesitated, then opened the door again, transferred the key to the outside, and turned it in the lock. He was putting the key in his pocket, with a rather guilty feeling, when Chalmers approached him.

"I may have done wrong, sir," he whispered; "if so I am willing to suffer for it. I followed my instinct, sir, if you understand what I mean, and there wasn't much time to think."

A look passed between them.

"You needn't say any more, Chalmers, I know you would never have acted as you did without a strong reason. I take it you heard something from Miss Rowe when you let her in."

"I did, sir, and I was fair paralysed with what she told me. What's more, I could take my oath she's as sensible as you or me, let them say what they will."

The old man's habitually wooden face showed deep emotion.

"See here, Chalmers, lock the door of my room and bring me the key. We'll see that no one gets in there to tamper with that bottle, just in case there's anything wrong."

"Yes, sir, and if you'll take my advice, sir, you'll keep an eye on that doctor. I don't think we can trust him, sir."

With this parting counsel, spoken in a tone of strong conviction, the butler departed on his mission.

Although burning to know what Esther had said to Chalmers on her precipitate dash up the stairs, Roger felt his curiosity must remain unsatisfied for the present. At the moment all that mattered was her safety, already he had left her too long. He suddenly realised that he had been away at least five minutes, and assailed by fresh fears he hurried at once into the boudoir.

He entered confident of finding his aunt in charge of the situation. The next instant he cursed his folly in ever leaving the room. The old lady was not there. Instead, the clumsy figure bending over the couch and concealing its occupant from view was that of Sartorius. To his excited brain there was a sinister suggestion in the heavy body that approached so close to the girl lately terrified into unconsciousness. Roger did not stop to think. He strode forward and with a brusque movement caught hold of the man's arm and pulled him away. As he did so his nostrils detected a familiar odour and he caught sight of some object held in the doctor's hand. Was it a hypodermic syringe? A sick feeling swept over him.

"What are you doing to her?" he demanded furiously.

The doctor straightened up and for a second the two eyed each other in tense silence. Then a shadow of contempt passed over the taller man's face.

"My dear Mr. Clifford," he replied deliberately, "if you go away and leave this woman in a critical condition for a considerable length of time, you can hardly expect me not to do what I can for her. You may even admit that my knowledge of what is best is perhaps more extensive than yours."

Steadily Roger's eyes met the gaze of the doctor's little cold greyish ones.

"I don't question your superior knowledge, doctor," he replied with careful emphasis. "But I am not convinced that you were trying to revive her. How do I know"—he paused a moment, then continued slowly—"that you were not doing something to keep her unconscious?"

The suggestion amounted to a slap in the face. He watched keenly to note the result, and saw the heavy figure draw itself up to its full height, seeming at the same time to swell out. The broad face with its sloping, flattish forehead betrayed little if any change of expression.

"You overreach yourself, Mr. Clifford. Your gross insinuation compels me to go at once to Lady Clifford and inform her that I cannot remain longer under the same roof with a person who has so offensively outraged my professional dignity."

He was moving away when Roger stopped him with a gesture.

"I am afraid in the light of what has happened I must make it plain to you that you are not to hold any communication with Lady Clifford for the present. I must ask you to remain at the other end of this room until I give you leave to withdraw."

A sudden gleam shot into the dull little eyes.

"May I ask by what authority you issue orders in this house?"

"I would prefer you didn't ask," retorted Roger with an unwavering gaze, "because the only answer is an extremely direct one."

As he spoke he slipped his right hand into his pocket with a movement there was no misunderstanding.

"This is intimidation, Mr. Clifford."

"You are at liberty to give it any name you like. The point is that only by doing as I say can you avoid at the moment a legal investigation."

A second or two elapsed while the doctor looked at him silently, evidently considering the matter. Then without a word he turned and walked heavily towards the fireplace, where he seated himself in the big arm-chair. At this precise moment Miss Clifford came back into the room with a basin of water and a towel. She glanced at the distant figure of the doctor with slight surprise, then at Roger as though scenting something amiss.

"He sent me to get these," she murmured uncertainly. "Is she coming around?"

"You shouldn't have let him come near her," he returned, shaking his head. "I thought you understood."

She glanced at him in distressed astonishment. Plainly her belief in the doctor remained quite unshaken; she had as yet not the faintest conception of the suspicions in her nephew's mind.

"Did I do wrong?" she whispered. "I didn't see how it could make any difference as long as the poor girl wasn't conscious, and I began to be frightened. Her pulse is so terribly weak!"

"We must get another doctor here as quickly as possible," announced Roger with decision. "Ring for Chalmers; he will attend to it. I daren't leave the room."

However, it was unnecessary to ring. Chalmers entered at that moment and slipped a key into Roger's hand.

"I'll telephone at once, sir," he said. "There is a doctor quite close by, a French one, of course, but I dare say he will be good enough."

"Yes, Chalmers, tell him to come at once, that it is serious. If you can't get him, try another one; don't leave the telephone until you've found someone. And send one of the maids for a hot-water bottle."

With a nod of understanding the butler went quickly out.

"I'm afraid Thérèse is rather upset by all this," remarked the old lady as she gently bathed the bloodstains from Esther's pale cheek. "She can't stand much of this sort of thing."

It seemed to Roger incredible that his aunt should not suspect something was wrong, yet it was true that she remained in ignorance of what had taken place in his bathroom a few minutes ago. She was merely aware that Thérèse had retired to her room without offering to assist them. Without comment Roger renewed his efforts to resuscitate the fainting girl. Her face was ashy, her lips bluish. There was no apparent change in her condition; she continued to lie there so limp and lifeless that Roger became more and more frightened. Yet great as was his fear he dared not call in the services of the man by the fire. Aware of his aunt's mystification and disapproval, he still considered the doctor the more serious of two dangers.

"It is the strangest case I have ever known," murmured old Miss Clifford in perplexity. "What do you suppose is the reason for her turning against the doctor so suddenly? Why, I thought they were on the best of terms? And where do you suppose she has been? Did you notice all this mud down the side of her clothes? And no hat, nor bag—so she must be without money."

He nodded gravely, watching eagerly for the least sign of returning consciousness. He could not tell whether Sartorius had administered a *piqûre* of some kind to her or not, and the uncertainty filled him with apprehension. He could not rid his mind of Esther's stricken cry, "If he does that again I'm finished!" What was it she meant? Was it possible that those red dots on her arm furnished the answer? She might have been out of her senses when she said that, of course. If what the doctor averred was the case, then it was part of her delusion to believe he was trying to injure her. How could one know the truth? She might die now, so easily; then one could never find out.

She might die—! The fear of this tortured him. The solution of the mystery, even the question of whether his father's death had been due to natural causes or not sank into comparative insignificance beside that terrifying possibility. Nothing could undo what was done, nothing could bring his father back—but here was this girl whom he loved apparently about to slip over the border-line before his eyes and he could do nothing to save her. The thought drove him distracted.

A maid brought the hot-water bottle: they put it near Esther's feet, which were icy to the touch, even through her thin stockings. They loosened her clothing, although there was not much to be done in that line, her slender body being innocent of stays. Presently Miss Clifford raised an anxious face.

"Don't you think we'd better get *him* to do something after all?" she whispered nervously. "I'm rather frightened!"

He frowned and shook his head, at the same time realising how strange his refusal must strike her. Before he could frame a reasonable reply Chalmers returned to inform him that he had found a doctor, who would be with them in a few minutes.

"Thank God! Dido, we'll wait for him."

"Very well, my dear, if you think it's safe."

She glanced doubtfully at the inert form under the pink coverlet.

"I know what you're thinking," he said softly, putting his hand on her shoulder, "but I believe I am acting for the best. You must simply take my word for it."

Purposely disregarding her puzzled glance he consulted his watch, then looked towards the figure seated in the armchair by the fire. Sartorius, perfectly self-contained, was making entries in a notebook, apparently little concerned with what went on behind him. A certain scornful touch about his absolute sang-froid unnerved Roger somewhat. It made him feel that perhaps he was acting the fool, jumping at false conclusions. Was Esther's dread of this man purely the creation of a disordered brain?

"Pardon, mademoiselle!"

A woman's voice in the doorway back of him made him start suddenly to find Thérèse's maid, Aline, eyeing them with a slightly hostile curiosity.

"La porte de Madame est fermée à clef. Je demande pardon se je dérange Mademoiselle et Monsieur!"

With a deprecatory manner that was irritatingly exaggerated she crossed the room on tip-toe, bestowing a single searching glance on the sofa and its occupant. Roger wondered how much she had heard in the kitchen. He was sure Chalmers would give nothing important away to the other servants.

"I wonder why Thérèse has locked her door?" Miss Clifford remarked wonderingly when Aline had disappeared into her mistress's bedroom. "She doesn't usually. . . . Listen, Roger, was that a car outside?"

Two minutes later Chalmers, with an air of relief, announced:

"Dr. Bousquet, sir."

CHAPTER XXXIV

"Bonsoir, Madame! Bonsoir, Monsieur! I hope I have not kept you long. I came as quickly as I could. This is the patient, I suppose?"

He spoke in excellent English, and had a brisk and businesslike air. He was a small and dapper man with ginger hair cut *en brosse*, and red-brown eyes behind thick glasses. Setting down his bag on a chair, he cast a professional glance at the prostrate figure under the pink quilt, then running his eyes over the room he discovered Dr. Sartorius. At once a look of puzzled recognition, tinged with deference, came over his sharp little face. He bowed stiffly.

"Ah, doctor, how do you do?" he greeted his colleague in a slightly diffident tone. "Am I to understand that . . . may I ask if I am intruding, or . . ." and he broke off, obviously uncertain as to the position of things.

Sartorius rose and stood stolidly beside his chair.

"Not at all, doctor," he replied coolly. "Mr. Clifford will no doubt explain why you were sent for. There appears to be a good reason."

Expectantly the little man turned to Roger, who, seeing the necessity of some explanation to satisfy him on a point of professional etiquette, said quietly:

"This lady, doctor, is a nurse who has been employed in our family until my father's death a few days ago. After the funeral she left the house, then this evening she returned suddenly in a very strange and excited state. A few minutes after she entered the room here she became unconscious. The reason Dr. Sartorius does not attempt to do anything for her is that when he did try she became much worse. It seems that she has taken a marked antipathy to him, we don't know why."

The Frenchman raised his bushy red brows.

"Ah, ah?" he commented. "May I inquire if you had any knowledge of this antipathy before she went away?"

"I had," replied Sartorius heavily. "I mentioned the fact to Lady Clifford. I had begun to suspect at the last that she might be suffering from some rather obscure mental derangement."

"I see, I see! I daresay you have come to no conclusion as to her present state, doctor?"

"I have not had an adequate opportunity of judging."

"Yes, yes, I quite understand the difficulty you were placed in. Very annoying, very annoying! With your permission, then, I will try to see what it is all about."

During this polite interchange Roger had difficulty in restraining his impatience. It seemed possible that Esther might perish while these two medical men discussed the situation. He watched tensely while the little doctor got out various instruments and bottles, changed his thick pince-nez for a pair of spectacles with tortoiseshell rims exactly matching his eyebrows, and finally proceeded with a maddening deliberation to study the patient, listening at her heart, feeling her pulse, turning back her eyelids. At last he raised a grave face.

"How long has this condition lasted?" he asked, frowning.

"About twenty minutes, I should say."

The Frenchman pursed his lips and shook his head slightly as he proceeded with the examination. Roger grew more and more alarmed. Thinking to facilitate matters, he pointed out the holes in the coat-sleeve.

"What do you make of those, doctor?" he demanded.

The bristling brows rose in astonishment.

"Ah, ah?" their owner exclaimed, sliding the two sleeves deftly off the shoulder and scrutinising the red dots on the skin, round which a bruise was beginning to form. "*Tiens, tiens,* this begins to be more clear. Doctor," he said, turning to Sartorius, "had you any suspicion that this young woman was addicted to the use of a drug?"

Roger glanced searchingly at the man by the fireplace. The sallow face showed no alteration whatever.

"I admit I did not come to that conclusion during the time she was here," the doctor made answer, "but her conduct at times might have suggested it. Those marks enlightened me."

In spite of his resolution to restrain himself, Roger took a step forward angrily.

"Do you mean to insinuate that she gave herself those injections— *through both sleeves*?" he burst out.

Sartorius turned slightly away without replying. Dr. Bousquet shrugged his shoulders and removing his spectacles wiped them carefully on a purple silk handkerchief.

"It would be unusual, monsieur, certainly, but not impossible. There is no accounting for the vagaries of these victims. Whatever the case, she is under the influence of morphia now. It appears to be morphia," he added cautiously.

"Then if she is," declared Roger, losing all control, "that man over there is responsible for it. He gave her the last of those injections not a quarter of an hour ago."

There is no describing the effect of this bombshell. There was shocked silence, during which both Miss Clifford and the little doctor regarded the speaker with a mixture of embarrassment and incredulous concern.

"Roger! My dear! Do you know what you are saying?" the old lady whispered in pained remonstrance.

Chagrined that he had committed himself so incautiously, Roger turned and stared down at Esther, biting his lip. Plainly this was not the time for straightforward speech. Besides, he caught a glance of sympathy mingled with scorn for himself exchanged between the two physicians.

"Never mind how she got any of the injections," he amended hastily, addressing Bousquet in a low voice; "all that concerns us now is how to save her. It was unwise of me to speak as I did."

The doctor's silence and a touch of asperity in his manner conveyed a definite reproof. Shaking his head dubiously, he put his spectacles into their case and blew his nose on the purple handkerchief.

"Well, Mr. Clifford," he said at last, "the best thing we can do at the moment is to get this young person undressed and into a bed. I can then ascertain if there are other hypodermic needle marks on her, and perhaps come to one or two other decisions about which I am doubtful. Can this be arranged?"

"Certainly. I will give orders at once to have a room got ready for her."

He rang the bell, then, returning, put a direct question to the Frenchman.

"Tell me, doctor, do you consider her in danger?"

The little man glanced towards the inert figure doubtfully.

"It is difficult, extremely difficult, to say anything with certainty until the effect of the drug has worn off. She appears to be suffering from severe nervous exhaustion as well as from morphia, which complicates matters. It also seems likely that she has gone without food for some time. Her vitality is very low, very low indeed—although I cannot say there appears to be anything organically wrong with her heart."

Again Roger visualised the dreadful picture of the girl wandering, out of her head, through the streets. It fitted in so aptly with this suggestion of her being without food and in an exhausted state. It was with an effort that he thrust aside the morbid idea to speak to Chalmers.

"Miss Rowe's room is ready for her, sir," the butler replied quietly. "I took the liberty of having it done, sir, thinking you'd want to put her to bed. Shall I lend a hand to carry her in, sir?"

It was an easy matter to transfer Esther from the couch to her former quarters. Roger remained in the hall within reach of the boudoir, and spoke once more to Dr. Bousquet before returning to resume his self-constituted guard of Sartorius.

"I think I ought to tell you, doctor, that before she became unconscious she made a very startling statement. We cannot tell whether there is any truth in what she said or not—but I may say that a great deal depends on the establishment of her sanity. I suppose you have no way of telling—?"

A pleasantly contemptuous smile hovered in the red-brown eyes behind the thick glasses.

"Monsieur, persons who form the morphia habit become, as you are aware, notoriously untruthful. They invent extraordinary stories, make incredible—and often convincing—accusations. I do not of course know anything about this young woman, but—" And he left the sentence unfinished.

It was a diplomatic way of damning in advance any evidence Esther might give. The man, on his own statement, knew nothing, had no prejudice for or against. He was merely voicing a medical fact.

With a mind torn by fresh doubts Roger walked slowly back into the boudoir. He could not help beginning to be afraid that he was acting foolishly. The high-handed manner in which he had dealt with his step-mother and Sartorius might yet land him in most unpleasant difficulties. Obviously he had no right to restrain their movements, and the fact that he had actually threatened Sartorius was sufficient to bring down punishment upon him. Still, he knew in his heart that if he had the thing to do over again he would behave in much the same way. Certainly he felt sure that whether they were malefactors or completely innocent, both Thérèse and the doctor had acted in a manner to arouse suspicion.

As he entered the room, from the opposite door Aline approached him. Her black gimlet eyes surveyed him with a baleful glare as with a distinct touch of irony she inquired if it were permitted that she should bring Madame something to eat.

"Naturally; bring Madame whatever she requires," he replied indifferently.

With a toss of the head she departed, hostility in every inch of her stiff body.

Finding it a disagreeable matter to remain in the same room with the phlegmatic figure still seated in the *bergère* by the fire, Roger crossed to one of the French windows, and opening the casement stepped outside on the narrow balcony. There was a misty drizzle of rain which cooled his burning face, the air was mild enough, but saturated with moisture. The leaves of the trees glistened with heavy drops. Along the balcony to the right showed the light from Thérèse's room in a bar across the wet stone. Her curtains had not been drawn, and for a few seconds he could see her silhouette framed in the window. . . . What was she thinking? what was going on in that brain, which he now felt he had never understood? Was it possible she was guilty of the cold-blooded act Esther had accused her of? His mind could not yet take in the enormity of it, the thought was too staggering. It scarcely seemed credible that so ethereal, so delicate an exterior could hide the consciousness of crime. It was far easier to believe there was some hideous mistake about it all, that Esther, if not deranged, had been misled by appearances. . . . What appearances? What could have given her this idea? He resolved to question Chalmers at once, to find out what he knew. Esther had certainly told the old man something which had profoundly impressed him, that much was evident.

He found Chalmers in the hall, on his way downstairs. Motioning him to approach, Roger spoke to him in a voice cautiously subdued.

"Let me hear, Chalmers, exactly what Miss Rowe said to you when you let her in. What did you think of her—how did she strike you?"

"You saw for yourself what she looked like, sir," replied the old man quietly, yet with an undercurrent of excitement that was not lost on Roger. "I almost took her for a ghost. She fell into the hall when I opened the door, hardly able to stand, she was, sir. I put out my hand to steady her. 'Lord, miss,' I said, 'where have you come from?' I said. She gave me a sort of wild look, sir, then she says, half-choking like, 'Chalmers, where's Mr. Roger? Has the doctor bandaged his hand yet?'"

"Did she ask you that straight off?" demanded Roger, frowning in deep thought.

"Yes, sir, she did. I believed as you did that she was quite off her head. I told her you were in this room with Miss Clifford, and that I thought the doctor was with you, though I wasn't sure. She went as white as a sheet, sir; I was afraid she was going to drop down, but she didn't. She took another sort of spurt, as you may say, and was up those steps so fast she left me behind. I heard her say, 'He's trying to kill him; he's going to give him lock-jaw, and everybody'll believe it's an accident.'"

"Lock-jaw!"

Complete bewilderment was in Roger's face as he repeated the word in a whisper.

"Yes, sir, I was as astonished as you. It seemed as though she must be raving, but then when she said . . ."

He was interrupted by a sudden peal at the doorbell, loud and long, supplemented by violent blows of the brass knocker. Both men jumped at the sound, then exchanged glances of puzzled apprehension. Who at this particular moment was in such a hurry to enter?

"Beg pardon, sir, I'd better see who that is, I expect."

"Yes, yes, Chalmers, you can finish telling me afterwards."

Revolving in his mind the astounding information he had just received, Roger re-entered the sitting-room. The ghastly audacity of the idea that Sartorius had a moment ago been on the very point of introducing the germs of lock-jaw—tetanus to give it its proper name—

into the wound on his hand seemed on the face of it beyond the bounds of possibility. Why, what man would dare to do such a thing? The risk of it! . . . Yet was there so great a risk? Hadn't the doctor repeatedly warned him of the danger he was running? Why, if there was nothing in it, did he examine him so carefully just now, paying special attention to his face and jaw? It had certainly given the impression that he suspected the beginning of certain tell-tale symptoms. Had he done it in order that later the eye-witnesses could recall every detail and make it appear like a purely accidental seizure? Then that bit of white something which Sartorius had dropped into the fire. It might have been of no importance, yet again . . .

He looked curiously at the ragged cut on his thumb and barely repressed a shudder. If such a thing was true, by what a narrow margin had he escaped a horrible death. . . . Across the room the object of his suspicions continued to sit calmly figuring in a notebook, never glancing around. His attitude was a declaration of the fact that the young man behind him was an excitable firebrand, whose behaviour was scarcely worth troubling about. Let him alone, he will come to his senses, that broad, imperturbable back seemed to say. . . .

Suddenly a revulsion swept over Roger. He felt a bit of an ass. Of course there could be no truth in this mad story, such things didn't happen. Though of course if it was entirely fiction, it put Esther in a queer light, however you looked at it. Either it was the result of those "confusional attacks" the doctor had hinted at, or she was, as both doctors now implied, a victim of morphia-mania. . . . Unthinkable! Esther!

What was this noise outside the door? Confused voices reached him speaking in French, together with the heavy tread of several men, who apparently were tramping up the stairs. The following instant Chalmers threw open the door, his face a study.

"The police, sir," he announced.

Roger sprang to his feet.

CHAPTER XXXV

"The police!"

"Yes, sir, three officers. They say someone telephoned for them, but I can't for the life of me say who it could have been, sir. Who would want to?"

In blank astonishment Roger stared as three men in uniform filed into the room and stood at attention. Two wore the regulation dress of sergents-de-ville, the third was clearly of superior rank. He was an aggressive, youngish fellow with a sharp, sallow face and a black, bristly moustache, cut very short. He began by eyeing Roger all over with a sort of dark suspicion, then addressed him in French.

"I take it that you are Monsieur Clifford?" he interrogated accusingly, keeping his smouldering black eyes fixed on Roger's face, while with his right hand he brought a notebook out of his pocket.

"Certainly my name is Clifford, but perhaps you will be good enough to inform me why you—"

"That can wait. You are English, monsieur?"

"Naturally. And I refuse to answer another question until you tell me how in thunder you come to be here," replied Roger, rapidly losing his temper.

"English, British subject," muttered the officer, writing busily with a stump of a pencil and ignoring utterly Roger's statement. "Occupation, monsieur?"

"Who sent for you to come here?" demanded Roger, more and more irate.

The question had an unexpected reply.

"C'était moi, messieurs, qui viens de vous téléphoner. Moi je suis Lady Clifford."

The voice, metallic and defiant, rang out from the door leading into the right-hand bedroom. The officer stared in surprise, while Roger wheeled with a brusque movement of incredulity to behold Thérèse facing them.

"*You* telephoned them?" he repeated, hardly able to believe his ears.

"Certainly. I simply reported the fact to police headquarters that I am being kept a prisoner in my bedroom."

She eyed him squarely, the yellow flecks in her grey irises plainly apparent. For two seconds she flashed him a challenge, while he regarded her steadily in complete silence. Then with a sudden softer air and a little gesture of appeal, she turned to the officer in charge and spoke rapidly in French.

"This is the gentleman, monsieur, my stepson, Mr. Roger Clifford."

"Your stepson, madame?" reiterated the man in a shocked tone.

"Yes, monsieur, the son of my late husband, Sir Charles Clifford, who has been dead less than a week."

There was a slight tremor in her voice, and, Roger could almost have sworn, tears in her eyes. The officers averted their eyes decorously, while

Roger gazed at her with aloof impersonality, simply curious. He watched her score her point and wondered just how far she intended to pursue the advantage. What was her plan? Was she, after all, technically innocent, able to prove the fact? Or was this a bold stratagem, to throw dust in his eyes? He was totally unable to choose between the two diametrically opposed theories.

The officer in charge shot a black glance at him and made ready to write further particulars.

"Pray proceed, madame. Will you kindly inform me as to the exact nature of this gentleman's conduct towards yourself."

"Monsieur, it is simply what I told you on the telephone. My stepson, who is a guest in my house, had the audacity to force me, under threats, to enter my room, after which he turned the key on me."

The man looked nonplussed, but intensely respectful.

"But, madame, permit me to suggest that you do not appear to be a prisoner."

"I will explain, monsieur. He did not lock that door there, it was not necessary, since he has never left the room. He has, in, fact, been on guard here. But the outer door, leading to the hall, is fastened, as you will see if you care to look."

At a sign from the superior officer one of the sergents-de-ville stepped into the hall and quickly returned to confirm Lady Clifford's statement. The chief representative of the police then drew a long breath and spoke to Roger in a threatening voice.

"Monsieur, you have heard Madame's statement to the effect that you, a guest in her house, forced her to remain in her bedroom by locking the door and removing the key. Do you deny this?"

"Not at all, it is perfectly true."

The reply was so cool that the interlocutor's self-possession wavered for an instant.

"Ah, indeed, then, monsieur, you make no attempt to contradict Madame's accusation?" inquired the man importantly the repetition giving him time to arrange his thoughts.

"It is true as far as it goes," Roger replied coldly. "If you wish to know the whole of the matter I must refer you to Madame."

There was an uncomfortable pause while the officer bit the end of his stubby pencil, evidently uncertain how best to proceed. Twice he glanced at Lady Clifford, and once he opened his mouth to speak, then closed it again. Suddenly, with an impulsive gesture, Thérèse turned directly to Roger.

"How can you say such a thing, Roger?" she inquired with an air of frankness and mild reproach. "I know only too well that in your heart you have always disliked me, have always been jealous of any little influence I may have had with your father, but how can you stand there and suggest that I can tell this gentleman why you behaved as you did when I don't know the reason?"

The stroke told; moreover, the absolute candour with its hint of lurking tears enhanced the strong appeal which her beauty had already exerted over the three limbs of the law. Not wishing to disclose anything more than was necessary Roger remained stonily silent, letting the officers think what they pleased. He felt the triumph in Thérèse's voice when she spoke again.

"You see, monsieur, Mr. Clifford does not care to reply. I leave you to draw your own conclusions. For me it is quite evident that he is unwilling to reveal his reasons for subjecting me to this treatment."

The man with the black moustache shifted from one foot to the other. From his expression it became apparent that he was growing ill at ease, scenting the presence, perhaps, of some purely domestic difference which lay outside his province. As he hesitated his roving eye caught sight of Sartorius, who had risen unobtrusively and was regarding the scene with dispassionate interest.

"May I be permitted to inquire, madame, who this gentleman is?"

"But certainly, monsieur. This is Dr. Gregory Sartorius, who for some weeks has been my husband's private physician. He is still staying here, as a favour to me, in order to be of service to my stepson, who has not been well."

The officer bowed, plainly as much impressed by the lady's generosity to her ungrateful relative as by the magnificence of having a private physician in attendance. He cleared his throat and turned again to Roger with a resumption of his truculent manner.

"Monsieur, the reasons for your inexcusable action have no interest for me. The point is that the law does not allow you to restrict the liberty of this lady in any way whatsoever. If you even attempt to do so, you will find yourself in serious trouble. Are you, or are you not, prepared to hand over the key to Madame's door?"

Without hesitation Roger put his hand in his pocket and took out the key.

"Here it is," he said simply, and held it out to the astonished officer, who shot him a puzzled and suspicious glance from under his black brows.

"Furthermore, monsieur, I warn you in the presence of witnesses that if you make a second attempt to molest Madame, I shall be compelled to give you in charge."

Roger offered no comment. The dark man looked from one to the other around the room, and although he had delivered his ultimatum in a hectoring tone, it was plain that he found himself dissatisfied with the situation. Perhaps he was uncertain whether or not the whole thing was a hoax and himself the butt of a joke, to be laughed at later for treating the affair in a melodramatic way. The faces before him told him nothing. At last he cleared his throat again with finality, and bowing to Lady Clifford with something approaching a flourish, extended the key to her.

"Voilà, madame!" he announced triumphantly. "I think there is nothing more that can be done at the moment." He moved closer to her and, speaking in a confidential tone added, "I fear it is impossible for me to arrest this gentleman, as he has withdrawn from his offensive position. All it is in my power to do is to warn him not to repeat the insult. I rely upon you, madame, to keep me informed in case of further trouble."

Thérèse smiled with a clear-eyed serenity which enslaved the posse to a man.

"Thanks to you, monsieur, I do not anticipate any further trouble," she replied with a glance from under her lashes. "Only this was the sort of thing I felt I could not deal with alone."

"Naturally not, madame," rejoined the officer, flattered but embarrassed. "While I am entirely in the dark as to the motives underlying this gentleman's conduct, I can safely promise that the law of France will protect you from him."

With another fierce glance in Roger's direction, he turned to go, making a sign to the *sergent-de-ville.*

"One moment, messieurs! It would give me pleasure to have you partake of some refreshment before you leave. Aline!" she called, and the maid appeared instantly from the open door behind. "Aline, show these officers to the dining-room and ask them to have a glass of port."

"Madame is most kind! With Madame's permission we will drink Madame's health!"

She flashed a gracious smile at the three who departed, led by Aline. Roger watched them go, conscious that Thérèse was regarding him out of the corners of her eyes. A moment later he felt rather than saw her withdraw, with a sort of elaborate nonchalance, to her own room once more.

As on former occasions Roger was revolted by what he considered her innate vulgarity, but this time he was puzzled as well, unable to decide whether it covered innocence or guilt. Quite possibly he was doing her the grossest injustice. In any case he now knew that he had acted foolishly in trying to restrain her movement. He had been moved by an impulse and regretted it. Until he had more trustworthy information he could do nothing whatever, take no step against either her or the doctor. It was lucky for him, indeed, that the latter had not seen fit to inform the police of the threat used against him. The fat would have been in the fire then and no mistake. Why had the fellow kept quiet? It argued against him, although perhaps he considered that even an unsubstantiated charge would do no good to a professional man. . . . Thérèse, too, had carefully avoided giving any details of the affair, for which he was heartily thankful. For a moment he had been paralysed by the dread lest the whole business concerning Esther should be dragged into the open. It was not a matter for the public yet, and might never be.

More and more did it become difficult to know what course to pursue. Yet some bulldog instinct within him made him unwilling to relinquish his watch over the two people concerned.

Two things he was determined Thérèse should not do. One was to find her way into his bedroom, the other to hold any communication with Sartorius. This in mind, he lit a cigarette with at least an outward show of calmness, and took his seat near the door. From here he could see what went on in the hall, in case Thérèse should attempt to come outside, and at the same time keep a quiet eye on the phlegmatic figure of the doctor.

A dozen small incidents, hitherto scarcely noticed, recurred to him. Moreover the disjointed words uttered by Esther as she had lain with her head on his arm now linked themselves together to form a coherent meaning. Could it be possible that what both doctors suggested had any foundation in fact? It seemed unthinkable. His whole association with the girl rose before him to assert her unimpeachable normality. And yet there was proof that Sartorius, a physician of standing, had cast doubts upon her sanity long before her attack upon him. The condition he had attributed to her could so easily account for her dramatic reappearance and her invention of a mad story of crime and persecution, as easily as it could explain the morphia injections, self-inflicted. His aunt had no doubt that the doctor was right in his belief; no one had any doubt except himself—and Chalmers. In his own case his opinion might be influenced by his love for the girl—for it was love, there was no question in his mind now.

He heard the representatives of the police take their leave, with voluble expressions of gratitude for the hospitality of the house. A few minutes afterwards Chalmers came up to bring him some food and a whisky and soda.

"No good starving yourself, sir," he whispered, setting down the tray on a small table. "It won't help us to find out what we want to know. Shall I bring him something too, or shall I let him have it in the dining-room?"

Roger signified the latter, and the butler approached Sartorius with a confidential air and formally announced that dinner was served. It was all rather absurd, Roger thought. With a nod the doctor rose and lumbered from the room. It was now after half past nine.

Left alone Roger found himself too disturbed to eat more than a few mouthfuls. To his relief Chalmers returned almost at once.

"I've left Marie to look after him, sir," he said in a guarded tone, "thinking you'd be wanting to hear the rest of what I was telling you when we were interrupted. I know what happened with the police, sir, for I took the liberty of remaining in the hall while they were here."

"What do you think of it all, Chalmers?"

The old man narrowed his lips into a cautious line.

"Well, sir, her ladyship may be as innocent as the babe unborn, in which case I've a deal to answer for. But I believe, sir, that her sending for the police was just a part of her game—to pull the wool over our eyes, sir."

Roger shook his head slowly and drank his whisky before replying.

"I don't know, Chalmers, I'm completely at sea. Go on, though, let me hear all that Miss Rowe said to you."

"Well, sir, it was very little, but I caught something about a plot she'd got wind of, a plan between her ladyship and the doctor to kill Sir Charles by giving him typhoid fever, and you too, sir. She said something about germs, and—mind this, sir—*Evian water*. That's what made me act as I did, sir, in regard to her ladyship. There was no mistake about it; she was just going to pour that water away, sir, when it came over me what she was up to, and quick as a flash I grabbed her arm and wrenched the bottle out of her hands. If I were to go to prison for it, sir, I'd still swear I did right."

Roger nodded slowly, his face hardening.

"If this should be true, Chalmers, and not, as they want us to believe, a fabrication of Miss Rowe's brain, then—"

He broke off and for a second his eyes met those of the old servant.

Then the latter bent forward and finished the sentence for him.

"Then it's murder, sir, no other name for it. Those two killed Sir Charles just as surely as if they'd put a bullet into him, and they meant to get you, sir, one way or another. I'd take my oath on it. It's my opinion the nurse got here just in time to save you."

"And yet, Chalmers, it's quite possible that business of the mineral water has some other, simple explanation. One must admit the possibility."

"Very good, sir, there's those who can examine into that bottle and say if there's anything amiss with it. I consider that bottle as evidence, sir, and I'm glad we've got it safely under lock and key."

"Yes, we can have it analysed. Perhaps I ought to have handed it over to the police. . . . I didn't do it because while the thing's in doubt one can't bring a horrible accusation, particularly against a member of one's family. My father's own wife—!"

The butler nodded understandingly.

"I suppose I'll have to be leaving here in the morning, sir: I sha'n't be wanted after what has happened. But I don't like leaving you alone to handle things, sir."

"We'll all go too, Chalmers, my aunt and I and Miss Rowe, if she's fit to be moved. You will come with us to an hotel for the present. I'm not going to bed at all to-night, I'm going to keep watch over Miss Rowe. If her story is true, Sartorius may try to get at her again; she mustn't be left."

"I shall keep about, too, sir, to know what goes on in this house."

"Right, Chalmers, it's a good idea. By the way, we'll keep as much as we can from my aunt, there's no good alarming her. I'll go now and inquire about Miss Rowe."

"Je demands pardon, monsieur!"

He jumped as the sardonic voice of Aline sounded in his ear, and the woman, with a covert glance of mock-servility, hurried past him with the empty tray. There were both malice and triumph in her bearing. Whether she knew anything or not—and it seemed impossible that she could surmise their suspicions—her manner conveyed unmistakably that she knew her mistress had scored a victory. A sudden misgiving swept over Roger. Supposing the hideous affair to be true, was it not extremely doubtful that they would ever be able to prove it? Might they not go on to the end of their days not knowing?

He crossed the hall and went along the passage to Esther's room. As he gently opened the door an odour of drugs or disinfectants met his nostrils, giving him a sinking feeling he had often experienced as a small boy on entering a dentist's room.

The little doctor was bending over the bed. From the other side Miss Clifford raised a white and tired face. Roger felt suddenly oppressed by fear. What were they going to tell him? He motioned to his aunt, who came towards him and answered the question he was afraid to utter.

"The doctor hasn't been able to bring her around, Roger, though he's done all he can. It's nearly an hour and a half, now, and she is still unconscious."

CHAPTER XXXVI

IT WAS nearly midnight when Dr. Bousquet at last took his departure. An hour before that time Esther became conscious, but was so utterly weak he would not allow her to speak or make the smallest effort of any kind. She made no comment on finding herself back in her old quarters, and after a short interval drifted back into a natural sleep. The watchers felt a degree of relief.

"I think I may safely leave her now, monsieur," said the doctor, drawing on his gloves. "I will come again in the morning about ten o'clock, and if any complication should arise in the meantime, you will of course telephone me. She is suffering now from shock, it seems, combined with the after-effects of morphia. Later when she is less exhausted she may be intensely nervous. One must see that she is kept absolutely quiet, with nothing to agitate her. A fresh shock might do great harm."

Roger glanced at the grey-white face on the pillow. It was thin and drawn; it was hard to understand how it could have altered so much in these few days' time. What had happened to her to give her that pinched look? The shadows under the closed eyes were deep violet.

"Tell me, doctor," he whispered. "Have you been able to come to any conclusion on the subject of her mental condition?"

He brought out the last words with a painful hesitation.

"I am not an alienist, at least not an expert," replied the little man cautiously, elevating the reddish tufts of his brows. "Of course I have a general knowledge. During the short interval when she was conscious she did not appear to be other than normal, but that, I fear, is not conclusive evidence. One would have to study her. If, as Dr. Sartorius suggests, she may be suffering from confusional attacks, she would part of the time be so completely sane that one would suspect nothing wrong. Subjects of that kind often live a sort of double life. They are apt to invent romantic or mysterious histories about themselves, intrigues in which they figure, often as a persecuted victim. They make these tales so extremely convincing that they frequently succeed in imposing their belief on other people."

"You mean there would be nothing about her to make one know she was not normal mentally?"

"Quite so, unless one happened to possess proof that her stories were untrue."

Roger's heart sank. Horrible as it was to contemplate the thought of the crime committed in their midst, it was to him infinitely worse to think of Esther as mentally unbalanced.

"Have you noticed anything yourself which you would regard as a suspicious symptom, doctor?" he inquired with difficulty.

"Only her violent antipathy to Dr. Sartorius. I should consider that rather a bad sign. It is the sort of thing these subjects are prone to, monsieur," and the little man shook his head disparagingly.

Roger risked one more question, dreading the answer.

"How can we find out about her? You say she will have to be studied?"

"Very probably, monsieur. There are certain tests. I should suggest that if the young woman is someone in whom you are particularly interested"—he gave a tactful cough which Roger understood well—"the best thing you can do is to place her for a few weeks in a quiet sanatorium. There is one near Grasse; either Dr. Sartorius or I could arrange it for you."

"I see, doctor. Well, we will think about it."

He watched the little man depart, grimly resolved never to let Esther be placed in a sanatorium, no matter what happened. Sartorius himself had mentioned the quiet place near Grasse. That fact alone was enough to decide him against it. He was alone now with Esther. A few minutes before he had persuaded his aunt to go to her room and try to sleep. She had demurred at first, but he had firmly led her to her door.

"I'll go if you insist," she gave in at last. "But you're so far from well yourself, it will be a great strain on you to sit up all night."

"Nonsense; this business has made me forget all about myself. If you insist on sharing watches, I will call you early in the morning."

She nodded reluctantly, then looked at him with a troubled brow.

"Roger, where in heaven's name do you suppose that poor girl has been these past two days?"

He shook his head slowly.

"If we knew that, Dido, we'd have the key to the whole damned mystery," he said.

Sinking down wearily in the chair beside the bed he painstakingly attempted to organise a plan of action. It was a difficult business when he had so little he could definitely go on. His efforts brought meagre results; moreover he felt confused, curiously fatigued in mind and body. In the dim light of the shaded lamp the figures on the Toile de Jouy danced incessantly before his eyes with an eerie effect; he felt himself enveloped in a phantasmagoria of which it was impossible to tell substance from shadow. Every few seconds his eyes kept gravitating back to the pale, fragile face of Esther, which was troubled even in sleep, the brow furrowed slightly, the muscles about the mouth twitching from time to time. Whatever the cause of her present state, he felt gravely apprehensive for her, afraid that she might be in for a serious nervous illness. Perhaps what she wished to tell him might be buried in oblivion for months, if indeed it ever came to light. It even occurred to him that she might wake up completely ignorant of everything that had preceded her collapse. In that case what should he do? how should he behave? He knew he could never rid his mind entirely of the suspicion she had planted there, yet how to prove it?

The door opened quietly, and Chalmers came in, bringing him a cup of coffee.

"The doctor's gone to his room, now, sir, otherwise I wouldn't be here. I've stuck about the hall and stairs the whole time, sir."

"What about her ladyship?"

"She's never tried to leave her room, sir. I've heard her trying to get on to someone on the telephone, it seems as though she's been at it for hours, but I fancy she hasn't got through."

"Has she had any chance of speaking with the doctor?"

"She has not, sir, at least not without my knowing, and I daresay she didn't want to risk that. Aline, though—that's a woman I never could stick, sir, I don't mind telling you!—Aline has been prowling around the end of the hall near your room a couple of times. I caught her at it, and she pretended to be looking out of the window."

"You think she was trying to get into my room?" Roger asked thoughtfully.

"I'm pretty sure of it, sir."

Roger drank his coffee in silence, mentally reviewing this information.

"There is another little thing I've noticed, sir," Chalmers continued. "There are a number of keys gone from doors about the house. I've counted seven missing, and I could take my oath they were in the locks earlier in the evening. There's never any reason for taking them out."

"Then you think Aline has taken them to see if any of them will open my door?"

"That's it, sir. I could have told her there's no two keys alike in this house," he added grimly. "She came to me very friendly like at about ten o'clock, and tried to pump me to find out what I knew. Had the nurse come to, and was she able to talk yet? Was it true she had staggered in so drunk she couldn't see proper, and had fallen in a heap on the floor? Things like that, sir. Not much change she got out of me. I shut her up in no time, sir. I knew what she was after."

Hours passed. Roger sat on alone in the half-lighted room, analysing his impressions and going over in his mind the whole course of his father's illness, from the moment he had entered the house. To save his life he could not think of one suspicious circumstance, nothing that appeared even particularly unusual. Yet, no! What about that cablegram which was never sent? With a start he recalled it, wondering how it could have slipped his memory till now. What if Thérèse had had another and more vital reason than he had thought of for keeping him away? Was it possible she had been afraid to have him in the house? It was a fact that he alone knew her relations with Holliday, he alone had always to an annoying extent seen through her. He recalled with a feeling akin to nausea her recent attempts to placate him, to turn him from an enemy into an ally. Had she done that in order to blind him the more completely to what was going on? The idea suggested a degree of calculating inhumanity appalling to contemplate. He lived over again the moment when she had clung to him caressingly and pressed her perfumed cheek against his breast. . . . How could he have been such an utter fool? He set his teeth with a feeling of intolerable disgust. . . .

A smothered scream from the bed caused him to start up.

Esther had suddenly sat up in bed, bolt-upright, her eyes glazed with terror, one thin hand clapped over her open mouth.

"Esther, my dear! What is it?"

She continued to gaze transfixed in the direction of the door, unutterable horror written on her face.

"S'sh," she whispered tensely. "S'sh—listen!"

Roger listened, but could hear nothing. The house was absolutely still. Very gently he took her hand and held it firmly in his. It trembled like a bird imprisoned.

"Darling—there's nothing to be frightened of. What did you think you heard?"

She swallowed twice, then spoke, her voice still strangely hoarse.

"It was the doctor. He was outside there, in the passage. I know he was there."

"Nonsense, there's no one about, or if there is, it's only Chalmers."

"Listen, though!"

Roger obeyed again, and for several seconds they both held their breath, straining their ears. At last from outside there came the very faint creak of a footstep, as though someone who had been standing still was now moving away. Roger made a movement to jump up, but in a panic she pulled him back.

"No, no, don't leave me!"

"Certainly not, if you don't want me to. But you're quite safe now; you have nothing to be afraid of."

She leaned closer to him, trembling.

"No," the hoarse voice whispered, "that's not true. I'm not safe as long as I'm in the same house with him. He is afraid of me. He wants to keep me from talking. He will do anything to keep me quiet, anything. He's only waiting for his chance."

A violent tremor seized her so that her teeth chattered. With his arm about her Roger forced her gently to lie down, noting with growing alarm the fixed glitter of her eyes and the moisture standing in beads upon her forehead, above which her bronze hair ruffled in damp curls. All at once it had become appallingly easy to believe that she was suffering from the delusion of persecution, that her brain, somehow disordered, had fabricated a whole history of terror. Sick at heart he yet recalled the doctor's counsel against allowing her to excite herself.

"Esther, dear," he said soothingly. "You must keep quite quiet and trust to me. Remember your nerves are bound to be upset after all that morphia you have had. You know that."

He stopped, afraid that he had said the wrong thing, but she only frowned thoughtfully as though considering his words.

"Morphia," she repeated to herself. "Yes, I suppose that is what it was. No wonder I feel queer. . . . And then of course I haven't had anything to eat for two days and a half—that makes it worse."

"Two days and a half!"

He stared at her aghast. This last speech of hers sounded amazingly rational. He burned to question her, yet dared not attempt it.

"The doctor said you were to have something if you waked up," he said quietly, as though there were nothing out of the way. "There's something here ready in a little saucepan. I've only got to heat it up. Shall I give it to you?"

She nodded and lay motionless, watching with languid eyes the blue flame of the spirit-lamp as he made ready a cup of broth, then submitted with the docility of a child while he put another pillow under her head and fed her the hot liquid, a spoonful at a time, slowly, for fear of making her sick. When she had finished she sank back with closed eyes, and he thought a faint tinge of warmer colour crept into her cheeks. For what seemed to him a long period there was complete silence. He gazed at her with searching eyes, tortured by doubts and questionings. When he had begun to think she had again fallen asleep, she quietly spoke.

"That was good," she murmured; "I needed that. . . . It's a long time to go without food, you get so weak."

He could bear the suspense no longer. So cautiously he said:

"My dear, how was it you didn't have anything to eat for two and a half days? What do you mean?"

She looked at him for a long puzzled moment, then drew her hand across her brow.

"Of course," she answered slowly, "you don't know about that. No. How could you?"

He hoped she was going to continue, but instead she raised herself on her elbow and whispered, "Tell me this. What have you done about him?"

"You mean the doctor? Nothing. He's in his room now, asleep, I suppose. It's about three o'clock, you know."

She drew in her breath sharply, her pupils dilating.

"Do you mean you haven't arrested him—after what I told you? Then he *was* outside that door! I knew it!"

He caught her hands in a reassuring grasp.

"No, no, my dear, you mustn't be frightened. Don't you understand it's impossible to arrest the man—without a reason?"

She gave him a piercing look.

"But I *told* you! Didn't you hear what I said? He's a murderer! He murdered your father, and he was going to kill you too, if I hadn't found out and got here in time! Oh, aren't people stupid! I thought I'd made it all clear!"

She tore her hands from his hold and covered her face for an instant, crying, "Oh, oh! Why couldn't you have him arrested at once, both of them for that matter? I can't understand! Why didn't you?"

There was no evading the sharpness of her question. He dropped his eyes in embarrassment, unable to reply.

"Oh!" she burst out as though the truth had suddenly dawned on her, "now I know, I see it all! You thought I didn't know what I was saying. You thought I was raving. The doctor made you believe it. He would;

he's always prepared for any emergency, even though he never dreamed I should get away!"

"Get away? What do you mean by that, Esther?"

Instead of replying, she lifted his right hand and examined it with feverish interest.

"Are you absolutely sure he didn't touch this place in any way? You didn't let him put anything on it?"

"No, no—nothing at all."

She sank back, exhausted.

"Thank God! I began to be afraid I didn't save you after all," she breathed, and laughed a little hysterically. "Oh, Roger, I shall dream for years of that terrible time I had trying to reach you! I honestly thought I should die on the way."

"Esther," he said, forcing himself to speak calmly, "where were you during those two days and nights? What do you mean by a terrible time trying to reach me?"

Her face contracted with a spasm of pain, as though the memory were unbearable. He pressed her hand, quick to spare her, and afraid, too, that he might do her an injury.

"It doesn't in the least matter; don't tell me now."

She lay silent another moment, then answered slowly:

"No . . . I will tell you. It won't hurt me now. You see, I have been kept a prisoner . . . unconscious . . . in the doctor's laboratory, you know, at the top of his house . . . in the Route de Grasse."

"A prisoner—!"

For the life of him he could not repress the utter incredulity he felt at this astounding statement.

"I don't think you believe me," she said, smiling the ghost of a smile. "I know it sounds impossible, but it's true. He never meant for me to leave there alive. He was going to do away with me so as to leave no trace."

Suddenly he knew that she was speaking the truth.

"Esther—do you know what you're saying?"

Cold horror gripped him. It seemed unthinkable that this tender young creature so close to him had lately passed through the hell she described. In a daze he listened to the dry, hoarse voice as it continued:

"Oh, I know all right. He kept me stupefied. I never knew how I got there; I didn't even know I was there . . . it was only through an accident that I came to at all, otherwise . . . Such a silly accident! All because Captain Holliday didn't give me the injection properly."

"*Holliday?*"

He wondered if he had heard aright. She did not answer, going off, at first softly, then with increasing vehemence into convulsions of laughter that shook her from head to foot. He clasped her close in his arms and held her to him, smoothing her rough curls and whispering:

"Steady on, Esther dear! It's all over now. You're safe with me; I sha'n't let anything happen to you!"

She subsided at last, the tears spilling over her lashes and down her cheeks unheeded. He wiped them away, realising how spent she was with the effort of relating, even so briefly, her terrible experience.

"Rest now, darling. You must keep absolutely quiet. I don't want to hear any more now, except . . . Esther, I wonder if I dare ask you one thing. Don't speak if you don't feel like it. But . . . you realise we can't make a definite charge of any kind until we know what we're about. You understand that, I know. Tell me, dear, are there any proofs of this horrible story? I mean proofs of the plot you spoke of to murder my father, and also of your being sequestered in the laboratory."

He saw her eyes narrow with thought. She lay very still, as though to focus all her strength to give him a connected answer.

"I understand, of course, there must be more than my word, for he'll do his utmost to discredit me. Listen: if the police or someone will go to the Route de Grasse before the doctor can get there, they'll find a good deal of evidence. Of course he'll get there as soon as he can—I'm surprised he hasn't gone already—and he'll do his best to cover up the signs. He can't mend that skylight in a hurry, though," she added thoughtfully.

"Esther, how does Holliday come into this? Was he in the plot?"

"No, not at all—not actively, that is. He was dragged into it at the last simply to stand guard over me and see I didn't get away. Even he had to see that it was absolutely necessary to dispose of me," she finished coolly. "It would have ruined everything if they hadn't."

"Good God . . ."

"Now about the proofs. I believe Lady Clifford has been giving you typhoid culture in your mineral water. I heard the doctor say so. I don't know that we can prove that, or that she gave it to your father in his milk, either; that's all done with. But there's one thing we can prove. There's a little chemist named Cailler—I can tell you where the shop is—who has an analysis of a hypodermic needle the doctor used on your father. It was what caused that sudden relapse. The needle had pure toxin of typhoid in it. I know, because I took it to the chemist myself."

"*You* did?"

"Certainly. It was too late to save your poor father—nothing could have saved him—but I was afraid they were trying to get you as well, and I had to be sure before I dared say anything. I didn't get the report till after the funeral, when I heard it over the telephone. Then I sent you that message by Chalmers."

"I see! Then what happened? I was only three minutes getting downstairs, but you were nowhere to be seen."

"Of course, that was because the doctor was waiting behind the door to grab me. He stuck that awful needle of his in my arm, and after that I can't tell you anything. I didn't know any more until two days later, when I found myself lying on a bed in the laboratory."

A slight fit of trembling overtook her again. He took her two limp hands in his and kissed them, moved by a new and overpowering emotion. With startling vividness he realised the whole stupendous thing, what she had done, what she had risked and suffered. Even that stupid incident of what the servant-girl had told about seeing her with Holliday in his car became clear as day. Of course—and he had suspected her of a flirtation!

"Esther, my own Esther—you splendid, marvellous girl! To think that I never knew, that you might have died, and I should never have known what became of you! Do you know what I was thinking? I spent two days searching for you in every hotel and pension in Cannes . . ."

"I know," she said softly, her eyes suddenly misty.

"I can't take it in yet, Esther; it's too overwhelming."

He buried his head in the covers beside her. She put her hand upon his hair and caressed it with a clinging touch that sent a thrill through him. Like this they remained for long minutes, and the communion was to him the sweetest he had ever known. Strange that this complete ecstasy should come to him at the very moment when he was shocked to the depths of his being by the disclosure of the vile crime perpetrated in their midst.

After a little while Esther drifted off to sleep once more, leaving him to face again the problem of those two murderers, as he now knew them to be, still at large and still under the roof with him. What was to be done? Would they make any attempt to escape, or would they brazen it out till the last? He had a strong suspicion that they would both adopt this latter course. He foresaw a long and difficult trail, a defence skilfully engineered by Sartorius, whose reputation would stand him in good stead. In his imagination he pictured a French jury swayed by the beauty and emotional appeal of Thérèse. Why, they might easily win; it was perfectly possible. He had an Englishman's contempt for French jurisdiction. As for the doctor, he felt sure that that man would employ every diabolical means in his power to discredit Esther's statement, to blacken her character; he would impute false motives to her or make a convincing case against her sanity, perhaps both. The very notion made him boil with rage. The cold-blooded infamy of the plot to do away with his father was as nothing compared with the wanton brutality of the attempt on Esther's life. To think of this fresh and lovely body, so near to him now that he could feel the throbbing of her heart, dismembered, defiled in the work of annihilation, filled him with unspeakable horror. He had to take a firm grip on himself to keep from forcing his way into the neighbouring room and wreaking personal vengeance on the author of so bestial an outrage. The man's stolid calm, which had appeared a proof of innocence, now made him seem a monster of insensibility. Sartorius was not human; he was the python of Esther's dream, slow-blooded, impersonal, relentless. . . .

The clock struck four. Some time after this he must have lost consciousness, for gradually his waking thoughts blurred imperceptibly into unreal, his head resting heavily on the bed beside the sleeping girl. He was roused by a touch on his shoulder and a voice saying tensely in his ear:

"Mr. Roger! Mr. Roger, sir!"

Dizzily he raised his head, blinking in the grey daylight that filled the room. Then he struggled to his feet, stiff and cramped.

"Yes, Chalmers, what is it?"

"Her ladyship, sir—she's not in her room. She's not in the house. She's gone, sir!"

CHAPTER XXXVII

"Gone! What do you mean? How could she get away?"

"That's what we don't know, sir. We—"

"Who is we?" demanded Roger sharply.

"I mean Aline, sir; it was she who found it out. I've been about the house the whole night, sir; I've never closed my eyes. No one could have got past me without my knowing it."

Roger glanced at the bed. Esther still slept, the rings around her eyes darker than ever in the cold morning light.

"Come outside," he said in a lower tone. "We mustn't disturb Miss Rowe. Now tell me."

"It's just as I say, sir. It seems she had told Aline to bring her some tea at six o'clock. I couldn't say what she had in mind to be wanting it so early; it seems as if she was planning to go out before anyone was up, but I don't know, sir. Anyhow, when Aline did bring the tea a moment ago, the room was empty; the bed hadn't been touched."

"You've searched the house?"

"Only partly, sir."

"What about the back stairs?"

"I don't think she could have come out of her room at all, sir, without my knowing; and in any case last night I locked the tradesmen's door and put the key in my pocket."

Roger rapidly reconnoitred.

"Stay here till I call my aunt," he ordered. "Whatever you do, don't stir from this spot. I am afraid to leave Miss Rowe alone for a single moment."

In a few minutes he returned with Miss Clifford, whom he had found wide awake, on the point of donning her dressing-gown to come and relieve him. He told her nothing about Thérèse's disappearance, merely cautioning her strongly against leaving Esther unguarded.

"You must grasp this fact, Dido," he said gravely, looking her straight in the eyes. "Esther is no more out of her mind than you or I. There is something very serious behind this, and that man Sartorius is a terrible menace to her safety. I can't explain now, but you'll know it all soon enough."

He left her bewildered and shaken, and rejoined the butler in the hall. Outside the boudoir door stood Aline, her brows drawn together under her ragged fringe of hair, her thin lips set in a line that betokened anxiety.

"*Monsieur, monsieur,*" she exclaimed accusingly, "*dites moi, qu'est-ce que vous avez fait?*"

"*Je n'ai rien fait, Aline,*" he replied coldly; "*je ne sais rien.*"

She gazed at him in a puzzled fashion. For all her habitual crafty appearance, he felt sure she had no knowledge of this dreadful business. In her way she had a certain loyalty to her mistress which might readily dispose her to regard him as an enemy.

"*Moi non plus, monsieur,*" she said with hesitation. "*Mais vous savez, hier soir Madame a été tellement fâchée contre Monsieur que je croyais . . .*"

"*Ça ne fait rien,*" he interrupted, striding past her impatiently.

With the muddled feeling of sleep still upon him he unlocked his own door and went through to the bathroom, where he hastily washed his face in cold water. Then as he dried it with a bath-towel he took a quick survey of the room. All was exactly as he had left it the night before: the full-length casement window stood half open, as it usually did; the bottle of Evian was on the shelf where he had placed it. That at any rate was still safe, he reflected. Thérèse had not been able to get at it, thanks to his precautions.

As he quitted the room, relocking the door, Chalmers approached him and spoke in a whisper.

"Do you think it's all right, sir?" he inquired. "She's gone to ask the doctor if he knows anything about her ladyship."

Following the direction of the old man's eyes, Roger saw the black-clad figure of the maid at the first door along the passage. Her voice, high-pitched with excitement, reached his ears, mingled with the doctor's heavy tones.

"Let her alone; it can't do any harm. You are still sure he didn't communicate with her ladyship at all?"

"Positive, sir. I'm sure he's never stirred from his room."

"We'd better make quite sure she's not in the house somewhere," said Roger slowly. "And then if we don't find her—"

"What then, sir?"

"Then I think there is nothing for me to do but communicate with the police."

"I see, sir. Then you've talked to Miss Rowe, sir?"

"Yes, Chalmers. I have heard more than enough."

As he spoke he realised suddenly that they were now plunged into the midst of a revolting sensation. In a few hours the newspapers would blazon it to the world, and all Cannes, all France, perhaps, would be searching for the beautiful Lady Clifford, wanted on the charge of murdering her husband.

"Aline," he said as the woman came towards him, "what was Madame wearing? Have you thought to look?"

"Ah, non, monsieur, mais tenez! Je vous dirai toute de suite."

She hurried into Thérèse's room and returned almost at once with a face still more perplexed. There was nothing missing from Madame's wearing apparel, as far as she could see, except the black chiffon gown Madame wore last evening. Madame had not undressed at eleven o'clock, when she desired to be left alone.

"Do you mean to say there is no coat gone? No wrap of any kind, nor a hat?"

"Monsieur peut regarder. C'est comme je dis."

The three exchanged puzzled glances.

"She may be in the house," hazarded Roger at last. "We had better find out."

In a few minutes they had made a tour of the entire villa. Roger himself tried the fastenings of all the windows on the ground-floor, and the doors leading onto the terrace from the salon. All was secure. There remained only the doctor's room, and Aline, who had been inside it a moment ago, was prepared to swear her ladyship was not there.

Roger shot a speculative glance at the maid. Was it possible she was lying? Was this all part of some scheme on Thérèse's part to allow her time to get away? Had Aline connived at her escape? The suspicion took root. They were now at the top of the house, where there were only servants' quarters and box-rooms. Two flights of stairs lay between them and the front door. What if the woman had led them hither in order to leave the lower regions unguarded?

"Listen, sir! Was that a car starting?"

All stood still, attentive to the sound below. Then with a sudden idea Roger strode to the small oval window in the mansard roof, and tried to see down into the garden. Far below an engine whirred, tyres grated on the drive. He caught sight of a car just disappearing out of the gateway.

"By God, Chalmers, they've gone! They've made off together."

"Was it the doctor's car, sir? I thought I knew the sound."

There was no good being upset about it, Roger reflected; certainly he could not detain the two unless he had a warrant for their arrest. Yet he experienced a feeling of chagrin at being so easily outwitted. The doctor's room, seen in disorder through the open door when they descended the stairs, told a story of a hasty departure.

"She was probably hiding in his room all the time," Roger remarked grimly as he eyed the untidy bed. "They've gone off somewhere together, though I'm astonished that they'd be so stupid. It's a damaging admission, or might be regarded in that light."

"For the life of me, I can't think how she got out of her room without my seeing her, sir," the old man commented with a rueful shake of the head.

"Well, there it is, and I believe this woman's been fooling us all along."

"Do you think their idea is to try to escape, sir?"

"Oh, I hardly think so! It is far more likely they are on their way to the police with some concocted story against Miss Rowe and against me. They will arrange it together, thinking to have the advantage of denouncing me before I can denounce them."

He became, aware that the sharp, black eyes of Aline were fixed on his face curiously. He wondered how much English she understood.

"It would have been difficult to prevent their leaving the house in any case," he added slowly. "But I believe I can circumvent them in another way. I have a plan of action, Chalmers. I am going first to a chemist Miss Rowe has told me about, and after that I intend to make a statement at police headquarters. You might get me the telephone book and a cup of coffee while I change my clothes."

As he spoke a subdued but pathetic whine reached their ears. It came from Thérèse's little Aberdeen terrier, who stood in the boudoir door, looking up with eyes of patient inquiry and uttering continuous plaints.

"*Il pleure tout le temps,*" murmured Aline. "*Ah, Tony, Tony, qu'est-ce que tu as? Ah, le pauvre!*"

"Come, Tony, old boy," called Roger, stooping to stroke the dog for a moment. "What's the matter? Put him outdoors, Chalmers; perhaps he only wants to go out."

The butler obeyed, and Roger entered his room to change his attire. His mind was heavily oppressed with the ordeal that lay before him, yet he was keyed up with a strange excitement. He felt there must now be no delay in the matter of laying a formal charge against the woman who for six years had been his father's wife and also against a highly respected member of the medical profession. That he would encounter a terrific opposition he did not question for a moment. He was not in the least sure that his case would be plain sailing. He saw himself, his aunt, Chalmers, and, last and hardest to contemplate, Esther in the witness-box—Esther, whose nerves were temporarily shattered by her frightful experience. . . . Had Thérèse been a party to the attempt on her life? Whether she had or not, she must have known about it and condoned it.

Outside in the garden the wretched dog continued to howl. What possessed the poor little creature? In the stillness of the early morning the long-drawn, disconsolate sounds rose and tell with a dirge-like hint of desolation. He must be silenced somehow; he would disturb Esther.

Presently the howling ceased, and a second later Chalmers came up bringing rolls and coffee, the dog at his heels, shivering and whining.

"I can't make out what's wrong with him, sir; he's regularly upset. He wanted to come in, yet when I opened the door he stood there looking as if he had something on his mind. Try to eat a bit, sir; you've been a long time without proper food, and you've a hard day ahead of you."

Roger forced himself to drink a cup of coffee. It was true he had given no thought to himself for days. He gazed unseeingly out of the window at the acacias, glistening with the wet of last night's steady rain, gloomy under the still grey sky. Oppression lay heavy upon his spirit.

"Yes, Chalmers, there's a bad time ahead of us. If we don't look sharp those two will find a way out."

"You think there's a chance of them escaping, sir?"

"Not that. I mean they may manage to be acquitted."

He put his hand absently on the rough black head of the Aberdeen, who had cowered close to his leg, still faintly whimpering.

"Will they exhume Sir Charles's body, sir, do you think?"

"What would be the use? There would be nothing gained by that. My father died of a well-known disease; as far as anyone could tell it was a perfectly natural death. So would I have died a so-called natural death if the doctor had succeeded in his plan against me. That was the infernal cleverness of his scheme. Of course in the case of Miss Rowe's detention it is a different matter, but even there we may not be able to prove anything conclusive. We are up against an extraordinarily clever man. Still, I don't yet know the extent of our evidence against him; it may be very strong indeed. That's what I've got to find out."

"And all for the sake of your poor father's money, sir—which she'd have got in a few years' time anyhow!"

Roger was silent, knowing better than Chalmers, perhaps, the reason why Thérèse was not willing to wait for his father to die. He put on the light overcoat the butler held ready for him, thinking he would take one look at Esther before setting out. It was still very early; the life of the house had not yet begun. He knew that he would not find the chemist's shop open, and it might be several hours before he could accomplish much, but his restless state would not permit him to remain inactive.

As he left his room followed by Chalmers, a loud ringing and knocking at the front door caused them both to start and look at each other, recalling the dramatic entry of the police the night before. What could it be this time, and at this early hour?

"That will be a telegram, sir, I should say, though they don't generally make such a row, especially this time of day. I'll just see."

The clamour continued without ceasing. Roger let the old servant precede him down the stairs and saw him draw back the bolts of the door, muttering, "All right, all right—what's all the fuss about?"

On the threshold stood the excited figure of a telegraphic messenger, holding in his hand a *dépêche* which he did not trouble to deliver. Instead he burst out at once in a harsh, strained voice:

"Monsieur! Monsieur! On n'a pas su—on n'a pas regardé dehors— là-bas—"

"Comment?" demanded Roger, frowning. *"Qu'est-ce qu'il y a?"*

"Un accident, monsieur. Regardez donc!"

With a tense forefinger he pointed over the low stone balustrade at the right-hand side of the steps. Both men leaned over to look. What at first appeared to be a sodden, black rag, beaten by the rain, lay upon the ground close to the wall of the house. What was it? It was half-hidden by a rose-bush. . . . Someone pushed rudely past Roger, thrusting him aside. It was Aline.

"Chalmers, what is it? It can't be—My God it is; it's . . ."

An ear-splitting shriek rent the air as Aline made the same discovery.

Scream followed scream as the woman beat her hands together, crying:

"Ah, nom d'un nom! C'est Madame, c'est Madame!"

It was indeed Lady Clifford. The body, clad in the black chiffon frock soaked by the rain, lay crumpled up in the angle of the steps. The face was hidden under the bush, but the hands were visible, flecked with mud, their short fingers curved rigidly inward like talons, grasping, clutching at the air. All around lay glittering fragments of broken glass. What did it mean?

"Quiet that woman, someone—Chalmers, see to her," Roger cried, vaulting over the balustrade.

He knelt and pushed aside the sheltering branches of the rose-bush so as to reveal the head and face, the messenger bending close to him, breathing heavily. The grey eyes were stretched wide with a stare of terror, the mouth hung open. On the temple over the right eyebrow gaped a deep wound from which a vast quantity of blood had poured, down the side of the face and neck and shoulder, where it now stuck clotted and dark. There was no doubt whatever that life was extinct. She had probably been dead for several hours. All the clothing was sopping with water and beaten into the soil.

"Do you think it's suicide, sir?" asked Chalmers in a low voice.

Roger shook his head without replying. Certain odd details now became apparent. Tiny red scratches marred the skin in two or three places, giving a scarred appearance. Broken twigs on the rose-bush told their story also, but it was not at these that Roger looked so fixedly.

"Qu'est-ce qu'elle porte autour de son cou?" whispered the messenger in a curious but awed voice.

Carefully Roger lifted a mauve, mudstained wet scarf, the two ends of which were knotted about the throat. Some object was fastened securely to the middle of the strip of silk, tied by a ribbon. He examined it wonderingly. It was the broken, jagged neck of a bottle.

CHAPTER XXXVIII

ALL the servants of the household, drawn by Aline's screams, now crowded upon the steps and looked on with frightened faces. From them issued a confusion of hazarded explanations, all wide of the truth. Madame had started to go out and had had a stroke of some sort; Madame had shot herself; Madame had been lured outside by a bandit and struck with a club, the object being to secure her pearls. Yet, no—the pearls were not missing, there they were around her neck, stained dark with blood. Ah! . . . what a terrible sight! Then it was not robbery after all. What could it be, then?

The neck of the bottle hung around her throat caused complete mystification, likewise the fact that upon the feet were no shoes, only the cobwebby black stockings, laced with delicate clocks, which she had worn the night before. What could have possessed her to venture out at night and into the rain as well, clad in the filmy, perishable gown and in her stocking-feet? It was a mystery wholly baffling; not one of the excited staff could offer a reasonable theory.

When the body was raised from the ground one fact at least was established, and that was that death had not been occasioned by the gash on the temple. At the first movement the head swung back like the head of a sawdust doll. The neck had been broken.

They bore the body upstairs and laid it on the gilt bed. Then at a word from Roger the butler picked up the receiver of the telephone upon the painted *table de nuit* and rang up Dr. Bousquet. The physician could do no good, but he would attend to certain necessary formalities. The servants crowded around, quiet now but avid with curiosity, until Roger with a wave of the hand cleared the room, at the same time issuing instructions to the chief of them. When he believed himself alone with Chalmers a touch on the arm reminded him that the messenger, who had followed the cortege upstairs, was still lingering on the threshold of the bedroom. With his grubby hand he held out the telegram he had brought, pointing to the name on the back.

"Leddy Cleefford? *C'est madame là?*" he whispered hoarsely.

Roger nodded and took the telegram, slipping it into his pocket. Then mechanically he handed the messenger fifty francs and watched him depart. At the door of Esther's room he encountered his aunt, her face full of alarm.

"What is it all about, Roger? Something dreadful has happened, I know it! I didn't dare leave the room after what you said."

"Close the door and come outside. Sartorius has gone, so Esther is quite safe from him, but she's in a very nervous state and I don't want her to know this yet. . . . Brace up, Dido; you must try to take what I'm going to say quite calmly. Thérèse is dead. She died last night."

He thought she was going to faint, but she clutched the door-knob and steadied herself.

"Dead!" Her dry lips formed the word. "Impossible! Why, last night she . . . what was it? Was she ill?"

"No. It seems to have been an accident. There'll have to be an inquest. It's going to be extremely painful, and a terrible shock for you. But remember this—if she'd lived it would have been infinitely worse for us all."

She moistened her lips, regarding him with an ashen face.

"Roger—I don't think I know what you mean."

"Simply this, dear. What Miss Rowe said last night was true, all of it. She wasn't raving."

"You mean that Thérèse and Dr. Sartorius . . . you can't mean that . . ."

"I do. They are murderers. They killed my father."

"Your father! But he died of typhoid fever—you know that as well as I do; there was nothing wrong about it."

"They gave him typhoid fever, by means of culture in the milk he was taking. When he was getting well, Sartorius brought on a relapse by means of injecting the pure toxin, deadly stuff. The old man hadn't the ghost of a chance. Yet it was all so hidden we should never have known anything was wrong if it had not been for Esther. She saved my life, you know. They were out to get me as well."

She put up her hand to her trembling mouth.

"Do you mean to say they would have murdered you too?" she faltered, on the verge of a collapse.

"There, dear, don't think about it too much. It's all over, thanks to that poor girl in there. Go back to her now; I'll come with you. Or no, hold on a minute—I'm going to get you a drink."

Quickly he fetched her a stiff whisky, which he made her force down. Then when she seemed somewhat recovered, he said:

"Don't say anything to Esther just yet; I'm going to break this to her myself. I want first to get you both out of the house. Chalmers is going to get a suite for us all at an hotel; then I'll leave you in his care for a bit. I depend on your help, Dido, so I may as well tell you right now that I intend to marry Esther almost at once—if she will have me."

This statement had the desired effect. He saw the old eyes light up with a faint spark, while the face was less stricken.

"Do you mean it, Roger?"

"I never meant anything more in my life. I've always wanted her, from the first day I saw her."

"I—I'm glad, I think. She's the only girl I've known whom I'd be willing to give you to."

A glance of affection passed between them; then, as she was about to enter the bedroom, she turned back for a moment, whispering:

"You haven't told me yet what—happened to Thérèse."

He hesitated, then replied:

"She fell,—from the narrow stone ledge beside the end of the balcony, on the second story. The wistaria is all torn away where she clutched at it to save herself. She broke her neck."

There was no shadow of a doubt that this theory was correct. Dr. Bousquet, who arrived in half an hour, declared that death must have occurred about four or five hours earlier. Therefore Thérèse must have waited till there seemed the least likelihood of her being seen or heard, then at perhaps two o'clock in the morning had crept out of her window and along the balcony, which ended a dozen feet from Roger's room. From thence on there was merely a decorative stone ledge, barely four inches wide. The closed window of the bedroom came first, its projecting sill offering something to cling to, but on each side of this was a space where the only support was the creeper on the wall. It was a perilous undertaking. In some fashion she had evidently made her way along the ledge. Roger did not yet know whether the accident had occurred on the journey to the bathroom or from it; he would not know for certain until the water in the Evian bottle was submitted to an analysis. All that one could tell was the spot where she had slipped and fallen, which was the first of the two dangerous places, almost immediately over the front steps. The wistaria to which she had clung was broken away in several spots, a whole spray of it fluttered loose from the wall. Here it was that she must have lost her balance. Her head had struck one of the ornamental stone baskets of fruit, after which it seemed that her body had ricochetted, her head doubling under her.

The broken bottle-neck caused the little doctor complete mystification. He scented some painful secret, though without venturing anywhere near the facts of the case. Roger refrained from enlightening him, not yet able to discuss the affair with a stranger, although knowing that in all probability the coroner would drag out a certain amount of the truth at the inquest. Ultimately, of course, it would be impossible to hush the matter up, since he had every intention of prosecuting Sartorius to the full extent of the law, and the man's guilt could not be established without implicating the dead woman.

By noon there was nothing more that could be done for the immediate moment. The police had been notified, the inquest set for the day after to-morrow. A warrant had been sworn out for the arrest of Sartorius, who was not to be found. There was reason to believe he had visited his residence in the Route de Grasse after leaving the Villa Firenze, but so far no one appeared to have any knowledge of his subsequent movements. His car was missing, which provided a likely clue. It seemed wholly improbable that he would long succeed in evading arrest; a foreigner of his unusual appearance presented an easy target. Yet Roger felt some degree of astonishment that he should think of disappearing. It argued a hopeless flaw in his defences.

Early in the afternoon Esther and Miss Clifford left La Californie in charge of Bousquet and descended by car to Cannes itself, where they took up their quarters in a comfortable and quiet hotel. Esther was promptly put to bed again. She was still too weak to sit up, and looked extremely ill. As yet she knew nothing of the catastrophe that had overtaken Lady Clifford, for the doctor thought her unequal to the strain of a fresh excitement. New surroundings and complete rest were now what she required to restore her, but even so it might be weeks before she was entirely herself. Although Bousquet had no idea of the reasons responsible for her present state beyond the fairly obvious effects of the morphia, he rightly surmised that her nervous system had sustained a severe shock. He saw, too, that while in the villa she had been the prey of some obscure but almost paralysing fear. Directly she was removed from the atmosphere of the Cliffords' house she began to be calmer.

At three o'clock Roger accompanied a small deputation of the police to Sartorius's house. In the main bedroom they found considerable disorder—drawers pulled out and their contents strewn about, various signs of hasty leave-taking, though how much of this was due to the doctor's own departure and how much to Holliday's was difficult to determine, as the two men had occupied the same room. However, under the bed was a small steamer trunk and a brown leather dressing-bag, both locked, and both initialled E. R. The trunk bore the label of a White Star liner, a Paris hotel, and the Carlton Hotel, Cannes. These pieces of luggage were the first bits of evidence to confirm the truth of Esther's story. In the laboratory above further confirmation awaited the investigators. Roger caught his breath as he stood in the open doorway and took in the corroborative details.

The hanging lamp was shattered as well as several panes of the skylight. On the table lay an overturned chair, the floor was littered with fragments of a glass jar mixed with a crystalline substance. Knotted to an iron bracket was the end of a ragged rope of crimson material, which disappeared through the open section of the skylight. The whole party gazed for some minutes in silence, making their own deductions. Then the chief retreated a pace or two and peered into the alcove.

"Regardez!" he said, pointing a significant finger at the narrow camp-bed with its tumbled army blanket.

Roger looked. The bed still bore the imprint of Esther's body; he felt that he could almost see her lying there, drugged, helpless. On the little table was a glass of dusty water and a murderous-looking hypodermic needle. How in heaven's name had the girl escaped? It was not yet clear to him, and seemed nothing short of miraculous.

The doors of both cupboards stood open, and sundry rings in the light coating of grime showed where bottles had recently been displaced. Suddenly it became clear to Roger that what had occurred was this: Sartorius, at the first opportunity, as Esther had predicted, had rushed here to find out what had happened. Seeing the hopeless extent of the evidence against him, he had relinquished any idea he might have had of putting up a fight, and had simply decided on the spot to attempt an escape. He had with great care and forethought erected a whole struc-ture, complete to the smallest detail; but one single brick at the base had become loosened, and the entire thing had toppled into ruins, beyond hope of reconstruction.

Two men remained on guard at the house, while the others returned to headquarters to make a report, Roger going with them to add his own statement to theirs. This done, he went to his new quarters in the hotel, worn out, but realising that he could do nothing more, so might as well take a rest. He found Dido anxiously awaiting him in the sitting-room of the suite.

"Esther is asleep at last," she said. "She still doesn't know anything, though I believe it would be better to tell her when she wakes up. She heard Aline scream this morning; it woke her up, and ever since then she has known something happened. She is terribly nervous, jumps at the slightest noise, and no matter what I say she is afraid you are running into some sort of danger."

"Is she?"

His eyes brightened for a moment.

"Yes. Do you know, she is really in mortal terror of Dr. Sartorius. I don't understand exactly why. I haven't allowed her to talk about things—the doctor said she mustn't—and I've tried too to keep her from seeing what a shock I've had. Has anything been heard of the doctor, by the way?"

"Not yet. He has completely vanished, but I don't think we need trouble about that. The morning papers everywhere are publishing a description of him, and all outgoing trains and motors are being watched, as well as the boats in the harbour. There is not much chance of his getting away."

She nodded with a degree of relief. Then with a sort of hesitation she said:

"Tell me, Roger. Do you suppose he knew about Thérèse's—accident—before he left the villa this morning?"

Roger frowned.

"Knew? Dido, one of the most ghastly things about this whole affair is that he must have known. He couldn't have avoided knowing. It was daylight, and when he came out he had to go around that side of the house to get to the garage. I myself noticed the print of his boot—a larger boot than anyone else wears—in the mould of the flowerbed, three feet away from the body."

"Roger! Then he saw her?"

"Of course. He took one look at her, realised what had happened, and saw in a flash that the manner of her death had, so to speak, given the whole show away. After that he didn't waste a second, but set about saving his own damned skin."

"How horrible!" she exclaimed, shuddering.

"You are right, it was horrible—but logical. He was only being true to his type. There is no sentiment about him; he has always despised the rest of us, even Thérèse, who was his accomplice."

In his own room Roger realised for the first time a sense of terrible fatigue. Up till now he had taken no account of the fact that he had had scarcely any sleep for several nights, and in addition to this had in actual fact been suffering from mild typhoid. His mind was still keyed up by excitement, but every muscle in his body ached with weariness.

Chalmers had laid out his dressing-gown only, as a plain indication that he should dine in his own room and go to bed. Slowly he turned on the hot water in the bath, and began to divest himself of his coat. As he did so he suddenly recalled the telegram handed him that morning, the message addressed to the dead woman. It had passed completely out of his thoughts. He drew the blue envelope out of his pocket and looked at it thoughtfully. The mark showed that it had been handed in at a small town on the road to Marseilles on the previous evening.

After some hesitation he tore open the flap and spread the paper out, then stared at it thoughtfully. The enclosure read:

SO SORRY UNABLE SAY GOOD-BVE SAILING MARSEILLES TO-MORROW AU REVOIR ALL MY LOVE. ARTHUR.

CHAPTER XXXIX

THREE days later Esther sat by the window in the hotel sitting-room of the Cliffords' suite, waiting for Roger. She had made rapid progress during the past twenty-four hours, but she still felt rather wan and tremulous, as though she had been through a long illness. Moreover she now knew all there was to know about the affair in which she had played a leading part. She had insisted on being told what had happened to Lady Clifford, and in spite of the inevitable shock to her nerves she had since felt steadier. She had now beside her all the papers containing accounts of the death of the Frenchwoman and the disappearance of Dr. Sartorius, both well-known figures in Cannes, and she had read with the keenest interest all the diverse theories which strove to connect the two events. Up till now not one report had hit upon the true facts of the case; all the stories were wide of the mark, and the general impression given to the public was that in some mysterious way the doctor was responsible for his employer's catastrophic end. There was one garbled account which mentioned her own name—gleaned, most likely, from one of the French servants at the villa—but so far Roger, in his determination to prevent the Press from persecuting her, had kept her well out of it.

It seemed almost unbelievable that after three whole days so little of the actual affair should be known. The sensation caused was a big one, but it remained in the nature of an enigma. Rumour in several quarters had it that Lady Clifford had simply committed suicide because of the desertion of her lover. The result of the inquest was not yet known.

and the fact that the death was due to an accident was difficult for most people to grasp.

Esther, however, knew how the awful thing had happened, and amid her complex emotions she was conscious of a sort of admiration for the Frenchwoman's courage in setting out as she must have done, in the darkness and rain, on her perilous mission—a mission she had all but accomplished, too, for it had now been established that the bottle upon the shelf in Roger's bathroom contained pure Evian water, innocent of contamination. Thérèse had therefore effected the exchange and was on her return journey when she lost her balance.

Looking out upon the Croisette and the harbour beyond, where the myriad lights of yachts began to twinkle in the violet dusk, Esther drew a deep breath and assembled her thoughts more calmly than she had as yet been able to do. The terrible experience through which she had passed had left its imprint upon her; she was still ready to jump at the slightest sound, or even, absurdly, to burst into tears. Yet deep within her was a warm consciousness of security, an earnest of happiness to come. No word of actual love had been spoken between her and Roger, she had not been alone with him since that night at the villa, yet it was enough for her to recall the pressure of his face against her hands and the hungry way in which his eyes had dwelt upon her. In that hour she had learned how much she mattered to him. She closed her eyes now and revelled in the delicious certainty of what was coming to her. Her heart beat almost as it had done during those dreadful moments in the laboratory which she was striving to forget; it thumped against her ribs with great blows, so that instinctively she put her hands upon her breast to quiet it.

"What an idiot I am to take so much for granted," she reflected, chiding herself. "Suppose I'm mistaken about him after all?"

She knew she wasn't mistaken. She also knew that old Miss Clifford scented a romance, was indeed keeping out of the way now to let her be alone with Roger. This was the first time that Esther had had her clothes on; the old lady had helped her to dress, unpacking with her own hands the little steamer-trunk that had been fetched from the Route de Grasse, and given orders to the chambermaid to press all its contents and put them in order.

Esther glanced down at her frock. It was the peach-coloured one she had worn that night when she had danced at the Ambassadeurs. It felt a little loose upon her now, for she had lost a good deal of weight, perhaps six or seven pounds, she reflected. Her hair needed trimming, the curly bronze locks played about her neck and ears in a fashion that stirred her displeasure. Still, that could soon be remedied; she would take herself in hand at once. She was glad to be in mufti for a bit, to indulge with a clear conscience in a riot of feminine distractions. Even to sit here quietly, her hands in her lap, after the storm she had passed through, was in itself a luxury. Her feeling of security and well-being was so acute that the realisation of it brought a little stab of almost pain, while tears, so close to the surface now, rushed into her eyes.

It was at this moment that the door opened and Roger came in, his arms filled with an immense bunch of pale pink roses. She rose hurriedly, brushing the tears away with a feeling of shame, and smiling at him. He came close and looked with a grave face at the drops still clinging to her lashes.

"What are those for?" he inquired in a serious tone.

"Nothing at all. If I tell you, you'll think me such a fool! I—I was only thinking to myself how happy I was to be alive, and—and all that."

He looked down at her for a long moment with so penetrating a gaze that she grew embarrassed.

"There—that's the look of yours I like so much," he said at last, watching her colour rise. "You know you are just a nice child, Esther— an awfully nice child! That's how I first thought of you."

With a gesture half-afraid he put up one finger and touched a tendril of hair that had strayed loose on her neck. She felt shyer than before, and turned her attention to the roses.

"For me?" she asked, burying her face in their cool depths. "How too beautiful! I don't think I've ever seen roses so lovely before. There's— there's something special about them, somehow," she added truthfully.

"There is," he replied gravely, as he deposited his burden on the table.

Suddenly tongue-tied, she made an effort to speak naturally of other matters, avoiding the personal.

"Any news of . . . of that man?" she inquired.

Stupid that she still could not speak of him easily!

Roger saw that a faint shadow had darkened her upturned eyes, and it cut him to the heart.

"No, nothing yet—but don't let that distress you. The fellow is bound to be caught; it's only a question of time. You are not to be worried about it. Look at me! You are worrying, this minute."

"I'm not at all," she denied stoutly. "Why should I bother about him—now?"

For answer he drew forward the biggest arm-chair and gently made her sit down. The slight hollow of her delicate cheek, the dark circles under the eyes, caused him acute suffering.

"Seriously, Esther, when I think of what you have been through, when I think that it must have left a terrible impression on you and that nothing I can do can remove that impression, it is almost more than I can bear. I feel it is all our fault."

"How perfectly absurd! It was nobody's fault. And you ought to be thankful it has turned out as it has. I am, I can tell you. As for me, I shall get over this, don't worry! I'm not neurotic or anything queer, whatever that man wanted to make you believe. I am really frightfully normal."

"Yes, thank God! I feel an ass to think I could ever have doubted it."

"I don't know. When I think what I must have looked like bursting in on you that night—a sort of Curfew-Shall-Not-Ring-To-night, I suppose—I don't wonder at anyone's thinking me a lunatic. How I ever got there at all is a mystery to me. I believe I was unconscious part of the time. I scarcely remember it; the whole thing seems like a sort of feverish nightmare. When the taxi came to a standstill I simply gave everything up for lost. I only set out to walk that last mile in a sort of dogged desperation; I never thought I should get there, or that if I did it would be in time. It was all uphill, too. I remember the perspiration running in trickles with the rain down my face, all in my eyes, so that I could scarcely see. Every little while I just toppled over altogether and lay on the sidewalk. It was the purest good luck that I wasn't run in for a drunken person. That would have finished it!"

"My dear!"

"Oh, well, let's not talk about it any more. I want to forget all that part of it—if I can."

He sat down close to her on the window-seat, silent for a moment. Then he said:

"Esther, tell me one thing. What first put the suspicion into your head that there was something not quite straight about my father's illness?"

She knit her brow and thought hard for a bit.

"I hardly know," she replied at last. "It's awfully difficult to say. There were certain tiny, unimportant things that I noticed, even before I took on the case, but taken separately not one would have meant anything much. I don't believe I can say exactly when I first began to feel uncomfortable about the situation. Perhaps I shouldn't have done so at all if it hadn't been for the pure accident of overhearing a conversation between your stepmother and Captain Holliday that afternoon I told you about."

"I know you saw them together, but you never told me you heard what they were talking about."

"Well, I did hear quite a lot. I listened hard, pretending not to, of course. I got tremendously interested. He was saying he had almost made up his mind to go to South America with his Spanish friend, and she showed very plainly that she was afraid to let him go, that she believed he wouldn't come back to her. Then she made it pretty clear that it was the attitude of a person she called 'Charles' which had caused all the trouble. Of course I didn't know who Charles was! But after that she said something which interested me enormously. She described a visit to a crystal-gazer, or a medium of some kind, and she said the woman saw 'Charles' lying ill in bed, with a nurse beside him and a doctor. And who do you think she said the doctor was? Sartorius!"

"You don't mean it!"

"You see, I had just come from Sartorius's house. I had gone there that afternoon to try to get a job. You may imagine how interested I was to find this woman was a patient of the man I expected to work for. And then . . . I got the idea that both Lady Clifford and the young man seemed disappointed because the medium didn't see anything further, and Captain Holliday was very bitter about it and said that Charles would recover and live to be ninety, which upset the lady very much."

"Do you think at that time . . ."

"No, I don't. What I believe is that Lady Clifford had no definite determination to do anything until she heard Holliday say he would probably be sailing on the 8th. I think it was the certainty of losing him so soon that drove her to take a positive step. No doubt she knew a good deal about the doctor through Holliday, and how he might be got at through his desire to be free from routine. As for him, human life as such meant nothing whatever to him—I heard him say so. All he cares for is science."

"Do you think Holliday had anything to do with it?" Roger asked tentatively, playing with the window-cord.

"I am fairly sure he hadn't, though he may have suspected something. At the last he was dragged into it quite against his will, or at least I got that idea. He was in a blue funk, too—simply dying to clear out."

"Just the same," remarked Roger rather grimly, "our friend Arthur is not going to be able to skin out of the affair so easily as he thinks. A wireless has already been sent to the boat he sailed on, and when he reaches port he'll be detained and sent back here. In any case, he'll be wanted as an accessory after the act, which may prove an unpleasant business for him. . . . Go on, though; tell me how you actually came to make up your mind that something was wrong."

"I never did make up my mind until it was too late—that was the awful part! When I think it all over, though, I can see that the thing that most roused my suspicions—not altogether by itself, but taken together with what happened later—was the doctor's flying into a passion with me for mislaying a hypodermic needle. I haven't told you that yet, have I?"

"No. Was it after *the* injection?"

"It was, and at the very moment when you cut your hand. I put the needle down to attend to you, and I completely forgot where I had laid it. He was fearfully angry, called me names and abused me in a way that got my back up. There seemed no reason for it; I couldn't understand it at all. Then the same day your father got suddenly worse, you remember, and I should have forgotten all about the beast's nasty temper, only . . ."

"Yes, what happened?"

"Why, quite suddenly, I found the needle! Where do you think? Inside a big book of drawings! I began wondering; I put two and two together. . . . You see, I didn't dare mention my awful suspicion—I couldn't! It might have ruined me for ever if I was wrong. So I did the only thing I could think of: I took the needle to that chemist and got it analysed. You know all the rest."

"If only you had confided in me, Esther!"

"Even so it was too late to save your father; nothing would have saved him. And you quite understand that if the suspicion had proved unfounded it would have finished me as a nurse for all time!"

He looked at her intently.

"Would that have meant so much to you?"

"Well, what do you think? I've got to earn my living."

"But as far as that goes you might have guessed—that is you might have . . ."

He broke off as a knock at the door heralded the entrance of a waiter bearing a tray with two frosty cocktails.

"Ah! here's something to put a little colour in your cheeks. You want bucking up, you know! Here's how!"

She took an appreciative sip, then set down her glass, turning on him a slightly troubled face.

"Roger . . . I suppose if this man is caught, it will mean a trial. I shall be wanted as a witness, sha'n't I? The chief witness, even!"

"Yes, my dear, you will," he replied reluctantly. "I hate the thought of it as much as you do. I wish there were some way to spare you."

"I expect he'll try to prove I'm insane," she said slowly. "Or else that I had some low motive in trying to fasten suspicion on to him. Perhaps he'll even suggest to his lawyer that I was out to blackmail him!"

"Esther, you're frightfully astute to think of such a thing. It's quite on the cards he will do that. He'll use every weapon in his power, unless..."

"Unless what?"

"Well, there's a pretty black lot of evidence against him. Thérèse's death in itself, the way in which she died, was a damaging admission. It seems to me possible that he'll give up the fight entirely. It's hard to predict anything. One doesn't know what cards he has up his sleeve."

Her clouded gaze strayed past him out of the window at the glimmering points of light.

"There is something still so terrifying to me about his machine-like efficiency," she said, "that I can believe him capable of anything. His whole plan was so perfectly thought out, down to the smallest detail. It only broke down through the purely accidental. Once through my losing the needle—though that wasn't so bad as his losing his temper!—and once because he let Holliday give me the injection instead of doing it himself. And yet when I think of what he may say at the trial..."

He leaned forward suddenly and took her two hands in his.

"Esther, listen to me! Will you promise to marry me, at once, before this beastly trial comes on?"

Once again the wave of colour swept over her face. She gave a little nervous laugh.

"But you haven't asked me at all, yet!"

"I'm asking you now. Besides, you knew I meant to. I've been making inquiries this afternoon. There are a lot of formalities that have to be gone through with: we have to see an English solicitor, sign a lot of papers, be *affichéd* two Sundays—a sort of banns, you know—and then we have to be married at the *mairie*. Altogether the business takes just over a couple of weeks, so the sooner one decides the sooner one can set about it, you see?"

She could think of no reply. Her home, her sisters, came into her mind; she stammered, then laughed again with a lump in her throat. Those tears again! She mustn't be so stupid...

There was a sharp rap at the door, more businesslike than the last.

"Who in hell is that?" Roger burst out in irritable annoyance.

It proved to be the valet, obsequious and apologetic, yet full of importance.

"There is a *sergent-de-ville* to speak with Monsieur," he informed them mysteriously, but with a Frenchman's full appreciation of the ruptured *tête-à-tête*.

"I'll have to go, I suppose," Roger informed her. "But I'll get it disposed of as quickly as possible."

Ten minutes went slowly by. She had tried not to let Roger see how much she dreaded the prospect of the witness-box. In her present state of nerves she felt she might be guilty of a hundred contradictions and indiscretions, if faced with the basilisk eyes and over-powering personality of the man she feared. At the very thought of him she began to tremble all over as though with ague. It was perfectly absurd, of course, but there it was. Still now, if she chose, she could face the trying experience as a married woman, as Roger Clifford's wife. That security somehow promised her a new strength. Roger's wife! And in a fortnight's time! A different sort of tremor seized her, a *frisson* of exquisite joy. . . .

The door opened. Roger came towards her, took her hands again in his, and looked at her closely. She grew apprehensive of what he had to tell her.

"What is it? What has happened?"

"Don't be frightened. They have caught Sartorius. They captured him aboard a fruit-boat in the harbour, about an hour ago. The boat was under sailing orders, bound for a port in Morocco; they think the captain was a friend of Sartorius's. Anyway, they surrounded the doctor in his cabin. He didn't put up any fight—simply looked at them, blew his nose, and followed them up without a word."

She stared at him blankly, wondering what more he had to say.

"Yes—go on. What then?"

"They handcuffed him, of course, and let him sit between two of them in the car. He was quite composed, had nothing to say. It was dark inside the car; they couldn't see him very well. One of the officers thought he leaned against him pretty heavily. When they got to the station he didn't get up, didn't move at all."

"What do you mean?"

"He did us a good turn, Esther. He was quite dead—poisoned, beyond doubt."

"Poisoned! I wonder how he did it?"

"It is amazing, isn't it? It was the stolid calmness of the fellow that put them off, I suppose. They think he must have taken something he had ready when he blew his nose."

She looked at him, her pupils dilated, trying to adjust her ideas to this new development. She felt strangely bewildered.

"It seems so—so stupid! I can't take it in. A clever man like that . . . first to run away, then to throw up the sponge . . ."

"I know, that's the way it strikes me, too; he seemed at the last so lacking in resource. Still, he was probably like one of those big, heavy cars that are wonderful on the straight, but can't turn quickly in a sharp corner. Take one of those two-ton Hispano-Suizas—"

"Or the Juggernaut," she suggested slowly.

"By Jove, yes, the Juggernaut . . . he was like that."

He looked at her with an awful realisation of how near her slender body had come to being ruthlessly crushed by the human machine— simply because it happened to put itself in the path. That he, too, had all unconsciously been in the path and had barely escaped destruction was now of minor importance.

For several seconds Esther stood with her hands against her heart, making an effort to grasp, to envisage, the whole of her strange adventure. Since she had set foot in Cannes two months before she had watched an old man done slowly to death, had saved a life that meant everything to her, and had been directly responsible for the events leading up to two deaths. What a part she had played! She could scarcely take it in. . . .

She came out of her reverie to find herself in Roger's strong arms, his lips warm upon hers. Thought deserted her for a breathless moment.

"Do you know what I'm thinking?" he whispered in what might be termed the first conscious interval. "There may not be any pressing necessity for an immediate wedding, and yet . . ."

"Yes?" she murmured, her face against his, her heart beating fast.

"Well, a fortnight is a pretty long engagement—at least for me. What do you say?"

Her answer, somewhat muffled, came after a longish pause.

"Since you force me to admit it," she whispered against his neck, "it's quite long enough for me—too!"

THE END